PRAISE FOR

THE ...

'Fast, skilfully put together ... full of life . . . has everything I look for in a thriller' *Len Deighton*

'Mr Molloy throws back cordial glimpses of Le Carré, Deighton, Anthony Price, even Buchan, in this brisk debut' *Sunday Times*

'Non-stop action-packed thriller . . . Great fun' *Mail On Sunday*

THE KID FROM RIGA

'An abundance of ideas and zestful writing' *Literary Review*

'Sure-footed, smack up-to-date and full of expertise' *Bloodhound*

'Don't leave Gatwick without it!' *Mail On Sunday*

THE HARLOT OF JERICHO

'Sex, violence, skulduggery . . . a very heady brew . . . I bet you won't put down this sizzling thriller' *Daily Mail*

'Adventure with a chilling dash of high-tech' *Mail On Sunday*

By the same author

THE BLACK DWARF
THE KID FROM RIGA

MICHAEL MOLLOY

The Harlot of Jericho

Futura

A Futura Book

Reproduced, printed and bound in Great Britain by
BPCC Hazell Books Ltd
Member of BPCC Ltd
Aylesbury, Bucks, England

Futura Publications
A Division of
Macdonald & Co (Publishers) Ltd
Orbit House
1 New Fetter Lane
London EC4A 1AR
A member of Maxwell Macmillan Pergamon Publishing Corporation

'And Joshua saved Rahab the harlot alive, and her father's household, and all that she had; and she dwelleth in Israel even unto this day; because she hid the messengers, which Joshua sent to spy out Jericho.'

Joshua 6.25

PROLOGUE

The barman stood with his back to the poker table, but his eyes never left the reflection in the mirror before him. Occasionally, when other customers called for his attention, he would wave them towards the two Mexican women who served at the far end of the bar, and continue to polish a crystal glass while he studied the seven men who sat in the cone of smoke-filled light.

At the poker table a cocktail waitress hovered patiently; when the new hand was dealt she leaned forward and swiftly placed fresh drinks before the players. The big man to her right casually tossed a twenty-five-dollar chip on her tray and said: 'The change is for you, honey,' in a slow Southern accent. She thanked him with a professional smile and raised her eyebrows to the watching barman as the players each placed fifty-dollar chips into the pot.

The betting was heavy: after the first round four of the men dropped out and watched the big man pile chips before him and push them into the centre of the table.

'Your thousand and up another two,' he said easily.

The remaining players studied their cards until one sighed and threw his hand towards the dealer. The other ran the tips of his fingers through his hair in a quick nervous motion and began to calculate the value of the chips before him.

While he was counting a uniformed figure entered the bar and stood beside the big man, who leaned slightly towards him.

'We're all ready, sir,' he said in a low voice.

'I'll be right there,' he replied and returned his gaze to the

7

table where the other player had began to slide row after row of neatly piled chips into the pot. When he was finished he looked up at the big man.

'Your two thousand and raise another five,' he said and he hunched forward to study the heap of different-coloured counters on the green baize.

Without hesitating the big man pushed most of the chips before him into the centre.

'Your five and up another ten,' he said in a bored voice.

'I'll call you,' the other player said after a long pause and the barman, who was still studying the game, could hear defeat in the voice.

The big man stood up and flipped over his cards to reveal four kings and an eight. He didn't bother to look at the other player's hand.

'Keep the money safe for me, gentlemen,' he said easily. 'I'll be back when I've taken care of a little business.'

The barman watched him walk to the door, and then he turned his attention to an insistent customer. Once outside, the big man stood for a moment in the pitch-dark shadow of the alleyway before he walked a few yards and turned into a narrow curving road. There were no street lights, but a nearly full moon in the clear sky glowed with enough brightness for him to see the group of men dressed in uniform who stood together in a parking lot on the other side of the street.

The group was silhouetted against a sheer rockface at the back of the lot. They watched him as he crossed the road to join them.

'Everything ready?'

One man stepped forward and gestured towards the two rows of vehicles that were parked with their hoods facing inwards to leave a wide space in the centre of the lot.

'Just exactly as you ordered.' He handed him a shotgun. 'They're on their way. Johnson called again.'

The big man nodded. 'Wait for me to make the first move. I want them all. Understand?'

The uniformed men murmured their acknowledgements.

'OK, let's go,' he said.

The group broke up and each of them made for a different

8

vehicle.

The big man waited by the entrance to the lot. When the last door slammed there was a deep silence; he eased the shotgun in his arms and listened.

Minutes passed and then he caught the distant drumming roar of engines. Gradually the pounding sound funnelled into the narrow street and he could see the powerful beams of headlights weaving towards him.

He stepped back and crouched beside a pick-up truck next to the entrance as the rumbling motorcycles turned into the lot. The engines were gunned a few more times and then cut.

Slowly he raised his head and looked across the bonnet of the pick-up to count ten bikes close together between the two rows of vehicles. The big man listened to the whoops and shouts until the last headlight was turned off. Then he rapped twice on the door of the pick-up with the barrel of his shotgun. Headlights snapped on and instantly the lot was floodlit by the other vehicles.

The black-clad figures caught in the blinding light reacted with bewilderment. Sensing danger, they twisted from side to side like a nest of giant insects, until the big man stepped from behind the pick-up and called out to them.

'The town's just been closed to you folks,' he said in a tone that was almost friendly.

One of the group shaded his eyes from the light and took a step towards him. He wore his long matted hair tied back to show the swastika tattooed on his forehead.

'Bullshit,' he shouted, just before a massive charge of buckshot punched into his leather-covered torso. The rest turned from the blast in panic, but the other men who had emerged from the vehicles began to pump their shotguns at point-blank range into the writhing group.

Caught by twenty-four seconds of twelve-gauge crossfire, their bodies were blown into piles of blood, metal and leather. When they were finally still the big man walked forward and checked the huddled mass for any sign of life. Satisfied there were no survivors he passed his shotgun to the figure standing nearest to him.

9

'Clean the place up,' he said. 'I've got to collect my winnings.'

Later in the night, when the moon had dipped behind the mountains and the last customer had left the saloon, the barman walked over to the poker table. After a moment's pause he picked up the pack of cards and spread them, face up, on the green baize. Then he studied the edges carefully for a few minutes while he sipped a glass of bourbon.

The only other person in the bar, a blonde woman, came and stood beside him. 'I guess we're not going to be bothered by bikers any more,' he said softly. 'Yes, sir. They've really put the lid on this town.'

The woman ignored his remarks and looked down at the cards.

'Did you figure out how he cheats?' she asked.

'Sure,' he replied.

'Does he mark the cards?'

'No,' the barman replied and he flipped over the pack. 'He's better than that.'

The woman thought for a time, while she inhaled heavily on a cigarette.

'Put the table in the storeroom,' she said finally. 'I'm closing the game down.'

Chapter One

The rust-stained minicab edged into a gap between the cars that lined the pavement and came to a halt as the last gold light of a September evening deepened the shadows in Lynton Road. Without much apparent interest, the driver glanced down both sides of the narrow suburban street before his gaze settled on the small bay window he was parked before.

When the semi-detached houses were built in the late Twenties, the gates and low brick walls had all matched, but over the years successive owners had substituted wrought iron, picket fences and scalloped privet hedges. Some had paved the gardens and others planted trees. Originally the window frames had been white and the front doors Prussian blue: now colours were as varied as the shrubs and flowers that filled the gardens. The road lacked the elegance of its neighbours in Bedford Park, but the houses were well kept and reflected the pride that ordinary people brought to the things for which they cared.

The minicab was used to meaner streets. One front wing was crumpled by an old collision, a wire coathanger served as the radio aerial and cracked yellow plastic covered the seats.

The driver looked towards Number 25, and the net curtains were parted by a hand waving to acknowledge his arrival.

He noticed that the house was shabbier than the others around it. The paint on the windowsills was cracked and the grass on the tiny patch of lawn had been allowed to grow long so that it blurred the edges of the flower beds, like untrimmed hair over a shirt collar.

11

The driver switched off the engine and let his tattooed arm dangle from the car window so that he could slap on the door in time to the music that came from inside the cab. When the piece ended he turned off the tape and laced his hands behind his head. Now the only sounds in the street were the soft rattle from a distant lawnmower and a gentle ticking from the car as the engine cooled.

As he watched the quiet houses, a blue Cortina turned into the street and came towards him. It slowed down as it drew close and he could see a young couple in the front seats. The man driving just managed to park in the remaining space before the minicab. He pulled a cricket bag from the back seat, slammed the door and walked quickly up the garden path of Number 27 so that the front gate swung back onto the fair-haired girl who followed him.

She paused for a moment and glanced at the minicab driver as if to make an appeal against the sulky young man's rudeness.

At the doorway he had put down his bag and thrust his hands into his blazer pockets while he watched impatiently as the fair girl fumbled in her handbag for the latchkey.

The driver watched the couple and tried to imagine the circumstances that had brought about their differing moods. Had the cricketer played badly, or the young wife flirted with one of the other players? She was pretty enough for men to flirt with her, and the backless cream dress that showed her suntan would provoke comments after a few pints of beer.

Finally the girl found her key and the door closed on their problems, just as Number 25 opened and two women stood for a moment in the doorway. The younger, who carried a canvas holdall, came out, turned at the gate and called to the older woman who stood in a flowered housecoat at the doorway.

'I'll ring you on Thursday.'

At the second attempt she managed to open the rear door of the minicab. The driver turned to her and she looked without enthusiasm into the dark features. The rough black hair and the dark stubble that covered his hollow cheeks reminded her of a boy she had met once who worked in a fairground.

'Where do you want to go to, lady?' he said in a South London accent.

'West End,' she replied in a clear voice. There was a harsh, grinding sound as he engaged the gears and they moved away, leaving a smudge of exhaust fumes.

The grey-haired woman in the housecoat watched the car drive the length of the street before she closed the front door.

When they stopped at the traffic lights in Chiswick High Road, the driver studied the woman's face in the rear-view mirror. Her features were too strong to be considered beautiful, but her mouth was full and sensual, and her dark hair was pulled back to accentuate the high cheekbones. She looked into the mirror and saw he was studying her.

'I didn't know that officers and gentlemen wore tattoos,' she said in a chiding voice.

Captain Lewis Horne glance down at the scrolled heart and dagger on his right forearm and then smiled back into the mirror.

'Fine artwork,' he said. 'Claude Henderson's people developed it. The trouble is, you have to rub like hell with pumice stone to get them off.'

The voice bore no trace of the South London accent that she had heard a few minutes earlier and Lewis Horne's features had lost their look of brutish slackness.

'You should have been an actor, Lewis,' she said as she reached into her handbag and produced cigarettes and a disposable lighter.

'I couldn't bear the rejection,' he replied and shook his head as she offered him the packet. She drew deeply and held the smoke in her lungs, but before it was half finished, she stubbed the cigarette out and folded her arms. He could feel the tension in her. It filled the car like the smoke from her cigarette. He decided to wait for her to speak.

Joyce Maynard looked out of the window again and for a moment a crease of concern, like a line drawn with a blunt pencil, appeared on her forehead.

'Turnham Green. Nothing ever happens here,' she said

13

softly but in a tone of reassurance rather than complaint. She looked back to Lewis Horne as if seeking agreement, but the lights changed and the car drew away.

'Even the battle didn't take place,' he said lightly.

'What battle?'

'The Battle of Turnham Green – during the Civil War.'

'Yes it did,' she said. 'We were taught about it at school.'

Lewis overtook a bus before he replied.

'No. Prince Rupert got here with men who were hung over from looting a wine cellar in Brentford the day before. Parliament sent out the militia from London and Rupert's men retired without a shot being fired. End of battle.'

Joyce Maynard smiled. 'That's the way to fight a war.'

Lewis nodded. 'It didn't continue in the same manner. Some time I'll tell you about Marston Moor.'

They drove on in silence until the traffic became heavier at Shepherd's Bush and they came to a stop. A silver Volvo he had been watching for some time swung into Wood Lane. He turned his head to follow the tail lights for a moment and then turned back. Across Shepherd's Bush Green twilight had deepened to night and dancing lights flashed through the darkened trees.

A black cab drew alongside them and Lewis casually turned to study the driver and his passengers. The man at the wheel returned his gaze with an aggressive stare. Lewis's eyes flickered back to the rear of the cab. Three women, heavily draped in black robes, their faces obscured by grotesque masks, were looking at him. For a moment his eyes made contact with one of them before she glanced away.

Using the car's mirrors he made another sweep of the lines of traffic behind them for any signs of a threat before he crunched the minicab into gear once again. The lights changed, and they began to crawl forward towards the bottle-neck of Holland Park Avenue. The black cab with its exotic cargo swung in front of him so that he had to brake sharply.

'Are we clean?' she asked.

'Yes,' Lewis replied. 'No-one's tailing us. What have you got?'

Lewis Horne glanced into the mirror again and saw her shoulders hunch before she spoke.

'An assassination. At least, it looks like it. The proposed victim is Marshall Cutter, an American industrialist.'

'Where?'

'Cap Ferrat on the Côte d'Azur.'

'When?'

'Tomorrow.'

'Tomorrow? Christ!'

'Sorry,' she said. 'It was a hell of a decoding job.'

Lewis turned off Holland Park into Norland Square and found a parking space. The interior of the cab was stuffy. He wound down his window and the roar of the traffic in Holland Park Road came to them as a distant throb.

'Get in the front seat next to me,' Lewis said.

She did as she was told and he turned to look at her.

'Now tell me everything,' he said.

Joyce Maynard lit another cigarette and paused briefly to order her thoughts.

'The agency got a coded telex from Tucson in Arizona on Friday. I managed to get a copy out.' She paused for a moment. 'It took me sixteen hours to crack it. Maybe I'm getting past it.'

'Twenty-six is still pretty young, Joyce,' Lewis said in a gentle voice.

She turned her head quickly. 'Is it? Not for mathematicians. Didn't you know we're over the hill by thirty?'

Lewis smiled. 'You should have been a musician. They go on for ever. What did the telex say?'

'Four hitmen trained to use sub-aqua equipment are to meet an American representative on board a motor yacht called *Marian* at Antibes tomorrow at noon. At five pm they will be dropped in the sea off the Cap so they can swim to Cutter's villa and make the hit.'

'How do they know he'll be at home?'

Joyce threw the half-finished cigarette from the window and a shower of sparks burst as it hit the pavement.

'They have a copy of Cutter's itinerary. He's one of these people who never stops work. His office know where he's going to be every minute of the day.'

Lewis reached out and put his arm around her shoulders when he noticed an elderly couple walking towards them. The pair seemed to be out for a stroll in the warm night air. Their arms were linked together and they took careful note of everything around them. As they grew closer, Lewis drew Joyce towards him and pretended to kiss her. It was an awkward thing to do. He could smell her face powder and the cigarette smoke on her breath. He brushed her cheek as the couple passed and as he drew away she touched the spot.

Lewis studied her profile in the light of the street lamp. She still looked preoccupied.

'Is everything all right, Joyce?' he asked.

She glanced at him. 'Fine,' she said. 'It's just that I found out the other day what the people at the agency had actually done. Two of them – Baden and Talgar – planted the bomb at Amsterdam Airport. Did you know that?'

Lewis nodded.

She started to take another cigarette from the packet and then she changed her mind.

'They knew all those children were going to be there.'

He looked up at the tall, terraced houses of the square. From one of the open windows the sound of someone practising scales on the piano came to them on the night air. She started to speak again. 'If they can do that to children . . . '

'Do you still feel able to cope with it all?' Lewis said carefully. 'I could speak to Charlie, get someone to relieve you?'

She hesitated for a moment. 'I can manage. I'm just surprised by what's happening to me.'

'What's that?'

She thought again before answering. 'I think I'm beginning to believe in the Devil.'

She waited for a comment but Lewis didn't say anything.

'I suppose it's being in the constant presence of evil,' she said, but the tone of her voice seemed to make the statement a question.

'Is that worrying you?'

She paused again.

16

'Not really – just surprising. I didn't expect four years of espionage work to bring about spiritual awakening.'

'I thought it was the Devil you were aware of?'

She managed a smile. 'Positive proof of the Devil is powerful evidence for the existence of God. I even went to church with my mother this morning.'

The scales on the piano came to an end and the anonymous pianist began to play a piece of Chopin which Lewis had not heard since he was a boy.

'How did you enjoy the service?' Lewis asked.

Joyce gave a short laugh.

'It was just as boring as when I was a child, but my mother was pleased I went with her. That was nice.'

'Are you worried about your cover?'

She shook her head. 'No. They have utter contempt for the typists. Sometimes I think they confuse us with the office equipment. Their arrogance is really extraordinary. I found out about Amsterdam by listening to Baden and Talgar talking. They took it for granted that none of us could understand them when they spoke German. They just stood there in the middle of the office and began to discuss how they had murdered thirty-seven human beings.' She shuddered, and to disguise the movement, folded her arms. 'How do you think they can justify that sort of hideous behaviour?'

Lewis shrugged. 'They argue that all acts of aggression are justified. They don't recognise civilians.' Lewis paused. 'Are you sure you're not in any danger?'

Joyce lit another cigarette and the car smelt of the acrid tobacco.

'Really, it's all right. They think I'm dumb Joyce Maynard, the secretary with the Brian Ferry and Clint Eastwood pin-ups on her stick board. If I put up a picture of Gaddafi they'd probably take me more seriously.'

'How's your mother?' Lewis said in a matter-of-fact voice.

Joyce opened her bag and put away the cigarettes before she answered.

'She's fine. She misses Dad, but I suppose that's understandable.'

'Does she still want you to move back home?' Lewis asked.

17

'Yes, she does. The trouble is, I can't tell her I live with Jeffrey. She's very old-fashioned.'

'What does he say?' Lewis said and he glanced up to the window where the piece of Chopin had come to an end.

'He wants to get married and have her to live with us.'

Lewis continued to look up at the window with a sense of anticipation. The first notes of a familiar piece of Mozart began. He was sure now that the child practising was using the same exercise book he had known as a boy.

'So what's the problem? Does it bother him that you're a Catholic?'

'No. He doesn't mind that. It's me that has the reservations.'

'I thought you were pretty keen on him?'

She sighed and massaged the back of her neck as she moved her head up and down.

'I am. It's just that I feel guilty all the time. I hate not being able to tell him what I really do. If I were to get married without him knowing, I would feel that I was violating the vows.' She sighed. 'Can you understand?'

'I think so, Joyce,' he said. 'It's not an unusual problem. We've all had to face something like it from time to time.'

'How do you and Hanna manage?' she asked, and Lewis had to think before he answered.

'She knows what I do.'

'So you don't have any difficulties?'

He smiled wryly. 'The truth is, she hates the job. Hanna wants me to quit the service, go back to Oxford and be a full-time historian.'

Joyce shook her head. 'But she's an intelligent woman; she's a doctor. Surely she knows how important our work is?'

'Logic tells her it's worthwhile, but emotionally she's repelled by the violence.'

'Does her being so rich worry you?' Joyce asked.

He smiled again. 'I think I can live with that, and at least we can talk about the job. That's more than you and Jeffrey have.'

'You're right, of course,' Joyce said. 'I know I'm just being self-centred.'

'Do you trust him?'

'Yes,' she said after a moment's hesitation.

'Then tell him what you do, Joyce.'

She didn't answer, so he spoke again.

'Look, we've vetted him. We had to. There's nothing to suggest he would be a security risk.'

She looked at him again and gave a rather sad smile.

'I want to, but I don't have the courage. I suppose I'm frightened that he'll think I'm some kind of freak. I don't want him to know I have a secret life.'

'Give him a chance. There's nothing else to do.'

She looked ahead and nodded.

Lewis watched her for a moment and then started the car again.

'Can I drop you near your home?'

'No. Leicester Square. We're going to the flicks.'

'Tell him this evening,' Lewis said.

Joyce smiled briefly. 'I'll try.'

He smiled back but he noticed that the line of concern still lingered on her forehead.

Lewis stopped in front of the closed doors of the garage behind Oxford Street and sounded the horn twice. The door opened after a moment and he edged the rusty cab down the ramp and into an empty bay deep in the echoing concrete cavern.

Jack Morris was on duty. He sat in the glass-panelled booth next to the gates watching a portable black-and-white television set, his feet on the table that was littered with teacups, spilling ashtrays and old newspapers. The warm air in the booth smelt stale as Lewis leaned into the aperture to hand over the keys.

'Pass me the telephone, Jack,' Lewis said and Morris did as he was told without looking from the flickering screen. Lewis dialled and after a long time there was an answer.

It was Sybil Mars. He could tell from the echo to her voice that she was using the extension in the hallway. The first words he heard were 'Get down', but he knew she was talking

19

to the two dogs that followed her about when Charlie was away.

Their house in Oxfordshire was so familiar to Lewis he could picture the scene at the other end of the telephone as clearly as if he were looking from the open doorway. The sun had been shining all day so Sybil would be wearing a cotton dress, something light-coloured to complement her blonde hair and pale complexion. If the night had cooled, she would have a coffee-coloured cashmere cardigan draped over her shoulders.

At first meeting, some people took Sybil Mars to be in her late twenties. Only by looking carefully at the tracery of lines around her eyes were they able to guess she had two daughters who were old enough to pursue their degrees, and their pleasures, as undergraduates.

'Charlie's eating at High Table tonight, Lewis,' she said. 'He's going to stay fairly late. They're entertaining Jeremy Bellingford's successor.'

There was a moment of pleasure when Lewis remembered that Bellingford, until recently their political master, had lost his seat at the General Election.

'Can you put me up tonight, Syb?' Lewis asked. 'I must come and see Charlie.'

'Of course. It's a pity you can't bring Hanna.'

'No chance, I'm afraid. She's working nights at the moment. A doctor's life is very hard.'

'Poor dear. It sounds as demanding as the life you and Charlie lead. Don't you wish you were both back at Oxford?'

'All the time,' he said. 'See you later.' He hung up and noticed that Morris's eyes still had not moved from the screen. Lewis snapped his fingers to gain his attention. Morris looked up at him.

'I think something has crept into your little room and died, Jack. You'd better check it isn't you.'

Morris looked around in a puzzled fashion as Lewis leaned in and took a set of keys for another car. On the drive to his home in Lamb's Conduit Street he thought about Joyce Maynard.

Despite her protestations he knew she was under tremendous strain. He decided to recommend that she go on leave, and he began to formulate a plan to have her replaced at the agency by one of their own temporary secretaries.

As he climbed the stairs to his own rooms he passed his sister's flat. It was on the landing below his own. He could see light beneath her door and as he paused he heard her laughter. He knocked and Janet opened the door.

'Hello, Lewis,' she said, her voice still full of humour. 'I'm just having a glass of wine in the kitchen with Roland.'

Lewis followed her into the tiny room. She had been ironing as well as entertaining Roland Perth, their landlord and proprietor of the Old Times Antique Shop which was on the ground floor.

Janet was wearing jeans and a pink shirt that was knotted at the waist. Her thick black hair was short enough to show the fine down on the nape of her neck. She had the same pale blue eyes as Lewis and there were similarities in their faces, but Lewis's features had a battered cast to them.

Roland Perth leaned against the sink, immaculate in grey flannel slacks and a light grey silk shirt. He would have been equally at home on the deck of a yacht.

'There's just enough for another glass, dear boy,' Roland said as he held up the bottle of wine, the cuff of his shirt slipping back to reveal the heavy gold watch on his tanned wrist.

'No thanks, Roly,' Lewis said. 'I just called to tell you I'm going away for a few days.'

He caught a fleeting look of concern on his sister's face.

'Anywhere interesting?' she said in a light voice.

He put his hand on her shoulder.

'Just routine,' he said, but she didn't look into his eyes. Instead she took up her iron once again.

'Oh, Hanna called. She'll be having a break at nine-thirty if you can get along to The Castle.'

He looked at his own ancient wristwatch.

'I'm not sure if I'll have time to make it.'

Roland shook his head in disapproval.

'The way you treat that delightful creature is disgraceful, and she only stays in this country because of you.'

Lewis shook his head: 'She stays here because she approves of the National Health Service.'

Roland smiled: 'Yes, dear, and if I was as rich as she was I could afford socialist principles as well. Would you like me to look after her while you're away?'

'Just keep an eye on my flat, Roland,' he said.

Perth raised his eyebrows in mock astonishment.

'I shouldn't worry, dear. If thieves broke into your bleak little rooms, they'd probably leave things for you.'

Lewis smiled. 'I forgot to ask if you had a good holiday in Greece,' he said.

Roland held up a hand, then let it fall onto the rim of the sink.

'I lost eight pounds. The natives were delightful, the beaches superb and the food was so wretched I couldn't eat a thing. I don't know why people go to health farms to lose weight when the cuisine in the Aegean will do the job for them.'

'No wonder Alexander the Great tried to conquer the world,' Lewis said. 'He was probably looking for a decent restaurant.'

Janet followed him to the door.

'Give me a ring if you're going to be longer than a few days,' she called out as he started to climb the stairs.

'If I get a chance,' he replied, and he let himself into his flat.

Lewis looked around the spartan rooms and thought of Roland's words. The plain, cheap furniture and the carpetless floors did make for a forbidding welcome. As he shaved and changed, Lewis remembered the tattoo on his arm, but decided that he did not have time to remove it. He buttoned the cuffs of the blue cotton shirt to obscure the livid emblem from view.

He was about to leave the flat when he stopped before an ancient, scarred upright piano that was next to the door. He raised the lid and played a sequence of chords with his right hand. The melancholy notes filled the cheerless room. On top of the piano was the carved wooden figure of an eighteenth-century rifleman. Propped against it was a Polaroid photograph of Hanna. He had taken it in the Boulevard St Germain a few months earlier. He studied the face for a moment then shut the piano with deliberation and hurried towards his car.

Twenty minutes later he noticed with satisfaction that there was a parking space outside the public house. The Castle was a heavy, tiled Edwardian building that had been modernised by the brewery in the early Seventies to coincide with the Victorian revival. They had chosen Scottish Baronial as the theme, so the walls were heavy with dark wood panels and the carpets woven into a vaguely tartan pattern.

When he entered the saloon, Hanna Pearce was standing with a tall bespectacled young man to the right of the doorway against a long, Formica-topped counter. Hanna looked up and smiled at him. He still had difficulty coming to terms with how attractive she was.

Lewis watched as the publican placed plates of baked beans and sausages on the counter before Hanna and her companion.

'I didn't know you were having dinner with somebody else,' Lewis said. 'Can you recommend the food here?'

Hanna pointed with a fork towards the gloomy-looking man who had served them and was now reading a newspaper he had spread on the bar.

'Meet Harry Cox, chef and master of the microwave oven.'

Lewis studied him for a moment. 'I don't think I'll bother,' he said before he turned to her companion. 'Hello, Nick. How's business?'

'Things are booming in our sector of the economy, old boy,' Dr Nicholas Hayward said through a mouthful of beans. 'Would you care for a drink?'

'No thanks,' Lewis replied but he took a sip of the orange juice from the glass before Hanna. 'I just dropped by to say I'm off for a few days.'

'Where to?' she asked and as she looked up at him Lewis noticed light blue smudges of fatigue beneath her eyes. He glanced at Nick who was slumped over his food. Both of them had the weary look that comes from long shifts of punishing work.

'South of France,' he said almost apologetically.

'Excellent,' Hanna said in a firm voice. 'I'll come with you.'

'Can you?' Lewis said with surprise.

Hanna laid down her fork. 'I've just switched some time with Sam Aldrich. I've got three clear days and my parents are at their home on the Cap – we can stay there.'

Lewis nodded with pleasure.

'Can you come with me to the car? I'm in a hurry.' He waved to her companion. 'Goodnight, Nick.' Hayward smiled a farewell before he turned again to his food.

Outside there were groups of young people dressed in summer clothes. They leaned against the wall of the pub relishing the warmth of an Indian summer night. Lewis and Hanna passed them by and stopped by the car.

'You look tired,' he said as they stood together on the pavement.

'We were short of staff this week. A couple of people are off sick.'

Lewis tried to think of something to ease her weariness. But all he could do was put out a hand and touch her cheek.

She smiled at the gesture. 'I'll be OK. A few days in the sunshine and I'll be ready to fight bears.'

He nodded and she could tell he was anxious to be on the move.

'Go on,' she said gently. 'I'll meet you at Heathrow for the morning flight to Nice.'

As he opened the door of the car, she spoke again.

'Incidentally, what kind of job are you on?'

'It won't take long,' he said.

'That doesn't answer the question, Lewis.'

He shrugged.

Hanna nodded. 'I know, I know. No questions, no rat pack,' she said.

'The expression is: No questions, no pack drill,' he said.

Hanna touched him on the shoulder.

'You stick to your version and I'll stick to mine.'

'See you at the airport,' Lewis said, and he got into the car.

Hanna walked slowly back to her supper, but she had lost her appetite for the food.

'Lucky chap, your Mr Horne,' Hayward said when he had scooped the last of the beans into his mouth. 'I wish this job took me to the South of France.'

'Yes,' Hanna said quietly. 'He gets to go all over the place. Sometimes I wonder if he's ever going to come back.'

Lewis made good time to Oxford. It was just before eleven o'clock when he crossed the dark waters of the Cherwell and passed Magdalen. Eventually he stopped before his own college. The lights of the Porter's Lodge shone through the open gates and showed a green sward of shaved grass in the quadrangle.

He paused beneath the familiar archway and looked into the office where Arthur Posgate was fussing with a notice board.

'Good evening, Arthur,' Lewis said to the white-haired figure who was wearing a grey cardigan of remarkable vintage. The old man turned slowly and peered suspiciously through a pair of spectacles that were repaired with sticking plaster. He blinked and smiled when he recognised Lewis.

'Captain Horne. Nice to see you, sir. You're a bit late for dinner.'

'I just came for a brandy.'

'If you're looking for the Provost, I saw him going to the house with Mr Mars and another gentleman a few minutes ago.'

'Thank you, Arthur,' Lewis said as he passed on and crunched along the gravel pathway that skirted the quadrangle.

All was quiet in the college. To his right the banks of Georgian windows that looked over the quadrangle were shuttered so that only cracks of light showed if the occupants were still awake. From the staircases broad shafts of light cut across the pathway.

Lewis approached the Provost's House that stood jutting out from the end of the pathway and saw that the black-painted door was ajar. He pushed it open and entered the stone-flagged hallway where he waited for a moment until he heard the low murmur of voices coming from the drawing-room.

Lewis knocked and entered. Three figures looked up from their easy chairs. Although they all wore dress clothes, each man was very different in appearance. Charles Austen Mars, tall and bony with grey-flecked hair and a long, lined face, wore an old, well-cut dinner jacket. He looked relaxed and very much at home in the atmosphere of the college. As head of the counter-terrorist unit of British Intelligence, his air of donnish calm created a useful impression among opponents in Whitehall who tended to underestimate some of the more ruthless aspects of his nature.

The short thickset figure of the Provost was clad in a double-breasted coat and the heavy, athletic body of Roger Kent, who sat on the edge of his chair as if to spring into action, was fashionably dressed in black mohair.

'Forgive me for calling at this hour, Provost,' Lewis said.

The Provost looked up, his round cheerful face dominated by thick spectacles.

'You're most welcome, Lewis. Will you join us in a brandy?'

Lewis nodded. 'Thank you. A small one.'

Charlie had unwound his long body from the chair at Lewis's unexpected appearance. He turned to Kent. 'Roger, may I introduce Captain Lewis Horne? A colleague of mine and a fellow of this college. Lewis, this is Roger Kent, who has taken over from Jeremy Bellingford.'

Kent got up and Lewis saw how fit he was. He leaned forward like a boxer as he took Lewis's hand.

'Captain, good to meet you.'

The smile was attractive, almost boyish and it was still possible to hear traces of a Tyneside accent in the deep voice.

'I enjoyed your book,' Kent said. 'Are you writing at the moment?'

Lewis was momentarily surprised by the question until he remembered that the junior minister had been a long time in politics for one so young. He had obviously mastered the flattering trick of remembering minor facts about people.

'Yes,' Lewis said.

'What about?'

'The private soldiers of the Civil War.'

'What interested you in that subject?'

Lewis looked into the broad dark face. The man had his head cocked to one side as he waited for Lewis to answer. There was shrewdness in the features and the look of pleasant anticipation schoolmasters get when they have posed a difficult problem for a bright pupil.

Lewis was careful with his reply.

'In the sixteenth century the King was the personification of the state. To persuade a common farm labourer that it was the right thing to defend the cause of Parliament instead of the Royal Family caused an interesting series of intellectual and emotional difficulties. I'm working on how they resolved those conflicts.'

Kent turned and smiled at Charlie and the Provost as if Lewis had passed a test.

'I wish I could get my civil servants to answer a simple question with such clarity,' he said. Then he turned back to Lewis. 'But I'm sorry. I imagine you want to talk to Charlie?'

The Provost got up and adjusted his rumpled suit. Lewis noticed that the collar of his shirt curled awkwardly. It wasn't that the Provost was badly dressed, more that his body resented clothes.

'Gentlemen, I suspect Lewis has some highly confidential information for you. I will take this opportunity to go to my bed.'

Roger Kent protested. 'Anything Captain Horne says can be trusted with you,' he said.

The Provost held up his hands. 'Please, no. I find new secrets too much of a burden at my age. Roger, you know where your room is. I will see you at breakfast.'

He turned to Lewis and paused for a moment, thrusting his hands deep into the pockets of his dinner jacket. 'I enjoyed your book, Lewis, but I think this one has greater potential.' He glanced around the room. 'I wonder if the country got the best bargain when you went for a soldier?'

He patted Lewis on the shoulder.

27

'Take care. The College Roll of Honour is already long. Try not to add your name to it. Good night to you, Charlie. My love to Sybil.'

When the door had closed, Charlie Mars walked across the room to a massive carved Victorian sideboard and poured himself another drink.

'Another brandy?' he said to Lewis as he added soda water to his own drink.

'Yes, a weak one. I'm driving.'

'Good,' Charlie said. 'I won't need a taxi. You can give me a lift home.'

'Not only that. I have Sybil's permission to stay the night,' Lewis said.

He glanced around the room while Charlie mixed the drinks. It hadn't changed since he was an undergraduate. The chairs and sofas were on the grand scale of Victorian opulence: carved walnut covered with grey-blue silk. The wood surfaces were dark and glowed from generations of regular polishing. The paintings in their heavy gilt frames were eighteenth-century landscapes, and the great fireplace of white and pink marble was massed with brass pokers and fire-irons. The light from the table lamps reflected from the silver frames of the photographs on the grand piano. It was a good room, with tables and desks and bookcases. A place you could spend a rainy day in.

Charlie handed him his drink and Roger Kent held up a hand. 'Before you begin, Captain Horne, may I put in a plea? As a new boy, I'm anxious to find out as much as I can about the work your department does. If you have the time, could you give me the whole picture?'

Lewis took a mouthful of his drink and looked towards Charlie Mars, who answered with a barely perceptible nod.

'Just how much detail do you want?' Lewis asked.

Kent gestured with his glass. 'Start with yourself, then the department and what you're doing now.'

Lewis took another swallow from his drink before he began.

'My father was an army officer. I went to a direct-grant grammar school. When I was at Oxford my father was killed on active service. I decided to follow a family tradition, so I went to Sandhurst. Eventually I was commissioned into the Rifle Brigade. Subsequently I transferred to the Special Air Service. Charlie and I kept in touch from the time I was an undergraduate here. When he was asked to form Gower Street section he requested me and I was seconded with other colleagues from the regiment.'

'How would you describe the work of Gower Street?' Kent asked Charlie without looking in Lewis's direction.

'We hunt terrorists and we fight those agents of other countries who use force in the pursuit of their political aims.'

'Is there much rough stuff?' Kent asked.

Charlie nodded. 'That's why I was asked to form the unit. Spying and espionage wasn't too dangerous before the Second World War. In fact, it was still something of a gentlemen's game. Novelists, travel writers, chaps with private incomes amusing themselves as they drifted around the world. A lot of it was making sure no-one was getting up to any mischief in the Empire. It all started to change with the rise of terrorism in the Sixties.'

'Are you saying that spying has changed?'

'No,' Charlie said. 'We're talking about different things. As far as spying is concerned, to a great extent the rules of the game still apply. As far as it goes, Russia is still the main competition. If we catch any of their agents we deport them if they're doing low-level economic stuff. A big catch is worth some propaganda value, although the general public is becoming more cynical about that sort of thing. But Moscow Central prides itself on bringing its people home, so a lot of swapping goes on. Of course, occasionally someone gets killed, but it is pretty rare and bad for business.

'What really altered things was the beginning of international terrorism. You know the sort of thing: gunning down people in a shopping precinct in Brussels because you disagree with the political situation in the Middle East. If an act of terrorism bears no relation to the victims and no relevance to the grievances, you can see how difficult it is to take protective counter-measures. It's impossible if everyone is a potential target. So we had to devise new tactics. We went

29

over to the offensive and decided we would actively hunt for them.'

'How successful have you been?' Kent asked.

Charlie Mars gave the question some consideration.

'We have prevented acts of terrorism. People are alive who would otherwise be dead. To a degree that must be counted as successful.'

'Anyone would accept that,' Kent said. 'Tell me, what kind of co-operation do you get from other countries?'

Charlie looked up at the ceiling as if preparing a careful answer.

'Good within the boundaries of other agencies' characteristics.'

'I don't follow,' Kent said.

Charlie shrugged. 'All Intelligence services by their nature are paranoid. If secrecy is your stock in trade you tend to extend that secrecy to everyone.'

'Even your own side?' Kent asked.

'In some cases, yes. In the secret world you tend to make deals with individuals, not organisations.'

'What's your unit's biggest asset?'

Charlie smiled. 'That's easy. Beyond question, Lewis and his colleagues. They're effective, and their reputation is a useful psychological weapon.'

Kent turned to Lewis. 'How do you chaps feel about that?'

Lewis put his glass down on the carpet at his feet.

'It's more interesting than NATO exercises.'

Kent took a charred pipe from his pocket and began to pack it carefully from a yellow oilskin pouch.

'So if Her Majesty's Government needs someone bumped off, we can call on you chaps?'

'Only if we know they're dangerous,' Lewis said quietly. 'We're not murderers or assassins. We're still soldiers. The only difference is the choice of battlefield.'

Kent put a match to the tobacco.

'I see the distinction. So what are you working on now, Captain Horne?'

'One of our operators has information about a terrorist attack.'

'Who is he?'

'It's her, actually. Joyce Maynard, code-name Skylark.'

Kent smiled. 'You actually use code-names these days?'

'You'd be surprised at how old habits linger on, Roger. We still use invisible ink on occasions.'

'Tell me about her,' Kent said.

Charlie ran his fingers through his hair in a brushing motion.

'She's a brilliant woman. A mathematician, and she has a genius for code-breaking. Claude Henderson recruited her. Claude is old-time MI5. He came to us from Curzon Street. Joyce was doing post-graduate work at London University.'

Kent interrupted again. 'How did you know how to recruit her?'

Charlie stretched out his legs.

'Claude Henderson does that side. He's got all his MI5 experience and the contacts. We have friends in most of the universities.'

'Why Joyce Maynard?'

'She seemed the right sort. Her father had spent his life in the Stationery Office printing high-security material. He died quite suddenly a year ago. Joyce did well at school and university. She was a straightfoward, uncomplicated girl. Her height caused her a few problems when she was young but once she got to eighteen and discovered tall boys like tall girls, that sorted itself out.'

Kent jabbed the stem of his pipe towards Charlie, who gazed for a moment with wistful longing at the trail of light blue tobacco smoke that curled from the bowl. 'None of these seem good enough reasons to recruit a girl into the Intelligence service.'

'I agree,' Charlie said. 'It was her choice of careers that caused us to make the approach.'

'Explain,' Kent said.

Charlie continued, 'When asked what she wanted to do she chose research, voluntary overseas work, teaching or the civil service.'

'So?' Kent said.

'They're all jobs that put dedication before self-interest.

31

She was worth the approach and Claude Henderson was right. She trained for two years, and for the last two years she's been on active service with us.'

'What's she doing now?'

Charlie shifted slightly in his armchair before he answered.

'She's working for a travel agency behind Wardour Street which is a front for a terrorist group.'

'IRA?' Kent asked as he put another match to the pipe.

'No,' Charlie said.

'Extreme left?' Kent said sharply.

'Just extreme. You can't apply the term left to these people. They're against all forms of government. They consider the Supreme Soviet and the leaders of the People's Republic of China to be enemies of the people.'

'Who are they for?' Kent asked.

'As far as we can gather, only those individuals who agree with their policies.'

'That's extreme,' Kent said with a grim smile. 'How did you find out the travel agency was a front?'

Charlie rubbed his hair again.

'Piece of luck, really. The floor below is occupied by a tailor's workshop run by a Mr Bernard Black. Inspector Light of the Special Branch has been going there to get his suits made for years. Mr Black thought a lot of suspicious people seemed to be using the place. Actually what he meant was a lot of Arabs. Then he wanted to take Mrs Black on a holiday to Israel. The agency didn't seem keen to do the booking and advised him to go elsewhere. So he told Inspector Light, who contacted us. We watched them for a bit and eventually spotted several people who were known to us. So we got Joyce a job there.'

'How? Jobs aren't easy to get anywhere these days,' Kent asked.

'We got one of their girls a better position and Joyce Maynard applied immediately the girl resigned. Until now the stuff she has given us has been good but fairly routine. We've been able to keep track of several people. Today we got a message from Skylark to say she wanted to make contact. Will you elaborate, Lewis?'

As he was about to answer, an owl hooted from somewhere in the Provost's garden.

'The Romans would have taken that for an omen,' Kent said from behind drifting clouds of pipe smoke. 'I'm sorry, Captain Horne. Please continue.'

Lewis leaned forward and picked up his drink. Then he rose to his feet before he answered.

'Sometime between the hours of four and five o'clock tomorrow afternoon four frogmen will swim ashore from a motor yacht off Cap Ferrat, land in the grounds of a villa and assassinate an American industrialist called Marshall Cutter.'

'Cutter?' Kent said with an edge of interest in his voice.

'Do you know him?' Charlie Mars asked in response.

'I know him,' Kent said and he rested his head back against the grey-blue silk chair and recalled what he knew about the Cutter family. 'His grandfather was one of those nineteenth-century robber barons. The fortune was founded on silver, then cattle. Marshall Cutter the First owned a town in Arizona. Probably the family still does. These days they're producing everything from drawing pins to space shuttles. The Cutter Electronics Corporation has some very large contracts with the Pentagon.'

'There could be a connection we don't know about,' Lewis said. 'The man who ordered the hit team is based in Tucson.'

Kent took a few thoughtful draws on his pipe and suddenly Lewis realised that he smoked it to make him look more mature, a necessary commodity in a politician.

'I think we had better involve the Americans,' he said finally. 'Good for relations, that sort of thing. How would you feel about working with them?'

Lewis shrugged. 'They're a lot easier to get on with than the DST.'

Kent looked puzzled.

'The Direction de la Surveillance du Territoire – the French counter-espionage service,' Charlie explained.

Kent widened his eyes. 'My God, the French. Will we have to involve them?'

Charlie smiled sympathetically.

'I will talk to René Clair, our liaison man. If anyone can help, he will.'

'And I'd better speak to Harry Selig in Washington as well,' Kent said.

He took an address book from his pocket, reached across for the telephone on the side table next to him and dialled a long series of numbers. 'I must remember to reimburse the college,' he said to himself as he waited.

'Hello, it's Roger Kent calling from England. May I speak to General Selig? . . . Certainly I'll hold.' Kent glanced at his wristwatch. 'He's having dinner. It's only six-thirty in Virginia. What extraordinary times Americans eat.'

While he waited, the owl hooted once again.

'Hello, Harry. Good to speak to you again. This is not a secure line but I have to talk. We have a problem. Someone nasty is coming our way from your country. We think your people should be involved.' Kent listened for a few moments. 'Captain Horne is handling this end. Oh, you know him? Good. Well, just a moment, I'll put him on.'

Lewis took the offered handset.

'Hello, Lewis,' the general said in a crisp voice. 'Still a captain? I thought you would have been promoted by now.'

'It comes slowly in our army, sir,' Lewis replied.

The general came to the point immediately. 'What are you looking for? Brains or balls?'

Lewis smiled. It always amused him that Charlie Mars's equivalent in the United States should be in such remarkable contrast. General Harry Selig had spent most of his life in the Marine Corps. It had not been a career that had smoothed the edges of his tongue or his social demeanour.

'Both,' Lewis replied.

The general paused. 'That nasty, eh?'

'Yes, sir. It could be.'

'Where is this nastiness coming from?'

'The hit team seem to be local talent but the orders are coming from Tucson.'

The general thought again. 'I've got a guy in Bonn who was born and bred in southern Arizona. Where do you want to meet him?'

'Noon tomorrow at the Negresco Beach Club in Nice.'
Lewis hesitated. 'Tell him I've got a big tattoo of a heart and
dagger on my right arm.'

The general chuckled. 'I'd like to have been with you the
night you got that. By the way, how's Charlie?'

'He's right here, sir. I'll put him on.'

Charlie took the telephone from Lewis and exchanged
pleasantries for a few moments, then hung up.

'Another drink, Captain Horne?' Kent asked as he raised
the brandy decanter.

'I think I can manage another weak one,' Lewis said and he
joined Kent at the sideboard while Charlie Mars started to
make a call to Paris.

From above the Porter's Lodge a bell chimed softly. The
drapes were back drawn from the windows so they could look
out over the Provost's garden. There was enough light reflected from the lake to show the trees at the water's edge. They
heard the bell chime twelve times.

Roger Kent looked at his watch. 'It's only seven minutes to
midnight,' he said. 'What does that bell signify?'

'The King's Minutes,' Lewis answered.

'What are they?' Kent asked.

Lewis took the glass of brandy before he answered.

'When Oxford was Charles I's headquarters during the
Civil War, he dined at this college. The other guests, being
syncophantic, assured him the war was as good as won.
Charles told them it was later than they thought and told
them to ring the midnight bell early every night as a reminder
of how little time there was.' Lewis continued to look out of
the window. 'So it goes on.'

Kent followed Lewis's gaze across the moonlit garden.

'It's very beautiful here.'

'Very,' Lewis answered.

'I got my degree at night school, you know. While I
worked.'

'Yes,' Lewis said. The story was well known: Kent had
started out as a coal miner and ended as the youngest member
of a Cabinet since William Pitt.

'The mine I worked is closed now,' he said and Lewis

35

noticed the Tyneside accent was more pronounced as he spoke. 'It's a bloody terrible way for men to earn a living.' He paused, still looking out over the darkened garden. 'All our people should know places like this,' he said quietly. 'There's a lot worth keeping in this country.'

Charlie finished his call and joined them.

'That seems to be all right,' he said. 'René thinks he can give you a clear run. Here's an address in Nice, near the flower market. He says they'll fix you up with the tools of your trade.'

Lewis slipped the oblong card into his pocket.

'By the way, I heard part of your conversation when I was on the telephone; that story of the King's Minutes is highly dubious, you know,' Charlie said.

Lewis looked up with interest. 'Really?'

'Yes,' Charlie said as he took more brandy. 'When I was an undergraduate, Giles Landis and I checked it out pretty thoroughly. The King hated this college because we didn't melt down our silver for the Royalist cause. So he would hardly have dined here. The more likely explanation is the one we discovered.'

'What was that?' Kent asked with interest.

Charlie took his time, secure in the knowledge that he had roused the interest of his audience.

'In the 1830s the Provost was called Bostock. He had a feud with the Head Porter, Belcher, who was related to Jim Belcher, the prize fighter. When Belcher was drunk he used to ring the midnight bell at various times to confuse Bostock. One night he rang it at seven minutes to midnight and Bostock was waiting with the Dean. They had synchronised their watches and they ordered Belcher to ring the bell at exactly the same time each night from then on. So Belcher never got another night off for eighteen years.'

Kent let out a bellow of laughter.

'This bloody country. How wonderful! So why didn't your story gain wider acceptance?'

Charlie shrugged. 'People preferred the King's Minutes version. It's a fact of life all historians have to face. The myths of the past are often stronger than the truth.'

Kent put down his empty glass and raised his shoulders as if to ease tension.

'Well, I don't think there is anything else I can do tonight,' he said, in a voice that had lost the sounds of the north-east once again. 'Good luck in your venture tomorrow, Captain Horne. You'll keep in touch, Charlie?'

'Of course, Roger. We wish you goodnight.'

Roger Kent took one last look over the garden and muttered, 'The King's Minutes.' Lewis could tell he was committing the story to memory.

They left him in the living-room, let themselves out of the Provost's House and walked slowly towards the Porter's Lodge. The quiet of the sleeping college was broken by the owl hooting once again.

Neither of them spoke on the drive home. Finally they reached the entrance to the lane that led to Charlie's house. The headlights of the car flickered from trees and shrubs until they lit the rose-pink bricks and the heavy wisteria that clad the Georgian frontage.

'What did you think of him?' Charlie asked as Lewis locked the car door.

'Kent? He seems pleasant enough. At least he can grasp an explanation quickly.'

Charlie opened the front door and his dogs wagged their greeting and jumped up at Lewis.

'Yes, his predecessor could be infuriatingly slow. It wasn't that he was stupid, just so preoccupied with himself he couldn't pay attention to anyone else. What about Kent? Is he the sort of chap you would go into the jungle with?'

Lewis remembered the handshake as firm and dry, but it had been many years since the hands had been roughened and dirtied by coal. They stopped for a moment in the darkened hall while Lewis considered his reply.

'People always get the wrong idea about jungles, Charlie. It's best not to crash about in them in a heroic fashion. Creeping like a coward is the way to stay alive.'

They climbed the stairs to the first landing before Charlie spoke again.

'Maybe he'll be good in the jungles of Whitehall. I hope he

37

doesn't prove to be a disappointment – I rather like him. Goodnight.'

Lewis climbed another flight of stairs to the room he knew Sybil had given him. One of the bare polished boards creaked as he walked upon it, just as it had when he had first slept in the room as an undergraduate. The water from the cold tap in the basin still ran slowly and the towel was as white and rough as ever when he dried his hands and face.

There were three books on the small mantelpiece above the gas fire: Chesterton's *Letters, Ruff's Guide to the Turf* and a collection of sermons by a Victorian ancestor of Charlie's. None of them tempted Lewis.

Instead he turned off the bedside lamp and lay awake for a few minutes. He hadn't drawn the curtains, so that moonlight filled the room from the big dormer window and he could make out the details on two drawings of Bath that were on the wall next to his bed. Something that Kent had said had seemed odd, and he searched through his memory to remember it.

After a few moments it came to him. 'Six-thirty, what extraordinary times Americans eat.' As a lad who started out in life down a coal mine, early in the evening would be the normal time to eat your evening meal. Lewis wondered at the affectation. He thought of the contradictions in Roger Kent: keeping his Tyneside accent; and professing surprise at working-class eating habits. I'll ask Charlie tomorrow, he thought, as he turned onto his right side and drifted into sleep.

Chapter Two

When the aircraft began its long turn over Marseilles, Lewis felt a familiar tightening in his chest. He consciously took deep breaths as he looked down on the sunlit coastline of the Côte d'Azur. The sea shaded from sapphire to Prussian blue where the ocean bed shelved into deep water, and tiny sailing boats cut the surface with white lines of foam, but the sight did not cheer him. Instead he focused on the aircraft's engines, which had begun a familiar grumble of changing roars as the pilot lined up for his descent to Nice airport.

Lewis glanced around with envy at the nonchalance with which the other passengers were treating the landing. An elderly man with glasses sat across the aisle from Hanna, calmly chewing his pen and studying the *Daily Telegraph* crossword, while three small children in front squabbled and squirmed as if they were on a Sunday drive in the family car. Hanna, next to him, was as cheerful and serene as the steward, who was making his final patrol.

Lewis hated the feeling of helplessness, the idea that he was trusting his fate to the hands of an anonymous pilot, who was lowering the aircraft so close to the water that it was as if they were about to settle on the gently chopping surface.

Unconsciously Lewis began to increase his grip on Hanna's hand. Eventually she winced at the pressure, so that he had to concentrate in order to slacken his hold. He closed his eyes as they hurtled towards the runway that jutted into the sea. The pilot touched down so gently there was not the slightest jolt to tell him they had landed. He opened his eyes when the engines reversed and they gradually rolled to a halt.

When it had stopped completely Lewis began to relax the muscles that had tightened in his shoulders and arms. He dabbed his forehead with the sleeve of his shirt and caught an expression of sympathy from the hostess, who smiled quickly.

'Warm, isn't it?'

Lewis smiled ruefully. 'It always is, flying.' He took his holdall from the baggage rack and allowed Hanna to go first as they shuffled to the exit. The three children ahead of them swatted each other with magazines despite their mother's feeble attempts to restore discipline.

They walked across the concrete apron towards the airport buildings and the air was warm and gentle with the mixed scent of pine, fresh coffee and aviation fuel. The combination cheered him, and he remembered that the old soldiers of the Roman Empire had retired to Provence; a soft billet after the harsh garrisons of the Rhine and northern Britain, Lewis thought.

'Flying doesn't get any easier for you, does it?' Hanna said at last. He shook his head and smiled.

Once through immigration and past a waiting family that had begun to embrace the mother and the three boisterous children with Gallic passion, they made for the taxis at a leisurely pace. The August crowds had gone, and, with them, the near-panic encountered at the height of the season.

'I'll ring later,' Lewis said when Hanna was settled into her taxi.

'If we go out for any reason, Connie and Vincent will be at the villa. They'll tell you where we are.'

Lewis nodded and gave a brief wave as her cab pulled away.

His own journey didn't take long. The airport was just on the edge of the city. Lewis had been to Nice before but he had spent most of the time then close to the Promenade des Anglais, the long, curving avenue where the best hotels and apartments looked over the sea.

The rest of the city to the north was unexplored territory. As he was driven along the magnificent palm-decked avenue skirting the bay, Lewis began to think about Hanna's parents and the meeting that was going to take place that evening.

Although he already knew odd details about them from Hanna, he realised that he had no idea at all of their physical appearance.

During the war her father had been a pilot in the American 8th Air Force, stationed in East Anglia, where he had met Hanna's mother, who was the daughter of a local landowner. They had married despite the opposition of both families and produced two children, Hanna and her brother, who had been killed in Vietnam.

He also knew that Hanna's father was one of the four richest men in America and that one day she would inherit quite a sizeable piece of the earth. Lewis realised they were going to show more than just a passing interest in him.

'Negresco,' the driver said.

'Drop me at the Beach Club,' Lewis instructed, and they came to a halt opposite the domed hotel. He paid off the cab and crossed the wide pavement to the steps that led down to the beach. There was no sand in the bay, just a massive sweep of pebbles, but the grand hotels had brought luxury to the water's edge. Open-air restaurants and shaded bars led to wooden decks and duckwalks, while mattresses and umbrellas covered the stony ground.

Lewis looked at his watch. He would have enough time for a swim before his meeting. One of the Beach Club attendants promised to look after his bag. He changed and waded into the warm water. Then he struck out hard away from the shore, each powerful stroke easing the tension his body had stored up during the flight.

After ten minutes he stopped swimming and trod water. When he turned to look back at the shoreline, it was as clear and crisp as a postcard. Three boats with brightly coloured sails moved in his field of vision. The sky was pale blue, but towards the Alpes Maritimes there was a long, dark smudge of smoke far beyond the fringe of palms and the roofs of the hotels that line the Promenade des Anglais. At that moment the dark shape of a fire-fighting plane droned over his head in the direction of the dark horizon, ready to dump its cargo of sea water on the distant burning mountains.

He floated contentedly for a few minutes and then swam

41

towards the shore in a leisurely fashion. As the beach came closer he began to yearn for a drink to wash his mouth clean cf the sea salt. Back on land, he padded up the wooden duckwalk between the geometric rows of mattresses and stood for a few minutes under the shower, each moment's delay enhancing the anticipation of the cold beer to come. Finally he rubbed himself down with the towel the attendant handed him and sat down on one of the stools against the shaded bar.

The only other customer was a solemn-faced little girl with sun-whitened hair who was carefully eating a peach melba. She stopped to observe him for a few moments and then returned to the task of spooning the melting icecream.

Lewis drank his beer quickly then asked for a coffee. The swarthy young man began to manipulate the hissing machine.

'Good season?' Lewis asked.

The barman made a rocking motion with his left hand, fingers spread open.

'Not too bad. Not so many Americans. But there are more Japanese now, and Germans. The British always. They tell us every year that Britain has finally had it, but back they come. Maybe nobody told them.' He put the cup of coffee down carefully. 'Where are you from? The north?' he asked.

Lewis took a sip.

'St Malo.'

The barman nodded with satisfaction as he turned away. 'I thought I recognised the accent.'

Lewis smiled at the remark. He was pleased that the barman had taken him for a native, but it was easy to fool the young man. His own version of the French accent was so heavy with the sounds of the south it was rather like expecting a Clydeside barman to know the difference between people from Devon and Cornwall.

Lewis took another mouthful of the frothy coffee and heard footsteps on the duckwalk. The man who slid onto the bar stool next to him pushed his aviator's sunglasses further up the bridge of his nose and stared down at the copy of *Nice-Matin* which he had spread on the bar before him. He was of medium height, with short brown hair and a deep ruddy tan.

He wore a dark blue sports shirt and pale grey slacks with black tasselled loafers.

Lewis judged him to be in his late thirties. He could tell from the man's slimness and the muscles in the forearms and the corded neck that he was very fit. Even his face looked hard. The nose was ridged and sharp, with flared nostrils, and the cheeks and brow were bony, the flesh taut across the plains and hollows. A black cigar was clamped between his teeth. It smelt cheap.

He asked for a coffee and continued to study the paper. The barman gave it to him and went off to chat with his friend who handed out the towels.

Without raising his eyes from *Nice-Matin* the American said 'Hi' in a quiet voice.

'Anything in the paper?' Lewis asked politely and the American raised it up to show the page.

'There are bad fires in the Alpes Maritimes. They've called in the army to help fight them.' The voice was deep and pleasant.

'It happens a lot,' Lewis said.

The American glanced down at Lewis's forearm.

'That's nice work,' he said. 'What is it, your regimental symbol?'

Lewis placed his left hand over much of the tattoo.

'I needed it for a job. It comes off.'

The American removed the cigar from his mouth and held out his hand.

'David Neil – but everybody drops the David.'

'Lewis Horne.'

They shook hands. The small girl finished her peach melba, watched them both for a few moments and then slid from her stool and rejoined her mother, who was one of the few people sunbathing. David Neil turned on his stool and looked without expression at the woman. She was wearing a tiny, orange bikini bottom, her naked breasts as darkly tanned as the rest of her body.

'Is it always this quiet?' he asked.

'August is their big month but this is quieter than usual for September.'

43

Neil nodded. 'This is my first time down here.' He turned to Lewis. 'Tell me, what kind of French was the guy behind the bar speaking?'

'The local patois,' Lewis explained. 'Until the Treaty of Savoy, Nice was an Italian city. The border was the River Var, not the mountains. They mixed Italian in with French.'

Neil carefully ground out the remains of his cigar.

'What's the job? All I got was an instruction to make contact; no information.'

Lewis looked at the towel attendant who lounged near them watching the woman sunbathing. He didn't like talking in one place for too long.

'Just give me a moment to get dressed and we'll take a stroll along the Promenade.'

Lewis dressed quickly, gave the attendant twenty francs and joined Neil at the foot of the stairs.

'Why do the English get the credit for this?' Neil asked as he gestured along the Promenade des Anglais. Lewis turned to the right at the top of the steps and they walked slowly in an easterly direction next to the sea.

'The English paid for it,' Lewis said. 'They developed the South of France as a winter resort. Nice, Cannes, Monte Carlo, Hyères. Nobody fashionable dreamt of coming here in the summer until the Twenties. There was unemployment in Nice round about the turn of the century. The British residents put up the money to build the promenade.'

'I see,' Neil said. 'So tell me more about the job.'

Lewis slung his holdall to the other shoulder before he began.

'Have you heard of Marshall Cutter?'

'The guy who owns the Cutter Corporation? Sure. I've seen him on the cover of *Time* magazine.'

'He's got a villa at Cap Ferrat just a few miles down the coast, towards Italy.' Lewis gestured in the direction they were walking. 'There's an organisation in London that puts hit teams together for people of the same broad political persuasion. Forty-eight hours ago there was a request from Tucson for four top operators who could use sub-aqua equipment to meet aboard a boat in Antibes today. They would then proceed to Marshall Cutter's back door and dispose of him.'

David Neil took another black cigar from the breast pocket of his sports shirt and cupped his hands protectively as he lit it, although there was no wind at all. When it was burning to his satisfaction, he turned to Lewis.

'I suppose they want us to bring one of these guys back alive?'

Lewis stopped and put his hands in his trouser pockets.

'That's right.'

Neil put one foot on the low wall. 'How do you feel about that?' he said as he looked out to sea.

'I've no objection,' Lewis replied, choosing his words with care. 'Providing they understand my priorities.'

Neil turned and looked at him.

'What are they?' he asked in a flat voice.

'It's simple – the first people we bring back alive are you and me.'

Neil smiled. 'I think we're going to get along just fine on this job.' He turned from the view and pointed to a dusty Golf with the hood down that was parked near them.

'That's mine.'

Every available inch of the car was packed with baggage. Lewis took a large canvas duffel bag from the passenger seat and rested his feet on a suitcase, with the duffel bag on his lap. Neil looked down at him with a grin.

'My God, you British Secret Service guys always look so damned debonair.'

He slipped into the driver's seat and quickly eased the car into the traffic.

'Why the hell do you need all this stuff?' Lewis asked.

Neil eased the car into the fast lane, earning a blast of disapproval from a big Renault that swung out to overtake them at the first opportunity.

'This is my last job in Europe. I was just going to deliver the car to a guy I've sold it to in our Paris station, before I got on a plane for the States. I'm going back to Langley and then I'll be a field instructor for a while.' He pumped on the accelerator and shot forward to stop a Fiat from cutting in.

45

'God, I'm going to miss the driving over here. Do you know we can only do fifty-five in the States?'

Lewis watched with alarm as Neil crammed the Golf almost against the rear bumper of the Renault.

'Fancy inventing something as dangerous as an automobile and then not letting anyone drive it over fifty-five miles an hour. I tell you, America's really getting middle-aged.'

Lewis indicated with his hand and shouted above the roar of the slipstream. 'Take the next right.'

Neil made a tight, squealing turn and Lewis looked down at the street map of Nice he had bought at the airport. After ten minutes of crawling through the streets of a fairly rundown neighbourhood, they turned into a narrow cobbled alleyway and stopped next to a long shop that sold discount shoes. Neil looked at the rows of dusty stock as Lewis checked the address once again.

'This is it,' Lewis said. 'The open gates there with the sacks of cement and stuff outside.'

The yard they turned into had an old peeling sign over the entrance to a large courtyard – *Paul Bouchet et Fils*. There was a clutter of stacked paving stones, piles of wood, barrels of nails, heaps of sand and large creosoted sheds with heavy metal locks on the doors. A decrepit dog with grey spiky hair lay in a patch of sunlight in front of a shed that served as the office. The windows were open to allow air to circulate.

Lewis and Neil got out of the car and walked towards a shadowy figure that sat in the gloom, listening to a tape of Edith Piaf, the curious throaty, warbling voice filling the deserted yard with its melancholy sound. They stood before the man seated at a desk made from a decorator's trestle and waited for him to speak.

The eyes that looked at them with disinterest were set like poached eggs in a baggy face that billowed with pouches of flesh. Short, cropped hair the same colour as the dog's topped a once-powerful body that had run to fat. The man wore a string vest and when he stood up they saw a pair of creased shorts and two unlikely thin legs.

'M'sieur,' he said and they noticed large, horse-like yellow teeth.

Lewis spoke rapidly with a southern accent.

'René Clair sent us. He says you can help us with a job we have to do.'

The fat man didn't reply. Instead he took a bunch of keys from a hook next to him and joined them outside. The dog got up and stood in a cringing fashion by his side.

Still without speaking, he gestured with his head for them to follow and led them across the yard, his sandals making a slapping sound on the cobbles. Slowly he selected the key to one of the locks on a pair of doors that were set into an ancient stone wall. They followed him into the dark interior, and their guide switched on the lights. They were inside a massive, windowless storeroom. The whitewashed walls reflected the light of the strips of neon overhead. A variety of vehicles was parked in rows against one wall of the warehouse, and on the other side were work benches and heavy metal storage cupboards.

'What do you need?' the old man said.

'This will do,' Lewis said, slapping a small, white-painted Ford truck with the sign *Service du Piscine* lettered on the side. 'Do you have any white overalls?'

'Sure,' their provider grunted. 'What about weapons?'

'Something small and light with plenty of firepower, preferably with silencers.'

'Uzis?'

'That's OK with me.' Lewis looked to Neil for approval.

'An Uzi is fine.'

The man unlocked one of the khaki-painted storage cupboards and took two squat little sub-machine guns from a rack and two bags with shoulder straps.

'The silencers and six magazine clips are here. Do you want handguns?'

They both nodded. He unlocked the cabinet next to them and swung it open so they could make their selection from the variety displayed before them. There must have been over a hundred guns in the cabinet. Neil chose a Smith and Wesson .38 Police Special in a leather shoulder holster. Lewis took his time and eventually found a Browning automatic. He checked the action and then sorted around until he found a

47

further two magazines and a box of nine-millimetre ammunition, which he put in the bag with his other items.

'OK?' the fat man asked.

Suddenly Neil whistled. 'What have we got here?' he said in an appreciative voice. Then he reached into the cabinet and took out a combat knife in a metal sheath. It made a zinging sound as he drew the carbon-black blade free from the scabbard. The back four inches of the blade were serrated so that you could saw wood – or through an opponent's pelvis. Neil sheathed the blade and tucked it into the waistband of his trousers.

'Do you want us to sign for this stuff?' Lewis asked.

The man shrugged and smiled.

'I wouldn't mind the van back. The weapons are untraceable.'

'Can I leave my car here?' Neil asked in halting French.

The man nodded.

'Do you do removals?' Lewis asked him.

'Not here,' the fat man said. 'Ring this number.' He handed Neil a grubby card with a Nice telephone number printed on it.

As Lewis drove from the yard they could see the mangy dog cocking its leg against the wheel of the Golf.

'I should have put the hood up,' Neil said gloomily. 'That dog is going to get to my luggage.'

Lewis looked at him with curiosity.

'What the hell do you want the knife for? I wasn't planning any hand-to-hand combat on this job.'

Neil took the knife from his waistband and held it up with evident pleasure.

'I've been meaning to get one of these babies for a long time. It's for my old man. They're great little hunting knives.' He put the knife away carefully and began to check the sub-machine guns, holding them low in his lap so that other motorists could not see what he was doing.

When they stopped at the lights, Lewis glanced down and watched for a few moments as Neil deftly made checks and adjustments. Lewis could see he was a natural with weapons, one of those people to whom a gun seems like a natural

48

extension of the body. When he was satisfied he packed them back into the satchels.

'OK?' Lewis asked as they turned back onto the Promenade des Anglais.

'Fine. The Uzis look as if they've only been test-fired. The .38's new. Your Browning's been around as long as I have.'

Lewis glanced at him again. When youth has passed, most men soften, muscles lose tone, the waist thickens. A few seem to get harder. Lewis found it difficult to imagine how David Neil would have looked when young. His age seemed to fit him like a well-cut suit.

'How did you get into this?' Lewis asked.

Neil gave a short, barking laugh.

'Drifted in, I guess. Reserve officer, training corps, when I was at Arizona University . . . they said I was a natural so I joined the Rangers.'

Lewis knew the rest. 'Fort Benning?'

'Yeah – jump school, then long-range recon. in 'Nam. After that I was an instructor for a while. Then my wife divorced me and I started to unravel for a bit. That's when the Marine found me. He kicked me back into shape. Since then I've been with the department.'

Lewis knew the Marine referred to was General Harry Selig.

'He said you were a good soldier, for a Limey,' Neil said with a grin.

Lewis laughed. 'Did he tell you about putting my regiment on the boat?'

'No, we didn't have that long to talk.'

Lewis eased the van into the slow lane as the road began to climb round to Villefranche. A Ferrari and a motorbike snaked past them and hurtled ahead along the narrow road.

Lewis checked the rear-view mirror before he resumed the conversation.

'One of General Selig's ancestors was at Yorktown with Washington. My regiment surrendered there. He likes to remind me.'

A small blue car weaved behind them like a wasp trapped against a window pane. Lewis eased over and the car buzzed past them.

'Are we going to turn up cold, or shall we call Mr Cutter?'

Lewis turned right at the sign for Cap Ferrat and slowed down.

'I thought we'd just talk our way in. If we telephone them they might get worried and send for the police. French cops can be difficult.'

'How are we for time?' Neil asked.

'OK,' Lewis said as he began to check the side of the deserted road. There was a gap in the pine trees and a dusty track of packed red earth that led away to the left. Stuck in the soil was a small sign that read Villa Picard in white lettering on blue enamel. Lewis swung down the narrow lane and the van bumped along the rutted road through the gloom of the shade from the low pine trees.

Gradually the trees thinned out on each side, and they could see that they were driving along a narrow strip of land with the sea on either side.

There was a screen of trees ahead. When they passed through them they emerged onto a paved courtyard. The Villa Picard was as wide as the strip of land it stood upon, and the flanks of the villa were built into the rocks that fell away to the sea.

It was a fortress. High small windows were set into a heavy stone wall blocked with spiked bars, and the door was of iron-bound wood with a metal bell-pull and a two-way speaker system. There were three cars parked in the courtyard – a silver convertible Rolls Royce next to a rather shabby Mini and a Range Rover.

Lewis and Neil studied the house for a while before they got out of the van.

'No wonder they're coming from the sea,' Neil said softly. 'You'd need artillery to get in this way.'

'Let's see if soft words can do the trick,' Lewis said.

They got out of the van and walked to the door. It was slightly ajar. Neil swung it wide and they stood in the doorway.

Across the cool dark hallway a slim man was talking on the telephone. He wore a dazzling white towelling robe which matched his carefully cut hair and even teeth. His skin was as brown as a leather wallet.

He spoke into the telephone. 'Hang on, Paul.' Then he gestured to Lewis and Neil. 'The first floor, OK?'

'I'm sorry?' Lewis said.

'You speak English? Great. First floor, on the right. The goddamn shower's blocked again.'

They stood without moving and the man turned to the telephone once again.

'I'll call you later, Paul.' He hung up slowly. 'Who are you guys?' he said in a flat voice.

Neil spoke in an easy voice: 'I take it you're Marshall Cutter?'

The man folded his arms and nodded.

'This is Captain Horne of the British Secret Service and I'm David Neil. I used to be a major, but I'm just plain mister now.'

Cutter looked at them both without emotion.

Neil turned to Lewis. 'I don't think he believes us.'

Lewis unslung his canvas satchel and handed it to the man.

'Give him yours,' he said.

Neil handed over the bag.

'You're definitely Marshall Cutter?' Neil asked.

'Sure,' he said.

'Look in the bags,' Neil said gently.

Cutter did as he was instructed.

'What the hell is going on here?' he asked in a tight, angry voice.

Lewis looked at his watch. 'Mr Cutter, any time now four frogmen are going to swim up to your backyard and try to kill you. We're here to try to prevent that unhappy eventuality.'

'Do you guys have any proof of identity?' Cutter said, his voice betraying his disbelief.

'We're in the *Secret* Service, Mr Cutter,' Neil said. 'I.D. would be kind of self-defeating.'

Cutter's self-confidence was growing as he held the bags containing the weapons. When he spoke again there was arrogance in his voice.

'You don't expect me to believe this crap? You sound to

me like a couple of con artists.' As he spoke he took the .38 from one of the bags and levelled it at them.

Then he picked up the telephone again. 'I'm going to call the cops.' He rattled the cradle. 'Have you guys cut this line?' he said in a harsh voice.

Lewis and Neil exchanged glances of concern and their sudden anxiety seemed to communicate to Cutter and convince him they were genuine. He lowered the revolver.

'I'll go out and take a look,' Neil said. He took one of the satchels from Cutter, extracted the sub-machine gun and snapped a magazine into the breach before he moved swiftly back to the open door and slipped out.

Cutter turned to Lewis. 'Jesus Christ, I've got guests here.'

'I think it would be for the best if we brought them inside,' Lewis replied.

Cutter studied him for a few seconds. Lewis looked at his watch again.

'This way,' Cutter said and led Lewis through the vast house into the garden. Cutter stopped to close a huge pair of French windows and Lewis walked ahead of him. The land behind the house was about sixty yards wide and approximately one hundred and fifty yards long. The ground was at least thirty feet above the water line near the house, but it sloped down until it was almost level with the sea. Most of it was lawn, fringed with cypress, olive and orange trees. In the centre was a shimmering rectangle of light-blue water. As he walked towards the pool Lewis could see two young women in bikinis lying on towels and a middle-aged couple sitting in easy chairs under a large sun umbrella.

The man was wearing light cotton sports clothes. Despite the dark grey hair that was cut short and the lines that emphasised his features, there was a boyish quality to his face. He watched Lewis's approach with shrewd, bright blue eyes. The woman, whose plain white sundress was as expensive as the man's sports clothes, had an even, light tan, the kind worn by people who lived in perpetual sunshine. Her fair, grey-streaked hair was piled on top of her head. When she looked up from the book in her lap Lewis could see how beautiful she had been in her youth.

One of the sunbathers was voluptuous, with an hour-glass figure, her dark red hair cut short and her face and body massed with freckles. When she looked at him he noticed large green eyes and a snub nose.

Her black-haired companion was slender and quite beautiful. She raised herself on to one elbow as they drew close and smiled.

'Hello, darling. That was clever of you to find us.' Before he could answer she rolled to her side and said, 'Mom, Dad, this is Lewis Horne.'

The girl with red hair smiled at him in a lazy, sun-dazed fashion and said, 'Hi. My name is Carrie.'

'Do you know this guy, Hanna?' Marshall Cutter said.

'Of course I do, Marshall,' Hanna said and she watched Lewis as he looked around the garden anxiously.

'You seem to have something on your mind, young man,' her father said as they shook hands.

'Forgive me,' Lewis said. 'This is not a social call. I had no idea Hanna would be here. I've come to warn you that you are all in great danger.'

'Really?' Pearce said with casual good humour in his voice. 'It all seems pretty peaceful to me.'

Cutter waved towards the sea. 'He says some goddamn frogmen are going to come out of the sea and kill me,' he said in a half-jocular tone.

'I thought you said this young man wrote history books, Hanna,' her mother said in a bewildered voice.

Hanna nodded. 'He does, Mother. But he's got another job as well, a secret job.'

'Are you sure this isn't some kind of gag?' Hanna's father asked in the same tone as his wife's.

'Yes, Dad,' Hanna said in an urgent voice. 'If he says we're in danger, you must believe him.'

To reinforce her words, Lewis took the Uzi from the satchel he carried and clipped in a magazine. The others watched his actions with a sense of mounting apprehension.

'Why should a gang of terrorists want to kill me?' Cutter asked. The anger had now left his voice and there was a sudden note of concern.

Lewis shrugged. 'I can't give you their reasons, only their intentions. Please believe me, my companion and I are sure that you are in grave danger. Now I must urge you all to go into the house.'

'Do as he says,' Hanna said, and the pleading in her voice finally convinced them.

The group reached the living-room as David Neil returned. Lewis introduced him.

'Two cars must have followed us along the track,' Neil explained. 'There are four men.'

'Who are they?' the red-headed girl said. There was a note of fear in her voice.

'It's my guess they're here to pick up the frogmen after they do the job,' Lewis said.

'Why go to the trouble of using frogmen?' Hanna's father asked. 'If the guys outside are armed, they could assassinate Marshall.'

'They couldn't be sure they could get past the front of this house, Mr Pearce,' Lewis explained. 'With the front door bolted it's as tough to crack as a pill-box. Do you have any weapons in the house, Mr Cutter?' he said.

Cutter hesitated.

'Yes, I think so. A shotgun . . . no, damn, Jean-Pierre's got it.'

'Who's Jean-Pierre?' Lewis asked.

'He's the husband of the couple who look after the place. They're not here just now,' Cutter said.

Lewis picked up the satchel Cutter had discarded and pulled out the Browning which he held up for examination.

'Do you know how to use this, Mr Cutter?'

'I've used automatics before, but not this one. Show me.'

Lewis snapped a magazine into the handle and jacked a cartridge into the breach.

'It's cocked now, so keep the safety on.' Lewis held the gun out on the palm of his hand while he demonstrated the mechanics. 'Here's the safety and this is how you change magazines.'

Cutter took the Browning and put two full magazines in the pocket of the towelling robe.

Neil handed Hanna's father the Smith and Wesson and the holster.

'I know how to use one of these, son,' Pearce said calmly as he slipped his arm through the holster strap.

Lewis spoke in a voice that was used to being obeyed. 'Gentlemen, take the ladies upstairs to one of the rooms with a window looking over the front of the house. If the people in the cars outside make any move towards the door, fire a couple of shots. Don't give them the benefit of the doubt. Understand?'

The two middle-aged men nodded. The group started to climb the staircase but Hanna lingered and looked down at Lewis.

'Go on,' he said quietly. 'I'll see you soon.'

She half raised her hand in farewell and then hurried on behind the others.

Lewis and Neil walked back into the living room and studied the garden through the picture window that ran the entire width of the house. The lawn and trees they looked out on could afford them no cover.

'Well, they can only come one way, partner,' Neil said lightly. 'I guess we'll have to bushwhack them here in the parlour.'

He looked around. It was a handsome room. There was a short flight of steps that entered through a wide archway from the entrance hall. To the right, a massive fireplace dominated the end of the room. The stone walls were covered with abstract paintings. In the centre of the room was a plain dark leather sofa facing an onyx and brass coffee table, holding a bronze Henry Moore statue of a mother and child. Behind the sofa was a long, bleached-wood table stacked with books, heavy pottery table lamps at each end. To the left of the sofa was a grand piano. Along the left wall was a carved mahogany bar with a copper top. There was a mixture of comfortable armchairs scattered around the room. Turkish rugs were arranged on the polished stone floor.

The room had been furnished to a personal taste. No decorator would have chosen such an idiosyncratic collection of objects and furniture. Nonetheless, the effect was impressive.

Lewis walked over to the piano and played a few bars.

'Nice tone,' Neil said. 'But there's too much echo in here.'

Lewis looked up. 'What do you think?'

They both glanced around the room.

'The fireplace and the bar,' David Neil said.

'Yes,' replied Lewis. 'Which would you prefer?'

'I'll try the fireplace. One of them might be Santa Claus.'

They both took their positions.

'OK?' Lewis called.

'OK.'

Lewis checked the action on the Uzi sub-machine gun once again and screwed on the silencer. He took a spare magazine and tucked it into his waistband, remembering that the Uzi had a rate of fire that could spray six hundred rounds of ammunition in sixty seconds. It was a squat, ugly weapon that was made for the job he was about to undertake – fighting in a confined space.

Lewis looked at his watch again. Three minutes before they were due. The angle of the bar against the wall gave him a chance to stand in shadow. The stone felt cool on the small of his back. The scent of pine came through the open glass doors to the garden. There was total silence.

Then there was a distant engine note and one of the fire-fighting planes came low over the bay, climbing to drop the payload of water it had sucked up into its belly onto the fires burning in the distant mountains.

'Three – coming from the left,' Neil said softly across the room.

Then Lewis saw them, like shadows on the sunlit lawn. They moved fast onto the patio in a zigzagging motion, their wetsuits still gleaming from the sea. Each one had a sub-machine gun slung across his chest and carried a handgun. Lewis searched for the fourth man, but there was no sign of anyone else as the three paused before slipping through the open windows.

Once inside they stopped to look and listen. They were all of medium height; one was pale, the other two had dark complexions and heavy moustaches. The pale one had a face pitted with scars.

Lewis decided to try them in French. He tensed his body to be ready for a hostile move and spoke in a clear voice.

'Halt, stay where you are and throw down your arms,' he commanded.

As soon as he started to speak the three moved swiftly. They were good, Lewis thought. Only one of them turned towards the sound of Lewis's voice. The others swung to cover the rest of the room. The one seeking Lewis crouched and fired two rounds from the automatic he held. Both bullets came close: the first shot slammed into the grand piano causing a curious singing chord as the nickel-plated nose of the high-velocity round cut through ivory, wood, felt and piano wire before it lodged in the copper lip of the bar next to Lewis's elbow. The second shot gashed a long scar in the stone wall two inches above Lewis's head before it ricocheted into the ceiling.

As he came under fire, Lewis measured the distance, took into account the crouching stance of the man aiming the handgun at him and squeezed the trigger of his Uzi for a two-second burst. The first round ploughed along the frogman's right forearm, splitting the wetsuit open to reveal the naked arm beneath and creasing the skin so that a bright red line of blood appeared. The man dropped the automatic which clattered onto the stone floor. Then Lewis's Uzi jammed.

The frogman scrabbled for the sub-machine gun slung across his chest and Lewis dropped his Uzi and threw himself at the crouching black figure. As he did so, he heard four shots, so close together they made a continuous echoing sound in the cavernous room.

Lewis hit his opponent with his right shoulder before the man could swing his own machine gun into line. The weight of the collision threw him across the room so that he cannoned into one of the other frogmen who were both firing at David Neil.

The shattering sound of their handguns firing in the confined space caused a ringing in Lewis's ears so that he could not hear Neil's silenced Uzi, but he could see the results as a spray of ammunition slammed into the two black-clad figures.

As they fell, Lewis's opponent had regained his balance once again and had started to bring his machine gun up to fire. Lewis aimed a kick at the man's throat but he snapped his head to one side and the blow glanced off its site.

The momentum of the kick caused the Turkish rug beneath Lewis's foot to slip on the polished stone floor so that he skidded and fell beside the leather sofa. Desperately he rolled back onto all fours, but it was too late. Triumph showed in the man's pitted face as Lewis crouched before him. But instead of firing the weapon now pointed at Lewis's head, he slowly pitched forward onto the rumpled carpet. David Neil stood over him, the combat knife in his right hand.

'I couldn't take a chance with the Uzi,' he said to Lewis who was breathing in short gasps. 'You were too close together.'

They stood for a while and looked down at the three casualties as blood leaked from their tightly-clad bodies and formed irregular dark pools around them.

'This one is still alive,' Neil said, looking down at the man he had knifed.

They turned him over carefully and he lay, his eyes unblinking, gazing through the glass wall into the pale blue sky that was lightly laced with fleecy clouds.

'Where is the fourth man?' Lewis asked in French.

The dying man gave no sign of understanding. Lewis tried again. The man's eyes flickered towards him and a puzzled expression passed fleetingly across his face.

'*Englouti*,' he said clearly. Then the life went from him.

'What did that mean?' Neil asked.

Lewis straightened up and shrugged.

'It sounded like "swallowed",' Lewis said.

As he spoke they heard six shots at even intervals come from above them. Lewis took the sub-machine gun from the hands of the dead man at his feet and they moved swiftly up the stairs to the room where the others were sheltering.

The door was opened by Carrie, the red-headed girl, who stood next to Hanna. They were still dressed in their tiny bikinis. At the swimming pool they had looked innocent, like creatures relaxing in natural surroundings. Here in a bedroom their nakedness seemed wanton.

Lewis looked past them to Hanna's father and Marshall Cutter, who knelt on a small bed beneath the bow windows. Both of them held guns.

'What's happening?' Lewis asked.

'Those guys are pulling out,' Cutter said as Lewis and Neil leaned across to look out of the window.

Above the trees that screened the front of the house they could see two cars kicking up reddish dust behind them as they jolted down the dirt road. There was only one man in each car.

'When you started shooting they moved towards the house,' Cutter explained. 'So I pumped a couple of rounds in their direction. It kind of changed their minds.'

They watched the cars rattle out of sight and then turned away from the window.

'What happened downstairs?' Cutter asked as he handed the Browning automatic back to Lewis who snapped on the safety-catch again and tucked the gun into the waistband of his trousers.

'I'm afraid you've got three dead frogmen in your sitting-room, Mr Cutter,' David Neil said bluntly.

'Is there much damage?' Cutter asked.

'Well, they're badly damaged. The only thing of yours that died was the piano,' Neil replied.

'Damn,' Cutter said. 'I was fond of the piano. It's a Bechstein.'

Lewis smiled grimly. 'Why don't you give it a Viking funeral – set fire to it and float it out to sea?'

Cutter looked at him coldly for a few moments. 'What do we do now? Call the police?' he asked.

'We can't call anyone until we get the line repaired,' Neil said. 'Do you have any equipment – insulating tape, that sort of stuff?'

Cutter thought for a few moments.

'Yes, I think so. In the kitchen. I'll show you where Jean-Pierre keeps the tools.'

Hanna turned to Lewis.

'I'll take a look at the men downstairs. Just to check your diagnosis.'

She pushed past the red-headed girl and he followed her down to the living room. As Hanna went about her work, Lewis glanced at the battleground. There was still a strong smell of cordite in the room, but otherwise it didn't seem too untidy, except where the frogmen lay huddled in their pools of congealing blood.

Hanna moved quickly from man to man, checking for any sign of life. She frowned slightly as she examined the last one.

'This isn't a gunshot wound,' she said. 'It looks as if it was caused by a blade.'

'It was,' Lewis said quietly. 'My gun jammed.' He pointed down at the body. 'This one was about to shoot me. Neil had to kill him with a combat knife.'

Hanna stood up slowly, pressing the fingertips of her right hand to the centre of her brow. For some time she seemed to study the man who had been knifed. Then she began to tremble.

'Oh God, Lew. Oh God. It could be you lying there,' she said, in a choking voice.

He wrapped his arms around her as she held both her hands to her face. Her body was cold to his touch.

'People dying, from natural causes or from accidents, I'm used to that. But killing as a job of work, I'll never get used to it – never.'

Lewis guided her gently to the bar and found a bottle of cognac. He poured a large measure and handed it to her. She drank it like medicine, in one gulp.

'I'll go and put some clothes on,' she said after a moment and walked out of the room with her head lowered as David Neil entered.

'The line's on. You'd better give removals a ring.'

Lewis felt in his pocket for the card the fat man had given him. The phone was answered the moment it rang.

'Alpes Maritimes Removals,' a crisp voice said.

'I have an emergency job,' Lewis said. 'Code-number seven zero nine five zero.'

'How many items?'

'Three.'

'Any repair work needed?'

'No.'

'What address?' the emotionless voice asked.

'Villa Picard, rue Clemenceau, Cap Ferrat.'

There was a brief pause.

'We will be there in thirty minutes.'

He replaced the receiver and walked over to the Uzi that had jammed and examined it curiously. After a moment's work he extracted the round that he caused the stoppage and weighed it in the palm of his hand. Then he walked out of the open window and threw it as far as he could into the dark blue sea.

The row of restaurants that lined the waterfront at Villefranche cast their lights onto the calm water of the bay so that the sea shimmered with their dancing reflections. The night was warm and still for the people who sat in the open air. At a table in Le Germaine du Maire, Marshall Cutter rapped twice to attract attention and raised a glass of wine.

'Ladies and gentlemen, without too much formality I would like to propose a toast and a vote of thanks to these two guys.'

The rest raised their glasses to Lewis and Neil, who smiled with slight embarrassment. After the toast, Lewis turned to Hanna.

'You still haven't told me how you happened to be at the Villa Picard,' he said.

Hanna looked down the table to where Marshall Cutter was leaning forward to listen to something her mother was saying. As she spoke, she touched Cutter's hand. It was the gesture close friends make.

'Dad and Mr Cutter have known each other for years,' she said.

Cutter heard what she said. '1942 to be precise. Monthar Davis Air Base, Tucson, Arizona.' He raised his glass again, this time to Hanna's father. 'I was training to be a bombardier and Hotshot here was learning how to drive a B17. God, we had a hell of a time.'

Hanna's mother looked at each of them in turn.

'A hell of a time, indeed. You were boys, just boys, even when you got to England.' She turned to Hanna. 'Your grandfather used to call him Lieutenant Andy Hardy. He wouldn't take him seriously at all.'

Lewis watched Hanna's parents with interest. They looked like rich people. Neither wore extravagant jewellery and their clothes were plain and rather conservative, but there was an aura of wealth. Both had clear complexions. Her father's hair had receded at the temples to accentuate his tall forehead and lean jawline. There was no fat on his body and he held himself like a man who kept fit. Hanna's mother had clearly been as attractive as Hanna in her youth, but it was a different kind of beauty – fair and very English, the kind associated with green lawns and afternoon tea.

'How did you win her, Dad?' Hanna asked.

'I offered her father money for her,' he said with a straight face. 'There's nothing old landed gentry won't do for dough.'

Mrs Pearce threw back her head and laughed.

'What rubbish,' she said. 'Mind you, he was impressed when he finally discovered how rich you were.' She turned to the table. 'You see, there was no way for us to tell the difference between Americans then. They all seemed to wear the same uniform, they spoke the same and they all had beautiful teeth. In England only the wealthy or the lucky had nice teeth in those days.'

'Money always makes a difference,' Pearce said, glancing in Lewis's direction. 'You know, when the other guys found out how well-heeled we were, they called our ship *The Silver Spoon*.' He looked down at the table and grinned at the memory. 'I wonder what happened to her?'

'I know,' Cutter said. He snapped open a Dunhill lighter and lit a cigarette before he continued.

'The Mexican Air Force bought her in 1946. Then in '68 she was sold south again to a guy in Honduras who used her to haul cargo.'

'How the hell do you know that?' Pearce said.

Cutter blew some smoke into the clear night air.

'Because four years ago his son sold her to me.'

'You've got her?' Pearce said in susprise.

62

Cutter grinned. 'Sure. For the last three years. I've been having her rebuilt. She looks better now than when you used to bounce her around Arizona in '42.'

'Well I'm damned. What do you think of that?' Peace said in amazement to his wife.

'Money can make your dreams come true,' Lewis said, and as he spoke he realised the light-hearted remark had caused Hanna's father to sit straighter in his chair.

Pearce looked from Hanna to Lewis and then said in a polite voice, 'I understand from my daughter you have a problem with money.'

'No,' Lewis said easily. 'I've never had enough for it to cause a problem.'

'Or for it to be a responsibility?' Pearce said pleasantly.

Lewis rested both hands on the table, then looked at Pearce without emotion.

'I'm a professional soldier. I have other responsibilities.'

'Come on,' Hanna said warily. 'Take me for a walk.'

She stood up and Lewis rose to take the hand she held out to him. They walked along the quay beside the water's edge in silence for a time, until Hanna spoke.

'So, what do you think of them?'

'Your parents?'

'Of course.'

'They seem nice people,' he said cautiously, 'but every now and again I catch your father looking at me as if I've got a dead cat under my arm.'

She threw back her head to laugh as he had seen her mother do earlier.

'Well, I am his only daughter, but he's expecting to lose me one day. If I was Mr Cutter I'd be worried about the flame-haired Carrie.'

'Why?' Lewis said with surprise.

'Haven't you noticed the way she's been looking at your friend?'

'No.'

'Marshall has. Every time she gives one of those sighing, sidelong glances, he grinds his teeth down a few more centimetres.'

Lewis turned and looked at her.

'And I always thought power and money were the great aphrodisiacs.'

Hanna put an arm around his waist and he held her to him. He could feel the warmth of her through the cotton dress she wore.

'What do you think happened to the fourth man?' she asked after a few minutes.

'I don't know. We found their sub-aqua equipment, but no sign of him.'

'Are you sure there were supposed to be four?'

'The rest of the information was completely accurate. Maybe he stayed aboard the boat. It was found abandoned in the marina at Cannes.'

They strolled on for a while until they came to the end of the quay. Away from the restaurants they could hear the water slapping against the sea wall they stood on, and in the distance the glimmering sea seemed to merge with a clear, dark sky. Suddenly a shooting star flared momentarily as it burnt across the horizon.

Hanna rested her head upon his shoulder.

'Did you wish?' she said.

Lewis nodded. 'You know something?' he said gently.

'What?' Hanna asked.

'If I had more than sixty or seventy pounds in the bank I'd think about making your father an offer for you.'

Chapter Three

It was just before twelve o'clock on Boxing Day and snow was falling from a pewter-coloured sky when Lewis and Charlie came out of the wood and crunched across a wide, sloping field down to the village which Charlie's family had lived near for more than two hundred years. Ahead of them the dogs stuck close to the hedgerow and startled a pheasant which rose with a clatter of wings from the brambled thicket.

Lewis had one hand thrust deep into the pocket of a duffel-coat. The other clasped an ash walking-stick with which he slashed at hummocks of snow-clad grass.

Charlie had both hands in the pockets of an old riding coat and carried his hawthorn cane under his arm. His chin was tucked deep inside the turned-up collar of his coat, and the peak of a new tweed cap was pulled down over his brow. Ever since they had left the house he had been humming 'Stompin' at the Savoy'.

Now their wellington boots made deeper footprints in the drifting snow as they approached the village. The only signs of life were the lights in The King's Head saloon bar which backed onto the field they walked over.

Charlie ended 'Stompin' at the Savoy' and turned to Lewis.

'How is the book going?' he asked.

'Not bad,' Lewis said. 'I got a good result from the appeal in the *Spectator*. A marvellous old boy wrote to me from York. His family have a dozen letters written by an ancestor who was a trooper with Fairfax.'

Charlie opened the gate that led to the pub car park and whistled for the dogs to come to him.

'Have they ever been published?' he asked.

'No – that's what makes them so valuable to me. You know most private soldiers were illiterate at the time. Plenty of officers wrote accounts.'

Charlie grinned as he led them to the front door of the public house.

'You remember I warned you of that difficulty when you started.'

They entered and passed along the narrow passageway that led to the saloon bar, and looked around before they saw a young woman in jeans who was kneeling before the inglenook fireplace. She stood up as they entered, brushing her hands together, and there was a crackling sound from the kindling in the newly lit fire.

'Hello, Mr Mars,' she said with a broad smile of pleasure. 'I wasn't expecting any customers for a bit. What can I get you?'

'Two large malt whiskies, Mary, if you please,' Charlie said. 'Oh, and Sybil said could you spare her three lemons?'

'I'll fetch them in a minute,' she said, as she poured the drinks from a bottle she took from the shelf, and placed them on the bar. 'These are on the house, Mr Mars.'

'That's very generous, Mary.'

'Jack's instructions. He said to thank you for renewing the lease.'

'Where is he?' Charlie said as he passed Lewis his drink.

'He had to go into Oxford to see his mother. He should be back before closing time. Oh, and that other stuff you asked for is in a tin box on the desk in the office.'

'Thank you,' Charlie said.

There was a noise from the public bar which called her away. Charlie and Lewis sat down on ladder-backed chairs before the fire and drank in silence for a few minutes. The dogs circled for a moment before finding the right places to settle in front of the hearth.

Lewis looked around the empty room. Horse brasses glowed on the heavy beams over the bar. The low ceiling was mellowed to a dark cream colour by age, and rugs were scattered on the plank floor. The polished table-tops reflected the framed photographs of village fêtes, cricket teams and ancient celebrations that crammed the Cotswold stone walls.

Lewis put one hand out towards the fire and held his glass with the other.

'I had no idea you were a landlord, Charlie,' he said in a slightly mocking tone.

'Why do you think I'm so enormously popular in the village?' Charlie said airily. 'Until my grandfather's day we even controlled the vicar's living.'

He took the cap from his head and examined the lining for a moment before leaning forward and putting it on the mantelpiece next to a heavy mahogany clock.

'I hate wearing new clothes,' he said with deep feeling. 'The grandfather I just mentioned used to have his valet wear things to break them in. He was one of the best-dressed men in the Home Counties.'

'Who, your grandfather?'

'No, the valet. The other servants called him Dandy Brown.'

The fire started to throw out more heat. Lewis took off his duffel-coat and laid it on the bench seat beside the fireplace. Charlie did the same with his coat.

'How was Ireland?' Charlie asked.

Lewis looked around at the mellow peace of their surroundings and shrugged.

'The same.'

They both looked into the fire.

'Connor's finished,' Lewis said and Charlie stirred and looked at him.

'In what sense?'

'It's not there any more. He's used up.'

Charlie grunted.

'How's Skylark?' Lewis asked.

Charlie paused before he replied.

'She's fine. The holiday did her good. The agency has been quiet for nearly two months but I think it's about time we pulled her out again and put in a permanent replacement.'

He stretched his legs out as he spoke and disturbed the dogs. The retriever moved its position closer to the flames.

'Do you see any cause for concern?' Lewis said.

Charlie slowly shook his head.

'No. I just don't like leaving a girl who is not much older than one of my daughters in that sort of danger.' He smiled ruefully at Lewis. 'I suppose that qualifies me as a hopeless chauvinist.'

Just then the door to the bar opened and a gust of icy wind blew in against them, followed by Claude Henderson and his wife. They were both bundled against the cold in matching sheepskin coats. Charlie and Lewis stood up to greet them.

Claude's wife, Edith, was a plump, pretty woman with dark, curly hair. She had very fair skin and wore deep red lipstick on her rosebud mouth. She turned her cheek for a kiss from Charlie as Claude took the sheepskin coats and hung them on the brass hooks behind the door. Lewis bought a glass of sherry for Claude, a gin and tonic for Edith, and more whisky for himself and Charlie. When Mary had given him his change he rejoined the party.

Claude was showing Charlie an article from a tabloid newspaper which he studied as Claude spoke.

'I think he's a bloody menace.'

'Who is, Claude?' Lewis asked as he pulled up another chair.

Claude gestured towards the newspaper.

'This damn fool, Dr Lionel Reece.'

'I'm sorry,' Lewis said. 'I don't follow.'

Charlie folded the paper and handed it back to Claude.

'You were away when the fuss started,' Charlie explained. 'There is a young scientist called Reece who announced that he could manufacture the most sophisticated chemical-warfare diseases in a suburban kitchen. The tabloids christened him The Chemical Warfare Cook.'

Lewis shrugged. 'Surely everyone knows the trick with chemical weapons is how you deliver the payload to the enemy and limit the distribution so you don't wipe out your own side?'

'Yes,' Claude said, 'but until now you needed a fairly well-equipped laboratory to manufacture them in the first place. Now this damned fool has shown how to do it in a kitchen.'

'You still need a method of distributing the virus,'

Claude's wife said. 'You can't make that in the kitchen, even if you've got an Aga.'

Claude took a sip of sherry. 'Quite right, Edith,' he said, and he turned to Lewis and Charlie. 'She has a degree in chemistry, you know.'

He gazed around the saloon bar. 'This really is a charming pub,' he said appreciatively.

'You're talking to the right man,' Lewis said. 'I bet you didn't realise that Charlie is the landlord of this splendid establishment, did you, Claude?'

'Well, I congratulate you,' Claude said. 'No jukebox, no fruit machine. In fact, no plastic of any kind. It should be called The Haven, not The King's Head.'

Charlie looked up at the ceiling.

'It wasn't always called The King's Head. The name was changed during the Civil War. Before that it was called The Rose.'

Lewis looked at him with interest.

'Why?'

Charlie leaned forward and threw a log onto the fire and watched as a cloud of sparks burst up the chimney. The red setter and the retriever opened their eyes at the noise but neither moved.

'A troop of Levellers were billeted here,' he said nonchalantly.

'What were Levellers?' Claude's wife asked.

'Parliamentary troops who believed in creating a society where everyone was equal,' Lewis replied.

'Communists?' she said with surprise.

'No. Christians, actually,' Lewis said.

'Too Christian for some people,' Charlie said.

'Are there any parish records?' Lewis asked.

'Oh, better than that,' Charlie said as he rearranged the fire with a poker. 'There's a tin chest in the office full of stuff. Jack dug it all out for you.'

In a moment Lewis was behind the bar and Mary led him to the tiny office next to the kitchen. There on the desk was a blackened tin chest with a broken clasp. Mary switched on the Anglepoise lamp that balanced on a metal filing cabinet.

'I'll give you some space,' she said as she eased out of the cramped little room.

Lewis opened the chest. It was full to the brim with papers, some written on parchment and, towards the bottom of the pile, some on vellum. He glanced at them quickly. They were records of the public house going back four hundred years. Bills of sale, contracts, records of employment and title deeds. Then he came to two thick ledgers bound in calfskin. He took them from the box and adjusted the lamp. When he opened the top book there was a plain white card inside. It read *'Merry Christmas. Sybil and Charlie'*. He put the card inside his pocket and looked down at the strong clear handwriting.

'May 1st 1651. I, Joshua Cullins, do solemnly swear to God that this shall be a true and faithful record of the thoughts, words and deeds of this troop . . . ' He read no more. Instead he carefully placed the ledgers and documents back in the tin trunk and carried it to the saloon bar.

He put it down on the bench seat with his duffel-coat, then took his glass of whisky and raised it to Charlie.

Before Lewis could say anything Charlie got up. 'Come on, who's for a game of darts? Sybil told me to keep you away from the house until one-thirty.'

'Not me,' Claude's wife said. 'I'm sure Claude will give you a game.'

'I'll keep Edith company,' Lewis said, as Claude and Charlie took their positions before the board and selected their darts from a rack on the windowsill.

When the game was under way, Edith leaned towards Lewis and spoke in a quiet voice.

'Do you know what Sybil is preparing for lunch, Lewis?' she said. There was a note of concern in her voice.

'Goose, I think,' Lewis whispered. 'Why?'

She raised her eyes.

'We spent yesterday with my sister and she gave us boiled fish for lunch. Can you imagine? Her husband has become a health fanatic. There we all were, pulling crackers over pieces of cod in parsley sauce. Claude was furious.'

Lewis looked towards the portly figure of Henderson who

was taking aim with great care. Finally he threw the dart.

'Well done, Claude,' Charlie said amiably. 'Your game.'

Henderson looked enormously pleased.

'Fancy a game, Lewis?' he called out.

'I'm no good, Claude,' Lewis said, 'but I'll chalk for you. Let Edith play.'

Even against his wife, Henderson played with ferocious concentration and won two more games. Lewis sipped whisky and did the subtractions on the blackboard, occasionally glancing with warm satisfaction at the black tin box on the bench seat.

Finally, Charlie looked at his watch.

'Drink up,' he ordered.

Claude won the last game and during the flurry of putting on coats, while the dogs bumped against everyone's legs, Mary handed Charlie a paper bag with the lemons. Lewis was left alone as he wiped the blackboard clean.

Three darts lay on the table. He glanced around to make sure Mary had gone back to the public bar, then threw the darts in rapid succession. Two hit the treble twenty, the third bounced on the wire and fell onto the rubber mat. He placed it on the table, picked up the black tin box and joined the others in the car park.

Claude's Volvo shooting-brake was so covered in snow everyone was brushing the windows clear. Eventually they set off along the narrow road, the windscreen wipers just able to cope with the heavy snowfall.

'Doesn't the house look lovely?' Edith said when they stopped in Charlie's drive. 'Ours is comfortable, but it does lack character.'

'The house we had in Highgate had character,' Claude said stiffly. 'You were the one who wanted to move.' Edith looked at him coldly and walked through the door Lewis held open for her.

Once inside the house Charlie went to deliver the lemons, leaving Lewis to bank the fire and Claude to offer drinks. Edith protested that she was already tipsy but she accepted another gin and tonic. Lewis had placed his tin box in a corner and was raking the fire when Hanna came into the

71

room with a piece of paper in her hand. She took a sherry Claude poured for her and turned to Lewis.

'Someone called Max Buller rang for you. He said he would be at this number after three o'clock.'

Lewis read the number and threw the message on the fire. Hanna watched him and grinned.

'I thought you guys were trained to eat pieces of paper?' she said as the dinner gong summoned them to the dining-room.

'Normally we do,' Lewis said, 'but I didn't want to spoil my appetite for the goose.'

'Sybil, I must say that was a splendid luncheon, splendid,' Claude Henderson said and he raised his glass in her direction. The others around the table joined in with their congratulations and Lewis felt a glow of relaxation from the rich food and the second glass of brandy. The fire in the dining-room made the room comfortably stuffy in contrast to the whitened garden they looked out on through the window.

Snow light filled the room and highlighted the counte-nances of Charlie's ancestors who looked down from the dark panelled walls.

'More pudding, Claude?' Sybil asked and he protested in a half-hearted fashion as she replenished his plate with sherry trifle.

'Where are the girls?' Edith asked.

'Gone to London this morning, to stay with friends,' Charlie said as he carefully lit a large cigar.

'I do hope they'll be all right,' Sybil said as she glanced out of the window at the still falling snow.

'I'm certain the City of Westminster can be relied upon to keep Knightsbridge free of snowdrifts,' Charlie said expansively as he blew a tiny smoke ring which he watched with evident satisfaction.

'Charlie, if you make any more pompous remarks like that I will set the dogs on you,' Sybil said and she served another portion of trifle to Edith.

Lewis took a cigar from the box and examined the dark,

almost oily skin before he sliced the end with Charlie's silver cutter and lit the aromatic tobacco with a thin spill of wood. At his second puff the delicate little carriage clock on the mantelpiece chimed three times.

Lewis made his excuses and went to the telephone in the hall. After the warmth of the dining-room there was a distinct chill in the hallway. After a long wait, Max Buller answered the telephone.

'Turn that bloody row down,' Lewis heard him shout and the noise of rock music diminished.

'Lew, I'm at my brother's. I wish I'd gone to work, a newspaper office would be a haven of peace after this place. There are enough kids here to start a protest movement. Jesus, I hate the young.'

'What's the problem?' Lewis asked.

'I've had a very interesting communication from Joe Roper,' Buller said. 'Just a minute.'

Lewis could hear him ordering the teenagers from the room.

'Roper's got a new bird,' Max Buller began and Lewis could hear a slight slur in his voice. 'Well, he's always got a new bird, but this one could be serious. She's got a bit of money. Anyway, he's taken her to a French ski resort for Christmas. Le Plesir to be precise. Two days ago they had an avalanche there. Some people were killed, it sealed off the town and brought down the telephone lines.

'This morning we got a telex at the office from Roper. It's in a sort of Cockney code – rhyming slang. What did he use to call you when you when we were in Belfast?'

'Rich,' Lewis said. 'Horne – Torn. Torn Curtain – Richard Burton.'

'I'll read it to you,' Max said. 'Got a pen?'

'OK,' Lewis said as he picked up the silver propelling pencil next to the telephone. Sybil's touch, Lewis thought; a gold one would be vulgar.

'Shoot,' Lewis said, and Max began to speak clearly at dictation speed.

'Message begins: "Give Rich the squeak. Cecil B definite. Avalanche old moody. Spooks banged up manor. Ear-

wigging dog. Rub-a-dub favourite. Same frog Taig gaff.''
That's it. We tried to get a telex back but got no response.'

'Le Plesir?' Lewis asked.

'That's it.'

'Thanks, Max. Have a happy Boxing Day.'

'The movie will be on in a minute. That should get me off to sleep,' Buller said.

'Be seeing you.' Lewis hung up the telephone and read the message again. It was easy for him to translate the code. The squeak was to tell. When they had been in Belfast, Roper always referred to big operations as Cecil B De Mille productions. Old moody was Cockney for nonsense. Spooks was used for Secret Service operators. Bang up manor meant to seal the town. Earwigging was eavesdropping, dog and bone was the telephone. Rub-a-dub favourite meant meet me in pub. Frog was for frog and toad – road. Taig was Protestant Belfast slang for Catholic. Gaff was a place people live in or meet. Lewis wrote a free translation down and went back to the dining-room.

They looked up expectantly as he entered.

'Work, I'm afraid,' Lewis said apologetically.

The three women groaned simultaneously and they all stood up to begin clearing the table.

When the door closed Lewis read the translation to the men. 'Tell Lewis Horne something big has happened here. The French Secret Service have sealed off the resort. The avalanche story is a cover. They are tapping the telephones. Meet me in the pub halfway up the road to the Catholic Church.'

'Who is this from?' Charlie asked as he tapped ash from his cigar.

'A photographer I knew from tours in Belfast.'

'Can you trust him?' asked Claude.

'He must have pictures he wants me to bring out for him. Joe Roper is as devious as a double-glazing salesman. I'm sure this is a trade.'

'How will you get in if the French have sealed the town?'

'They can only seal the road, Claude,' Lewis said with a smile. 'They can't seal the mountains.'

'Will you take anyone? Gordon or Sandy?' Charlie asked.

74

'No, I don't think so,' Lewis said. 'I've got a friend who knows the area. I might get him to come along.'

Hanna came back into the room to collect more of the silver and crockery.

'I've got to go to work,' Lewis told her.

'How long for?' Hanna asked in an easy voice as she piled the pudding plates.

'Maybe a couple of days.'

'Oh, well,' she said with an attempt at cheerfulness. 'It could have been worse. You might have been a sailor.'

'I'm sorry, Hanna.'

She walked to the door without looking at him. 'I know you are, Lewis. So am I.'

Claude opened the door for her and Charlie shot Lewis a glance of sympathy.

'Maybe it could wait until tomorrow?' he said.

Lewis shook his head. 'No. Roper wouldn't exaggerate. It's big. I'd better take a look.'

'Where will you go from?' Charlie said as he patted the setter who had come to put a paw on his knee.

'Heathrow via Brize Norton,' Lewis said. 'We store a few bits of kit there that I shall need.'

He went out into the hall again and found Hanna putting on a camelhair coat.

'I'll drive you,' she said and as he stood before her she suddenly put her arms around him and kissed him hard.

'What's that for?' he said with surprise.

'That's for being a good person, you jerk,' she said in a voice full of tenderness. 'What did your dad use to say to you?'

'Chin in, chest out and look to your front like a soldier.'

She took him by the lapels and rocked him gently.

'Well, you look to your front, Lewis Horne, and keep your butt down too.'

'You sound like the Marine.'

'Who's he?'

'General Harry Selig of the United States Marine Corps. Sergeants envy the roughness of his language.' Lewis reached out to the coat-rack and pulled on his duffel-coat.

'I'm ready,' Lewis said.

Hanna looked up.

'Aren't you taking anything with you?' she asked.

'No, I'll pick up everything I need at Brize Norton.'

Hanna opened the door and bright reflected light from the white landscape flooded into the hallway. The last flurries of snow were falling as she edged the car carefully into the lane at the end of the drive.

They drove slowly through the hushed countryside, their tyres cutting deep ruts in the fresh fall until they came to the main road where there had been sufficient traffic to melt the snow. The macadam showed through the whiteness like wet licorice.

Hanna remained cheerful and kept up a flow of small-talk until they arrived at the main gate of the airfield.

'I'll get out here,' Lewis said.

She kissed him quickly and turned round and drove on the moment he had closed the door.

Lewis watched the car for a few seconds, then he felt through his pockets for his identification. Hanna had been cheerful and he had found that almost more disturbing than her hostility to his work. It played on his mind as he handed the cardboard oblong to the sentry on duty.

'And the same to you, sir,' he said.

Lewis looked at him, puzzled. The sentry held out a card to him that read, '*Merry Christmas. Sybil and Charlie*'.

Lewis could see three skiers on the mountain making the last run of the day as the train from Interlaken slowed down to enter Grindelwald. It came to a gentle halt at the buffers and he got off and stood in the space between the tracks. Above him rose the north face of the Eiger, which dominated the village and the surrounding mountains like a cathedral over-looking a medieval city.

On the next track a crowd of skiers disembarked from one of the little mountain trains. They began to unload their equipment from an open truck. Lewis was reminded of a regiment of soldiers as he watched the heavily booted figures scrambling to recover their skis like troops making sure they had their own equipment.

Standing quite still on the platform was a Swiss railway official. He looked as imposing as a general, in his elegant black greatcoat with a gold-trimmed scarlet cap pulled at an angle over one eye.

Lewis liked the Swiss train service, but his real affection was for the Jungfrau system that chugged through the mountains in Lilliputian splendour. He remembered this was the area where the English invented winter sports. The Swiss peasants had gazed in amazement as tweed-clad foreigners crouched on racing toboggans or poled themselves vigorously down mountainsides with slats of wood strapped to their feet.

While he paused to study the grandeur of the surrounding mountains, a group of Japanese went chattering by. Lewis watched them and smiled. There was something very Japanese about skiing. Hurtling down an icy mountainside without protective armour or helmet, and with only two sharp poles to aid you, would appeal to the Samurai spirit.

He stored his kit at the tiny station and entered the Hotel Derby that was next to the platform. The bar was modern, chrome and smoked glass. One of the tables was reserved for the old men of the village, who sat and talked quietly among the noise of the holiday-makers relaxing in the warmth. A wiry figure sat at a table near the door wearing old-fashioned woollen ski trousers and the red jacket of the ski instructors. He was draining a glass of what Lewis guessed was café Lutz, a Swiss concoction of coffee and fiery liquor. His companion sat with a litre of beer before him, smoking a Havana cigar.

Mike Elders was a bear-like man with a wind-burnt skin and wiry red hair. His heavy beard and moustache were matted with ice that was just beginning to thaw. As he looked up from the cigar he caught sight of Lewis and smiled.

'My dear fellow, how good to see you,' he said affably as Lewis joined them at the table. 'Let me introduce you.' He turned to the red-jacketed figure who looked at Lewis with grave interest. 'Lewis Horne, this is Fritz Lehmann.'

Lewis took the hand and felt skin as tough as leather.

'Hello,' the man said with a brief smile, then he turned back to the red-bearded figure.

'So you will call me tomorrow?'

'Yes. I'm not sure about my movements for the next couple of days,' he said. The mountain man held a hand up as a half salute and departed. Lewis sat down in the chair opposite and waved to catch the attention of the hurrying waitress.

'Cognac and coffee,' he ordered. He pointed to the beer in front of the bearded man. 'And another beer.'

The waitress returned almost instantly with the order and Lewis prepared his coffee with sugar and cream.

'I rang your home,' he said. 'They thought you might be here.'

The bearded man nodded. 'I've been far from the madding crowd with Fritz.' He took a large swallow of beer and clawed at the ice in his beard. Then he cocked his head and studied Lewis. 'Now, what can I do for you?'

'I need some help,' Lewis said. He shuffled his chair next to Elders's and produced a map from the patch pocket of his duffel coat.

'Do you know Le Plesir?' he asked.

Elders looked down at the alpine area indicated by Lewis's finger.

'Yes, I skied it twice last year.'

Lewis glanced around the bar and moved closer.

'The French have sealed the road,' he said in a low voice. 'I want to get in.'

The heavy figure stirred with interest.

'Without them knowing, I presume?'

'Exactly.'

'It'll be expensive.'

'That's OK. How can I do it?'

Elders puffed on the cigar some more until the two of them became enveloped in the blue smoke. Finally he picked up Lewis's coffee spoon and pointed to a position on the map.

'If the weather holds we can get in here by helicopter.'

'Any problems with detection?' Lewis asked.

Elders shook his head and rivulets of melting ice ran down to soak into his blue sweatshirt.

'There are so many helicopters dodging around these mountains at this time of year, no-one can keep an eye on them.'

'Will we need any special kit?'

Elders thought for a while.

'Only skins for the skis when we walk uphill. We could get killed, but no special equipment would prevent that eventuality.'

He stopped talking for a moment as a tall blonde girl in a peach-coloured ski suit squeezed past their table with an apologetic smile.

'By the way, how good are your legs?' Elders said as they watched the girl leave the bar.

'They're OK,' Lewis said. 'Not Olympic standard but they'll last out.'

Elders swallowed the last of his second beer and caught the arm of a passing waitress. He placed the empty glass on her tray and asked for another.

'Just a cognac,' Lewis said as he leaned forward and studied the map for a few minutes. 'So where will he put us down exactly?' he asked and Elders rocked forward on his chair and picked up the spoon once more.

He pulled the map at the edges to smooth out a crease and pointed precisely with the tip of the spoon.

'That's a mountain away from the resort,' Lewis said.

Elders nodded. 'It depends on the conditions. If he drops us this side of Le Plesir and the wind happens to be in the wrong direction, we'll make so much noise they'll be able to hear us in the discos of Paris. If we come this route, we land on the blind side of the mountain, climb for a while, traverse around and cross a small glacier.' He traced the route with the spoon. 'Then we can ski down into Le Plesir and do your business.'

'Are you coming?' Lewis said.

Elders looked at him with an amiable grin.

'I think you'll need someone to hold your hand on the ice bridge.'

'What ice bridge?' Lewis said with suspicion.

'It's a little trick Mother Nature has pulled up there.'

'Oh, Christ,' Lewis said softly. 'How do we get out?'

Elders sat back and took a mouthful of his third litre of beer.

'The hard way, old boy. We take skins for the skis and walk out.'

'And across the glacier?'

'No, we can get the chopper to pick us up at the top of Le Plesir. It won't matter if they hear us on the way out, will it?'

Lewis shook his head. 'When can we go? I've got to be in the village as soon as possible.'

'Let me make a call,' Elders said, and rose to his feet.

'I'll do the same.' Lewis gestured to the waitress and when he had paid for the drinks he changed a note for coins.

Charlie answered the telephone. 'All's well,' Lewis said. 'I've found Mike Elders. We may go in tonight.'

'Who's Elders?' Charlie asked.

'A friend of mine. He spends most of his time skiing during the winter.'

'What's he like?' Charlie asked with interest.

Lewis thought about the ice bridge for a moment.

'He's a good sort but he's got one bad fault.'

'What's that?'

'He doesn't scare easily,' Lewis said with feeling. He could hear Charlie's sepulchral laughter echoing as he hung up the telephone.

Slowly and with great care Elders edged along the narrow bridge of solid-packed snow that connected the glacier above a great split in the ancient ice. Around them all was perfect stillness. Beneath the bridge the sharp, ugly walls of the crevasse descended into darkness.

The only sounds were the rasping of Elders's breath and the creak and rustle of his equipment. Each of them wore thin, white cotton camouflage suits over their ski clothes. They carried knapsacks and their skis were slung from their shoulders.

'OK,' Elders called as he turned and gestured for Lewis to

make the crossing. At that moment the glacier began to groan as the pressures of rock and ice responded to minute changes in temperature. Then there was stillness again. Lewis closed down his imagination like a stoker slamming a furnace door. He forced himself to forget everything except the thin strip of whiteness before him, knowing that once he was upon the path his life was committed, and no skill or stroke of good fortune would help him to avoid death if that last shift had weakened the bridge and caused a fissure that had not had time to heal in the sub-zero temperature.

'Look on it as a stroll along Piccadilly on a summer's afternoon, old boy,' Elders called out by way of encouragement, as Lewis moved out and began each careful step in the footprints Elders had made in the snow-covered surface.

Eventually the narrow strip of ice merged, once again, with the surface of the glacier and Lewis eased his shoulders with relief.

'Not far now,' Elders said, and he gestured towards a long black sliver of rock that stood out from the snow. 'When we get to that we begin our traverse to the descent.'

Lewis nodded and Elders took the lead and carefully prodded the snow before him in case there were any crevasses hidden by the drift.

When they reached the rock, they lay back against the dark surface and Lewis looked up at the moon. It seemed sharp and close enough to reach out and touch. The brightness it brought to their surroundings gave everything a surreal quality, like the clarity of a Salvador Dali painting.

'How are you?' Elders asked.

'OK,' Lewis grunted in reply, but he could feel an aching weariness in his legs as if they had been squeezed in a massive vice. Since the helicopter dropped them, they had climbed through snowfields for two and a half hours, and then picked their way with infinite care across the edge of the glacier.

'Come on,' Elders said and they began to work their way along a ledge about eighteen inches wide until they entered a shadowed hollow shielded from the moonlight. In Lewis's judgement it was about a hundred and fifty yards across.

'Can we cross on the skis?' Lewis asked.

'Too risky. This is the last part of the walk.'

Once they had begun, Lewis could tell why. Beneath a fine layer of snow, the rocks were jagged, interspersed with drifts of soft, powdery snow.

It was back-breaking work after the first climb, but eventually they scrambled the last few yards out of the hollow and onto a great, wide snowfield bathed in moonlight. Panting for breath they stood and looked down to the lights of the village.

Elders unslung his knapsack and produced a small pair of binoculars. He handed them to Lewis and continued to search in the bag until he found a small silver flask from which he took a longish drink. Nudging Lewis, he handed him the flask.

'Irish,' he said. 'There's one good drink left in it.'

Lewis took the flask and drank gratefully. Then he trained the binoculars on the village. He traced the road to where he could see arc-lights. The road was blocked by huge pieces of machinery and he could make out police vehicles and tiny figures walking purposefully between them. The elevation was so acute, the village was almost like a map beneath them. Carefully, Lewis scanned the streets and located the church by its spire. Then he swept the slopes down to the edge of the little resort.

'There are no police patrolling these slopes,' he said.

Elders grunted with satisfaction.

'Is there any activity on the lifts?' he asked.

Lewis retrained the binoculars. Far to their left across the snowfield he could see the spidery lines of the ski lifts. Nothing moved in the moonlight.

Elders pointed with his ski pole. 'We cross this, and there where you can see the trees start we pick up a red run which will take us straight down to the village.'

Lewis followed the line Elders indicated and nodded. Methodically they set about adjusting their equipment. Lewis carefully knocked the packed snow from his boots with a ski pole and snapped shut the bindings on his skis. He gave the inside of his goggles a final wipe, clipped up his ski-jacket at the throat, made sure his knapsack was set comfortably, and looked to his companion.

'Let's go,' Elders said, and they launched themselves out onto the virgin slope of the great snowfield and leaned into the rushing air. After a few moments Lewis's weariness was forgotten as he felt a familiar surge of exhilaration. Side by side they hurtled down the mountainside, their skis making ruler-straight cuts in the snow until Elders began a wide swing to the right, like a fighter pilot turning from formation.

Lewis followed him and they gradually reduced speed until they turned again between fir trees and onto the impacted snow of a machine-made piste. Almost immediately they hit ice where the slush of daytime had frozen in the cold night air.

With the caution of expert skiers they slowed to make a steady descent. When they were about a mile from the village Elders stopped.

'You see where the cable-car station is?' he asked.

'Yes,' Lewis answered.

'There is a pathway there which cuts across this run. Just before it there's a spot under a house where we can hide our kit. Then we can get on the path and walk down into the village past the station and find your friend.'

When they got to a clump of trees before the pathway they stopped and stripped off their white camouflage, put their ski boots in their knapsacks and donned heavy shoes. Shouldering their skis they walked along the narrow pathway through high banks of cleared snow until they reached the house.

The chalet was built against the steep slope of the mountain so that the front elevation was on high stilts and the rear rested on the mountainside. Piled around the base were heaps of neatly sawn logs.

Stealthily Lewis and Elders concealed their equipment. They were so close to the people in the house Lewis could make out snatches of the conversation being spoken between the couple in the room above their heads. They were arguing. From the lack of enthusiasm they brought to the subject it was an old theme. She attacked him for his lack of manners towards her mother. He attacked the woman's lack of compassion and femininity.

Quietly Lewis and Elders stole away past the cable-car station and crossed a stone bridge over a narrow, rushing stream. Recently heavy snow had fallen on Le Plesir. It lay deep on the rooftops and piled high each side of the little streets that were bright with lights and neon signs.

There were crowds of people milling about the roadways in bright multicoloured après-ski clothes. Lewis could see police everywhere. They wore heavy anoraks and carried sub-machine guns slung at their sides. It looked as if the town was under martial law.

'They're searching for someone,' Lewis said.

'How do you know?' Elders asked.

Lewis nodded towards one of the uniformed figures.

'There's a difference in the way they look at a street when they're just there to keep order.' He held out a hand to guide his companion. 'This way,' he said and indicated a street that led to a spired church. A weary-looking man and woman were locking the glass door of a gift shop on their left.

'Pardon, is that the Catholic Church?' Lewis asked the woman in French.

'*Oui, m'sieur,* ' she said quietly, without bothering to look at him.

After a few minutes' walk they saw a sign for The Red Lion. Pounding rock music poured from the open doorway.

'I suppose this is the place,' Lewis said.

Inside the entrance a girl asked them if they wanted a ticket to the disco in the basement. They smiled and shook their heads as they pushed open another door that led into a bar that was packed solid with people. Customers stood four deep at the bar, hoping for service. The wooden floor, which Lewis could feel but not see because of the proximity of bodies nudging against him, was slippery with melted snow and spilt beer. It was a young people's place. Most of the customers were teenagers or barely into their twenties.

'Rich, Rich,' Lewis could hear someone calling above the roar of conversation and the barely muffled rock band thumping away below them.

Scanning the bar he saw Joe Roper standing on a stool to gain his attention. Lewis and Elders squeezed through the crowd and finally got to a tiny table that was covered with glasses. Joe Roper sat with a girl who had a pretty, pouting face and a deeply bored expression.

'Do you want a drink?' Roper shouted about the noise.

'How the hell will you get served in this chaos?' Lewis shouted back.

Roper reached beneath his feet and produced a bottle of Scotch and six cans of lager held together with plastic rings. Lewis unscrewed the cap from the bottle of Bell's and used it to swallow a measure of the whisky. He passed the bottle to Elders, who raised it to his lips and took a long swallow. They both took cans of lager and gulped them down. Lewis could feel the effects of the liquor spread through his body.

'This is my fiancée, Karen,' Roper shouted.

The girl looked at Lewis and a smile flashed across the bored features with the speed of a bird passing a window.

'Delighted to meet you, Karen,' Lewis said.

'What?' she replied.

'I'm delighted to meet you,' he repeated, louder.

'Yeah,' Karen said.

'This is my friend, Michael Elders.'

Karen repeated the fleeting smile and continued to shake her shoulders in time to the music that came from beneath their feet.

'Let's go for a walk,' Roper said. 'Karen, look after Mr Elders.'

Mike raised the bottle of whisky in salute as Roper led the way. Lewis welcomed the icy air that greeted them when they stood in the narrow street. 'Up here,' he said and they began to walk towards the top of the road.

'What do you think of Karen?' Roper asked.

'She seems very pleasant,' Lewis answered carefully. 'She's a bit young for you, isn't she?'

'Young?' Joe said with surprise in his voice. 'She's nineteen. I was that age when I got married for the first time.'

Lewis looked to see if he was making a joke, but it was

clear that Roper was quite serious. 'Besides,' he went on, 'I'm still only thirty-seven.'

Lewis snorted with laughter.

'Joe, you were thirty-eight when Sandy Patch and I did our last tour in Belfast.'

'Well, I only feel thirty-seven,' Roper said with conviction. 'And it's a well-known fact that women age faster than men – at least that's what my last wife said to me. "Joe," she said, "you've made an old woman of me." '

Lewis looked into the smiling face beside him and marvelled at his stamina in the pursuit of lust.

'Where did you meet Karen?' he asked as they picked their way carefully along the icy road.

'I'm a mate of her old man.'

'Her father?' Roper said and a note of confidentiality crept into his voice. ''Course, she doesn't know that. Vic Reagan is a bit of a local hero in my manor. He's a Paddy who started a building firm with nothing, but he's been doing a bit of porridge recently. Well, five years actually. Anyway, I got friendly with his wife, Doreen, and a couple of his mates came to see me. Said they were looking after things for Vic while he was away, like. Anyway, Doreen gets dead nervous and suggests I say it's Karen I'm really interested in.' They plodded on for a while longer. 'Trouble is,' Roper continued, 'now I have got interested in her – Karen that is – and Doreen's got the raving hump. There's no pleasing some women, you know.'

Lewis could think of no comment to make. They passed more police.

'Where are we going?' Lewis asked eventually.

'The church,' Roper said.

'Will it be open?'

'Yeah, a door at the side. I told the priest that I had a lot of worries, so he gave me a key so as I could go in and pray when I needed to.'

Lewis thought for a few moments of Roper's tangled love life and conceded that if anyone was in need of spiritual guidance it was he.

The path was just wide enough for them to walk in single

file. The snow was higher than their heads. Roper opened the side door and they entered the church. It was a small, modern building with white walls and plain, long pews on a red-tiled floor. The single huge window behind the altar was decorated with an abstract stained-glass design.

Roper slid into one of the pews and Lewis sat down beside him. Roper reached into the pocket of his jacket and handed Lewis a black plastic film container.

'Give that to Max Buller, will you?' he said and Lewis slipped it into his own pocket.

Joe Roper sighed and looked towards the altar. Then he turned to Lewis. 'Are you a Catholic?'

'Church of England,' Lewis said.

'Yeah, so am I,' Roper said. 'Well, I think I am. I don't remember ever going to any church.'

'What happened here exactly?' Lewis asked.

'God only knows,' Roper said appropriately and he began to tap with his nails on the back of the pew in front of them. 'We got here three days before Christmas, Karen and me. On Christmas Eve there was an avalanche. I saw the rescue squads going out, so I tagged along with them. You know I always carry a camera.'

'How did you manage to get them to take you?' Lewis asked.

'I nicked one of the ski instructors' jackets. We were next to the ski school when the word of the avalanche came. A couple of minutes later I was in one of the helicopters.

'They took us over to the north side of the valley. There was one big dump and two trickles. They split us up into parties and the main body stayed where the big dump had been. It had covered about fifty yards of a wide run, so they thought there could be bodies buried. Me and another fella went over to the left where a smaller amount of snow had come down. He was one of those French mountain cops, three or four of them came along with the rescue teams. Anyway, he kept shouting at me in French and I kept pretending I couldn't hear him. One of the dogs was going crazy so we both started digging and then we found it. God, it gave me a turn.'

87

Roper stopped and lit a cigarette. Then he remembered where he was and almost put it out before he shrugged and drew deeply on the pungent French tobacco.

'What was there?' Lewis asked.

'A bloody frogman,' Roper explained. 'The works – sub-aqua equipment, total wet suit, and he's only carrying a sub-machine gun. It gave me and the other geezer a right turn, I can tell you.'

Roper drew on his cigarette some more and the glow gave a rose-coloured touch to his small, neat features.

'So what happened then?' Lewis asked.

Roper stubbed out the cigarette on the tiled floor and then brushed the ashes away with his hand. He hesitated for another moment, then put the cigarette end in his pocket.

'The cop indicated that he was going to get the others, so the second he was gone I took pictures of the body – that's the film I've just given you.'

'And?' Lewis said, knowing there was more.

'I thought I'd move the body a bit to improve the composition,' Roper said. 'I managed to turn him on his side and that's when I saw he had a waterproof satchel clipped to him, so I nicked it and scarpered.'

'How did you get away?' Lewis asked.

'As soon as I was out of sight, I buried the ski instructor's coat and took off the hat. Then I pissed off back down here.

'Later I heard the French cops were doing their pieces. It seems the frogman had a passport on him and he turned out to be wanted by Interpol for terrorism. They worked out I'd nicked something. The Chief of Police wants to make a name for himself so he's refused to call in the big boys. Instead he's banged up the village and he's got his own boys looking for the satchel.'

'Where is it now?' Lewis asked.

Roper got up and walked to the altar and searched beneath the base of the lectern that stood to one side of the stained-glass window. After a few moments he stood up and placed a thick oilskin wallet about twelve inches by ten into Lewis's hands with the care of a priest delivering the sacrament.

Chapter Four

Claude Henderson stood on the pavement in Gower Street and kicked his heavy shoes against the iron railing to clear the clinging snow. When the door opened he crossed the black-and-white chequered floor of the hallway towards Sergeant Major Watts, who glanced up from the door release switch and looked impassively at Henderson's new clothes.

The sheepskin coat was ordinary enough but Claude also wore a Russian hat made of tightly curled fur that had been dyed to a bluish tinge so that it resembled the hair of an American matron. Sergeant Major Watts took Claude's key from the rack and handed it to him in silence as he continued to study the fur hat. It took all of Claude's self-control to refrain from snatching the article from his head and stuffing it out of sight, but he knew such a gesture would be construed as victory by the man who confronted him with the basilisk stare.

Claude took the key without speaking and was on the second step of the staircase when Sergeant Major Watts's voice came to him.

'Nice 'at, Mr 'Enderson. Christmas present, was it?'

Claude only paused for a moment.

'From my wife, actually,' he said in defeated tones as he continued his upward climb.

At the top of the house he met Penny Rose standing in the narrow corridor.

'Good morning, Mr Henderson,' she said cheerfully. 'Mr Mars said would you spare him a few minutes as soon as you're free?'

Claude Henderson studied Penny for a moment. He prided himself that he was an observant man and he was aware that there was something different about her. The dark blonde hair was the same; then he realised she wasn't wearing her customary spectacles.

'Good heavens, Penny,' he said in a flattering voice. 'I'd never realised how blue your eyes are.'

She smiled, showing very white teeth.

'These are my new contact lenses, Mr Henderson. They're a bit of a cheat. They're tinted.'

Claude handed her his coat and hat and the keys to his office.

' "Blind were mine eyes, till they were seen of thine".'

'I'm sorry, sir?' Penny said.

Claude smiled. 'Just a line of poetry. Can you put these in my office and leave a cup of coffee on my desk? My secretary is away today,' he said as he gave a light knock on Charlie Mars's door and entered without waiting.

It was a room that could have been mistaken at first glance for a secondhand bookshop. Lewis sat on a battered leather chesterfield with his feet up on a coffee table, studying a large black and white photograph. It was of a black-clad figure sprawled grotesquely in the snow. The harsh contrasts of the picture gave it the appearance of a woodcut.

'I suppose your friend Max Buller will put the headline "FROZEN FROGMAN FOXES FROGS" on that page when he prints it,' Charlie Mars said as he leaned over to fan a newly lit fire. The lumps of smokeless fuel seemed reluctant to ignite.

' "Blind were mine eyes, till they were seen of thine",' Claude repeated as Charlie looked up.

' "And mine ears deaf by thy fame healed be".'

'Who wrote it?' Henderson asked as he rubbed his hands together.

Charlie thought for a moment. 'Michael Drayton or Samuel David,' he said.

'Michael Drayton,' Lewis said. ' "Some atheist or vile infidel in love . . . " '

Claude nodded his appreciation. 'Nothing yet?' he asked.

90

'No. I'll give them another ring.' Charlie picked up the telephone and dialled an internal number. 'Mars here, how's it going? Good.' He replaced the receiver. 'Gordon Meredith is on his way up with it.'

Claude looked at the photograph which Lewis had discarded.

'This really is a most extraordinary picture,' he said. 'How on earth could he have turned up under an avalanche?'

'Something biblical perhaps, Claude? A plague of frogmen falling on the Alpes Maritimes? They have found fish on mountain tops, you know.'

'I think I've got it,' Lewis said with a note of surprise in his voice.

The other two looked at him expectantly.

'It's the fourth man,' he said with conviction. Claude and Charlie did not follow his chain of thought.

'I remember now,' Lewis said and he stood up, hunched with excitement, his hands thrust into his pockets. 'There were massive fires in the Alpes. It was the lead story in *Nice-Matin*. The French were using those bloody great aircraft that suck up sea water and drop it on the flames.' He held his hands out to Charlie and Claude. 'Don't you see? One of the planes must have drawn him inside it. The hitman who spoke before he died said the fourth man was swallowed.'

They all looked down at the photograph again and considered the bizarre nature of the man's death until the door opened and Gordon Meredith entered the room carrying the satchel Lewis had been presented with by Roper.

'They took a damned long time,' Charlie said, rubbing his scalp roughly with bony fingers.

'Nico said it is one of the most beautiful jobs he's ever seen,' Meredith said as he placed the waterproof satchel on the coffee table. 'It was bloody difficult to get into. Everything triggered off a self-destruct mechanism. He finally cracked it a few minutes ago.'

'How?' Charlie asked.

'Look here,' Meredith said and he applied pressure with the ball of his thumb to the oilskin where it ran beside the lock. The skin lifted to reveal a row of small perforations in the metal. Meredith took a pin from the lapel of his jacket and inserted it into one of the holes, then he snapped open the flap. 'It's all right. Nico removed the charge, it's quite safe.'

Charlie Mars exchanged glances with Lewis then reached inside the satchel. He withdrew six large cream-coloured envelopes made of stiff, expensive hand-made paper. Each one bore a single name in large type. Charlie spread them on the table. The names were instantly familiar to them. They were all leaders of terrorist organisations operating in Europe. Charlie took an ivory-handled knife from his desk and carefully slit open the letters. Each contained a single sheet of the cream paper with the same message in a variety of languages.

'Sir, the final instalment of your fee is due. If the bearer of this letter receives $250,000, we shall continue with the completion of our course of studies.'

The heading on the sheets of paper read:

The Jericho Institute
Jericho
Arizona USA

Charlie Mars went to the bookshelf to the right of the fire-place and pulled down a world atlas. He scanned the map of the southern states of America for a time, flipped open the index, then slammed the book shut.

'Nothing there,' he muttered as he replaced the atlas and continued to search the shelves.

'Ah!' he said triumphantly as he pulled down a thick volume with heavy Edwardian binding and turned to the index. 'Yes,' he said in a contented voice. 'Jericho, in a gazetteer for 1901 . . . two thousand, three hundred and twenty-four people lived there then.'

As Charlie finished speaking there was a sharp rap on the door and Penny Rose entered. She held a cassette in her hand.

'Signals have just received this, sir. They say it's urgent,' she said as she handed the tape to Charlie.

He glanced at the time written in felt-tipped pen on the

label. '9.47am. Seven minutes ago,' he said as he checked his watch. 'Can you find that machine for me, Penny?'

Immediately she went to one of the cupboards below the bookcase and produced a cassette player which she placed on Charlie's cluttered desk. He inserted the tape and there was an expectant silence in the room until Joyce Maynard's voice came to them.

She spoke quickly and they could detect anxiety in her tone. 'Skylark emergency. Repeat, Skylark emergency. This group has achieved some kind of major coup, a kidnapping. I don't know who it is, but it's concerned with their operations in America. The telex traffic has been heavy. I haven't had the opportunity to decode anything, but a few hours ago the head of this station talked to Tucson on the telephone. I overheard part of the conversation. He said: "I'm sure we can rely on his co-operation. In fact, I can guarantee it. We expect no interference from the police or security people." ' Her voice became even more urgent at this point. 'I must go – I'll call later.'

The recording ended and Charlie Mars wound back the tape and played it again. Then he picked up the telephone.

'Signals? The Skylark tape. Do you have a voice print yet? Yes? Definitely her? Thank you.'

He sat deep in thought for a couple of minutes while the others waited. Then he looked up and said in a quiet, precise voice, 'Claude, get on to Harry Selig and tell him we shall need the help of his man from Arizona again. Lewis, you'd better go to Tucson and liaise with him. I want to know exactly what goes on at the Jericho Institute. Gordon, contact Inspector Lear at Special Branch and inform him of Skylark's message. Ask him if the police have any information about a kidnapping or the disappearance of anyone interesting or noteworthy.' He turned to Penny Rose. 'Ask Operations to set up a special unit. Everything connected with this project must go through the same desk. I want it manned twenty-four hours a day. Tell Curzon Street that I will have a Minister's clearance for the overtime.'

Penny hesitated and Charlie looked at her quizzically. 'Will the project have a code-name, sir?'

Charlie smiled. 'Yes, if you like, Penny.' He threw his head back and thought for a moment. 'We'll call it Ragtime.'

'Ragtime, sir?' she said.

Charlie smiled again. ' "I'm a rootin' tootin' hi falutin' son of a gun from Arizona, Ragtime Cowboy Joe." '

Penny left to do his bidding, and only Lewis remained with Charlie in the office.

Charlie ejected the tape from the cassette recorder and placed it on top of the cream envelopes. Then he tipped back his chair and thrust his bony hands deep into his jacket pockets.

'Do you get a feeling they're connected?' Lewis asked.

Charlie nodded. 'Much as I hate hunches, yes, I do.' He got up restlessly and walked over to the fireplace where he scattered another small shovelful of fuel onto the pitiful fire and gazed down in contemplation of his work.

'At least it will be warm in Arizona,' he said as he watched the tiny flames.

Lewis grinned as he walked to the door.

'You know what General Crook said about it?'

Charlie looked up at him expectantly.

' "If I owned Hell and Arizona, I'd live in Hell and rent out Arizona." '

David Neil was not as tanned as the last time Lewis had seen him, but he was dressed the same – light slacks and a dark blue sports shirt. He stood on the concourse with his arms folded as Lewis came from the baggage carousel.

'I heard it was snowing in England. I expected you to be dressed like Nanook of the North,' he said as he took one of Lewis's bags.

'I changed out of my snow shoes at Los Angeles,' Lewis replied, as Neil guided him to the exit.

When they stepped into the open it was like breathing inside a brick oven. Lewis could feel the dry air in his lungs. 'I thought it would be more humid at this time of year,' he said as they walked towards the car park.

Neil looked up at the star-filled sky. 'Yeah – we're getting freaky weather, the kind of storms we usually get in August.'

They stopped by a gleaming, dark grey Range Rover with tinted windows which caused Lewis to whistle in appreciation.

'Beautiful, isn't it?' Neil said. Lewis nodded. 'I won it in a poker game when I was in Las Vegas two weeks ago.'

'Who were you playing, an Arab prince?' Lewis said as he felt the soft leather upholstery.

Neil chuckled. 'No, it was some kid whose old man turned out to be a Mafia chieftain. The whole thing is customised. It cost as much as a Rolls Royce. It's bomb-proof, bullet-proof and gas-proof.' Neil turned on the ignition. 'In fact, if they nuke Tucson in the next half-hour, we're probably in the safest place. Four-wheel drive,' Neil explained. 'It's the best thing if we need to get off the road.'

Lewis stowed his bags and sat next to Neil on the front bench seat. He fastened his seat belt automatically although Neil didn't bother with his. Neil turned the vehicle onto the highway and immediately Lewis noticed how sedately everyone drove in comparison with the motorway traffic in England. Neil's comments about the slowness of the traffic in the States came back to him.

'Are you used to American driving habits yet?' Lewis asked.

Neil smiled. 'Used to them, yes. Happy, no,' he said as they drove in the centre lane at a steady thirty-five miles an hour.

Lewis looked at the low buildings that lined the streets they drove through and was reminded of other cities in the south west of America. There were palm trees, and harsh lights shone on shopping malls and adobe walls. Gradually the street became lined with houses which eventually petered out, and then they were driving on a straight deserted road that stretched in the direction of low mountains on the horizon.

There were scrublike trees each side of them and the road began to rise and dip like a fairground ride as they followed the contours of the land.

Neil sensed that Lewis was puzzled by the roller-coaster

effect. 'It's because of the rains,' he said. 'If they made a level road, the water would just wash it away so they let it go up and down with the land. They get a couple of inches all at once. It rips across this county like a chain-saw. Anything in the way just goes.' Neil made a sweeping motion with his hand to emphasise the point.

After a time the rise and fall stopped and gradually the road began to rise slightly but steadily. The macadam surface became a red dirt track and the headlights of the car showed that the scrub had given way to a fantastic landscape of different cacti. Standing above all were the tall saguaros with arms like rubber men. Massed around them was an astonishing variety – shapes like knives, small cannon, sheaves of wheat, bundles of sticks.

Neil turned off the track onto a branch dirt road and stopped on the edge of a clearing against a low white-painted porch that was thick with vines. The porch extended across the front of a large low building. To the right was a car port. Lewis could make out the squat blunted shape of a World War II weapon carrier that had been stripped down as a desert vehicle.

They got out of the car and Neil held up a warning hand and whistled a long rising note before he crossed the deep porch, opened an insect screen and unlocked the door.

Then Lewis saw the reason for his caution. Standing quite still in the entrance to the house was a massive, black Great Dane.

It walked forward a few paces and its claws made a tapping sound on the wooden floor.

'Hi, Duchess,' Neil said softly. 'It's OK, he's with me.'

Lewis stood still for a moment and the giant beast stepped forward to sniff him. The huge head came level with his solar plexus as he looked down into the eyes that glowed like orbs of polished stone. After a moment the dog was satisfied. She butted him gently in the stomach and he reached out and scratched the mighty head.

'That's OK,' Neil said. 'She likes you.'

'I'm glad of that,' Lewis said dryly. 'What do they keep her for – in case a rogue elephant attacks the place?'

Neil laughed as he switched on some of the lamps in the room.

'Paul and Florence just like big dogs.'

When Lewis could take his attention from the Great Dane that was now nudging him in an affectionate manner, he looked around the large square room that opened, in the American manner, straight from the porch.

He could tell that the single-storey building had evolved rather than been designed. To the left was a large fireplace, and half the room was at a higher level, divided by a wooden railing. The wide windows were of different sizes. There were large leather sofas, easy chairs, and the heads of horned animals on the whitewashed walls along with paintings and drawing of Western subjects. Vivid, geometrically-patterned Indian rugs were scattered on the floor. Dominating the room was a magnificent row of saddles mounted on stands: Indian saddles, with embroidered cloth fringed with buckskin; ancient Spanish and Mexican equipment, some plain and workmanlike, others chased and inlaid with silver decoration, cowboy rigs and military kit.

Neil could see Lewis's interest. 'Paul collects them. He's an artist and a historian. This is one of his paintings.'

Lewis examined the picture. It was of an Indian scout. He could see every detail of the weapons, equipment and clothing clearly. The meticulous piece of work had been a labour of devotion.

While Lewis examined the rest of the pictures Neil brought his bags in from the car. 'Are you hungry?' he asked as he came from the kitchen with two large bottles of beer. He handed one to Lewis who took a long swallow. It was strong – more like an English ale than the usual light American beer. He glanced at the label.

'Mexican,' Neil said. 'They make damned good beer. Can I get you anything to eat?'

Lewis shook his head. He realised suddenly that he was drained by the long journey and he thought how many weeks it would have taken the Indian scout to cover the thousands of miles he had travelled in the last twenty hours.

'Is there anyone else in the house?' he asked.

'No. Paul and Florence are away up north. A Mexican maid comes in each day to keep an eye on the dog.'

Lewis stretched and then drained the last of his beer.

'I think I'll turn in,' he said.

Neil nodded towards a door. 'You can use that room.'

Lewis thanked him and handed Neil the empty bottle as he held out his hand for it. A few minutes later he was beneath a patchwork quilt counterpane in a small room filled with rough pinewood furniture. As he closed his eyes, a distant owl hooted and the sound came to him across the desert silence. He thought for a moment of the Provost's drawing-room in Oxford before he slipped into sleep.

Sybil eased Charlie's old Jaguar from the slickened surface in the centre of Gower Street into the yellow slush at the side of the road and they came to a stop. Charlie leaned across and kissed his wife.

'I'll send one of the duty drivers for you at seven,' he said, as he opened his door and cold air gushed into the warm fug they had created inside the car since leaving home.

'Will that give you time to change?' Sybil asked.

Charlie hesitated as he was about to get out. 'Is it dinner jackets?'

'Of course it is, darling.'

Charlie swung his feet into the slush in the gutter.

'In that case you had better make it six-thirty,' he said in a resigned voice. Then he looked back at Sybil. 'Do you realise I'm putting on special clothes for the ambassador of a country that is small enough to fit into my living-room?'

The snow on the pavement was packed into ice so Charlie picked his way gingerly to the steps as Sybil drove off. Inside the house he made for the operations room.

George Ward was duty officer. He sat at a large old partners' desk that was covered with papers in wire baskets. His spotted bow tie was undone and his light brown hair, normally combed with great care, was tousled in disarray.

Gordon Meredith seemed more composed. He sat next to

Ward, frowning in concentration as he examined a long telex report. Finally he folded it into a concertina and placed it in an already full wire basket at the centre of the desk. The room was stuffy from the heat coming from the iron radiators that lined the walls.

Charlie was always reminded of an old-fashioned schoolroom when he was here. The illusion was helped by a massive map of the world, showing the British Empire of George V, that hung on the far wall from the duty officer's desk, which faced the rest of the room. Behind the desk was a blackboard with information about operators and rosters chalked in hieroglyphics and abbreviated codes.

Charlie unbuttoned his thick tweed overcoat, took the blue cashmere muffler from around his throat and stuffed it into a pocket.

'Got anything?' he asked as they both looked up.

'Nothing so far,' George Ward said. He gestured to the surface of the table. 'This is just the stuff that isn't on computer. Mary Brown's department is checking that end.' Ward massaged his closed eyes with a thumb and forefinger and Charlie could see the stubble on his jaw. 'I asked all the local constabularies for anyone reported missing in the last forty-eight hours. Some of them have sent their lists for the last six months. One genius even sent us a report of a missing dog – an Airedale to be precise.'

Charlie smiled in sympathy. 'Well done. Give me a shout if you get anything interesting.'

Charlie reached his room as Penny Rose was placing a cup of coffee on his desk. He threw his coat onto the sofa, picked up the cup and sipped appreciatively.

Claude entered the room. 'It's nice and warm in here,' he said plaintively. 'How do you manage it?' He looked at the heater in the fireplace, which blew hot air into the room. 'Ah, new equipment, I see.' He reached down and rubbed his hands together in the warming stream.

Charlie sat at his desk and snapped on the light. He glanced through the papers and checked the arrivals that Penny Rose had placed there that morning. Satisfying himself that there was nothing that needed his immediate attention he looked up at Claude who now stood with his back to the fan heater, rocking on his feet as if he was before a roaring fire.

'Any word of Joyce Maynard?' Charlie asked, careful to keep the anxiety he felt out of his voice.

Henderson shook his head slowly. 'No check calls. She hasn't been to her flat.'

Charlie picked up his cup and held it for some time before he drank some more coffee. Neither man spoke, the only sound in the room was the whirring noise made by the new heater. Charlie looked through one of the dormer windows at the laden roofs. The sky was a luminous white that promised more snow. Then the telephone rang.

'Yes?' Charlie said. It was Penny Rose.

'Mr Kent is here, sir. On his way up. Sergeant Major Watts called.'

'Thank you, Penny,' Charlie said and as he replaced the receiver there was a sharp rap on the door and Roger Kent entered.

He was wearing a light-coloured Burberry trenchcoat. Charlie wondered if everyone he knew had received new clothes for Christmas.

'This is an unexpected pleasure, Roger,' Charlie said as Kent flopped down on the chesterfield.

'That's all right,' Kent said with a wink at Henderson. 'I've got something for you so I thought I'd bring it personally.'

'That's kind of you. We appreciate such courtesy.'

Roger Kent sensed that Charlie was not going to ask him what it was, so he rummaged in his trenchcoat pocket and pulled out a folded piece of paper. He stretched towards Charlie, who half leaned across the desk and casually took the paper from him. Charlie read the message and looked up at an expectant Claude Henderson.

'Dr Lionel Reece, the Chemical Warfare Cook, has been mising from his home for nearly three days.'

'Reece?' Henderson repeated. 'How do you know?'

Roger Kent got to his feet, peeled off his trenchcoat and patted his pockets in search of tobacco.

'I got Special Branch to keep an eye on him after his kitchen speech. It's a pity it wasn't an armed escort.'

Charlie tapped on his desk with a forefinger as Kent attended to his pipe.

'Was he kidnapped or did he walk away of his own accord?'

Kent looked up from tamping his pipe. He struck a match and puffed clouds of smoke into the room. Charlie inhaled the fragrant aroma and glanced at the pipe enviously.

'Reece doesn't drive a car. A minicab picked him up from his flat. He was carrying an overnight bag. The policeman on duty rang his wife and said he was from the minicab firm. He told her the car's radio was out of order and he wanted the check the destination. Mrs Reece said he'd gone to his mother's house in Edgware for a few days. They checked the address. So far, no sign of Dr Reece.'

Charlie held his fingertips together and touched his lips with them for a moment, then he turned to Henderson and said in a quiet voice, 'Claude, would you be so kind as to ring down to the Duty Room and order a car?'

Lewis came out of a deep sleep and for a moment could not remember where he was. Then his eyes focused on the patch-work counterpane. He rolled over and gazed into the glowing inquisitive eyes of Duchess, who sat patiently beside the bed looking down at him. For a moment he felt he was taking part in a fairy-tale where the mighty dog was guarding a hidden treasure.

'Good morning,' he said politely.

The dog sighed and lowered her chin onto his chest. He reached out and patted the great head.

'I'd like to stay here talking to you,' Lewis said, 'but duty calls.' He got up and found the bathroom. When he had showered he made for the smell of coffee which he tracked down to a large kitchen.

Duchess came with him, her claws clicking on the red stone floor. There was a massive black iron range in one corner. David Neil stood by it cooking eggs. A pile of toast and thin strips of crispy bacon were keeping warm on the hob.

Lewis took the blue enamelled coffee pot from the stove

and poured a mug of coffee. He added sugar and had taken three deep draughts of the brew before Neil spoke.

'Go out on the porch. This is almost ready.'

Lewis walked to the verandah and sat down at a table that had been laid with a red gingham cloth. There was silverware, good crockery and even a small bunch of flowers. It told him a great deal about David Neil.

Lewis was one of the spartan school of bachelors. Neil had the patience and inclination to make life comfortable for himself. Perhaps it was the after-effects of his marriage, Lewis thought, as he looked towards the low mountain range that the morning air seemed to bring close in crystal clarity. The sun was just touching the mountain tops.

Across the semicircular apron of packed red earth before the house, the cacti and mesquite trees grew in such attractive profusion Lewis wondered if they had been planted by a gardener. He enjoyed the last minutes between dawn and morning.

Neil pushed open the flyscreen with his shoulder and placed a heavily laden tray on a side table. Lewis helped himself to more coffee and a plate of eggs and bacon.

The two men ate in silence, enjoying the food and the early quiet of the day. As Lewis pushed aside his empty plate, two tiny hummingbirds whirred up to the potted flowers that dangled above his head and dipped their long beaks into the open blooms.

'That was good,' Lewis said contentedly. Neil rocked back in his chair and rested the mug of coffee on his thigh. 'You cook well.'

'My ex-wife used to say the same.'

There was silence for a time, then Lewis spoke. 'What happened to her?' he asked, sensing from Neil's tone that it was no longer a delicate subject with him.

'She ran off with a drummer.'

'A fairground drummer?'

Neil grinned. 'No – a drummer in a rock band. American women stopped running off with fairground drummers when Herbert Hoover was President.'

Lewis said nothing. He knew that Neil would talk when he was ready.

Finally, Neil began to speak in an easy, flat tone, without emotion. 'I met her when I was at Fort Bragg. She was a stenographer. God, she was beautiful.' He stopped for a moment. 'We married, then I had to go overseas for a while. She wanted to be near her folks, so we got an apartment in St Louis. That was where she came from. When I got home she was in hospital with a broken nose, cracked ribs, multiple bruising. This guy she knew had beaten her up.'

His voice remained flat but Lewis could begin to hear an edge in it.

'I went looking for him. Eventually I found him in an hotel in New Orleans. The room was a sewer. He hadn't been out of it for days. He was only a kid. The manager of the band told me she'd started to get it on with the kid – the drummer – then when he was hooked, she screwed the rest of the band.'

He smiled at Lewis but it was a terrible smile.

'It seems I'd married a regular Lucrezia Borgia. I went back to St Louis, but she'd discharged herself from the hospital. I heard two days later that she'd gone to New Orleans and found the kid. The next night I was in a liquor store when three punks tried to rob it. They had shotguns and Police Specials.'

He stopped and looked towards the sun which was now beating down with all the promise of a sparkling day.

'Go on,' Lewis said quietly.

'I killed two of them,' Neil said remotely. 'The one that lived was the son of a prominent citizen. I didn't get a good press. After that, I drank for a while. Then the Marine found me.'

There was another silence until Lewis said: 'Any regrets?'

'Yeah,' Neil replied and this time the smile was healthy. 'I'm sorry I didn't bust her nose as well.' He got to his feet and stretched. 'Come on, I need a hand with the dishes.'

When the crockery was stacked away, they went into the living-room. Neil produced an old briefcase from which he took a large-scale relief map and spread it out on a round table near the window. He pointed with a pencil.

'We're here just outside Tucson.' He traced a line south.

'Just below Tombstone near Bisbee is Jericho, close on the Mexican border.'

Lewis studied the map for a moment.

'How big is it?' he asked.

Neil shrugged. 'About the size of an aircraft carrier. The place is a freak. It lies in the mountains like this.' He cupped his hands together.

'Because it's up high it doesn't get so hot. They rebuilt the entire town in 1902 because Marshall Cutter's grandfather went on a visit to Italy and liked Florence. They planted cypress trees and gave the whole place an Italian look. They even had an opera house. The main seam of silver ran out in the Thirties and the place practically became a ghost town. Some people stayed. The Cutter family kept the Jericho Company going with a skeleton staff just in case someone hit another major lode. They still get some silver out of the mine, but a guy called Brady bought the town from Cutter about three years ago and founded the Jericho Institute, which has been making big profits in the last two financial years.'

Lewis scratched his chin thoughtfully.

'So why would the Jericho Institute put together a hit team to get rid of Marshall Cutter?'

Neil threw the pencil in the air and caught it again.

'Company politics? Business can get pretty rough in the States. Maybe Cutter wanted to get back into the action when Brady started to make big money.'

Lewis got to his feet and stood by the window.

'Where's Marshall Cutter now?' Neil asked as he folded up the map.

'He was in London when I left, but he's in Los Angeles most of the time. We kept an eye on him for a few weeks but he insisted that his own security people take on the job. There hasn't been another attempt at a hit since September.'

Lewis watched a hawk drifting in the sky for a moment.

'So how do we get into Jericho?'

Neil folded his arms and looked up at the low ceiling of the verandah.

'We could put camouflage cream on our faces and climb over the mountain. However . . . ' He looked at his wristwatch. 'In a couple of hours we've got an appointment at the Jericho Institute Tucson office. They're hiring labour for the mine.'

Neil picked up the briefcase again and took out a large bulky envelope which he handed to Lewis.

'Courtesy of the United States taxpayers.'

Inside was a used wallet, the corners wrinkled and creased. Lewis opened it and took out a Diner's Club credit card, an American driving licence in his own name, a social security card, a letter from a fictitious mother and two snapshots of a middle-aged American couple in front of a trailer.

'This says I'm from New England,' he said.

'Yeah,' Neil replied. 'Tucson's growing so fast hardly anyone comes from around here any more except the Indians.'

He studied Lewis for a few moments.

'I think we'd better get you some other clothes. You're a bit Ivy League for a working stiff.'

Lewis looked down at himself.

'I've got a pair of jeans in my bag,' he suggested.

Neil nodded. 'OK, but chew gum as well and slouch a bit more.'

'Like this?' Lewis said and he let his shoulders slacken and opened his mouth slightly.

Neil studied him.

'That is very good . . . you just took about sixty points off your IQ. Now let me hear if you can manage the voice.'

Lewis recited the first fifty words of the Declaration of Independence.

'Good,' Neil said. 'A bit more New York than New England, but no-one should notice. Get changed, we've got to do some work on the Range Rover.'

Neil brought a large brown paper bag with him from the house and they stood side by side in front of the gleaming paintwork and chrome of the vehicle.

'Just taking a last look for a while,' Neil said. 'If we turn up in a hundred-thousand-dollar job like this, someone will blow the whistle on us.'

Neil took a couple of spray cans of paint and a container of heavy grease from the bag. They set to work, and half an

hour later stood back to admire their labours. The Range
Rover looked a long way from the showroom.

'OK, let's give it a final coat,' Neil said after he had
dumped a couple of buckets of water over the bodywork.
They coated the car with fine dust and let the windscreen
wipers cut fans across the filthy windscreen.

'The inside still looks pretty ritzy,' Lewis said.

Neil went into the house and got some old tartan rugs
which he threw over the expensive upholstery. Lewis
scattered some empty beercans on the floor. A few handfuls
of dust finished the job.

Neil made some final checks to the house and Lewis said
goodbye to the Great Dane, who watched them from a
window with rapt attention as they drove away.

As they came to a halt at some roadworks on the outskirts
of Tucson, Neil looked up into the clear sky. Two black jet
fighters flew in a gently curving turn towards the Ricon
mountains.

'It could rain again today,' he said, almost to himself.

'Does it make much difference?' Lewis asked as he
watched a great machine flanked by workmen and engulfed
in clouds of dust cutting the way for a new road through the
edge of the undergrowth.

A workman waved Neil on and he eased the Range Rover
forward. 'You have to see it to believe it. The desert sucks up
the water, then everything just bursts into colour. It's not
usually as hot as this at this time of year,' Neil said as he
made some adjustments to the air-conditioning, 'and the
rains are heavier. It's real summer weather.'

After a few more minutes Neil eased the Range Rover off
the main road onto a slipway in front of a parade of shops
and parked. They walked a few yards through the ferocious
sunshine to a low, white-painted building fronted by a tiny
lawn of coarse grass which grew around a fat-bodied palm
tree. Neil pushed open a door of dark-tinted glass and they
entered a small pastel-coloured office where a young man in a
blue short-sleeved shirt sat at a desk, reading a copy of
Arizona Highways. He looked up as they entered, a bored
expression on his face.

'We came about the jobs,' Neil said.

'Jobs?' the young man repeated as he looked at Neil's unshaven face and plaid working-man's shirt.

Neil nodded. 'Yeah, at the mine. I called here and someone said we had to come and take a test today.'

The young man got up and walked to a filing cabinet where he took out a sheaf of forms. He handed two of each to them and then gestured to an empty desk in the corner. They sat down and began to write laboriously. The first asked for personal details; the second was a general intelligence test which required the subject to tick boxes in answer to simple questions.

After half an hour the young man said, 'Time's up,' and collected the papers. Lewis and Neil sat with folded arms while the young man checked them.

'OK,' he said after a while. 'These seem in order.' He took two slips of paper from a drawer, filled them in and signed them. 'Report to the pay shack at Jericho and give these to the duty clerk.' He took two more plastic squares from the drawer. 'These are your identification cards. Go next door to the department store. There is a photo machine. Get mug shots for these.' He held up the ID cards. 'OK?'

'Next door?' Lewis said slowly. The young man nodded.

'Photographs – mug shots – for these,' the young man said with exaggerated care.

When they left the young man picked up the telephone on his desk and punched out a number.

'Corelli? It's Ellis here. I'm sending you two more hands. No, I wouldn't say they were morons – just barely literate idiots. One of them has a tattoo on his arm; he can hardly spell his name. I tell you, if anyone wants quiz-show contestants in this country they should come to me. Yeah, talk to you soon, Corelli.'

Lewis and Neil returned with their strips of colour photographs and the young man stuck them onto their cards and handed them back with a flourish.

'There you are, gentlemen. You are now employees of the Jericho Institute.'

'I hear there's a great cathouse in Jericho,' Neil said as he stuffed his card into the pocket of his shirt.

The young man shrugged and picked up the magazine once more. 'Like everything, it's a matter of taste,' he said, as he glanced at the two of them with evident contempt. 'The ladies of the Grand Hotel don't rely on gentlemen such as your-selves for the major part of their income. You're the salt of the earth, I'm sure, but hardly the Las Vegas carriage trade.'

'Well thanks, buddy,' Lewis said as he switched his wad of chewing gum around his mouth. 'You've been a lotta help.'

The young man didn't even watch them as they made for the filth-encrusted Range Rover.

'That thing doesn't work.' The voice was young, cheerful and very English. Claude Henderson and Charlie Mars turned on the top step of a short flight that led to the entrance of a block of mansion flats and looked down at the young woman who had spoken to them.

'I beg your pardon?' Claude said in the formal tones he used before an introduction.

'Those bells are broken,' she said. She was wearing a navy-blue coat with the deep collar up against the thin flurries of snow that melted on the black wet pavement. She had a face to match the voice: fair skin, a snub nose and a wide smile.

Charlie walked down the steps and took the pushchair she was manoeuvring up the stairs by the axle. The small child, who was a mirror image of the mother, stared at him with interest.

'Thank you,' the woman said when they reached the doorway. 'You don't meet many gentlemen in this part of Earl's Court.'

'We're calling on Mrs Reece. She does live here, doesn't she?' Charlie asked.

The girl looked at them both for a moment.

'Yes, on the third floor, flat nine. Do you have any identification?'

Charlie smiled. 'I'm afraid we're just teachers at the same university as Dr Reece. All I have is my driving licence.' Charlie produced the document from his wallet and handed it to the young woman.

108

'Claude?' he said as she studied it.

Henderson fumbled inside his bulky suede coat. 'I've got a letter from my bank manager.' He searched some more. 'And a ticket for the London Library.'

The woman shrugged. 'All right.' She opened the door and allowed them to enter the spacious hallway.

'Thank you,' Charlie said with a fatherly smile.

'I shall call the police if I hear any screams,' the woman said as she let herself into a ground-floor flat.

Charlie and Claude climbed the wide staircase to the third floor. The door to Number 9 stood wide open. Charlie lifted a small brass knocker that was tarnished with verdigris and let it fall once.

'I'm almost ready,' a female voice called out. 'You're a bit early. Come in.'

Charlie and Claude exchanged glances of surprise and then entered the cluttered hallway. There was a large coat-stand bulky with clothes, four large cardboard cartons filled with rubbish and a pile of bulging black plastic bags.

They squeezed past and entered a long narrow room with tall windows at the far end. The high ceiling was heavily decorated with plaster scrollwork.

Every surface near the doorway was cluttered. Piles of books lay by the fireplace, clothes, newspapers and magazines lay discarded on chairs and tables. But there was an oasis of order under the tall windows. Within it were a pink velvet chaise-longue and a Victorian table draped with white lace and adorned with brass lamps with delicate floral shades.

'Who the hell are you?' a voice demanded in a Birmingham accent.

Charlie and Claude turned and looked down upon a tiny woman in very high stiletto heels who stood with hands upon hips and gazed up at them defiantly. She wore nothing except shoes and a minute pair of panties. The woman began to smile as they desperately sought some focus of attention other than the splendid breasts she thrust before her like the prow of a sailing ship.

'Forgive the intrusion, Mrs Reece,' Charlie said as he fixed his eyes on the light switch behind her head. 'We're civil servants. We want to talk to you about your husband.'

Mrs Reece reached over and took a housecoat that was thrown over the back of a chair and pulled it on. Immediately she was transformed. The fullness of her breasts now made her look plump, small and homely. She swept the newspapers from a sofa and dumped them on the floor and gestured for them to sit down.

She sat on a straight-backed chair and crossed her legs. The housecoat fell away to reveal the small, shapely legs and once again she became an erotic figure.

'I'm sorry about the mess. We've only just moved into the flat and the people who were here before us left the place like a tip.'

Charlie studied her as she spoke.

Thick, shining dark hair hung past her shoulders and a heavy fringe framed her heart-shaped face. She had high, wide cheekbones, large uptilted brown eyes and a bow-shaped mouth that was emphasised by pink lipstick. In spite of the heavy make-up he could see the skin was flawless. She laughed and wrinkled the tiny nose so that he could see small even white teeth and the pinkness of her tongue.

'I expect you're wondering what Lionel is doing married to a girl like me, aren't you?' she said as Charlie and Claude sat gazing at her in some discomfort.

Claude made a curious noise as he cleared his throat. 'You don't seem to be the usual kind of wife for an academic, Mrs Reece,' he said politely.

She shrugged and the housecoat parted once again to reveal one of the magnificent breasts. Casually she pulled it close.

'That's what my friends said when we got married. Call me Sheila, by the way. Everyone does.'

'How did you meet?' Charlie asked.

'At university.'

'University?' Claude managed to say in an incredulous voice.

She turned to him. 'Yes, Lionel was at Birmingham University. I was working in Marks and Spencer's – I was trying

110

to get into modelling as well, but I wasn't getting anywhere. He was doing his PhD. We met at a dance.'

Charlie noticed that as she spoke her accent softened.

'He was a right wally. He used to follow me around everywhere. Not that he was bad-looking, it was just he couldn't speak without tripping over his tongue. He just used to blush, and everything he wanted to say came out wrong.'

'What altered your feelings towards him?' Charlie asked.

She looked at him steadily for a moment. 'My sister.' As she spoke a call came from the hallway.

'Sheila – it's me.'

A man entered the room. Two large leather bags hung from his shoulders by straps, and he was carrying a large folded aluminium tripod. He wore a black silk bomber jacket with a portrait of Marilyn Monroe embroidered on the breast, washed-out blue jeans and trainers. His thick hair was brushed forward, so that at first glance Charlie took him to be young, but as he unloaded his equipment he realised the man was much older than the clothes implied.

'Barry, these two gentlemen are friends of Lionel. This is Barry Day.'

Charlie and Claude stood up to shake hands.

'My name is Mars and this is Mr Henderson,' Charlie said.

Barry Day nodded cheerfully. 'You're not wearing anything tight under that frightful housecoat, are you, Sheila?' he asked.

She stood up and opened the housecoat to him. He examined her remarkable body as a car dealer might look upon a vehicle for sale.

'Good girl. No crease marks.'

'Make some coffee, will you, Barry? I've still got some business with these gentlemen,' she said as she closed the housecoat once again. Mr Day made for the kitchen.

'This place is a bloody slum, Sheila. Where's your Filipino slave?' he called out.

'She's due back tomorrow, thank God,' Sheila Reece shouted towards the kitchen.

'You mentioned your sister,' Charlie said insistently.

Sheila Reece thought for a moment.

111

'Oh, yeah. It was my sister's husband, Tony. She was crazy about him. Big, good-looking feller. Lots of laughs. He used to cart our Karen around like a mascot. That was twelve years ago, when they got married. He's got a beer belly on him now like a sack of nutty slack and he's pissed all of the time. Karen spends every day on the twelfth floor of a block of flats. She eats Valium. I could tell they were going that way when I first met Lionel. So I thought, what kind of a life do I want? Walsall for the rest of my life, apart from two weeks every year on the Costa del Sol? Lionel was my chance to become middle-class. At least, that's what I thought. He told me he was going to be in a university for the rest of his life.

'It's funny. I worked at Birmingham but I had this idea we'd get married and live in a sort of castle in the country. Lionel would wear his gown and I'd be nice to the boys. I think I got it mixed up with "*Goodbye, Mr Chips*". Anyway, we got married, and a year and a half later Lionel was teaching at London University and we were living in a bed-sitter in Tufnell Park.'

Barry Day came into the room with a mug of coffee which he handed to Sheila Reece.

'Would you gentlemen care for anything?' he asked.

Charlie and Claude both declined with thanks, and turned back to Sheila.

'He seems to be doing much better now,' Claude said. 'I was wondering how you could afford all this on your husband's salary.'

Sheila looked at him in amazement for a while and then she laughed.

'I'm afraid I pay for all of this,' she said. She paused. 'You don't know who I am, do you?' She looked from Claude to Charlie. 'Either of you?'

They exchanged puzzled glances.

'I'm the Bullring Venus now.'

'Bullring Venus?' Claude said in a confused voice.

'Just a minute.' She left the room and reappeared almost instantly with a large scrapbook which she handed to Claude.

'I was spotted in Oxford Street by a press photographer.

Lionel doesn't like it, but it means we can live here. I'm even going to buy him a car.'

Claude opened the scrapbook and they looked down at the huge pictures of Sheila Reece cut from tabloid newspapers.

'That's what they call me in the tabs,' she said. 'The Bullring Venus.'

Claude cleared his throat again. 'Is this why your husband has left you, Mrs Reece?'

She looked up in astonishment. 'Left me? Why do you think he's left me? We're very happy.'

Claude looked around. 'Where is he, Mrs Reece? Where is your husband?'

She looked at the pair of them and they could see there was an air of uncertainty after her previous poise.

'He's visiting his mother.'

'Why didn't you go with him?' Charlie asked.

'She hates me,' Sheila Reece said. 'Lionel is her only child; her husband left her years ago. She's very respectaable, lives in Edgware. I don't go there in case any of the neighbours recognises me.'

'Why did he go to his mother's house?' Charlie said. 'Please give me every detail you can remember.'

She thought for a time.

'He got a telephone call. He told me it was a neighbour, who said his mother wasn't feeling too well. He packed an overnight bag and told me he'd be home in a few days.'

She looked at them both and they could see the fear beginning to grow inside her.

'Where is he?' she said, her voice breaking. 'What's happened to him – is he in danger?'

They stood up.

'We're not sure, Mrs Reece,' Charlie said as gently as he could. He handed her a card. 'If he rings you at any time, these people can get in touch with me. One last thing – does he have any special friends? Anyone close, apart from yourself?'

She sat almost in a crouch in the chair and clutched the card Charlie had given her.

'There's only George Selby,' she said.

'Who is he?' Claude asked as he made a note of the name.

'He was Lionel's best man.'

'Do you have his address?'

'I think so,' she replied and she began to search amongst the chaos of books piled by the fireplace. As she searched, Claude could see she was crying.

Chapter Five

David Neil drove with one hand on the steering wheel at a steady fifty miles an hour. Ahead of them the deserted road cut across the bleak brown plain towards the distant mountains like a black scar.

Lewis had become drowsy facing the monotony of the featureless landscape and the glare of the sun. The air-conditioning kept the temperature of the car at an even coolness but the interior smelt stale and metallic. They had been on the road for nearly two hours. At first Lewis was interested by the landscape which seemed to change with astonishing frequency. But now they had come to this massive flat expanse which had once, millions of years ago, been the bed of a great sea, and the sameness of the view was beginning to bore him. He began to appreciate the vastness of the continent and thought how lightly people had sketched their presence on the land.

His mind turned to home and he compared the way the English countryside had been altered by generations of care. But for the road they travelled upon, this part of America was as nature had shaped it: harsh and hard, an unforgiving land.

'They must have been remarkable people,' he said almost to himself and David Neil glanced towards him for a moment. 'The settlers,' Lewis said, aware that his first remark would have sounded obscure.

Neil nodded. 'It wasn't just the weather. The locals made rough neighbours.'

Lewis looked towards the mountains that seemed to stay

the same distance from them despite the motion of the car.

'Were the Apaches really that tough?'

Neil nodded again. 'Geronimo kept an army pinned down in Arizona. They chased him around for years.' He gestured ahead. 'Once they got into those hills, no-one could find them. Mind you, it was good for business in Tucson. Government contracts kept the town going.'

As they spoke, dense clouds, the colour of lead, began to rise above the mountains. Within minutes they had rolled across the bright blue sky as if blinds had been drawn against a summer day. The first crack of thunder was quickly followed by others, like artillery being fired. Lightning jabbed down in jagged spears and suddenly they drove into rain that fell with a force Lewis had seen before only in the tropics.

Despite the sweep of the heavy-duty wipers, such was the power of the wall of rainwater that the windscreen blurred and distorted their vision. Neil turned on the headlights, switched off the air-conditioning and eased the speed down.

After some time the plain gave way to rising ground, and occasional trees grew beside the road.

'We didn't see any cattle,' Lewis said above the noise of the rain drumming on the car's roof.

'The big herds went a long time ago,' Neil said as he peered forward to see his way through the lashing storm. 'They overgrazed the country. It takes forty acres to feed one head in some parts now, and the land's getting drier.'

'Drier?' Lewis said with a laugh.

'Sure, don't let this rain fool you. Arizona used to have more water a hundred and fifty years ago. Some of the rivers are almost gone now except in the monsoon seasons. Hell, we used to have a lot of beaver once,' Neil said as he continued to study the road.

Lewis looked out through the blurred windscreen. There were trees and grass on the high ground around him.

'So the Apaches lived up here?' he said.

Neil shrugged. 'Yeah, sometimes. Other times they moved about. It's pretty hard to generalise about Indians. The tribes and nations are all so different.'

116

'How do you mean?' Lewis asked.

Neil thought for a moment. 'Well, take the Papagos. The name means the bean eaters. That's what we used to call them when I was a kid. They changed their name recently. I can't remember exactly what it is now. Something like "People of the Desert". They're almost black and all of them are heavy. They have a gene that causes them to store fat. For centuries they lived here and had a cycle of plenty followed by famine, so they were ready for the bad years. Now they get enough to eat all the time so they have a weight problem.

'Here we go,' Neil said, pointing at the sign for Jericho which had appeared, and he turned into a slip road on the right.

As the road climbed, the landscape became greener and there were more trees. Eventually the rain started to ease and had come to a stop when they entered the mouth of a wide tunnel cut in the side of the mountain. The interior was bright with orange-coloured sodium lights. After fifty yards, they halted at a gate made of tubular steel and linked mesh.

There was a glass inspection booth. Inside were two guards who wore blue military-style uniforms. One stayed inside the box, the other came and stood on the island in the centre of the road and held out his hand. They produced their identity cards and held them out to the impassive guard, who nodded his shaven bullet-shaped head.

'The pay-shack is the last building in the town at the mouth of the mine. Check in there.'

The guard inside the box operated the switch and waved them on as the gate swung open. They drove on down the tunnel for another hundred yards before they came into daylight once again.

The road they drove on lay halfway up the side of a narrow valley. To their left, just below, sparkling fresh in the sharp sunlight that followed the storm, were the rooftops of Jericho. Neil stopped the vehicle under the shade of a small oak tree that grew by the side of the road and they got out.

Lewis looked down with fascination on the tiny piece of Italy that nestled between the narrow cleft of the surrounding mountains. Spires and domes broke the lines of red-tiled roofs. Some of the buildings were dark red brick trimmed with granite, others were of fine stone or pastel-shaded plaster. Laced through the streets and on the hillsides were lines of cypress trees.

'Fantastic, isn't it?' Neil said as Lewis studied the sight before them. 'It's like finding a chunk of Tuscany up here.'

They got back into the Range Rover and drove slowly down the hill, following the road signs that directed them to the mine. The road passed between a high, slanting cleft in the bare granite of the mountain. When it emerged from the narrow gorge, they entered a landscape of rubble excavated from the mine.

No vegetation grew on the lunar surface but different minerals from the bowels of the earth stained the surroundings, colouring the mountains of slag with red, ochre, lavender and emerald green. At last they came to a wide, flat, open space where clattering machinery brought ore from the depths of the mine. Huge tracks stood in a line as the conveyors tipped loads of crushed rock into their dumpers.

As each truck received its load, a supervisor waved it on its way and the lorries took an exit road that Lewis assumed led to the smelting works.

Neil parked the Range Rover beside a row of vehicles outside a long, low building on the opposite side of the perimeter to the mine entrance. The ground was puddled and muddy from the rain but the swirling dust from the conveyor belts and the loaded lorries had coated everything with a layer of fine, whitish dust.

Neil and Lewis entered the pay-shack. There was a counter running the length of the room and positions for desk clerks. Two were deserted but at the third a woman in her early thirties with an elaborately shaped hairstyle sat listening to a powerful figure in the blue uniform of a guard who leaned on the counter.

Lewis and Neil walked over and stood behind him. As they did so, the heavy-set young man took a muscular arm from the counter and rested it on the varnished butt of the Colt .44 he carried in the black leather holster he wore around his waist.

As the arm moved, they could see the great slabs of muscle across his back shift through the blue shirt.

'Git down by the wall,' the guard commanded in a soft voice that managed to be both emotionless and yet full of menace.

'What's that you say, buddy?' Neil said in a friendly tone and the guard turned slowly to look at them. He had a round, almost baby face, except for the knots of muscle that worked at his jaw.

His hair was cropped close to the skull and his eyebrows and eyelashes were bleached almost white against his tanned smooth skin. The eyes were very pale grey and flickered between them. Instinctively Lewis balanced himself evenly and let his hands hang free at his sides as he looked into the round, even features. He knew he was looking at the face of a psychopath.

The guard smiled without warmth, showing small, very white teeth. He took his hand from the butt of the revolver and rested both palms behind him on the counter, then slowly studied each of them in turn before he pointed with a thick, stubby finger. The hands were heavy and powerful. Small white scars showed on the tanned knuckles. Lewis noticed that the fingernails were bitten very short.

'I said git down by the wall. Now that ain't too hard to understand, even for you dumb assholes, is it?'

As he spoke he nodded towards the far end of the shack where a solitary figure sat at the end of a row of chairs.

'Sorry, mister,' Lewis said.

The guard flicked his head in Lewis's direction.

'I didn't talk to you, shithead.'

Lewis tugged at Neil's sleeve. They walked to the far end of the shack and sat down on the chair next to a man who wore stained workclothes. His face was seamed with age and the hands that held a piece of paper were gnarled like old tree roots.

'That's Bull Reicher,' the old man said in a voice as soft as featherdown. 'Watch out for him – he likes to beat people into hamburger.' The man spoke without appearing to move his mouth.

119

'Thanks,' Lewis whispered.

The guard leaned forward and muttered something in the woman's ear and she laughed with him. Then he turned and looked down the room at the three of them for a few moments before he ambled slowly from the shack. When the door closed the old man turned to them.

'He walks around like he was Wyatt Earp, don't he?' The voice was thick with bitterness.

'I got other things to do but wait for you guys,' the woman called out in a Southern accent.

The old man got up and walked to her position and handed her the piece of paper he held. She ignored him and turned to Lewis and Neil.

'Are you the new hands?'

'Yes,' Neil replied.

'Come here,' she ordered contemptuously.

They joined the man at the counter.

'This here is Jim Davies,' she said, gesturing towards the old man. 'He'll show you around. You start tomorrow – eight o'clock.'

She lowered her head as if they no longer existed. The old man leaned forward.

'I'm on vacation tomorrow, Miss Elliot,' he said in a pleading voice as he held out the sheet of paper. 'Here's my leave docket.'

She took the paper and looked at him with distaste.

'Your vacation starts at 6 a.m. tomorrow. Now do as I say and show these guys around.'

Davies paused for a moment as if he were going to speak again, then he shrugged and led them out of the shack. They stopped by the Range Rover.

'That road only goes two places,' he said, pointing to the exit from the perimeter that the trucks used. 'The smelter on the other side of the mountains and a trailer park where the married guys live.'

'What happens to the refined silver?' Neil asked.

Davies pointed back to the pay-shack.

'They keep it in the big safe out back. A chopper lands here and they take it to Tucson every couple of days.' He looked at the Range Rover for a moment as if deciding something he was unsure of. 'I guess it's OK to take this up there.'

'You don't sound too certain,' Lewis said.

The old man looked at him with watery, red-rimmed eyes.

'Mister, you don't understand.'

'What's the problem?' Lewis asked.

The old man scratched his head. 'Somebody might not like the idea of us riff-raff driving around town in the daytime. You see, what we got here in Jericho is a good old-fashioned class system. The bosses and the guys at the Institute, they're the upper classes. They live in The Silver Queen, which is a pretty fancy hotel. At least, I hear it is, because I ain't never been in there. Then we got the guards – the middle classes. Us working stiffs live in the trailer park.'

'What about the cathouse? Is that off limits?' Neil asked.

The old man cackled with laughter.

'Nobody calls the Grand Hotel a cathouse, mister. It's a pretty fancy place. They ain't all hookers up there; some of 'em are genuine cocktail waitresses. Yes sir, Kate's place is pretty high class.'

'But does she keep guys like us out?'

The old man shook his head. 'The guys from the mine go there but they generally behave themselves.'

'What happens during the day?'

'Can't say. I ain't never been there during the day.'

'Well, now's your chance,' Neil said as the three of them climbed into the front seat of the Range Rover. Neil switched on and engaged the gear. The old man laughed again.

Neil spun the Range Rover around and headed up the hill through the centre of Jericho. 'How come Kate decides what goes on in the Grand Hotel?' he asked.

'Because she owns the place,' the old man said. 'The Jericho Institute owns every other damned building in the town but Kate's old man had the deeds to the Grand and they say she ain't never gonna sell.'

As they drove up the main street, Lewis could see gushing streams of rainwater, flowing from the sides of the mountains, that fed into the main street and then into the storm drains set into the sides of the roadway.

121

'That's The Silver Queen,' Davies said, and Neil slowed down so they could see the hotel which was set back from the road and higher than the buildings around it. The mountainside rose steeply behind. It had a very long flight of steps to a verandah, and four white pillars contrasted with the rose-coloured brick of the facade.

Davies pointed again. 'That's the Institute where I work and that's the barracks.'

The first building was gorgeously decorated with scrolls and intricate carvings in pink marble. The police barracks was suitably faced with rough-cut granite.

'What do you do there?' Neil asked.

'Janitor,' the old man replied.

'In here,' Davies indicated, and Neil turned off the street and into a car park.

'That's Kate's place,' Davies said.

It was a wide brick building with delicate iron balconies on each of the three floors. Window boxes filled with red and white geraniums relieved the austere frontage. The main doors were rounded at the top. They were of white wood and had swirls of *art nouveau* glass set into them.

The three men looked down the narrow, curving road and Lewis noticed that the buildings, although grand in design, were scaled down in size. Lewis was of average height but the proportions of the street made him feel somehow taller and more in command of his surroundings.

The scent of the cypress trees was heavy on the breeze that came down the narrow valley. They stood for a moment and listened as the sound of Dolly Parton singing about broken hearts drifted across from the Grand Hotel. When the music ended, the silence was filled with a long high-pitched scream of pain.

Claude Henderson came out of the telephone booth at Earl's Court tube station and picked his way through the crowd to the car which waited for him in the roadway. He slid into the back seat next to Charlie Mars and shook his head.

'Reece's mother hasn't seen him since Christmas,' he said

as he gazed balefully through the misted window at a youth in a studded leather jacket who had stopped for a moment next to the car, a huge blaring radio resting on his shoulder.

'What about Selby?' Charlie asked.

'He's moved from the address Reece's wife gave us. He and his wife are living with their daughter and son-in-law in Chiswick.'

'Did you ring?' Charlie asked.

'Yes,' Claude said rather irritably. 'You know, Charlie, we really ought to have telephones in these duty cars. It would save enormous amounts of trouble.'

'I shall apply with renewed vigour, Claude,' Charlie said in placating tones as Claude consulted a street guide.

'Go to the Hammersmith flyover, driver,' Claude instructed. 'I'll direct you from there.'

The journey didn't take long. Fifteen minutes later they stopped in front of a large stucco Victorian villa in a wide, quiet street lined with lime trees. They walked up the snow-covered gravelled drive and rapped on the oak door with a large brass knocker. The door was opened by a slim woman Charlie judged to be in her thirties. She was drying her hands on a tea-towel and there was a smudge of flour on her cheek.

Charlie and Claude took off their hats.

'My name is Henderson, Mrs Trent. I telephoned a few minutes ago. We would like to talk to Mr Selby. I presume he's your father?'

'Dad? Oh, yes,' she replied in a pleasant voice and opened the door wider so they could enter the hallway. 'Would you like to go through? He's in the garden.'

She led them across the marble-floored hallway, down a passage and into a large, cheerful kitchen that was decorated in pine, with bunches of herbs and large glass containers full of dried flowers. Mrs Trent went back to the pastry and the rolling pin on the table.

'That way,' she said, indicating the kitchen door. 'You can't miss him.'

They walked along the covered passageway and into a high walled garden that was dominated by three large pear trees. It was a good garden for children. There were laurels, a conservatory, huts, bushes and trellises that made secret places. On the oval of lawn before the conservatory a tall thin man, dressed in a black overcoat and trilby hat, was making a snowman. He stopped as Claude and Charlie approached and put a match to the pipe clenched in his teeth.

'Mr Selby?' Claude asked when they stood before him.

'I am,' the man said clearly.

'We're sorry to interrupt your task. My name is Claude Henderson and this is Charles Austen Mars.'

Selby studied them with very bright blue eyes. His face was narrow with a lantern jaw, the flesh ruddy from the cold. Finally, he took the pipe from his mouth and pointed the stem at Charlie.

'Did you write a book about the exile of Charles II?' he asked in a sharp voice.

'Guilty,' Charlie replied and Selby smiled with pleasure.

'Then I'm delighted you disturbed my work.' He waved at the snowman. 'What do you think?' he asked.

'It's definitely a snow*man*,' Claude said and Selby nodded his approval.

'Correct – my grandson was instructed to call them snow-persons. I intend to demonstrate that we glory in a precise language.' He scraped snow from his wellington boots and gestured for them to follow him into the conservatory, where he took their coats and sat them in wicker chairs.

'Would you care for some tea?' he said.

'I would, Mr Selby, if it isn't too much trouble,' Charlie said.

'No trouble at all – if you don't mind it in mugs and made with teabags,' Selby said and made for the kitchen.

When he came back with a tray after a few minutes, Charlie asked his first question.

'Do you remember Dr Lionel Reece?'

Selby banged out his pipe as he answered.

'Oh, yes, I still see him quite often.'

'Have you seen him recently?' Claude asked.

Selby fixed him with the bright blue eyes.

'Is this to do with the university?' he asked.

'We're from the government, Mr Selby. We're civil servants not academics.'

'Really?' Selby said. 'I seem to remember you taught at Oxford.'

'I did,' Charlie explained, 'but I have another job now.'

Selby put his mug down and looked out at his snowman.

'Does this have anything to do with his claims about generating germ warfare in the kitchen?'

'It could,' Charlie said.

Selby sighed.

Charlie shifted in his chair and took another sip of tea.

'Can you tell us about him? What kind of a person is he?'

Selby routed out his pipe with a small penknife and filled it again from a wooden tub of tobacco on the wicker table beside him. When he spoke he did so carefully.

'Lionel Reece is typical of a certain type of boy. He came from a broken home. His father left his mother when he was very young and his mother was – is – very possessive and at the same time rather cold. Some hold that this background will often influence boys to become homosexuals. I couldn't say. In Lionel's case he sought a father figure which he found in me, and the need for affection, which he found in his wife.'

'Do you approve of his wife, Mr Selby?' Claude asked.

Selby looked at him sharply.

'I said he looked on me as a father figure, Mr Henderson, but I am not his father. It would be an impertinence for me to pass judgement on his wife.'

'Do you like her?' said Charlie.

'Yes, actually I do,' Selby replied without hesitation. 'Very much.'

'Can you tell us more about him?' Charlie asked insistently.

Selby puffed on his pipe before he answered.

'He wasn't popular – too clever – and he didn't care for sport. In fact, he was rather badly co-ordinated. He seemed to miss adolescence altogether, but in many ways he has remained a boy. I don't know if you were familiar with the type at Oxford?'

Charlie nodded. 'Yes, I think I know what you mean.'

Selby examined the chewed stem of his pipe for a moment.

125

'I often found that when part of a boy's mind raced ahead with such astonishing speed, the rest of him seemed to suffer from arrested development. Again, Lionel is typical in that respect. Even today, his colleagues find him bumptious and arrogant, which I'm sure he is; except with me, to whom he shows exaggerated deference.'

Selby took the pipe from his mouth and examined it once again in an abstracted fashion.

'I'm afraid I must take the full blame for his outburst about manufacturing viruses.'

'Why is that?' Charlie asked, sitting forward in the chair.

'We saw them before Christmas. I'd had a few glasses of sherry and I said in rather flippant terms to forget about nuclear weapons – we would never see world disarmament until something made people think about the horror of chemical warfare. He took my remarks literally. It was stupid of me. I ought to know by now he doesn't think I'm capable of a silly statement.'

Charlie stood up and stretched his long legs. He turned and looked out at the snowman. The garden was almost monochromatic. The bare trees and dark shrubbery stood in stark contrast to the shadowless snow. When he spoke, his voice was carefully neutral.

'What about politics, Mr Selby? Did you pass any views on to him?'

Charlie watched Selby's face as he answered.

'I tried to give him some guidance, but I had to be careful. Lionel really wants to see life in extremes: good, bad, black, white. I suppose in many ways he is the type that is attracted to fascism or any form of totalitarianism. It was difficult to convey to him the impossibility of absolutes when you are dealing with human beings. I'm not sure he could assimilate my brand of pragmatism.'

'So what are your politics, Mr Selby?' Claude asked.

Selby turned to look at him.

'For many years my wife and I were staunch members of our local Labour Party. Once, I was even considered a firebrand of the left.' Selby smiled sadly. 'Of course, these days we are accused of being very right wing.'

126

Claude and Charlie thanked Selby as they pulled on their coats. He was about to show them from the house when he remembered something and excused himself. A few minutes later he returned with a book.

'Would you be so kind as to sign this copy of your book?' he asked, offering it to Charlie.

As he wrote his signature Charlie thought of another question.

'In your opinion, Mr Selby, could someone put pressure on Dr Reece?'

'What sort of people?' Selby asked.

'Very ruthless people.'

'Oh, yes,' Selby said as he opened the door for them. 'All they would have to do is to threaten me or his wife. We are the most important things in his life.'

Charlie and Claude walked down the snow-covered drive and stood for a moment on the pavement next to the car. The sky above the suburban street was dark and ominous.

Across the avenue a bay window was bright with lights and Christmas decorations. The street reminded Charlie of north Oxford, where he had taken his daughters to parties in their childhood. He wondered whether the world had been as innocent as he remembered it then.

Lewis and Neil looked towards the Grand Hotel from where the sound of the scream had come, and then exchanged questioning glances. Lewis was aware that the old man who had guided them was attempting to edge away. He reached out and held a handful of his shirt to restrain him.

'Who could that be?' Neil asked softly.

'Hell, I don't know,' the old man whined. 'It came from the bar.'

'What bar?' Lewis asked and he screwed more of Davies's shirt in his fist to emphasise the question.

'Round the side there and down the alley. You can't see it from here.'

The old man wriggled free as Lewis relaxed his grasp.

'I'd keep away if I were you guys. Bull Reicher goes there

most afternoons. The scream sounded like his kinda work.'

'Thanks for the tour,' Neil said. 'You can run along now.'

The old man began to shuffle away and then he stopped again.

'I ain't kidding. They say Reicher's killed guys – beaten them to death. They dump the bodies out there, beyond the mountains.' He gestured towards the north west.

Lewis nodded to the old man.

'Thanks. We'll take care,' he said, and the old man watched them cross the road and enter the alley before he walked away at a fast shuffling pace down the narrow street.

The alley rose at a steep angle from the roadway. A torrent of water rushed down a deep culvert cut in the centre of the passageway and flowed into the storm drains.

They entered a lobby painted matt black. A door opened onto a short flight of steps. Inside was a great dimly lit cavern with a strip of lighting running the length of a long bar that stretched down one side of the huge room.

As their eyes became accustomed to the gloom they could make out groups of tables with banquettes dividing the space, padded chairs upholstered in red artificial leather. Massive fans ticked slowly around on the dark painted ceiling. At the far end of the room there was a small bandstand and a jukebox that flashed and flickered primary colours that lit the area around it.

Old posters of wanted men, general stores, railroad services, steamship lines, patented machinery, all advertising the booming years of the nineteenth century, were varnished to the walls. A group of people were gathered in the light at the end of the bar. Lewis recognised Bull Reicher, who broke away and walked over to the jukebox. The same Dolly Parton record began to play again. As they drew nearer the group, Lewis could see that they were mostly women.

A grey-haired man tended the bar. He wore a white shirt with an open red waistcoat, a black, flowing bow-tie and pale blue garters as armbands.

Sitting on a stool opposite him was a woman with her back turned to Lewis and Neil. She wore a white buckskin shirt-dress decorated with fringes and rhinestones, which suited her heavy, voluptuous body. Pinkish blonde hair in ringlets was piled on top of her head. Bull Reicher stayed by the jukebox and watched them as they approached.

Around the table at the edge of the dance floor and close to the bar were six other women. They wore casual clothes. To Lewis they had the look of a chorus line, leggy and fit. Each girl was different, clearly chosen for the colour of her hair and skin. One dark girl crouched in her chair, her head almost touching the table top. It was clear from the huddled position that she was in pain. Another girl with tumbling dark red hair and pale skin tried to comfort her. The others looked on, their faces showing a mixture of sympathy and fear.

Bull Reicher still stood before the jukebox, his arms spread, resting the palms of his hands on each edge of the machine. Dangling from his right wrist was a policeman's night-stick. The barman watched Lewis and Neil without moving his head. His gaze caused the blonde woman to shift her position and turn to look at them. She wore an expression of cold anger but after a moment she smiled professionally.

'What's your pleasure, boys?'

'Two beers, please,' Neil said politely.

The barman looked at Lewis, who nodded his head in confirmation. Moments later, heavy chilled glasses stood before them.

'You guys new here?' the blonde asked in a cheerful voice that was clearly forced.

'Yes, ma'am,' Neil replied.

Lewis studied her. She had big features that matched the proportions of her body, but they were regular and, in a way, beautiful. There were lines sketched around her mouth and eyes. Lewis judged her to be in her middle forties. Unlike the girls at the table, she wore heavy make-up.

'Are you miners or truck drivers?' she asked huskily.

'We're gonna work down the mine, ma'am,' Neil said.

'My name's Kate,' she said. 'I own the place.'

'I'm Neil and this is Lew,' Neil said.

'Your friend don't say a lot,' she said. Then she shrugged. 'Hell, what do I care? Those are on the house. You can buy the girls drinks and talk to them, but they don't start work until eight o'clock.'

She took a cigarette from the pack in front of her and leaned forward to the barman who lit it with a bookmatch. She took a deep draw on the cigarette and then coughed explosively. When she had recovered she looked towards Bull Reicher who still gazed into the lights of the machine. When she spoke there was a rough edge of bitterness to her voice.

''Course, you won't be able to keep Juanita company. She ain't gonna be in the mood to work for a few days, is she, Bull?'

Reicher turned slowly and looked towards her, then he walked to the crouching woman and reached out to take her chin in his hand. He raised her face to look at him.

The other girls around the table drew away from him. Reicher turned the face from side to side. Lewis could see the girl's eyes were open wide with fear.

'Juanita's OK, aren't you, honey? After all, she hasn't any more feelings than a hog.'

As he spoke he took the night-stick and worked her blouse loose so that he could run the tip of the truncheon slowly up and down her body. The record finished and the room was locked in silence.

'Still too good for old Bull, huh?' He turned his head to look at the others. Then he gestured with the night-stick towards the red-haired girl who was looking at him with open contempt. 'Why don't you tell this cocktail waitress what she's missing, Juanita?' He jabbed the stick towards the red-haired girl again.

'My name is Annie, Reicher,' the red-head said, 'and I just want you to know I'd rather live in a leper colony than be touched by you.'

Reicher studied her for a moment and then spoke slowly. 'Girl, I'm tired of being nice to you. It just don't get me anywhere. I think it's time you learned what it means when you speak to me like that.'

Reicher's body swayed towards the girl as if he were about to strike out.

'Thank God that damned record is over,' Lewis said in a

130

conversational tone. The eyes of everyone flickered to him as he drained his glass and placed it on the bar. 'Same again, barman,' he said.

Like a ballet arranged by a choreographer, the people in the bar began to move away as Bull Reicher turned from Juanita and began to walk slowly towards Lewis. The girls rose from their seats at the table and edged from the light into the shadows.

'You dumb son-of-a-bitch,' Kate said sadly as she slid along the bar to join her girls in the darkness. The barman watched with interest as Neil carried his glass further down the bar.

It was clear how Bull Reicher was going to conduct himself. He stood before Lewis with his left hand resting easily on the bar. The night-stick in his right hand hung at his side. He spoke his line of dialogue.

'You talk too much, scumbag,' he said with a smile. It was a mistake. Lewis was working from another script. Instead of replying to the insult, he casually reached out and broke the little finger of Reicher's left hand as it rested on the bar.

The guard's eyes widened with surprise. He didn't move for a moment, then he bellowed with pain and swung the night-stick at Lewis's head. The truncheon missed its target. Lewis ducked beneath the swing and Reicher smashed into a row of glasses on the bar which exploded into a glittering shower of splintered glass.

Reicher was expecting a punch into the exposed side of his heavily muscled body. He was wrong again. Lewis stepped back and kicked him just underneath his right kneecap.

As Reicher collapsed to the floor, his left knee rested on the bar rail. Lewis jumped forward and landed with his full weight on the lower leg. The loud crack of Reicher's tibia and fibula breaking was like dry wood snapping. He gave a sighing groan and flopped back in a dead faint.

The night-stick rolled from his open hand across the bar floor and came to rest at the feet of the red-haired woman. She crouched down and picked up the truncheon and took a few paces to Reicher. She stood over the body for a moment and then dropped the stick next to him. Gradually the others in the room drew close to the supine body and stood in a circle staring down at the broken Goliath.

'Jesus,' a blonde girl said softly. 'I ain't never seen anything like that before, 'cept in the movies.' She looked up at Lewis. 'Are you a movie actor, mister?'

Lewis shook his head.

'He's coming round,' Kate said. Lewis bent down and took the massive black revolver from Reicher's holster. He flipped open the chamber, ejected the cartridges and dropped them behind the bar before sliding the gun back into the holster. Reicher's eyes flickered open. There was a moment of shock and then the pain hit him. He looked up at Lewis with pure animal rage and drew the Colt. The hammer clicked against the empty chambers.

'Call the barracks,' Kate said to the barman. 'Tell 'em to come and get him.' She turned to Lewis and Neil. 'You'd better come with me.'

As they walked away, Reicher called after them in a voice choked with anger and pain.

'You're dead, mister. You hear me? You're a dead man.'

The room ignored him. Neil watched as the red-haired girl helped Juanita from the bar.

'Thanks, mister,' Annie said before they passed on.

Kate led them to a table in the gloom and switched on a lamp. She waved away some of the girls who attempted to join them.

'They're on their way, Kate,' the barman called out.

'OK, bring some drinks.' She turned back to Lewis and Neil. 'Would you care for anything else?'

'Beer's fine for me,' Lewis said and Neil nodded.

Kate looked from one to the other.

'What is it with you guys? You gotta take it in turns to speak?'

They smiled at her grumbling tone.

'What the hell,' she said in a more relaxed tone. 'I heard enough talk to last me the rest of my life.'

The barman placed beers in front of Lewis and Neil and a club soda before Kate.

'You guys veterans?' Kate said.

'Yeah,' Neil said easily. 'Marines.'

Kate looked at Lewis shrewdly.

'Funny, I've seen a lotta Marines fight in my time, in fact I've wrestled some myself, but I ain't never seen one fight like you do.' She leaned back in her chair and kept staring at him. 'Mister, you've caused me a big problem. Let me see if you can do something about it.'

Lewis put down his glass and folded his arms.

'Go ahead,' he said.

Kate glanced across the room to where Reicher lay moaning in pain before she spoke.

'Bull is one of the most sadistic sons-of-bitches I ever came across and I've known some of the worst.'

She drew deeply on her cigarette and studied them both to see their reaction. She looked again to Reicher who still lay by the bar watched by the curious circle of girls. Then Kate turned back to them and rapped on the table to emphasise her point.

'But he was a lotta use to me.' She waved around the dark room. 'This place might get outta hand if there ain't someone like Bull around.'

Lewis looked at her steadily.

'Go on.'

'Look, the guys I get in here are rough. They come here to have fun and find trouble, and they drink like sailors. I give Bull a hundred bucks a week and a free ride on the house to keep the peace. Now you've broken my peace officer.'

'So how can I help?' Lewis said.

Kate leaned forward and blew two streams of blue smoke through her nostrils.

'This is the deal. I'll pay you what you would get at the mine plus Bull's hundred and you can board free. Most likely the girls'll hump you for nothing as well, so what do you say?'

'You're taking a chance, aren't you? We've only just met.'

She smiled a little bitterly and drew in more smoke.

'Honey, taking chances with men is my profession – so what do you say?'

'Can I speak with my partner alone?' Lewis asked.

'Sure,' Kate said as she rose to her feet. 'I'll be at the bar sympathising with Reicher.'

While Lewis and Neil spoke, a guard arrived with two white-clad medics.

'Holy Christ,' he said as he looked down at Reicher. 'I thought we'd come to get someone who had tangled with Bull.'

There didn't seem to be much sorrow in his voice. Reicher made a lot of noise as the men got him on to the stretcher.

'They ain't gonna like this, Kate,' the guard said as they struggled with their bulky load.

'That doesn't fill me with a great deal of concern, Eddie,' Kate replied as they manoeuvred the stretcher between the tables.

Lewis and Neil rejoined her at the bar, and Lewis shook his head as the barman raised his eyebrows and pointed at his empty glass.

'Well?' Kate said.

'Tell me some more about the men you get in here,' Lewis said.

Kate automatically reached out and lit another cigarette, then looked at it as if it had appeared in her hand by accident.

'Mostly they're the guys from the Institute.'

'What are they like?' Neil asked as he cradled his glass of beer. Kate shrugged and gestured with the cigarette.

'The miners and the truckers are OK. They ain't choirboys but they generally behave themselves. The men from the Institute, they're all foreign. Well, most of them are. Sometimes they get Americans.'

'Are they regular guys?' Neil asked as he took one of Kate's cigarettes.

'Who's regular?' she said with a lopsided smile. 'They seem like a bunch of crazies to me. Mai Li . . . ' She pointed towards a black-haired woman with golden skin who sat a few tables away. 'She worked in Saigon when she was thirteen and she says most of the Institute dudes act as if they've been in combat for a long time.'

'How's that?' Lewis asked.

'Mai Li,' Kate called out and the black-haired girl came over. 'Tell these guys what the men from the Institute are like.'

Mai Li spoke in an Oriental accent with strong American overtones.

'The teachers are OK, but those students – you never know what you're gonna get with them. Some just talk, cry, they get rough or they can't get it up. Some act as if they haven't seen a woman for ten years . . . All of them have got lousy nerves. They sleep bad.'

'Thanks, kid,' Kate said and Mai Li slipped away.

Lewis leaned on the bar and looked around the room.

'These men, did they ever start fights with Bull Reicher?'

Kate and the barman looked at each other for confirmation and after a few moments the barman said, 'Only those bikers Bull cleaned up a couple of years ago.'

'Bikers?' Lewis said.

'Yeah,' Kate said. 'Before they sealed up the town we used to get a biker gang in here. They were running drugs across the border. We had a lot of trouble with them. But Reicher saw them off.'

'And since then you've had no trouble?' said Lewis. 'Why do you think that is?'

Kate and the barman glanced at each other again.

'I guess they just took one look at Reicher and decided not to bother,' Kate said.

'Exactly,' Lewis said. 'Now take a look at me.'

The barman and Kate studied him for a while. They saw a slim young man of medium height with short, rough black hair and pale grey-blue eyes. The hollow cheeks and rather battered features did not look particularly brutal.

'I see what he means, Kate,' the barman said finally. 'Just to look at him, I reckon I could take him.'

Lewis turned back to Kate.

'He's got the idea. You put me in as bouncer and this place would be like Madison Square Gardens every night – with me as the main event.'

Kate didn't say anything but they could see from her expression that she was convinced.

'So, you got any suggestions?'

'Hire Dave as my back-up man.'

'No way,' Kate said. 'Reicher cost me a hundred a week. You're talking nearer a thousand.'

'Who runs your poker table?' Lewis asked.

'We don't have a house game any more,' Kate said.

Lewis waved towards the corner of the bar where there was a piano next to a telephone.

'Does that work?'

'The telephone?'

'No, the piano.'

'Sure,' Kate said. 'We get a band in, Saturdays.'

Lewis walked over and sat down on the bench stool and began to play, deliberately choosing a repertoire of melancholy standards. By the time he had finished, the girls had surrounded the piano and were gazing at Lewis with sad eyes. He looked up at Kate and he closed the lid. She seemed a little doleful as well.

'I never met a violent man yet who wasn't sentimental,' she said. 'Or a hooker,' she added. 'Do you play poker as good?' she asked Neil.

Neil folded his arms and smiled.

'Lady, did you ever meet a man who said he was a lousy poker player?'

Kate gave a barking laugh. 'If you're that smart you must be good.' She looked from one to another. 'OK, it's a deal.'

Lewis looked at his wristwatch and calculated the time in London.

'Can I make a long-distance call? I'll pay for it.'

'Sure.'

Lewis dialled and eventually the number came through.

'Ronnie Scott's Club,' a voice said clearly.

'Can I speak to Charlie Mars?' Lewis said. 'He will be at his table or at the bar with David Bradbury.'

'Hang on,' the distant voice said and after a few moments he was on the line.

'Uncle Charlie?' Lewis said. 'It's Lew here. This is where you can call me in Arizona.'

He read out the number on the dial.

'How are things?' Charlie asked.

'Just great,' Lewis said. 'Tell Ma I've got a good job at last.'

'What's that?' Charlie asked.

Lewis paused and looked around at the group of girls who watched him with interest.

'I'm playing the piano in a whorehouse.'

Chapter Six

'You're in here, honey,' Kate said as she unlocked the door
and stood aside so that Lewis could enter. He took four paces
forward and stopped in the centre of the room where he tried
to look unconcerned by the elaborate vulgarity of his surroundings.

Before him was an ornately carved coffee table next to a
chaise-longue flanked by two deep-buttoned velvet chairs.
Beside each chair were tiny side tables covered with dolls in
flowered dresses. Behind him, next to the door, was a sideboard that rose to the ceiling, carved and scrolled as intri-
cately as a medieval cathedral. The shelves and pigeon-holes
held a collection of delicate china figures in various stages of
lovemaking.

The windows behind the chaise-longue were framed in
heavy damask curtains that folded and flowed like a
ballgown. The hammered copper fireplace was shaped into
birds and flowers and from the ceiling, thick with plaster
decoration, hung a chandelier of carved glass and brass.

Every surface was cluttered and fussed with ornaments.
The coffee table was covered with carved glass bottles with
round attachments at the necks.

Lewis picked up one of the bottles and squeezed the rubber
bulb. A cloud of fragrant mist squirted from the bottle.

'The last girl who lived in here collected scents,' Kate
explained. 'Pretty, aren't they? – smell nice, too.'

Lewis put down the bottle and looked around.

Antimacassars covered the chairs and tasselled fringes
hung from shelves and cupboards. The blood-coloured walls

138

were crowded with paintings of scenes from a New Orleans sporting house, where slaves waited on fully-clothed gentlemen who were entertained by half-clad women.

Dominating the room with the looming menace of a battleship was a four-poster bed of awesome proportions. Red and purple velvet drapes were drawn back to reveal a white lace counterpane piled with heart-shaped pillows finished with scarlet ribbons. It was the most claustrophobic room Lewis had ever known.

'Well, what do you think?' Kate said with a crooked smile as she closed the door and held out the key.

Lewis took the heavy brass-ringed handle and paused before he replied.

'Cute,' he said after some thought.

Kate chuckled through the cigarette she kept between her lips.

'Honey, you fit in here like a hog in a beauty parlour.'

'He nodded. 'It's fancier than a Holiday Inn.'

She moved to the bed and patted one of the great carved posts.

'The girls call this the Titanic,' she said affectionately.

'Why?' Lewis asked in a distracted voice as he examined an engraving of a girl being helped into a bath.

Kate walked across the room before she answered. 'Because so many folks went down on it.'

Before she closed the door behind her she looked at Lewis for a moment.

'Why, honey, I do believe you're blushing,' she said. She was about to close the door when something else occurred to her. 'When you're ready, come down to my office. I've got something for you.'

'I'll be there,' he said as he began to make a further examination of the room. When he had made a thorough study of the intricate clutter, he lay down on the massive bed and the ancient springs twanged like an untuned guitar at the pressure of his body.

Once the discordant notes had died away, he lay still and listened. There was no sound from the street through the half-opened window. Somewhere in the hotel he could hear water gushing and then a high clear voice singing. The melody was strange and unfamiliar. He thought it must be one of the Mexican girls.

For a time he tried to relax by tensing and releasing the muscles in each part of his body, but the over-ripe opulence of the room continued to oppress him.

He decided to go and see how Neil was quartered. Along the corridor, four numbers from his own, he found an open door and Neil sitting in very different surroundings from the room he had just left. The walls were crowded with the mounted heads of animals . . . moose, puma, antelope, even a tiger snarled down on him. Old sporting guns formed a geometric pattern over the fireplace. A chair made entirely of antelope horns stood next to a military chest, the fittings and furniture were edged and trimmed with brass.

David Neil sat at a small table shuffling a pack of cards. He looked up as Lewis entered, and grinned.

'How do you like your boudoir?'

'You've seen it?' Lewis said as he sat down in the chair made of horns.

'I had a look at them all. The place is incredible – every room is different. There's even one like the inside of an Indian tepee.'

Neil gestured at the tiger's head.

'This one is called the Teddy Roosevelt Room on account of his hunting prowess. Yours is called . . . '

'I know, the Titanic,' Lewis said in a melancholy voice.

Neil's laughter was interrupted by a single knock on the door.

'Come,' Neil called out and the door opened slowly to reveal the barman. He stood and watched for a moment as Neil continued to shuffle the deck of cards.

'What can I do for you?' Neil asked.

The barman leaned against the doorframe and scratched his chin before answering.

'We've got a real nice poker table stored away. If you guys give me a hand we can set it up for tonight.'

'Sure. Do you want to do it now?'

'Good a time as any,' the barman said.

140

He led them along the corridor and down a wide flight of stairs that led to a mahogany-panelled hall that was lined with ferns in heavy brass containers. Lewis pointed to a door next to the reception desk.

'Is that Kate's office?'

'Yeah,' the man said.

They followed him to the end of a short corridor and turned to descend a flight of stairs. The walls were of rough-hewn granite and they could feel a drop in the temperature. The door at the bottom led into the dark, cavernous bar at the opposite end from the alleyway entrance.

'This place is cut out of the rock,' Lewis said.

The barman held the door open so they could enter and slapped the wall.

'Sure is. This place would make a damned fine atom-bomb shelter. We've got enough booze to last for ten years.'

He walked across the dance floor of the saloon and opened another door that was hard to see in the darkness.

'Of course, some of the girls would be kinda old, one or two of 'em are nearly thirty now.'

He turned on a light to reveal a storeroom piled with crates of liquor. In the corner of the room was a stack of wooden chairs.

'Under there,' the barman said.

They lifted off the dusty jumble and found a green-baize poker table.

'Ain't she a beauty?' the barman said.

'She sure is,' Neil replied, and he ran an appreciative hand along one of the seven sides. Lewis examined the brass troughs set into the surface before each player's position and a spring clip to hold paper money. Below the surface was another shelf for drinks.

'Why do you keep it in here?' Lewis asked.

The barman tested one of the clips before he replied.

'You know how excited some guys get when they play. It was always causing trouble, but mostly it was Bull Reicher's big brother.'

'Big brother?' Lewis said after a pause.

'Sure,' the man said. 'Didn't anyone mention him?'

141

Lewis shook his head.

'He's Brady's right-hand man. He really liked to play poker. Trouble was, he just hated to lose. He hasn't been around much since Kate had the table put away – tended to stay at The Silver Queen – but now a game's starting again, we're bound to see him down here. Most likely tonight. News travels fast in Jericho.'

There was a short thoughtful silence. Then Lewis spoke.

'When you say big brother, do you mean older?'

The barman leaned against the table and thought for a moment.

'I guess I mean older – and bigger – and I mean meaner,' he said slowly. 'Bull Reicher's a nasty, cunning son-of-a-bitch but deep down he's dumb. Ram, well he's smart. Some people say he's as psycho as Bull, but not when he's around.' He suddenly banged the poker table with his fist and chuckled. 'I guess he's gonna be around some now.'

'How good is his game?' Neil asked.

The old man cocked an eye at him. 'What makes you think I'd know?'

Neil reached out and took the man's right hand by the wrist. Lewis could see that the long slender fingers had been broken at the knuckles so they were white and misshapen.

'You've got card mechanic's hands, mister,' Neil said. 'Somebody broke your dealing equipment, didn't they?'

Neil released the wrist and the barman held it up and looked at the hand dispassionately.

'It happened in Reno, fifteen years ago. I took a rancher for thirty grand but I didn't know he'd be a bad loser. Some of his cowhands picked me up. They did this with a pair of pliers.'

Neil brushed the surface of the table with his hands.

'It can be a rough game.'

'What are we going to do about Bull's brother?' Lewis asked.

'We're not going to make friends with the guy,' Neil said.

Lewis nodded. 'Let's go for him. If we make him really angry he might make some mistakes.'

'So how good is Ram Reicher?' Neil asked again.

The barman shrugged. 'OK for an amateur, better than most. He cheats a little.'

'How?'

'Four of a kind. Ram palms aces or kings till he makes four. It's the only trick he does but he ain't bad at it.'

Neil thought for a moment. 'Can you cold deck me?'

'What's a cold deck?' Lewis asked.

'After a shuffle, a new pack of cards is substituted so all the hands dealt are prearranged.' Neil nodded to the barman. 'He'll know when Reicher has won a hand by palming cards. We change to a fresh pack and hit him.'

'What do I get?' the man said and Lewis could see the flash of enjoyment in his eyes.

'Ten per cent of my end,' Neil said.

'OK, but it's got to be my way.'

'How will you work it?' Lewis asked.

The barman turned to him. 'Ram Reicher likes to drink when he's playing. So I'll serve the table. When he's won a big hand he always asks for another shot. It's customary to call for a new deck after four of a kind. When you've given the new cards a good shuffle, place the pack on your left and distract him with your right hand. Drop cigar ash on the table and brush it away. That'll be enough. I'll cover the deck with the drinks tray. That'll give me an opportunity to switch and drop you the cold deck.'

Neil thought for a moment.

'Yeah, that's nice and simple. Let's try it now.'

They set the table near to the bar, close to where the piano stood. Lewis would be able to see the main room and watch the play.

'Come and sit here,' the barman said to Lewis. 'Ram always sits to the dealer's right.'

Lewis did as he was told.

'There'll be seven players,' the barman said. 'When I drop the cold deck, he'll get a low running flush, pat. You'll get four to a better running flush. The guy to your left will have four to a good straight. The other guys will have nothing.'

Neil pondered. 'Suppose one of them feels like playing a lousy hand?'

143

The barman looked at him thoughtfully.

'Can you deal just one off the bottom?'

'No – not against good players.'

'OK, we'll just have to take the chance that the other guys know how to play properly if they foul up. I'll drop another deck when Reicher cheats again.'

Lewis sat in the spot where Ram Reicher would sit and watched carefully as Neil and the barman practised the routine. After they had rehearsed the action half a dozen times it was faultless.

'I've got to see Kate,' Lewis said and he left them still polishing the drop. When he had made his way back to the hotel entrance hall, he knocked on the door of the office and entered without waiting to be invited.

Kate sat at a roll-top desk reading a copy of *New York* magazine by the light of a green glass lamp. She looked up at him and then down at the magazine.

'When were you in Manhattan last?'

'In the fall.'

'Lord, I wish I was there now,' she said and closed the magazine.

'It's cold in New York in January.'

'Mister,' she said, 'I'd rather be a snowball in Central Park than Jane Fonda in Jericho.'

Lewis folded his arms and leaned against the door.

'You didn't tell me about Ram Reicher.'

Kate got up from the swivel chair.

'Yeah, well, life's full of little curves and twists, honey. A straight road would drive a man like you crazy.'

Lewis thought for a moment.

'Look, Kate,' he said slowly. 'Ram Reicher's got a lot of big guys around. He knows what I've done to his brother so he'll try and jump me. What am I going to do if they use guns? Throw the piano at them?'

She moved to a massive safe in a corner of the room and dialled a combination. The heavy door swung open and he could see stacks of banknotes held in thick rubber bands. She took two slabs of money from the top shelf and carelessly laid them on the roll-top desk. Then she bent down again and

144

reached inside to search for something. While she did this Lewis studied the painting that was above the desk.

It was a fine piece of nineteenth-century work, life-sized and heavily framed in scrolled gilt. It showed a naked girl reclining on a buttoned couch holding one finger to a dimpled cheek. An Arab slave fanned her with a long palm-frond while another offered her a bowl of fruit. Curled at her feet was a sleeping tiger.

When he turned back Kate was holding a soft suede sack out to him. He took it and felt the weight of the contents. He looked at her with an inquiring glance.

'Go ahead,' she said as she lit another cigarette from the packet that lay on her desk.

Lewis loosened the drawstring and reached inside. He drew out a gunbelt with two holsters. The heavy black leather was studded with tiny silver rivets to make a design that flowed over the rich leather. He laid the belt down beside Kate's cigarettes and drew the two revolvers from their holsters. They rested in his hands with the comfortable balance of duelling pistols. The matched pair of Colts gleamed with their heavy plating of silver. The surface of the pistols was etched in a mass of beautifully cut designs that swirled along the barrels and chambers. The mother-of-pearl handles glowed with opalescent light. They were quite beautiful, and at the same time totally vulgar, like a fairground ride made by a master craftsman.

He released the catches on both guns and checked to make sure the chambers were empty, then snapped them closed again and cocked the hammers to test the action. They were featherlight. The merest touch on the triggers caused the hammers to fall.

Kate pulled open one of the pigeon-holed drawers in the desk and handed him a box of cartridges. 'The guns were made in 1876,' she said. 'The bullets were made last year.'

Lewis took the ammunition and slid six rounds into the chambers. Then he filled the loops on the gunbelt.

'Now you've got a pair of gentleman's guns, you don't have to throw the piano at Reicher,' she said.

145

'General George S. Paton said only a pimp wore pistols with pearl handles, Kate. A gentleman wears ivory.'

'Did he now?' she said in a dry voice. 'And where did you research that piece of information? The Marine Corps boot camp?'

'I must have heard it somewhere,' Lewis said warily.

Kate flicked the ash from her cigarette into a brass spittoon at her feet.

'Honey,' she said in a soft voice, 'if there's one thing a hooker gets to know, it's men. You may be able to fool the guys around here, but it won't work with me.'

He said nothing. She waved him away.

'Don't worry – it's none of my business. Just take the guns.'

'Thanks,' he said, 'but if I wear these I'll just be a walking invitation for someone to call me out.'

Kate nodded. 'Yeah, they are pretty fancy. What the hell, you keep 'em, anyway. You might need them some time.'

'I appreciate the thought,' he said as he returned the guns to the soft leather bag. 'I'll be on my way.'

Kate lit another cigarette and returned to her magazine.

When he got to his own room, he wondered where he could conceal the weapons. After a time he stood on the edge of the bed and slid the bag into the gap between the canopy and the ceiling. Then he looked at his watch. There were two hours before he had to go to work. He locked the door and lay down on the bed. Within minutes he had fallen asleep.

He woke at the first crash of thunder. The temperature dropped in the room as the rain began to fall in a pounding monsoon. He got up from the bed and stood by the open window to look down on the narrow road. Despite the wide storm-drains that were cut into the high gutters, a torrent of water overflowed and washed around the parked cars. Lights from the hotel gave the darkened street a harsh, dangerous quality.

He shivered in the cool air and closed the window against the storm. Next to his room was an alcove that had been made into a bathroom. He showered quickly and ran his hand around his chin. It had been early morning since he had shaved and it was going to be a long night. Fifteen minutes later he knocked on David Neil's door.

'Time for work,' he said and together they made their way to the saloon. They found Kate sitting at a table near the bar drinking a cup of coffee, the remains of a chicken salad in front of her.

At the sight of the plate Lewis remembered that they hadn't eaten since early morning.

'Sit down,' Kate said. 'Dolores will fix you something.' She nodded towards a heavy, silent figure who had appeared at the table and was clearing the remains of a meal.

'What have you got?' Neil asked and the Mexican woman pointed to a blackboard that was over the bar.

After a brief study Neil ordered in Spanish.

'What was that?' Lewis asked.

'Chilli and salad.'

Lewis smiled at the woman whose expression did not alter.

'I'll have the same.'

The woman nodded and moved away from the table with her loaded tray. Neil cocked his head in the direction of her retreating figure.

'Wet-back?' he said to Kate.

'Sure,' she replied. 'Most of 'em head for Tucson. We don't have many here. I guess it's too close to the border for them to feel secure. I've got five girls to do the cooking and cleaning and they help at the bar.'

'What about the mine?' Lewis asked as Dolores returned and poured them cups of coffee.

'Brady won't use 'em,' Kate said. 'At least, that's what Ram Reicher tells me. Ram keeps trying to get me to get rid of them. Says he doesn't want the border patrol hanging around. I told him: you hire me five white girls to work as servants in a whorehouse and I'll take 'em on.' Kate thought for a moment. 'Funny, isn't it? You don't have any trouble hiring white girls to be whores.'

'Is it easy to get across the border?' Lewis asked.

Kate dipped her finger in her coffee cup and drew a line on the table top.

'Mister, there's an open door from Texas across to

147

California and only a handful of border guards trying to keep it shut. It's not just the wet-backs. A lot of people make a living trading across the border and a lot of drugs get hauled in this way.'

Two bowls of chilli arrived and Lewis spooned several mouthfuls down before he was aware that Kate and Neil were watching him with interest. Neil had swallowed a glass of water and was pouring more from the iced pitcher on the table.

'That's the hottest goddamn chilli I've ever tasted,' Neil said. 'You must have a mouth lined with asbestos.'

'It's a bit like vindaloo,' Lewis said.

'What the hell is vindaloo?' Kate said with interest.

'Curry,' Lewis explained and noticed the look of incomprehension on her face. 'Indian food.'

'What tribe?'

'I meant the subcontinent of India.'

Kate smiled. 'I'm just pulling your leg, honey. I've heard about curry. I just didn't realise it was hot.'

She looked at him shrewdly for a while. 'Where did you get to eat curry?'

Lewis gazed back with an expression of guileless innocence.

'When I did my hitch with the Marine Corps, I was on embassy guard in London for a time.'

Kate rose from the table. 'I guess that's where you learned about General George S. Patton, huh? Well, I've got to go and take a look at the girls. Give them a chance and they start dressing like hookers. I like them to look like cocktail waitresses. It gives the place more class.'

'What did she mean by that?' Neil asked as he took a tentative mouthful of the chilli.

Lewis glanced around before he answered.

'She has her suspicions about us.'

Neil put down his fork and sipped some more iced water.

'Can we trust her?' he muttered.

Lewis shrugged. 'We're going to have to.'

He looked towards the bar and saw that the barman had arrived and was beginning the ritual that all men of his trade go through before the onslaught of customers. Cloths were distributed along the bar and ice troughs filled. The till was checked and primed, glasses racked and set in gleaming rows, dishes of sliced oranges, lemons and limes positioned and shakers put in place.

As he worked he would take occasional draws from a cigarette that rested in an ashtray on a corner of the bar. Finally he gave a long, sweeping gaze to make sure everything was to his satisfaction before he carefully stubbed out the cigarette. Then he cleaned the ashtray with his bar-cloth and poured himself a large measure of whiskey into a long glass filled with ice.

'Gentlemen,' he called out to Neil and Lewis. 'Would you care to join me in a drink before the evening's ordeal begins?'

Lewis had finished his chilli. Neil pushed his aside and they walked to the bar. They sat down on stools before him and asked for Mexican beers. The barman took an appreciative pull from his glass and placed it in front of him with slow deliberation.

'Irish whiskey,' he said with relish.

Lewis's eyes swept the bottles behind the bar and came upon a familiar black label. For a moment his thoughts wandered to Belfast and he remembered other bars that served dangerous customers. But for the moment all was peaceful. It was a quiet time like twilight. The girls slowly drifted into the bar, walking slowly and muttering to each other. They scattered around the tables.

Lewis finished his beer, walked over to the piano and sat down. His back was to the bar and above his head a mirror was set to show the length of the counter without him having to turn his head. He began to play softly, running melodies into each other to keep a flow of sound.

Gradually the room began to fill and cigarette smoke hazed the air. The customers were mostly young men who came in pairs. Occasionally there would be a man and a woman.

Lewis played for an hour and then took a break at the bar. He sipped beer for a few minutes until one of the girls came over to him and covered his hand with her own.

149

'The guy I'm with asked if you can play the same tune again,' she said and handed him a ten-dollar bill.

'Which tune?' Lewis said as he looked down in surprise at the bank note.

She began to hum and after a while Lewis thought he recognised 'Satin Doll'. He sat down at the piano again and played the opening chords and looked towards the table where the girl had rejoined her fair-haired companion. The man raised his glass to signify it was the correct melody. The girl who had given him the money walked onto the dance floor with the man who had made the request and they began to dance. After a while other couples joined them. The barman leaned over and placed an empty glass on top of the piano. More requests were made and the glass was soon filled with money.

Lewis watched the dancers. The girls who worked the saloon were professionals. They managed to convey an interest in the customers but at the same time he could see they kept a certain detachment. He was reminded of an air hostess's smile.

The men were different. He recognised the atmosphere they generated. They were like troops resting from battle. The civilian clothes they wore looked new but the drink and the attentive women loosened ties and jackets were being discarded. There was a sense of desperation in the way they appeared determined to enjoy themselves.

Kate came and stood beside him as he watched the couples sway and clutch each other.

'Here comes the carriage trade from The Silver Queen,' she said.

Lewis looked in the mirror and saw a group of older men laughing with each other as they came down the staircase. They were close enough to Lewis for him to hear the barman pointing out the poker table. Immediately four of them bought drinks at the bar and made for Neil. Lewis watched as he began to deal. A few spectators drifted towards the table as the cards flicked across the green baize, and Neil read out the hands as they were dealt.

Lewis knew that Ram Reicher had come into the saloon

before he glanced around and saw him standing at the bar. There was a momentary pause in the level of conversation as if the volume had been turned down on a radio set, then the babble of voices rose even higher than it had been before. The big brother was unmistakable. He leaned against the bar with one foot on the brass rail, close enough for Lewis to see the snakeskin band on the pale grey stetson and the gold and silver belt buckle. The man was so like Bull they could have been twins, were it not for the heavy creases each side of his mouth and the lines around the eyes.

The light grey whipcord suit was well cut in Western fashion and he wore a bootlace tie with a silver ram's head fastening at the throat. The polished black high-heeled cowboy boots made him taller than his brother. When the barman poured his bourbon on the rocks he took the tall glass in a massive fist and walked forward to lean on the top of the piano.

He was so big the two great forearms occupied most of the space. Lewis looked up at him without showing any interest and Ram removed his stetson and looked towards the poker table so that Lewis could study his right profile as he spoke.

'I hear you met my brother this afternoon,' he said in a clear, low voice.

Lewis continued to play softly and waited until Ram Reicher looked down at him before he nodded. Reicher looked to the poker table again.

'I wouldn't want you to get the idea we're the same sort of person just because we look alike.'

Lewis nodded again. This time Ram Reicher smiled and Lewis could see a hardness in him. Bull had the same features as his brother, but he was more controlled, capable of great cruelty and used to acting in cold blood.

'I'll remember that,' Lewis said.

'I'm sure you will,' Reicher said.

He replaced the stetson and moved to the poker table. Despite his size Ram Reicher walked like an athlete. Neil glanced up at his approach and continued to deal. He had kept an empty seat at the table. Reicher took the place and drew a thick wad of money from his inside pocket which he clipped to the green baize.

'Welcome,' Neil said in a professional dealer's voice. 'We're playing poker: seven card stud, five card stud and draw. No wild cards. The game changes every seven hands. There's a raise limit of double the pot and a twenty-dollar ante.'

Reicher waved towards Kate who was sitting at a table with two sober-looking middle-aged men. She walked over to him and he took one of the bills from beneath the clip. Lewis could see it was a thousand-dollar note. He handed her the money then he leaned forward and whispered something before he scooped his cards up and began to concentrate on the game.

Lewis watched the poker table for a while and eventually Kate came and stood near to him. She spoke softly.

'He's paid Juanita a thousand bucks for what Bull did this afternoon, and he asked for her to have the evening off.'

Lewis nodded almost imperceptibly but he kept his eyes on a table across the dance floor. He was aware that one of the men sitting there had been staring at him for some time and he could feel that he was looking for trouble. Lewis had known the man worked for Ram Reicher from the moment Reicher came into the saloon. He and his companion were the only people in the room who had not stared at the massive figure.

For the last hour the man had drunk beer steadily and kept his eyes on Lewis even when he raised his glass to his mouth. For the last quarter of an hour or so, the stare had gradually changed from an expressionless gaze to a contemptuous smile. Lewis knew it was only a matter of time before he made a move.

Lewis got to his feet and walked towards the lavatory. The man got up as he passed, and followed. A sign saying Rest Rooms glowed in the dark. Lewis glanced back before he entered the swing door beneath the notice. There were two of them behind him now. He slipped through the door and switched off the light in the narrow hallway.

Then he waited behind the door for it to open. The two men came into darkness.

Lewis reached into his jacket pocket as the two men lunged towards him. He squeezed the bulb attached to the carved-glass perfume bottle he had taken from Kate's collection, and the evaporating alcohol seared into their faces with the shock of tear-gas. They both turned away with the same reflex action and clutched their hands to their burning eyes.

Lewis placed his foot in the back of the first man and thrust him through the swing door into the saloon where he crashed into a table scattering the contents before him. He took the other by the hair and jerked his head back. There was a thudding sound as he cracked the head against the rough stone wall, and the man slid to the ground in a floppy heap.

The first man was still rubbing his stinging eyes. Lewis stepped forward, seized him by his shirt front and thrust one of the cut-glass edges of the perfume container against the man's throat.

'This is an old-fashioned razor, boy,' he said in a harsh, breathless voice. 'Do as I say or I'll cut your throat.'

The man said nothing.

'Get down on your knees,' Lewis ordered and kept the edge of the glass against his opponent's throat until he was on all fours.

Then Lewis stood up quickly and kicked the man on his jawline so that his head snapped to one side and he collapsed onto his face.

A ring of people stood watching him as he straightened up. Kate broke through and looked at the two bodies. She turned to the barman who had joined her.

'Take care of these guys.'

The man nodded to Kate as she reached out and took the bottle of scent from Lewis's hand.

'I guess that's the effect the manufacturers wanted,' she said, nodding down at the unconscious men. 'OK, folks, show's over. Carry on with the fun,' she called out to the people at the surrounding tables who had looked up at the disturbance.

'Who were they?' Lewis asked as he walked back to the piano.

'The one with the lumpy face is called Mike Reagan. The guy you kicked in the head is Johnnie Priest. They're guards, friends of the Reichers.'

The barman had a Mexican beer waiting for Lewis. He took a long swallow and looked towards Ram Reicher who was studying his hand of cards. He lifted his eyes and looked at Lewis without smiling. Then he laid the hand carefully in front of him and raised his glass of bourbon in a salute before he finished the drink in one swallow.

Neil looked up from his own hand and winked at Lewis then lowered his eyes to the pile of bank notes that had increased considerably since the beginning of the game. He made sure that Reicher noticed the exchange.

'What do you have?' Neil asked.

Reicher took his hand and spread the cards and showed four kings. As he pulled the money in the centre of the table towards him, he smiled in triumph.

He called for another drink and Neil looked towards the barman and pulled on the lobe of his left ear. Lewis watched as the drinks were carried to the table. Neil dropped the ash from his cheroot and made an elaborate show of brushing the baize. The barman dropped the rigged deck of cards, Neil dealt, and Reicher took the bait.

The hand was played as they had rehearsed it. At first the betting was brisk but as the amounts pushed into the pot grew larger, there was more deliberation to each bet. The tension from the table seemed to ripple through the room.

Conversation petered out as a crowd gradually congregated around the table. The barman was leaning on the counter behind Lewis. He stood up and rested his elbows on the bar so his head was close to the grey-haired man's.

The other player had dropped out and now Reicher and Neil sat with their cards before them on the green baize, leaning back in their chairs and looking down through the blue haze of tobacco smoke that drifted in the harsh pool of light thrown onto the scatter of money and cards.

Slowly, with one hand, Reicher reached out and counted

from the wad clipped before him. He tossed the notes into the middle of the table on top of the considerable pile that had already mounted in an untidy heap.

'Your five thousand,' he said in a casual voice and he counted more money. 'And another ten.'

There was a murmur of muttered comment through the crowd ringing the table. Neil looked at the pot for a while then slowly took a pull from his small black cigar. He looked at Reicher who gazed down impassively at the cards before him. Then he carefully counted out his own cash.

'Your ten and raise twenty,' he said in a low voice.

The crowd responded with the same muttered chorus of excitement. Reicher bet again and raised another twenty thousand. No one spoke at the size of the new bet. There was just a sharp intake of breath as if the room was one animal reacting to the smell of danger.

Neil looked at Reicher's bank roll and then at his own money.

'You've got thirty-five grand left,' he said in a cold voice. 'I'll set you in.'

He counted the same amount and pushed the money to the centre of the table. Reicher did the same with a dismissive motion of his hand.

Neil nodded down at Reicher's hand and the room waited in total silence as Reicher flipped over his cards. A chatter of released excitement greeted the two, three, four, five and six of spades. Neil turned his hand and spread the cards.

'Flush,' the word was whispered in a slight tone of disappointment as the spectators saw the cards were also running. Then a second shock as a voice said 'Another running flush, by God,' and the onlookers saw that the cards were the three, four, five, six and seven of diamonds.

Lewis watched Reicher carefully. His expression did not change but his pale complexion gradually suffused with blood. For a moment his massive body seemed to slump as if he had received a body blow. Then he took a deep gasp of breath and stood up quickly so that his chair would have fallen over had it not been caught by one of the people behind him.

He walked stiffly away from the table like someone who had received a severe beating. The spectators parted to let him through the ring. When he had passed and climbed the stairs, there was absolute silence until Lewis began to play once more and the people returned to their tables.

Gradually the tempo of the room returned and couples started dancing again. The poker game resumed, but Lewis could see the stakes were back to modest amounts.

The girls plied their trade and slowly the crowd settled down and finally began to thin out.

When most of the customers were gone, the barman brought over another drink and Lewis noticed he had poured one for himself.

'What's that you're playing?' he asked as he placed the beer on top of the piano.

' "Don't Blame Me",' Lewis said and the barman listened to the melody for a while.

'Oh, yeah. Nat King Cole used to sing that number.'

'That's right. He used to play it as well.'

The barman drank some of his whiskey.

'Is that so? I didn't know he played piano.'

'He certainly did.'

The barman looked to the poker table where Neil sat alone counting the stack of money.

'Reicher was gutted. Did you see how hard it was for him to get to the door?'

Lewis looked around the room. There were none of the girls left except for Kate, who sat at a far table with a black tin cash-box beside her.

As she stacked money in the box she made entries in a big green-bound ledger. Two of the Mexican women emerged from behind the bar and began to move quietly around the room cleaning away the debris of the evening. Neil walked over to the piano with two bundles of money. He handed one to the barman who slipped it into the pocket of his trousers and moved away to the table where Kate sat. Neil lit another of his small black cigars and took a few contented puffs.

The Mexican women had opened the doors and the big fans in the ceiling caused a gentle draught of cool air that blew through the basement room and gradually cleared the smoke-laden air. Lewis stood up and took the money from the glass on top of the piano and counted it.

'One hundred and thirty-five dollars,' he said in a surprised voice.

'How did *you* do?'

Neil examined the end of his glowing cigar.

'Fifty-seven thousand bucks,' he said.

Lewis nodded over his shoulder.

'Here comes your major contributor.'

Neil followed Lewis's gaze and saw Ram Reicher slowly walking down the stairs. He had his thumbs stuck in his belt and he took each step with deliberation. There was something satisfied about the man. They could see it as he walked towards them. He raised his stetson to Kate with an exaggerated display of courtesy.

'He looks like an old dog after he's eaten all the other dogs' feed,' Neil said softly.

There was a swagger about the way the man walked. The normal colour had returned to his face. His eyes glittered from the fleshy face. Something seems to have restored his good humour, Lewis thought as he looked into the bloated features.

Reicher laid a hand on the bar and drew his lips away from his teeth in the imitation of a smile.

'You're a lucky poker player, boy,' he said to Neil, who watched him for a moment and then smiled back.

'That's what my daddy taught me. Save your luck for when you really need it.'

Ram slapped the bar and gave a short barking laugh like a dog snarling.

'Well, your daddy was a wise man, son. Now how about you two? How wise are you?'

The eyes flickered to each of them in turn.

'We get by,' Lewis said.

Reicher turned and called down the bar.

'How about some service, here. I wanna buy these desperados a drink.'

The barman returned and took the order. Reicher put

down his glass after a long swallow and looked at them again.

'According to your records, you guys were in the Marine Corps.'

They didn't answer so Reicher tried another approach.

'You've caused me some problems today. How do you feel about that?'

Neil shrugged. 'We didn't plan to.'

Reicher sighed and took off his stetson and wiped the inside of the brim with a silk handkerchief.

'Yeah, well it ain't what you intend that counts in life, boy – it's what you do. And I just can't have tomorrow turning out the same. Now, I'm a reasonable man, and just to show you how tolerant I am, I'm gonna make you a good offer.'

He placed the stetson back on his head and gave a quick glance in the mirror behind the bar to make sure it was adjusted to his satisfaction.

'You broke up my little brother and damaged two more of my boys. But, as I said, I'm a tolerant man and some of that's my fault because I get the feeling I underestimated you.'

As he spoke he folded the silk handkerchief into a neat square and put it back into his jacket pocket. The action was done with deliberation like the words he spoke.

'Let's say we start again, and I want you to listen carefully because I'm gonna make you a generous deal. You pay me the money you took out of the poker game as medical expenses for the grief you brought to my boys and you can both come and work for me as guards.'

He smiled in the same mirthless fashion and raised his glass as if to seal the bargain.

'What do you say to that?'

Lewis and Neil exchanged glances before Neil turned back to Reicher.

'We're obliged for your kindness, but my partner and I are happy here at Kate's place. You've got to remember, we've already had two jobs in one day. We wouldn't like to get a reputation for being gadflies.'

They could see the anger building up in Reicher once again. His head settled in the barrel-like body and his chin and

158

shoulders came forward, but he made an effort of will and subdued the rage. When he spoke, his voice seemed to escape from the bulky body like steam released from a valve.

'OK, boys, you've decided. I won't be making any more offers.'

He pushed himself away from the bar and walked to Kate's table, where she was locking the cash-box. He bent down and whispered something to her and she watched him without replying as he walked from the room.

Kate joined Lewis and Neil. She took a cigarette from a pack and screwed the paper and cellophane into a ball which she placed in a large ashtray on the bar.

'That's the end of the fourth pack,' she said and she leaned forward to cup her hands around the match that Neil held out for her.

'Now I know it's time to go to bed.' She glanced at Lewis's watch. 'Goodnight, boys.'

The barman heaved the cash-box onto the counter next to her.

'Are we going to lock this up, Kate?'

'Sure,' she said. 'Come on.'

Lewis gestured towards the door.

'We're going to take a walk and get some air,' he said. 'Can you leave a door open so we don't disturb anyone?'

Kate reached over the bar and handed him a key which he slipped into his pocket.

'Come on, killer,' Kate said to the barman who heaved the box from the bar. 'Let's lock up the money and put the cat out.'

Lewis and Neil let themselves out onto the alley and strolled down to the street. The air was cool but the sky was bright and clear. There were few lights left burning in Jericho, and the only sound was the clip of their footsteps. They walked without speaking for a while down the narrow curving street. The silver light of the moon showed every detail of their side of the road but the buildings opposite were shrouded in inky darkness.

Lewis was glad of the chance to stretch his legs after the hours he had spent at the piano. His elbow was sore where he had caught it against the rough wall when he had banged the guard's head. He massaged it as they walked along the empty street. Neil stopped and lit a cigar and from an alleyway a prowling cat hurried past them hugging the wall, cautious of other night creatures. They continued walking.

Finally Neil spoke. 'What did you make of them?' he asked.

Lewis knew he was referring to the customers at Kate's saloon.

'It looks as if they're part of some kind of terrorist training programme,' he said.

Neil nodded. 'It's easy to bring them in this close to Mexico. The border guards have got their cookie-jar full chasing wet-backs. Nobody's going to bother about some white guys dressed in sharp suits with more than twenty bucks in their pockets. The only people around who look guilty are the Mexicans. The whole place is as tight as a fortress, but then there's a silver mine to protect. It's damned good cover.'

'So how do we close it down?' Lewis asked reflectively.

They stopped again and looked beyond the buildings to the ring of mountains that showed darkly against the starry sky.

'Well, the cops can't just come in and arrest everyone,' Neil said. 'If they were smart enough to put this idea together, they must have worked on a pretty good way out. If we're going to hit the place, it's got to be fast and overwhelming.'

They both considered the job.

'You'd need an army corps to hold a perimeter outside these mountains,' Lewis said.

They walked on slowly, each deep in thought.

'We're going to have to get into the Institute and find out what they've got planned,' Neil said. 'Or work on someone inside who can tell us what we need to know.'

'Did you pick up anything when you were at the table?' Lewis asked.

'Yeah, nothing positive, but it might help. No one knows what the big boss looks like. He never appears. Two of the players are engineers at the mine. When Brady took over he brought in Ram Reicher, who gives all the instructions.'

'No one ever sees him?' Lewis asked.

'That's what the engineers said,' Neil repeated.

As he spoke there was a chattering sound in the distance.

'Chopper,' Neil said and they watched the helicopter descend behind the rim of rock that led to the mine.

They both moved to the dark side of the street and stood in the doorway of a building. About fifty yards down the street the main door of the Institute opened and light flooded into the street. A blue-clad guard hurried down the steps and stood at the kerbside, accompanied by Ram Reicher.

Lewis glanced at his watch. It was exactly 2am. He looked up again to see headlights and a Mercedes with black glass windows stopping outside the Institute. The guard stepped forward to open the car door, and Reicher obscured the figure who walked beside him into the building.

They drew further back into the doorway as the headlights swept up the street as the car moved away.

'That could be Brady,' Neil said.

Lewis was about to answer when the sound of the helicopter came to them again, and they watched as it rose into the air and swung away to pass over the mountains and head towards the north.

'You know,' Neil said in the same soft voice, 'this place is getting to be very spooky.'

Lewis had the same feeling.

Neil's hand tightened on Lewis's shoulder and they looked up at the Institute building. Lights appeared at a row of windows and shadows began to play against the yellow blinds. Suddenly, one figure was silhouetted clearly.

The shadow was of a misshapen man holding a long stick which he brought down in three slashing motions as if the bulky distorted figure were testing the instrument. Then the flurry of shadows began again.

'Let's get back,' Neil said and they turned and walked swiftly back to the hotel.

They let themselves in and they were crossing the darkened hallway when they noticed that the door to Kate's office was slightly open so that a crack of light showed on the marbled floor. They turned from the stairs and went to the door.

Lewis pushed it open and they saw she was sitting staring at the desk. Before her was a thousand-dollar note.

'Everything all right, Kate?' Lewis asked gently and she turned to look at them.

She had removed the heavy make-up so that she looked very vulnerable by the glow of light from the lamp.

'The girl – Annie,' she said in a voice so low they could hardly hear.

'What about her?' Lewis asked.

Kate stood up and the thousand-dollar bill fluttered to the floor, but she ignored it.

'Reicher had two of the guards take her away. They left the money for her.'

Lewis didn't have to look at Neil – they were both thinking of the shadowy figure against the blinds.

Chapter Seven

They stood in the darkened hallway and watched Kate stoop down to pick up the thousand-dollar bill. She held it before her and then crumpled it into a tight ball and threw it aside as if it was one of her discarded cigarettes.

'Whores and money,' she said in a tired voice. 'We sell ourselves to get it and then give it away to pimps.'

She looked into their faces and they could see the bitterness. When she turned away they stood in awkward silence. The moment was ended by a sound that was familiar to them both. It was the metallic clicking noise of a hammer being cocked and the chamber of a revolver turning.

'Don't move until I say so, boys,' said a confident voice with a Southern accent, and they knew the speaker was close to them. 'Now put your hands behind you and lace your fingers together.'

They hesitated for a moment and they felt a gentle prod in each of their backs.

'That's a pump-action shotgun my man Reagan is aiming at you. Just so's you'd know how foolish it would be to disobey me,' the Southern voice continued. 'Now he'd really like to kill you, boy,' he said and he tapped Lewis on his shoulder with the long barrel of the Magnum revolver, 'on account of you spraying him with perfume and banging his head against the wall. So my advice to you is to do exactly what I say.'

Lewis felt handcuff bracelets snap around his wrists.

'You can turn around now,' the voice said.

Three men stood before them. The two Lewis had

encountered earlier in the evening held shotguns in a businesslike fashion. They flanked a smiling man of medium height who wore his black guard's stetson on the back of his head and held a large revolver level with Lewis's stomach.

'Forgive me for not introducing myself,' the young man said in the same menacing tone, 'but we won't know each other long enough to get acquainted, so it hardly seems worthwhile.'

He took the keys to Neil's Range Rover from his breast pocket and held them out without taking his eyes from theirs.

'Reagan, bring the car outside.'

Kate came out of her office and stood next to Lewis.

'Over here, ma'am,' the young man said.

Lewis could feel her anger.

'This isn't company property, Jethro,' she said. 'You've got no right to arrest anyone in my place.'

'You're right, Kate, and I feel downright ashamed of myself,' he said and he gestured with the revolver for Neil and Lewis to walk to the door. 'If I were you I'd file a complaint to Mr Brady.'

The sound of the Range Rover's engine came to them and the young man took Neil by the chain of the handcuffs and prodded him towards the doorway with the Magnum. They all climbed into the Range Rover and drove slowly down the main street until they arrived at the entrance to the Institute. Reagan indicated with the shotgun they were to enter the marble lobby. While Jethro pressed the button for the elevator, they stood waiting by an ornately gilded open cage that rose in the well of a grand staircase. Lewis glanced around at the splendour of the entrance hall. Two of the high walls were decorated with murals depicting the benefit that silver-mining bestowed upon the nation.

There was a monumental quality to the depictions of brawny farmers and industrial workers who gazed across the lobby to a heroic miner who held up a symbolic silver chalice against a Western sunset. It reminded Lewis of paintings he had seen in the Soviet Union.

The lift juddered to a halt and Jethro pulled open the gates. They rose slowly to the fourth floor and disembarked.

Their footsteps echoed along the marble floor until they stopped before a heavy door made of dark wood, with brightly polished brass fittings. Set into the wall beside the lock on the door was a small illuminated panel of buttons. One of the guards tapped out a combination, and as he pressed each digit a musical note played. They entered a room that was quite small, and in darkness.

Beyond an inner door they could hear muffled conversation and a sudden burst of laughter. Jethro switched on a light and they saw that they were in a secretary's office.

'Over there please, gentlemen,' Jethro said and indicated a red leather sofa under a window. Reagan sat down in the swivel chair behind the secretary's desk, with his weapon over the crook of his arm and pointing in their direction.

Jethro opened the door to the other room and Lewis was surprised to hear a brief snatch of Mozart before it closed once again. They sat in silence. Lewis studied the engravings of mine equipment on the wall for a while, and tried to recall the rest of the piece playing in the next room. To avoid useless speculation about their fate he began to think of music he was taught as a child.

The hymn 'Jerusalem' came to him and he remembered a cold Sunday morning after church when he was a boy. His sister Janet being held by his mother as his father pointed into the lions' cage at London Zoo. The scent of his father's pipe tobacco and the sharp rankness of the big cats came back to him.

The door to the inner office opened and Ram Reicher stood looking down at them. He had a full glass in his hand and the deliberation of his movements told Lewis that he had been drinking heavily.

'Bring 'em in,' he said to the guard. Reagan gestured with the shotgun for them to follow. The room they entered was long and aggressively masculine, in contrast to the delicate piece of Mozart that came from concealed speakers. To the right was a bank of windows and the shuttered blinds against which they had seen the shadows earlier. A bar and bookshelves lined the opposite wall. The green and red leather bindings contrasted with dark polished wood.

At the far end was a pool table flooded with light and a rough stone fireplace. Above the mantel was the skull of a longhorn steer. A carved desk covered by inkstands and ornaments shaped as horses and buffalo stood across the corner near the door. Nineteenth-century paintings of ranch life hung on the walls, lit by heavy brass lamps.

The floor was scattered with Indian rugs. Lewis glanced around the room and noticed a display case of weapons: mostly flintlock rifles, but there was also bows and arrows, lances, clubs and knives.

Jethro watched his glance with amusement and said in a low voice: 'Now I know what you're thinking, boy. But I advise you against it. Old Reagan here is the best damned shot I ever did see with a Winchester pump gun, and he'd just love to leave pieces of you lying all over the room.'

Lewis turned his attention to the six other men who sat in the leather armchairs. They were dressed Western-style and held drinks in their hands, but they looked as if they lived sedentary lives. He tried to imagine the clothes they would normally wear, and suddenly he knew that these men were academics – used to tweed, flannel and corduroy rather than the jeans and embroidered shirts they now affected. One of them was considerably older than the others. He was so thin the clothes seemed to hang on his sticklike body, and his face and hands were chalk-white and delicate like porcelain. He noticed Lewis's examination and looked back at him with expressionless pale blue eyes. Then he suddenly smiled without humour, revealing large yellowish teeth.

Bull Reicher sat among them in a wheelchair, his blue uniform trousers split to accommodate the plaster-cast on his right leg. He held a heavy cane with a gold top in his right hand. The chairs were grouped around a magnificent saddle, heavy with silver decorations. It stood on a mounting stand that was part of a curious piece of machinery.

Ram Reicher leaned against the desk and watched them, as Neil and Lewis studied the room. Then he pushed himself away from the desk and stood with his face close to theirs, so they could smell the bourbon on his breath and see the whiskers growing on the smooth skin.

'Get 'em some chairs,' he ordered, then he turned away and took a lariat that was coiled on the desk top.

He threw the rope to Reagan.

'Tie 'em down,' he said. The guard bound them to the seats while the men in the room watched in silence.

Ram Reicher nodded his satisfaction when the final knot was tied. 'Bring the girl,' he ordered.

The other men shifted in their chairs like an audience when an orchestra begins the overture. Reagan walked the length of the room to another door. Lewis could see that Bull Reicher was watching him with an expression of enjoyment.

Reagan returned, holding the red-haired girl by her arm. There was a defiance about her that impressed Lewis. She held her head high so that her mane of dark red hair fell back from her face. She turned to look at him for a moment and he thought, fleetingly, there was something familiar about her.

She was dressed in an imitation of a debutante's ballgown. Her shoulders were bare and the peach-coloured rayon dress was slit to the waist to reveal her legs as she walked. The low lights in the room lit her face from below, and emphasised her jaw and high cheekbones. It was like a scene from a Victorian melodrama – the captive princess brought before savages.

Ram Reicher stood behind Lewis and Neil.

'Boys,' he said in a voice loud enough to gain the attention of the room. 'I want you to meet our two guests.'

He placed a meaty hand on Neil's shoulder first.

'This here is Major David Neil of the United States Special Forces, and his buddy, Captain Lewis Horne of the British Special Air Service.'

Lewis and Neil exchanged a brief glance and Reicher chuckled.

'That surprises you, doesn't it, boys?' he said with good humour. 'Well, let me tell you, this ain't a piss-assed organisation you've been dealing with.' He pointed towards the door. 'Down there we got a computer that can tell me what time the Director General of the CIA took his morning crap. Finding out who you soldier boys really are was no trouble at all.'

Reicher paused and waited while the murmur of comments went around the room. He tightened his grip on their shoulders before he addressed the other men.

'Now, I can tell what you dudes are thinking . . . You're thinking, well, they don't look so tough, ain't ya?'

There were mutters of agreement from the room before Ram continued with his speech. He sounded like a fairground barker selling tonic from the back of a medicine wagon.

'Well, let me tell you, these boys are just about as tough as can be. You see, they've been trained so they can do just about anything. Why, they can jump out of airplanes and swim underwater. They can live in jungles eating bugs and snakes. They can shoot like Wild Bill Hickock and they can sneak up on you like Geronimo.'

Reicher slapped them on the shoulders.

'And you'd never believe it by looking at them, now would you?'

The men in the room laughed appreciatively. One of them called out: 'Come on, Ram, you must be exaggerating.'

Ram shook his head ponderously.

'No sir, no sir. Old Ram wouldn't lie to you. Now you all know my little brother here.' He gestured towards Bull, who was smiling as he fondled the cane in his hand.

'Big Bull, fine figure of a boy. You all know what Bull can do to anyone who gets sassy. Well, this little itty-bitty guy, Captain Lewis Horne of the British Special Air Service, put Bull in that wheelchair.'

He paused and when he spoke again his voice was edged with suppressed anger.

'Of course, he didn't do that in a fair fight, 'cause we all know what would've happened then. No sir, no sir, he used a lot of funny little tricks to break my brother's leg.'

He stopped and shook his head.

'And you know, boys, it ain't worthwhile trying to hurt him in return. Do you wanna know why?'

This time the room remained silent.

'I'll tell you. Because these guys – Major David Neil and Captain Lewis Horne – don't feel pain. Leastways, not like you and me. You see they've been trained. Trained to resist

168

torture, trained to go on when ordinary folks like us would quit, trained to disregard pain.'

Once more there was the murmur of conversation among the other men.

'So I tell you what we're gonna do.' He beamed around the room in triumph. 'We're gonna let the little lady take their pain for them.'

Reicher waved towards the girl.

'Tie her on, Reagan,' he said in a satisfied voice.

Annie was mounted in the saddle and her handcuffs removed before Reagan lashed her hands to the pommel and then her feet were tied into the stirrups.

'She's ready, boss,' Reagan said after he had tested the strength of his bindings.

'OK, boys,' Reicher called to the room. 'Let's get ourselves another little drink and start the show.'

The men milled around the bar and filled their glasses. The girl sat in the saddle looking ahead, her face expressionless. Lewis could see how determined she was. He knew she had an inner strength that had nothing to do with her physical body. It was the will to survive, and he knew she would die before her spirit broke. Reicher came from the bar and selected his seat with care. Lewis could see he wanted to be able to watch their faces as well as the planned entertainment.

Gradually the guests settled down again and looked towards Ram Reicher.

'Are you ready, Bull?' he called out.

'Ready, brother,' Bull replied and swung the cane in a slashing motion.

'OK, Reagan,' Reicher called. 'Let her go.'

He manipulated a switch on the stand beneath the saddle, and a motor slowly turned into motion. The machinery was designed to imitate the action of a wild horse. Within seconds the girl in the saddle was being thrown in a wild bucking motion that twisted and whirled in the centre of the room.

The men began to shift uneasily in their seats as Annie jerked and bucked in the saddle like a demented puppet, but Lewis could still see the expression of grim determination on her face. Then Bull Reicher began to play. As the machine whirled the girl close to him he slashed at her with the cane. The first few times he missed and Ram shouted encouragement.

Then he started to catch the repetitive timing of the machine and more of his blows began to land on her body.

Lewis and Neil sat stiffly in their seats and looked ahead. Bull Reicher's face was now slicked with sweat, and dark patches had appeared in semicircles around his armpits. He was now slashing at the girl with demented fury. Such was his ferocity that only occasional blows landed on her body but eventually he caught her a cutting blow on the head and she slumped forward into unconsciousness. The machine whipped her in a wide swinging circle, and blood from her wound sprayed the men around her.

'Stop,' Reicher called out and Reagan turned off the switch. 'Get something,' he ordered. 'She's bleeding on the furniture.'

Reagan hurried to another room and returned with a towel which he wrapped around the girl's head. There was a sudden silence and Lewis's voice cut through the room.

'Do you think old Bull enjoyed that? He's started to smell like a sewer.'

'I think so,' Neil replied. 'It's probably because he can't manage sex.'

'Is that so?'

'Yeah, a girl at the Grand Hotel told me his pecker's so small she used to have to put it in her belly button.'

Bull Reicher let out a bellow of rage and manoeuvred the wheelchair in front of Lewis. He raised the cane and slashed at his head. Lewis turned so that the blow landed on his shoulder. At the same moment, Neil stood up taking the chair with him and butted against Bull with his body. The wheelchair toppled sideways and Bull sprawled onto the floor. As he lay on the floor Lewis could tell the screams he emitted were of rage rather than pain, and he guessed Bull had taken some powerful drug as a painkiller.

Reagan and the other guard cocked their revolvers and placed the barrels against the two prisoners' heads. The others helped Bull Reicher back into his wheelchair and placed the cane back into his hand. For a time he sat panting as he fought to control his rage. When his breathing returned to normal, he was facing Lewis once again.

Then he turned the head of the cane and slowly withdrew a long narrow steel blade from the stick. For a few moments he held the needle-sharp point against Lewis's chest, with just enough pressure to prick the skin and cause a tiny rivulet of blood to trickle down his shirt.

Ram Reicher came and stood behind his brother's wheelchair.

'Take it easy, Bull,' he said in a soothing voice. 'These guys are from pretty fancy outfits. If the authorities find their bodies, we don't want them to have any unnecessary holes in them, do we now?'

Bull grinned and snapped the blade back into the cane. He looked at both prisoners in turn and spoke in an almost cheerful voice.

'I want to watch!'

Ram looked down at his brother and said in a solicitous tone, 'Now it's a long way for you to drive with that leg, boy.'

'I want to see it,' he said in a petulant, stubborn voice. 'I want to see their faces.' He looked up at his brother. 'They caused me a lot of heartache, Ram. I don't mind the ride. They gave me painkillers.'

He turned back to Lewis and Neil.

'I'd walk for a week on this leg,' he said, tapping the plaster-cast with the cane, 'just to see these two mothers die.'

Ram slapped his brother on his shoulders.

'Well, you'll see it, brother. That's for sure. If you want to see it – OK.' He turned to Reagan. 'Make sure you take it easy on the journey.'

He gestured first to Lewis and Neil, then swept his arm around to include Annie who had been laid out on a leather sofa, her head still swathed in the towel that had staunched the flow of blood.

'Keep them alive. Understand?'

Reagan nodded. 'I understand.'

171

Ram Reicher looked at his victims again and considered his last statement.

'But, on the other hand, if they seem as if they're going to give you real trouble, make sure you beat them to death. I don't want bullet wounds if it can be avoided.'

Reagan nodded again. 'I'll do as you say.'

Reicher continued. 'And get them some other clothes so it'll look natural if anyone ever finds them.'

'We've got all their stuff outside,' Reagan said.

Reicher nodded. 'Good. You can get going, then.'

There was a quiet moan of pain from the girl on the sofa and they turned to see the skeletal old man walk to her side.

'How is she?' Reicher asked.

The old man came over to them when he had finished his examination. 'Her wounds are superficial. Maybe a few cracked ribs and some concussion from the blow to the head. I think she's capable of undertaking any journey you think necessary.' He spoke with a heavy German accent. Neil looked at him with interest.

'Where did you take your medical degree, Doctor? Was it Belsen?' Neil asked in a conversational tone.

As the man turned towards him, Lewis could detect a spark of displeasure; two small red spots appeared on the lined, paper-white cheeks.

'A pity to make your acquaintance, Major, even for such a short time,' he said curtly.

'Maybe we'll meet again, Doctor,' Neil said with the same formality.

'I don't think so, Major,' Ram Reicher said as Reagan released them from the ropes. 'You're going to the Road of Death and that's been a one-way ticket for two hundred years.'

The final call for the flight to Malaga came over the address system as Charlie Mars walked with Sybil to the glass doorway. It was hot and stuffy in the departure lounge despite the grey coldness of the morning. He bent forward and kissed her so briefly that a casual observer might have thought they were not particularly close, but he watched until she reached a point where the corridor turned off before he walked swiftly away.

At the control desk two men were showing their passports to the duty officer with blasé familiarity. Charlie knew they would be standing at the bar of an international Hilton by nightfall. He watched them slip their documents back into the expensive leather travelling bags they both carried, and overheard a snatch of their conversation. It was about sharing a hire car when they got to Frankfurt.

The girl at the desk nodded him through, and he paused for a moment feeling very lonely as he thought of Sybil's departure. He looked at his wristwatch and saw that he had time to spare. On a sudden impulse he made for a door in that no-man's-land between the security people who searched hand luggage and the desks of the passport officers.

Reaching the end of a corridor he walked into an office where a woman with heavy glasses looked up casually from the telephone and then, recognising Charlie, replaced the phone and stood up.

'Is he in?' Charlie said pleasantly and he walked towards the opposite door.

'Yes, Mr Mars,' she said.

Charlie entered and looked around at plain walls that were covered with portrait photographs. Harsh fluorescent lights lit the room which had the permanent feeling of a closed cardboard box. The only other feature in the cubicle was a tin desk where a dishevelled figure in a dark green corduroy suit and no shoes sat with his feet on the desk, asleep.

Charlie shut the door gently but the noise was enough to wake the man who made a snorting noise as he came to. He blinked and ran both hands through his tousled hair.

'Hello, Charlie,' he said through a yawn. 'How are you?'

Charlie smiled as he sat down in the chair opposite.

'Pretty well, Guy,' Charlie said, 'but not perfect.'

Guy Landis rummaged around under his desk searching for his battered suede brogues which he eventually found and began to ease onto his feet.

'What's your problem, Charlie? Tell Uncle Guy,' he said wearily.

Charlie picked up a photograph from the desk and studied it for a moment before he placed it back on the pile.

'I can't find Skylark and Sybil's had to go abroad for a while. I don't know how long.'

Landis banged his feet on the floor and flexed his arms.

'Funny old world, isn't it? Personally, I'd be delighted if my beloved Muriel had to go abroad for an indefinite stay.'

Charlie looked around the walls once again.

'How are things going here?'

Guy Landis shrugged his shoulders. 'We've stopped twenty-seven illegal exits including two bank robbers on their way to the Costa Blanca, three suspicious Hungarians who turned out to be smuggling extremely boring trade secrets and a gang of IRA nasties, but no slim, attractive dark-haired woman of above average height with strong features.'

Charlie noticed the paleness of his face and the dark shadows beneath his bloodshot eyes.

'How long is it since you were home?' he asked.

Landis shrugged again. 'Don't worry, Charlie. If I'm in need of any home comforts, the delicious Mrs Wilmot will be more than generous with her favours.'

He swung his feet back onto the desk and called 'Betty' in a croaking bellow. The door opened instantly and the secretary backed into the room with two mugs.

'Coffee?' she said in a voice women use with spoilt children. She placed the mugs on the table and Landis opened a drawer in the desk and took out a bottle of malt whisky.

'One advantage of working at the airport, old boy,' he said cheerfully. 'You can get your hands on the good stuff tax-free.' He glanced at Charlie's face and laughed. 'Only joking, Charlie. I paid the full price for this.' He poured two large measures into the mugs. 'What's taken Sybil off?' he asked.

Charlie took a long swallow and placed the cup back on the table. 'An old aunt of hers has become ill so she's going to look after her. There's an uncle as well so she'll have her hands full for a while.'

They both sipped their coffee in silence for a time and then Landis spoke.

174

'So there's no leads to your Skylark's whereabouts?'

'No. You'd think it would be bloody difficult for a woman and five men to vanish in this country, wouldn't you? We've had good coverage in the papers and on television but so far, nothing.'

'What makes you so sure there are five men?'

'We aren't sure but it would seem logical that the minimum amount you would need to guard two is three people if they're going to get any sleep.'

Landis scratched his head.

'Why just three?'

Charlie folded his arms. 'It's just a guess but any more would make concealment even more difficult.'

Landis rummaged through his pockets and took out a packet of tipped cigarettes and a book of matches. He lit one of the cigarettes and pulled a metal wastepaper bin closer to his chair to use as an ashtray.

'So what have you got exactly?' he asked.

Charlie stood up and walked to the end of the room to distance himself from the temptation of the cigarette smoke.

'Exactly? Nothing.' He paused for a moment. 'We got a message from Skylark that the people at her agency had snatched someone important. It's even conjecture that the person is Dr Lionel Reece. We know that three other people at the agency where Skylark worked are missing.'

They drank some more of the mixture. The peaty flavour of the whisky tasted good through the weak coffee.

'What about Reece – no leads there?'

Charlie shook his head. 'We've got watchers on Reece's wife and his mother and the old schoolteacher he cares so much about.'

'Now that's odd,' Landis said. 'Of all the people I've met in life the least likely collection I'd want to keep in touch with were my old schoolmasters.'

He stubbed out the cigarette on the inside of the bin and poured the dregs of his drink on the sparks that smouldered on the screwed up pieces of paper.

Charlie sat down again, deep in thought, and Landis leaned

back in his chair with his hands thrust into the pockets of a brown woollen cardigan he wore beneath the jacket. After some time, Landis suddenly said:

'Funny, I keep thinking it's Thursday.'

'What did you say?' Charlie asked sharply.

He repeated the sentence.

'The old joke – *Punch*. Don't you remember? One hippopotamus saying to the other as they're basking in the tropical pool. "Funny, I keep thinking it's Thursday." '

'The cartoon was Tuesday,' Charlie said.

'Was it?' Landis replied. 'I was sure it was Thursday.'

But Charlie had got up and gone to the door.

'Mrs Wilmot,' he said. 'Do you think you can get me a Dr Hanna Pearce on the telephone? She is working at the Hammersmith Hospital at the moment.'

While he waited for the call he began to whistle softly.

'What's that tune?' Landis asked him.

Charlie thought for a moment.

'It's called "When the World Was Young",' he said. 'Eartha Kitt used to sing it.'

He smiled at Landis.

'Her autobiography was called *Thursday's Child*.'

The car edged forward in the heavy traffic which had slowed to a crawl in the snow that fell like thick clouds of whirling confetti. At the Hogarth Roundabout, Charlie Mars directed the driver to turn from the main stream down a narrow road, and instantly the surroundings changed.

The narrow irregular lane was a charming mixture of architectural styles, so that this jumble of buildings that lay only a few yards from an arterial road was as quiet and peaceful as a home counties village.

They turned left at a church and the car drove at an easy pace along Chiswick Mall. To the left, gardens ran up to fine old houses, and on their right, the bare trees fringed an embankment that half concealed the grey, choppy waters of the Thames.

'Over here, George,' Charlie said eventually and the driver

parked in front of a row of red-brick houses. Charlie checked the time.

'I'll be about half an hour,' he said.

'Right, sir,' the driver replied, and he reached into the pocket in the door and took out a paperback novel.

Charlie buttoned the collar of his tweed overcoat and walked along by the river in the direction of Hammersmith. Eventually the road became a narrow, brick-lined passageway that led to The Doves, an ancient riverside pub that Charlie entered, brushing snow from his hair and shoulders. The pub was crowded and noisy with lunchtime trade, so he had to wait behind other customers at the bar.

When it was his turn to be served he ordered a pint of bitter and took a chance on Hanna's order. A couple slid out of a corner seat and Charlie moved in quickly. He raised the pint to his lips and saw Hanna enter the bar.

'I got you a glass of wine,' he said as she squeezed beside him.

He could feel how tense she was and he noticed that her hand trembled as she raised the glass.

'Are you all right, my dear?' he asked gently.

She turned her head and he could see the worry in her eyes.

'What's happened to him?' she said.

'Happened? To whom?' Charlie asked, bewildered.

She lay her hands flat on the table and looked down at the wine glass.

'To Lewis.'

'Why do you ask?' he said in a suddenly anxious voice. 'Have you heard from him – something to cause you concern?'

Hanna took a sip of wine.

'Charlie, I haven't heard from him or seen him since lunch at your home on Boxing Day.'

Immediately he was full of contrition.

'My dear, I'm so sorry,' he said in a solicitous voice. 'Lewis is fine. At least he was when I last spoke to him.'

'Where is he?' she asked.

Charlie hesitated for a moment. 'America,' he said and took a drink from his beer.

'America?' Hanna said and there was an edge to her voice. 'Where in America?'

'Arizona,' Charlie answered and glanced around at the other customers.

'On a Dude Ranch, I suppose,' she said, and the earlier concern had been replaced by a strong tone of irony. She laughed with relief suddenly and took a good swallow from her drink. 'And I thought you were going to break some bad news to me.'

She leaned back against the wall so that her face was in shadow but Charlie could see the line of her shoulders alter and he knew how anxious she had been.

'No,' he said. 'Actually I wanted to ask a favour of you.'

She looked at her watch.

'If it doesn't take too long. I'm back on duty at three o'clock.'

'That should be long enough,' Charlie said. 'When you've finished your drink, we'll go.'

The snow still fell heavily, coating their hair and coats. Hanna slipped her arm through Charlie's as they walked huddled together to the car.

'Where are we going?' Hanna asked.

'There's a young woman who works for us,' Charlie said as he chose the path they walked with care. 'She's been missing for a few days and we're rather anxious to find her. We're going to see her mother who lives near here.'

'Do you think her mother knows where she is?' Hanna said.

Charlie thought for a little while before he answered.

'I don't know. You see our girl is a dutiful daughter. The mother, Mrs Maynard, is a widow but she leads a pretty active life. She takes lessons at night school and she's a member of a local dramatic society. But Skylark, that's our agent, goes to see her every Thursday without fail.'

They walked on for a few moments.

'Skylark would have seen her mother on Thursday if everything had been normal.'

'Maybe she telephoned,' Hanna said.

178

Charlie shook his head so that snow fell inside the collar of his coat.

'We have the telephone tapped. If Skylark had called her mother we would have known. And, conversely, if Mrs Maynard had made any calls we would know about it.'

'So you think Mrs Maynard may know what's happened to her daughter?' Hanna said, and her voice was beginning to show her interest.

'It's a possibility,' Charlie said. 'Forgive me if I sound patronising, but I really do want a woman's observation on how she reacts when I question her. You may notice nuances of behaviour that are meaningless to me.'

Hanna smiled and squeezed his arm. 'I get the picture. You just want a Dr Watson for filling in the bits mere mortals might notice.'

'Really, no, Hanna,' Charlie protested. 'I assure you I need your expertise.'

They had reached the car and Charlie opened the door for her.

'This girl – Skylark – could she be in real trouble?'

Charlie didn't answer immediately. The car drove back along Chiswick Mall and the layer of snow thinned out, leaving a fresh coat of white like a dusting of icing sugar on the embankments. The grey-coloured river flowed through the landscape, looking rough and dangerous in comparison to the gentle prettiness of the newly decorated houses and trees.

Beyond the thin strip of island that lay close to the road, two crews of boys fought the shells of their racing eights against the strength of the tide. Grimly they feathered their blades above the ruffled surface, and the relentless power of the river drained their effort. Charlie watched the two crews contract their bodies and haul the long oars through the swirling water.

'I think she could be,' he answered finally.

Hanna followed his gaze and began to watch the two crews.

'I didn't realise you had women in your line of work, Charlie,' she said.

'Oh, yes,' he replied with a quick smile. 'Contrary to popular myth, women are excellent at keeping secrets.'

Charlie leaned forward. 'Stop the car, George,' he said and he watched the race for a few minutes more.

'I bet the nearest boat is going to win,' Hanna said.

'I think not,' Charlie said and almost immediately the far crew began to pull ahead. 'Drive on, George,' he said and leaned back into the upholstery.

'How did you know they would do it?' Hanna asked.

'Damon Runyan,' Charlie said.

'I don't follow.'

Charlie recalled the quotation: ' "The race does not always go to the swift nor the fight to the strong – but that's the way to bet." '

Lewis, Neil and Annie lay huddled in the back of the truck as it moved along the highway. There was a strip of wooden seat running along one side, too narrow to give any comfort. The floor was studded metal. Despite his handcuffs, David Neil held Annie in his arms to try and protect her from the shock that conveyed every tiny vibration to their numbed bodies. Occasionally she would moan as she shifted, but mercifully she remained unconscious.

It was almost pitch black in the truck but the luminous dial on Lewis's watch told him they had been on the road for more than two hours and that dawn was close. The first sign of the sun came through the tiny grilled windows set into the doors and played a small square of light above Lewis's head.

There was a brief period of respite before the cool dawn air began to warm, and then the truck started to feel like the inside of a lighted stove. Perspiration began to pour from their bodies, so that their clothes became soaked, while their mouths dried and they ached for water.

After a time they felt the truck swing to the left, and from the bumping they began tó endure it was clear that they had taken a dirt road. The truck stopped and the rear door opened. Blinding sunshine flooded in.

Lewis held up his handcuffed hand to shield his eyes from

the light and squinted as one of the guards tossed three water-bottles inside before he slammed the doors and they resumed the jolting journey.

Lewis and Neil drank thirstily from the bottles, and then Neil supported the unconscious girl as Lewis trickled water down her throat.

'Where do you think they're taking us?' Lewis said.

'Reicher said the Road of Death, but that doesn't mean very much. It really means a general trail that was part of the old Spanish trade route that led up from Mexico and headed towards California from Tucson. It's rough country – as rough as it comes out here.' He paused for a while. 'But the Apaches aren't a problem any more.'

Lewis got to his feet and looked through the rear window. The convoy of vehicles threw up a thick cloud of dust from the dirt road. To each side of them the grey-brown desert stretched, pockmarked with stunted shrubbery. To the far south he could see mountains. He slid down next to Neil once again and they carefully eased Annie from his embrace so that Lewis could relieve Neil for a while. As soon as he released her, Neil slid flat onto the floor and, despite the discomfort of the surface, wedged himself into the corner and fell asleep.

Lewis did his best to ease the pain of the journey for the girl but it was like nursing a bird that had broken a wing. Although she remained unconscious, the jolting penetrated her sleep so that she continued to whimper and moan as the truck swayed and banged from side to side.

Eventually the weariness that seemed to penetrate his bones caused Lewis to pass into a state close to sleep. For a night-mare period he would doze and dream vividly, only to be jolted back to consciousness by the pounding ride. Finally the truck halted and they listened as voices called to each other. Gradually Annie started to come round as they trickled water into her mouth.

'Where are we?' she finally whispered.

'In the desert,' Neil said in a low voice. 'Your only hope is to play as dead as you can. Will you be able to manage that?'

'Sure,' she said and she closed her eyes, and Lewis felt her go limp in his arms.

For a long time they lay in the sweltering gloom, until the doors of the truck were opened and immediately their senses were alert to the smell of coffee and steaks cooking. Reagan stood silhouetted against the light, holding a shotgun.

'Bus ride's over – get out,' he ordered.

Lewis and Neil clambered out and stood stiffly at the rear of the vehicle while one of the guards unlocked their handcuffs.

They were positioned on a flat rock surface that fell away to a dry wash below them. A row of mesquite trees shaded Neil's Range Rover and a truck, which were parked next to an area where a fire was burning and food was being prepared.

A row of safari chairs had been set out beneath a canvas awning which gave a wide swath of shade from the fearsome sun.

Bull Reicher sat in one of these safari chairs drinking a can of beer. Reagan gestured with the shotgun for them to join him.

'What do you bet me he crushes the can when he finishes?' Neil whispered to Lewis as they approached the seated figure.

As they got closer they could see that Reicher had a sporting rifle with a telescopic sight across his lap. From Neil's Range Rover emerged the sound of Country and Western music on the cassette player.

'Turn off the music, boy,' Bull Reicher called out. 'It's time to hear the weather report.'

One of the guards fiddled with the radio and a fast voice began to read out the local news for Tucson. Lewis watched Bull finishing his beer, and half listened to the warning of an impending storm coming from the south. Reicher grinned as he lowered the can from his mouth and, as Neil had anticipated, he crushed it in his hand and threw it over the side of the bluff and down into the dry wash.

Then he raised the rifle and snapped off a shot at the can that now lay on the dry river bed. The can jumped from the

182

impact of the bullet, and as Reicher fired and hit it three more times, it skipped across the dusty wash.

'Great shooting, Bull,' Neil said.

'They're dangerous bastards, those beer cans,' Lewis added.

'How's the cocktail waitress?' Reicher asked.

'She's just about dead, you bastard,' Neil said angrily.

'Is that so?' Bull asked.

'She looks pretty bad,' Reagan said.

Reicher nodded with satisfaction. 'Lay her out on there,' he said, indicating with his rifle a higher slab of rock near by. 'There's plenty of vermin around here that'll appreciate a good feed, and they ain't particular where their meat has been.' He turned to the guard who was cooking the steaks on the barbecue. 'How's the chow?'

'Couple more minutes, boss.'

Reicher looked at his watch. 'Looks like we've timed it pretty well.'

Lewis and Neil turned to follow his gaze and saw smudges of grey cloud on the horizon.

'Get their pick-up down there,' Reicher said to Reagan.

They watched from their vantage point as he manoeuvred the Range Rover down a slope and onto the bed of the dry river. He parked it to face their position.

'Chow's ready,' the guard called out as Reagan reached the top of the slope once again.

'Sorry you can't stay for dinner, boys,' Reicher said, 'but it's time for you to go for a ride. Go down there and get in the truck.' He lifted the rifle slightly. 'And remember the beer can.'

They began the walk down to the wash. Halfway down the slope, Lewis spoke in a low voice. 'Is it worth trying for a break now?'

'No,' Neil replied. 'Get into the Range Rover.'

By the time they reached the vehicle the grey clouds had spread even further, and they could feel the drop in temperature that precedes a storm. When they were seated, they could see Reicher and the others sitting on the row of chairs beneath the canvas awning.

'I feel like a duck in a rifle range,' Lewis said. As he spoke, rain began to splatter on the windscreen.

'Did you notice the ammunition Reicher was using?' Neil said.

Lewis nodded. 'Soft nose, light charge.'

Neil leaned forward and switched on the ignition.

'Fasten your seat belt,' he said and at the same time he rapped on the windscreen. 'Armalite glass,' he said. 'That dumb son-of-a-bitch would need a bazooka to get through it.'

The engine coughed and refused to start and Lewis watched as Reicher raised the hunting rifle and aimed at him with careful deliberation. Time seemed to stop, and he thought of Hanna turning to greet him, her dark hair swirling to frame her face. Then he could hear a roaring sound that was like percussion behind an orchestra. Rain began lashing down.

Neil pumped at the engine and Lewis glanced towards him. Through his window he could see a wall of water hurtling down the river bed towards them.

As the engine caught, Lewis was aware of shots hammering into the Range Rover. Neil spun it around and the vehicle swerved for a moment on the slick of mud on the river-bed. Then the wheels gripped and they accelerated away. Neil swerved to avoid a rock embedded in the bottom of the wash, and the Range Rover slid to the left. Lewis watched helplessly, as the wall of water hit them. The force of the torrent knocked the vehicle onto its side and they were caught in the roaring maelstrom. Like a cork the Range Rover began to tumble and turn in the heart of the raging flood. The two men were held loosely by their seat belts, so the force of the river was throwing them about like dice in a cup.

'Drop us here, George,' Charlie Mars said and he indicated the corner of Lynton Road.

He held the door open for Hanna to get out, then they walked through the fresh snow to Number 25. There were no footprints on the path, but the doorstep had already been

184

swept clear and five empty milk bottles, sparkling clean, stood in a row.

'Are you sure she's in?' Hanna asked.

'No, I didn't want to risk a phone-call in case she put me off. It's hard for someone to turn people away from the door – unless they're selling something, of course.'

The bell chimed twice and they could see a light in the hallway through the roses entwined in the stained-glass window. They waited for some time before the door was opened by a tall woman with a strong mane of hair. Charlie could see immediately the resemblance to Joyce.

'Mrs Maynard? My name is Professor Mars and this is Dr Hanna Pearce. We're old friends of Joyce from London University. We're doing a field study on Bedford Park and Joyce has some valuable books of mine that I need urgently.'

Mrs Maynard looked disconcerted. 'Surely they'll be at her flat,' she said.

Charlie was at his most persuasive.

'No, I spoke to her some days ago and she particularly mentioned that they were at her mother's home.'

'You'd better come in,' Mrs Maynard said reluctantly.

They followed her past a flight of stairs and along a narrow passage into a rear room with a view of a white-clad garden through the small French windows. There was a small bookcase in a corner of the room and a plain table with six chairs. The walls were covered with blown-up black-and-white photographs. They were rather self-conscious artistic studies of parks and local buildings.

'What fine photographs, Mrs Maynard. Are they yours?'

'My husband's.' She looked at them for a moment. 'He printed and mounted them himself,' she said in a quiet voice.

'I'm passionately fond of photography myself,' Charlie lied.

'Really?' Mrs Maynard said without interest. 'Do you see your books?'

Charlie slowly checked the shelves while Hanna gazed at the gloomy photographs.

'No, I'm afraid not. Do you keep any others?'

Mrs Maynard frowned slightly. 'There are some in her old room, but they're all piled in the corner.'

Charlie boomed, 'Splendid,' and walked quickly out of the room and up the stairs before Mrs Maynard could protest. By the time she had caught up with him he had opened the three bedroom doors that led off the tiny landing.

'Ah, here we are,' he said and began to sort through the pile stacked in the corner of the small room.

'Yes, these are the ones I need.' He thrust three books under his arm and took Mrs Maynard's hand.

'I can't thank you enough. We must dash now.'

Hanna waited for him at the bottom of the stairs.

'Incidentally, Mrs Maynard, has Joyce gone away? I rang her office, and they said she'd taken a short holiday.'

'Yes,' the woman said quickly. 'She's staying in Norfolk with my sister for a few days. I'm afraid she's not on the telephone.'

Hanna opened the door and they both said goodbye. Charlie walked so fast Hanna almost had to run to keep up with his long strides. After twenty yards he glanced at the books he had taken from Skylark's bedroom.

'*Little Women, Portnoy's Complaint* and *The Mill on the Floss*. A Catholic taste in literature.'

He slowed down when he realised Hanna had difficulty keeping pace with him.

'What do you think?' he said.

Hanna paused before she spoke.

'At first I thought they might be there.'

'Why?' Charlie asked.

'She seems to be drinking a lot of milk for a woman living alone, and when you went upstairs I checked in the kitchen. The refrigerator is full of food.'

Charlie nodded as they walked to the corner where the car waited. They slipped into the back seat.

'Did you see anything interesting?' Hanna asked.

'Two indentations in the carpet outside the bathroom.' He held out his hands. 'About this far apart and approximately three inches long.'

Hanna looked hard at him. 'You know something, don't you?'

'Possibly,' Charlie said. 'See if you can work it out.'

Hanna looked out of the window at the shopkeepers clearing the snow from Chiswick High Street. Charlie glanced down at his watch. It took her three minutes.

'The photography,' she said suddenly. 'Her husband used the attic for a darkroom.'

Charlie nodded.

'Are they up there?'

'I think there's a strong chance,' Charlie said.

'What will you do?' Hanna said.

Charlie smiled. 'In the absence of Lewis, I shall get Gordon Meredith and Sandy Patch to pop into the attic.'

Chapter Eight

The force of the torrent tumbled the Range Rover along the bed of the flooded wash, as if Lewis and Neil were on a nightmare ride in a fairground, until suddenly they were jerked to a halt as the bonnet drove itself into an obstruction.

The Range Rover lay on its right side, and David Neil sprawled half across Lewis, jamming him against the door that rested on the riverbed. The flood waters continued to roar over them, causing debris caught in the stream to bang against the body of the car. It was as if they were being stoned by a maddened crowd.

In the faint light that filtered through the muddy, rushing water Lewis could just see Neil reaching for the interior light, and to his astonishment, it still worked.

'Can you move your hands?' Neil shouted above the roaring waters.

'A bit,' Lewis shouted back.

'Under the dashboard – to your right.'

Lewis thrust his arm forward and almost immediately found a metallic object clipped there. Jerking it from its hiding place he looked down at the fighting knife, in its metal scabbard, which Neil had first used in France. The razor-like edge parted the heavy nylon seat belts and they were able to move once again.

'How long will the main flood last?' Lewis shouted.

Neil cupped his hand to Lewis's ear and bellowed: 'It depends on the length of the storm – sometimes a short while, but if it's heavy . . . '

They examined their tomblike surroundings. So far there

was no evidence of a leak. They both leaned back and started to breathe lightly. Lewis guessed that the Range Rover had jammed against the bank at a curve in the wash, so protecting them from the main force of the river. He calculated that they would have a couple of hours of air if the vehicle remained watertight.

The roar of the river, accompanied by the drumming of floating debris against the vehicle continued, but they remained embedded in the embankment. As Lewis forced himself to relax, he began to examine the options for survival. It would be impossible to break out of the vehicle if the toughened glass was strong enough to resist a bullet: no amount of effort would smash the windows. The rear door faced the full pressure from the river's current, and the weight of the water that flowed across the door above them would be too great to allow them to force an exit.

Then the lights from the dashboard flickered and went out and they were plunged once again into the gloom of the river-bed. Now Lewis knew that their only hope was for the level of the water to fall soon. Deliberately he refused to allow his imagination to come into play. Instead he thought only of how to deal with his immediate physical environment.

Gradually the air turned foul. Neil edged his way over to the two spare wheels and sawed through the walls of the tyres with the serrated edge of the knife, but it did not seem to alter the atmosphere. Then Lewis noticed that there was a lessening of noise, and the inside of the car seemed to grow lighter. The level of the river was dropping.

Neil reached up and tried the electric switch to operate the window above them, but the water had conquered the car's electrical system, and the bullet-proof glass remained firmly closed.

'I'm going to try and break out,' Lewis shouted, and positioned himself so as to brace his shoulders against the door that faced the surface. He could feel how the lack of oxygen had sapped his energy, so that each movement required a massive act of will. He pulled back the handle set into the door and heaved. Nothing happened.

Lewis counted to ten, concentrating all his physical and

mental resources. His head began to pound as his body called for him to surrender. There was no pain, just an overwhelming desire to stop and rest.

Calling on that last deep reserve of will that lies in all human beings, he made the final effort. The door moved a fraction; water began to trickle into the car. His head swam hazily from the thick air and he knew that if he gave up now, the pressure from the river would slam the door shut and they would never escape.

He summoned up the memory of Bull Reicher savagely striking out at the defenceless girl, and with a shout of rage he heaved the door open against the water that now poured down on him. Despite the flood gushing in, he managed to haul himself out of the car. The current was still very strong but he could hold himself steady as he reached down to seize Neil's arms and pull him from the interior of the car.

Above him, spreading from the muddy embankment, where the water level had dropped, were the roots of a mesquite tree. They managed to grab a hold, and with their last strength, the two men scrambled up onto the bank and lay gasping on the stony, uneven ground.

For a time they gazed up into a sky that was now clear blue but for the smoky-white trails of a fighter plane that soared far above them across the desert.

When their oxygen-starved bodies were ready to work once more, they stood up and looked down on the river from the crumbling bank. The water level had continued to drop, and the Range Rover was now only two-thirds submerged. The heat of the sun had dried a thin coating of mud on its surface.

'And to think I nearly traded it for a Mustang,' Neil said.

'Sometimes it pays to buy British,' Lewis replied in a croaking voice.

They began to study the territory around them, and Lewis was surprised at how quickly the desert had sucked up the water from the storm. No damp earth remained, for the fierce sun had dried the landscape like a giant blowtorch. Back along the course of the river they could see, in the far distance, the rocky plateau where Reicher had made his camp. The terrain between was broken by hills and rocks, so it would be impossible for Reicher and his companions to follow the wash and find the Range Rover. Already Lewis's clothes were nearly dry, and he knew that the power of the sun would evaporate his perspiration. People who knew nothing of this kind of heat fainted from dehydration before they became thirsty.

They stood very still, watching the land about them, when there came a rustling sound from a clump of scrub that grew close to the wash.

As they both sank to a crouch, Lewis noticed that Neil had kept hold of the knife despite their struggle to escape from the car. As they looked towards the strange sound, there burst from the bushes a group of snorting, snuffling creatures on spindly legs, dark and heavy with bodies the size of pigs and heads the shape of warthogs. They were the ugliest creatures Lewis had ever seen, and surrounded the two men with evident curiosity. A rank smell came off them.

'Desert hogs,' Neil laughed. 'They make Reicher look handsome, don't they?'

When the men stood up again the creatures scattered away from them.

'Time to go to work,' Lewis said.

Charlie Mars sat next to the fireplace in the gallery of the Reform Club and watched Roger Kent walking towards him. He noticed how Kent had the ability to look as if he was concerned with some important business. It was an actor's technique but he did it very well. The preoccupied air, a quickness to the stride, shoulders hunched forward, one hand thrust into the jacket pocket of his well-cut suit, and a frown of concentration which broke into a brief smile as he recognised the Permanent Secretary of the Treasury, who was seated with two other members at one of the other tables that lined the gallery.

'What news on the Rialto?' Kent said as he chose a chair that was perceptibly higher than the one Charlie occupied.

'We might be getting somewhere,' Charlie said. 'I'm

waiting for Gordon Meredith who has been doing some digging about Mrs Maynard's next-door neighbours.'

As he spoke Gordon appeared at the top of the stairs and Charlie half-raised his arm to wave him over. By the time Gordon reached the table, a red-coated steward hovered over them, and Charlie ordered whiskies for Kent and himself and a glass of claret for Meredith.

'Begin, Gordon,' Charlie said.

Meredith paused to organise his thoughts.

'Well, they seem to be a perfectly decent young couple, Anthony and Pamela Hurst. He's twenty-nine, she's three years younger. They've known each other all their lives. Their parents were friends – used to go on holiday together when they were children.'

'How do the parents know each other?' Charlie asked.

'The fathers were in the Air Force together. The girl's father is a contract builder. His father's an architect. Anthony went to a local grammar school, then trained to be an accountant. Pamela became a secretary at the John Lewis Partnership. They got married four years ago. No children as yet.'

The steward arrived with their drinks, and during the pause in Gordon's narrative Roger Kent took the opportunity to light his pipe. Gordon watched the figure of the steward retreating before he resumed.

'Two years ago, Anthony chucked his job and opened an antique shop. Well, some antiques – it just about qualifies. They had to borrow from her father to get going.'

Charlie interrupted. 'Where is the shop?'

'In a side street off Chiswick High Road. They're not making a fortune, just getting by.'

'Are they there now?' Charlie asked.

Gordon nodded. Yes. He was at a sale in Buckinghamshire yesterday but today they're both in the shop.'

Charlie looked up at the glass dome above their heads, deep in thought.

Roger Kent gestured with his pipe. 'So all you have to do is drop in on them and explain that Her Majesty's Government wants to commandeer their house.' He applied another match to the bowl of his pipe.

'Will that be difficult?'

Charlie shrugged. 'It might be. The awkward part can be persuading people that we are what we are. They are just as likely to believe we're from some sort of television show and are pulling their legs for some fatuous stunt. A decent bribe can often work wonders.'

Kent puffed on his pipe a couple of times and Charlie was engulfed in fragrant tobacco smoke.

'Would it help if I went with you?' Kent said in a rather hopeful voice.

Charlie and Gordon exchanged glances of surprise.

'I rather think it would,' Charlie said with a smile. 'But won't we be keeping you from affairs of state?'

Roger Kent stood up and finished his whisky.

'My dear chap, that is the entire attraction in the escapade.'

Pamela Hurst sat at a dining table that occupied a great deal of the space in the tiny shop. Around her a jumble of furniture – tables, chairs, stools, wardrobes, desks – rose in towers that seemed likely to tumble from their precarious arrangements.

She was polishing a large and very tarnished canteen of cutlery, and so far she had not completed the forks. The work had caused a small knot of pain to form in the nape of her neck. She stopped for a moment to stretch and flex her shoulders to relieve the ache.

It was cold in the shop despite the small electric fire beneath the table that warmed her legs, so she wore a woollen ski-hat and an old sweater that belonged to her husband. She looked down at the newspaper that protected the surface of the table from the metal polish.

Smiling up at her was the photograph of a girl whose shiny, tousled hair framed a face as flawless as a plastic doll's. Her hands were clasped behind her head so that her perfect breasts thrust forward. Pamela Hurst read the caption and sniffed. 'The Bullring Venus,' she said with a disdainful shrug.

'Well, Miss Venus, we'd all look better if we could go

around looking like that all day,' she said and then she renewed her polishing. The door of the shop opened and the cold draught enveloped her.

The first man who entered was tall and slim. He wore an old-fashioned heavy tweed overcoat with no hat, so that his thick, greying hair was flecked with snow. Under his arm he carried an odd-shaped object wrapped in plain brown paper. The second man, who wore a dark blue cashmere coat with the collar turned up, seemed familiar to her. At first she thought he was an actor, until he smiled, and then she recognised Roger Kent and she felt a stab of excitement. She stood up and Kent held out his hand.

'Mrs Hurst?' he said in a deep voice, and he smiled so that the lines around his eyes crinkled.

Pamela was so flustered she almost took his hand before removing the rubber glove she wore.

'My name is Roger Kent,' he said with warmth and she noticed the laughter lines around his eyes.

'Yes,' she said quickly. 'I recognise you.'

'Is your husband here?' Kent said.

'No.' She looked around as if he might be concealed among the crowded furniture. 'That is, he won't be long. He's just popped out to buy something.'

Kent turned to Charlie.

'May I introduce a colleague of mine – Mr Mars.'

Charlie shook hands.

'Do you think he will be very long, Mrs Hurst? We really would like to talk to both of you.'

She looked from one to the other.

'I don't think so; the shop he's gone to is only just around the corner. Would you like to sit down?'

They both took chairs at the table.

'Is there any kind of trouble?' she asked with sudden concern.

Kent laughed. 'None at all, Mrs Hurst, I assure you.'

For a moment there was an awkward silence, but Roger Kent was used to making conversation with total strangers. He glanced around the shop and said in an easy voice: 'How is your business prospering?'

194

Pamela Hurst looked down at the cutlery before them in a sudden careworn fashion.

'Not so good, really. We've had a pretty rough time since, oh, last November.'

'I'm sorry to hear that,' Kent said. 'What's the reason?'

She gave a slight wave to the surroundings.

'We really only deal in furniture as you can see. Yesterday Tony bought this.' She indicated a Victorian sideboard with a glass-front display case. 'He thought it was better than it turned out to be.'

She picked up a couple of the pieces from the canteen.

'There was some other stuff in it like this, but it's only plate.'

'Perhaps we can help you, Mrs Hurst,' Charlie said and he got up from his place at the table, slid open the glass front of the case and placed the brown-paper parcel inside.

Pamela Hurst watched his actions, then looked to Roger Kent who smiled again and nodded to the parcel. She got up, opened the case again, took out the bundle and unwrapped a heavy chalice. She held it for a few minutes, then turned it over to examine the base.

'You say you only deal in furniture, Mrs Hurst,' Charlie said. 'Do you know anything of silver?'

'Not much,' she said.

'Then I have some good news for you,' he said as she placed the object carefully before her. 'That piece is Elizabethan. There's hardly any left in this country. The best examples are in the Kremlin museum. Most of the English bullion was melted down to pay for the Civil War.'

'Why are you doing this?' she asked with sudden suspicion. 'It's some kind of television joke, isn't it?'

Roger Kent shot Charlie a glance of sympathy.

'No, Mrs Hurst, this is not a game. We simply need your co-operation. You can consider this by way of a fee,' he said as he tapped the chalice.

As he finished speaking, the door opened once again and Anthony Hurst came into the shop in a flurry of snow. He stamped his feet before he looked up, and an expression of astonishment came to his face at the sight of his wife holding

195

the large cup to her breasts. He looked down at the two men seated at the table.

'You're . . . ' His voice trailed away as he recognised Roger Kent.

'Yes, Mr Hurst,' Kent said.

Anthony Hurst placed a container of Duraglit on the table next to the cutlery.'

'What are you doing here?' he said.

There was a brief silence, then Charlie Mars spoke.

'We would like to hold a party at your house, Mr Hurst.'

With their faces and exposed skin smeared with dried mud to protect them from the fierce sun, Lewis and David Neil moved with the stealth of hunting animals towards the Reicher encampment. It was good country to hide in. Broken ground, sudden depressions, rock formations, cactus and shrub. Most of the surface was like compacted gravel.

The desert air was so clean that Lewis could smell the camp as they drew closer. Car fumes, burnt wood and cooked meat, but Reicher and his men had departed. The tracks of their vehicles had ripped through the desert leaving ugly signs of passage.

They had left precious things for Lewis and Neil. The canvas awning was still there and a discarded white plastic gallon drum. They had not eaten the meal. The cold cooked steaks and a pan of beans were next to the barbecue that was still warm. There was a six-pack of beer and half a bottle of bourbon.

'I'll take care of the girl,' Lewis said and he made for the rock where Reicher's gang had left her, with her hands and feet secured by the handcuffs that Lewis and Neil themselves had previously worn. She looked like some sacrificial victim, Lewis thought as he stood by her. She still wore the tattered remains of the evening gown, and her hair was spread out, framing a face that showed the pain she had suffered. He looked down at her and was filled with pity.

Automatically but without much hope he reached for the pulse at the side of her throat, and to his astonishment felt the throb of life.

'She's still alive,' he said to Neil who had now joined him. Neil unscrewed the pommel of the knife and extracted a slim strip of metal from the handle. After a few minutes they had unpicked the handcuffs.

They carried her to the shade of the canvas awning. Her face and much of her body had been blistered by the sun. Lewis took the plastic container down to the river that was now flowing with sluggish reluctance. They strained the contents through a piece of her dress into an empty beer can and Neil started to dribble it into her mouth. Like the desert, she sucked thirstily at the water.

'We're going to have to take her with us,' Lewis said.

Neil nodded. 'It lengthens the odds some.'

'It's your desert,' Lewis said. 'Tell me about it.'

Neil thought for a while then took one of the unburnt charcoal bricks from the barbecue and drew a large circle with a line running through from top to bottom.

'That's the road. It's maybe ninety to a hundred miles away.' He drew a cross to the left-hand side. 'We're around here. If it was summer we'd be in real trouble.' He waved around. 'This would be a furnace. A lot of stuff lives here – snakes, lizards, the desert hogs we saw earlier, jackrabbits, big-horned sheep, antelope, coyotes, no people.' He looked around for a moment. 'We head east and look for Child's Mountain. There's a big white concrete building on it that stands out for miles. It's an abandoned radar station.' He looked up at the sky.

'What are our chances?' Lewis asked.

'Better than even with the girl.' He paused again. 'As long as it rains again.'

'When do we travel?' Lewis asked.

'Morning and late afternoon,' Neil replied. 'This terrain is too rough to try walking at night.'

'We'd better get started.' Lewis said.

Working together they fashioned a stretcher from the canvas awning and the support poles. When they were satisfied with the job, they loaded Annie and the pieces of equipment they had found in the camp and set off for the return journey to the Range Rover. Carrying the cumbersome burden was exhausting and they made frequent stops to take drinks from the muddy water they carried in the plastic container. By the time they reached the wreck, their shoes were already cut about by the sharp rocks that littered the ground.

The river had subsided to a trickle by now and the Range Rover lay on its side, still filled from the torrent. They prised open the rear door and the water gushed out. Inside were the canvas holdalls. They laid the contents out to dry and set about stripping the wreck.

The seat belts made shoulder straps for the makeshift stretcher. There was a can of lubricating oil which Neil took and gently smeared over Annie's sunburnt body. Her pulse was strong now and her breathing regular. Lewis found a torch in the glove compartment. The water had ruined the mechanism but he unscrewed the lens and tested it for a moment. The point of intensified sunlight it produced was sufficient to start a fire. They ripped out several lengths of wire from the engine and stripped off the plastic coating to make traps.

Neil sliced the leather covers from the seats and made gaiters to protect their lower legs from the cacti they would have to walk through. Then he fashioned crude rubber sandals from the tyres. When he had finished, he held up a pair for Lewis's inspection.

'We'll get through our shoes in no time,' he said. 'The North Vietnamese used to make out OK with these in 'Nam. About twenty million pairs must have walked down the Ho Chi Minh Trail.'

Finally, they were ready. Lewis wore an Arab-style head-dress he had made from a shirt. Neil looked at him in amazement.

'You look like a goddamn Indian,' he said.

'We'd better see if we can get some food into Annie,' Lewis said.

'She's still too weak to chew steak,' Neil replied. 'Chop up a piece real small and mash in some beans. If we mix it with beer we might get it down her.'

They made a small fire and used a couple of beer cans to

cook the mixture. Neil sliced the remaining steaks into thin strips and laid them on a sunbaked rock to dry. They filled every container they could find with water from the trickle that was all that now remained of the torrent that had almost killed them.

Then each took the half of a circle about a mile wide and worked across the ground, carefully looking for the signs of animal runs. When they located one they set a wire coil trap. As they worked their way back to their camp, they gathered dead wood.

Night came and the air gradually cooled. They built a fire and moved Annie closer to the warmth and then each of them ate a small amount of the dried meat and washed it down with beer. After the meal they sat and gazed into the flickering flames.

After a long time of silence Neil suddenly asked:

'What was the worst spot you've been in?'

Lewis poked at the fire with a stick before he answered. 'In a desert.' He looked up at the star-filled sky. 'Not like this one – in the Middle East. It's bleak, nothing but rocks and sand. Seven of us went in to find a group of guerrillas. We'd got information they were raiding a village to kill the head man. We did the job, but when we were coming out their main party hit our chopper with a missile. Three of us got out alive. We had hardly any ammunition. They attacked and, eventually, they overran us. The other two lads were troopers; they saved me till last because I was an officer.'

He paused for a while and then went on in a matter-of-fact voice.

'They chopped them up with swords.'

Lewis stopped again. Neil waited.

'They decided to keep me for the following day. So they pegged me out where they had left the other two. That night the dogs came from the village . . . ' He paused again. 'Anyway, my sergeant, who is an insubordinate bastard called Sandy Patch, came and rescued me.'

He poked the fire and a cloud of sparks rose in the still air.

'Funny, since then I've really hated flying.'

Lewis carefully placed some more wood on the fire and looked over at Neil, who was trimming the handle of a slingshot he was making.

'How about you?'

Lewis guessed what he would say even as he had asked the question. Neil continued to work on the slingshot while he spoke:

'After my wife left me, when I realised she didn't care, it was as if I was sliding down sheet ice. I just couldn't get a handhold. Every time I got close to being sober, I'd remember how she was when I first met her, the good times we had.' He stopped for a while. 'It was the thought of those other guys.'

He finished the slingshot and slid the knife back into the scabbard before he spoke again.

'Just vanity, I guess.'

They both stayed silent for a while, until a voice said: 'I know this is usually my job, but do you think one of you gentlemen could get me a drink?'

Annie had managed to raise herself on one elbow. Lewis mixed her some water and bourbon which she drank with a grimace.

'How do you feel?' Neil asked.

She lay back and looked up at him.

'One summer vacation I worked at Disneyworld. I used to feel like this every night.' She held out a hand. 'Here, see if you can get me to my feet.'

Lewis got her up and she took a few tentative steps.

'What's this goo all over me?' she asked.

'Oil,' Lewis said. 'You've been burnt pretty badly by the sun.'

She tried a lopsided smile.

'My Momma always said I should avoid a tan with my kind of skin.'

'We don't know if they broke anything. Does it hurt much when you move?' Neil said.

She placed a hand on his shoulder.

'Mister, it sure hurts when I just breathe.'

'Lie down,' Neil ordered.

200

She smiled again. 'I'm just a cocktail waitress, honey. You'll have to ask one of the other girls.'

'Do as you're told,' Neil said. 'On your back.'

'Where else?' she said but she obeyed him.

He began to massage her body feeling for any broken bones. She winced occasionally but she never cried out with the pain.

'You're in good shape,' he said eventually.

'Thanks,' she said easily. 'I'll be OK in a while. I've taken worse punishment.'

'When?' Lewis said.

She looked at him in a direct fashion. 'Your voice has changed. You're not American, are you?'

'No, I'm English,' he said.

'I thought so,' she said. She looked at the pair of them crouching by the firelight and the clothing they had fashioned. 'Do you two know what you're doing, or are you just getting it off being Red Indians?'

They didn't answer, but she looked around the camp and then she nodded. 'Thank God for the Boy Scouts of America.'

'Why didn't they kill you?' Lewis asked.

'Reagan wanted to,' she said. 'But Reicher thought it would be more fitting if I was eaten by coyotes and buzzards, so they left me out in the sun.'

'You got lucky. Get some sleep now,' Neil said. 'Tomorrow, Scarlett, we return to Tara.'

They made her a bed by spreading the canvas over chopped brush. Lewis lay awake for a while by the fire, thinking of Hanna. He began to drift into a state of half-sleep, and suddenly in his mind's eye he could see the New Model Army moving in battle order across a winter landscape. It was bitterly cold so that clouds of steam rose from the horses and the mouths of the men. He could hear the creak of leather and the clink of steel, and the grim faces of the troopers turned to look at him as they passed.

The vision was interrupted by the girl calling softly.

'Hey, mister.'

'Yes,' Neil answered quietly.

'Were you two guys going to carry me on the stretcher?'

201

'Sure,' Neil replied.

'It would have slowed you down, wouldn't it?'

'Some.'

'Why were you going to do it then? We all could have died in this desert.'

'Good-looking women are hard to find. We didn't want to waste one.'

There was a silence, then she said: 'Your wife must have been crazy.'

This time Neil didn't answer.

They were awake at first light. Lewis and Neil went to check their traps while Annie rekindled the fire from the embers. By the time they returned she had boiled water and had gone through the clothes in their bags to make for herself a similar outfit to theirs.

Lewis's traps had been empty but Neil's had yielded two jackrabbits. Neil cleaned them and cut one into small pieces which he placed in a hubcap full of water that was boiling on the fire.

'What do you think Reicher will do when he gets back?' Neil asked.

'Send a chopper to look for the Range Rover and check if we're dead,' Lewis replied.

'Yeah, that's what I figured,' Neil said. 'They'll start at their camp and then come along the wash.'

They thought for a while.

'If a chopper lands it'll be over there,' he said indicating the only flattish area of ground near to them.

'Let's see if we can prepare a surprise,' Lewis said.

Two hours later, the helicopter came from the east. It turned a wide curve and hovered over Bull Reicher's campsite, then it began to follow the dried-out wash. Within a few minutes it was hovering over the wreck. The two men inside looked down and saw the remains of a fire and three figures grouped around it, sprawled face down.

They swung away and the pilot settled the chopper on the bare patch of level ground, but kept the engine turning. They both had automatic rifles across their laps.

After a pause, the man accompanying the pilot got out and scuttled from beneath the turning blades. The wind from the downdraught plucked at his clothing.

Lying against a jutting rock that concealed him from the helicopter pilot, Lewis concentrated the light from the sun through the lens of the torch and aimed the needle of light onto a rag that hung from the bourbon bottle.

Petrol he had drained from the Range Rover's tank filled the bottle and soaked into the rag. In seconds the evaporating fumes burst into flames. Holding the Molotov cocktail with great care, Lewis stepped from behind the rock and hurled it into the cockpit of the helicopter. The bottle exploded and the burning rag ignited the petrol. In moments the chopper was a fireball. The other man turned in panic and as he did so, David Neil rose from beneath the canvas sheet that had been covered in earth and stones. The passenger saw what he thought was an Apache warrior as Neil plunged the knife into his body.

Lewis joined Neil and they began to search the body for anything of value. Lewis took the automatic rifle and the bandolier of magazines the dead man had slung across his chest. Neil unbuckled the black leather gunbelt he wore around his waist and buckled it on himself. He took out the revolver, snapped open the chamber to check the load, and then wiped the blade of the knife on the dead man's shirt.

Annie watched them with a certain amount of apprehension. She had been shocked by the violence of the attack.

'He didn't stand a chance,' she said in a voice low with shock.

'That's right,' Neil said without emotion. 'Take a look at him. He's one of the guys who carried you to a rock and spread you out for crowbait. Do you think he came back to tell you he was sorry?' He took hold of her shoulders. She looked into his eyes and he could see how young she was.

'I never saw anyone get killed before.' She turned away from the body. 'Dead people never look like that in the movies.'

Neil pointed towards the three dummies they had made from the extra clothing in their bags.

'That's the movie version,' he said. 'Now people see dummies as the real thing.'

Reginald Tyson stood in the hallway and adjusted the scarf his granddaughter had bought him for Christmas. He set his grey trilby at just the right angle, buttoned and belted his gaberdine raincoat and clipped the poppers at the wrists of his fur-lined gloves. It was only a few minutes' walk from Her Majesty's Stationery Office in Atlantic House across Holborn Circus to Chancery Lane tube station, but it was a bitterly cold evening and his wife, Irene, would nag if he hadn't wrapped up in the correct fashion.

'Goodnight, Reg,' Molly Patterson, a secretary in his department, called out as she swept past in her light macintosh and high heels. She'll catch her death dressed like that, he thought until he saw her stoop to get into her boyfriend's Mini. He stepped out into a biting wind and turned for the station – but a heavy, dark-haired man dressed in a black overcoat stood in front of him.

'Mr Reginald Tyson?' the man asked him politely enough, but there was an edge of authority in the tone that Tyson recognised from his years with the Civil Service.

'Yes,' he replied guardedly.

The man showed an identity card and said, 'My name is Chief Inspector Lear of the Special Branch. We would like you to help us with some inquiries.'

Reginald Tyson felt a terrible dread. It was a fantasy of his that he would be arrested and convicted of some crime of which he was totally innocent, and now his nightmare appeared to have become reality.

'What's it about?' he said in a voice that was already filled with guilt.

'Let's talk in the car, Mr Tyson. We'll be more comfortable there.'

'Am I under arrest?' he said as Inspector Lear guided him across the pavement.

'No, sir. There's nothing to worry about. We just need your help,' the Inspector said and they slid into the back seat of the waiting Rover.

'How long will I be?' Tyson asked in a braver voice. 'My wife is expecting me home at the usual time.'

Inspector Lear lit a small cigar and opened the rear window of the car a fraction so that a thin draught of icy air caught Tyson on the right side of his face. Instinctively he turned up the collar of his raincoat.

'Now don't you worry, Mr Tyson. Your wife has been informed that you have had to work late this evening. She even sent you a message to say that everything is all right and she has gone to babysit for your son and daughter-in-law. Incidentally, your supper is on a low gas in the oven.'

Inspector Lear's words reassured him and the dread passed away to be replaced by another emotion. Lamb stew, Tyson thought, that's what she's got me. Bloody lamb stew. She knows I hate it. He glanced at the policeman who smiled in a friendly manner and suddenly he felt a surge of elation. An adventure! I'm going to have an adventure. To hell with lamb stew! If there was time after the mysterious task he was about to perform he would call in at The Red Lion and have a couple of pork pies. There were bound to be some people there that he knew.

The police car waited to turn right into Gray's Inn Road and Tyson watched the people pouring down the entrance to Chancery Lane tube station.

The driver was clearly annoyed by the heavy traffic and Tyson could feel his bad temper, but he was enjoying himself now. The car was comfortable. The journey could last for ever, as far as he was concerned.

'We're here,' the Inspector said finally.

Tyson looked out at the street. He knew he was somewhere in Bloomsbury but he wasn't sure exactly where. The driver opened the door for him and the Inspector indicated that he should follow him up a short flight of stairs into a rather old building that looked like a private house. They crossed a small hallway to where a uniformed commissionaire nodded in recognition to the Inspector.

'Sergeant Major Watts, this is Mr Tyson. We are expected.'

'Yes sir, Mr Mars said would you go straight up?'

They climbed quite a lot of stairs and eventually reached the top of the house. Inspector Lear knocked and entered a large room with a pitched roof and dormer windows. There was a fireplace with a good fire burning and a lot of furniture that, to Tyson's eye, had seen better days. Books were everywhere, lining the walls and piled on tables and chairs, so that the room had a musty smell that reminded him of a second-hand bookshop.

He thought how his wife would disapprove. She didn't hold with books and had often remarked in the early days of their marriage that they were a trap for dust, and that old books had germs as well.

A group of men were gathered around a table at the end of the room, where an Anglepoise lamp shone down on papers they were studying. Two of the men straightened up from the table.

One of them was tall and dressed like a gentleman. Tyson had been a batman during his National Service and he had retained the ability to tell when a man's clothes had been made in Savile Row. Despite their age these still held the shape that only a good cutter gives to his work. Tyson glanced down at the man's shoes and his judgement was confirmed. They were hand-made Oxfords. Old and good for many more years.

The other man's clothes were expensive but off-the-peg. They looked well on him because he carried himself with importance. He didn't have the self-confidence to slouch like the tall man did.

It was only after he had studied their clothes that Tyson realised the shorter man had a famous face. Roger Kent, Junior Minister, he thought with mounting excitement. Now he was determined to call in at The Red Lion.

'Mr Tyson?' the tall man said. 'How good of you to come at such short notice.' He turned so that the Minister could stand beside him. 'My name is Mars. May I introduce the Right Honourable Roger Kent?'

Tyson shook hands.

'Why don't you take off your coat?' the thin man said and he indicated a young woman with long fair hair who had joined them. 'Can Miss Rose get you anything? A drink, a cup of tea?'

The young lady took his trilby, scarf and raincoat and smiled at him.

'A cup of tea would be very nice. Two sugars, please,' he said, and he sat down on a leather sofa that was before the fire. Roger Kent and Mr Mars sat in two chairs facing him.

'You have signed the Official Secrets Act as a civil servant with Her Majesty's Stationery Office?' Roger Kent said.

'Yes,' Tyson replied. 'Sometimes I have to deal with documents of a secret nature.'

'Yes, we know that, Mr Tyson, and we know that you can be trusted,' Kent said. 'But we must emphasise to you that anything we tell you in this room tonight is of the utmost national security.'

Tyson felt another surge of excitement, followed by a slight sense of disappointment as he realised his trip to The Red Lion would have to be postponed.

The tall man leaned forward and said, 'We understand you were friends with the late John Maynard, Mr Tyson.'

'Yes,' he replied in a puzzled voice. 'John and I knew each other a good many years.'

The tall man paused and exchanged glances with Roger Kent.

'Did you ever visit his darkroom at 25 Lynton Road?'

'Yes,' Tyson said, bewildered. 'Often. We were members of the same photography club.'

'Do you think you could describe the room to us?'

Charlie could see how baffled Tyson was becoming by his questions.

'It was just the attic,' Tyson said. 'There was nothing special about it.'

'Yes,' Charlie Mars said soothingly, 'but we really need to know exactly how it is arranged.'

Tyson was beginning to feel disappointed. He had imagined all sorts of extraordinary possibilities but these questions seemed ridiculous. The girl returned with his cup of tea and he took a few sips before he answered.

'Well, you get up to it by one of those contraptions that lowers from the loft – a sort of folding step-ladder. John had his enlarger and developing tanks against one of the walls or ends of the attic. There was an old sofa under the eaves on one side. He had his record-player up there as well, you know.'

Charlie nodded. 'Yes, he liked to play music without disturbing Mrs Maynard below.'

'That's right,' Tyson said.

'Now can you remember *exactly* how the room was arranged?'

Tyson drank some more tea.

'Not really,' he replied and he could feel their disappointment.

Two other men to whom he had not been introduced had now joined them. One was stocky with thinning red hair, and the other was a good-looking lad with a fair moustache. He looked up at their expectant faces.

'I've got some photographs of it,' he said.

'Photographs?' the others echoed.

'Yes,' he said, putting his empty cup on the book-littered table before him. 'John's wife goes in for amateur dramatics. When she was playing Elvira in *Blithe Spirit* we took a whole series of trick photographs of her with double exposure. You know, so you could see through her. Would they be any help?' he said.

'Where are these photographs?' Charlie Mars asked.

'At home,' Tyson said.

'Could you find them easily?'

'I think so.'

Penny Rose checked her desk and locked the door behind her. She knocked lightly on the door of Charlie Mars's office and put her head round to say goodnight. He was sitting on the sofa watching the fire, with a glass of malt whisky in his hand.

'Goodnight, Penny. Thank you,' he said, and as he spoke the telephone on his desk began to ring.

She started to enter the room to answer it, but he waved her away.

'You go home, I'll get it.'

She smiled gratefully as she closed the door.

'Mars,' he said and Guy Landis's voice came to him.

'Charlie, we've got something here.'

'Yes?' Charlie answered in a preoccupied tone.

'Not the people you're looking for, but a couple of dubious characters coming in.'

'Go on,' Charlie said.

Landis paused and Charlie knew he was taking a drink.

'Remember that fellow Cutter we were watching in the autumn?'

'Marshall Cutter, yes,' Charlie said with a faint stirring of interest.

'That's him. Well, two men have just come in from Frankfurt. They had his photograph in their baggage, and one of the other American – Pearce.'

'Why did you stop them?' Charlie asked.

'Routine drug search,' Landis replied. 'But Lloyd was on duty and he saw the snapshots in their personal possessions.'

'Where are they now?' Charlie asked.

'We've still got them on hold. They're not suspicious yet. What do you want me to do?'

'Let them go, but make sure Lloyd doesn't lose them.'

Charlie thought for a few minutes after the call, and then flipped through a leather-bound address book on his desk. He dialled a number, and after several rings an answering machine clicked on and Hanna Pearce's voice informed him that she was out at dinner for the evening but could be contacted at another number. Charlie redialled, and got the Connaught Hotel.

After a short wait Hanna came on the line.

'It's Charlie, Hanna. I'm sorry to disturb your evening.'

'Have you heard from Lewis?' she asked quickly.

'No, not yet. Actually I'm ringing on another matter. Do you know if Marshall Cutter is in this country?'

Hanna laughed. 'Holmes, you amaze you. I'm about to have dinner with him and my parents.'

Charlie paused long enough for her to sense that something was not right.

'What is it, Charlie?' she said in a flat voice.

'I'll explain later,' Charlie said. 'Are you in the bar?'

'Yes,' she said.

'All of you?'

'Yes, we are.'

'Stay there,' he ordered. 'Do you understand?'

'I understand,' she said.

He rang off and picked up an old-fashioned red telephone and dialled two numbers. The call was answered instantly.

'Duty officer,' a voice answered.

'There's going to be a possible assassination attempt at the Connaught Hotel. There are four people in the bar. Dr Hanna Pearce, her mother and father, and Marshall Cutter. Their pictures are on file. Get a team to the hotel right away and make sure Signals are on the ball.

'Tim Lloyd is trailing a couple of suspects from Heathrow. If he calls in he may need back-up. Got that?'

'Yes, sir,' the duty officer said in an emotionless voice.

'Bring them in,' Charlie said.

When he had replaced the receiver Charlie took a sheet of plain white paper from the drawer of his desk and began to doodle. Soon the paper was covered with odd words and hieroglyphics. He gazed down at it for a while and then screwed it into a ball and dropped it into the leather waste-paper basket beneath the desk before he dialled a long series of numbers on the telephone.

After a few minutes he was speaking to General Harry Selig.

'Charlie, I hope this is important,' the Marine said. 'I just got pulled out of a reception line for some bunch of African potentates. The President looked at me as if I'd farted while they were playing *Hail to the Chief*.'

'It's the real thing, Harry,' Charlie said. 'Can you get your computer magicians to track something for me?'

'Sure,' Selig answered and Charlie Mars dictated his requirements.

When he had finished, Charlie could hear General Selig passing on his request.

'That OK, Charlie?'

'Excellent,' he said and hung up the telephone.

Immediately the red telephone rang.

'Signals, sir. Lloyd reports that the two men he is trailing stopped for just a few minutes at an hotel in Earl's Court. They got into a waiting taxi and they both had new luggage.'

'Good,' Charlie said.

He flashed the signal for the duty officer.

'Tell Tim Lloyd's back-up team to take the two suspects.'

'Right, sir. Incidentally, the four people from the Connaught Hotel will be here in a few minutes.'

'My secretary's gone home. Will you show them up when they arrive?' Charlie said, then he got up from his desk and shovelled more fuel onto his fire.

When the duty officer showed the group into his room, Charlie was sitting on his scruffy leather chesterfield with his feet on the coffee table. He took his hands from his pockets, got to his feet and ushered his guests to the seats he had available. Hanna had been in the room before, but Mr and Mrs Pearce and Marshall Cutter were clearly intrigued by the clutter of battered furniture and mountains of books.

'Would you care for a drink?' Charlie asked. 'The coffee would be instant but I've got a decent whisky, or sherry if you prefer.'

When he had distributed the drinks, Charlie stood before the fireplace with a malt whisky in his hand and addressed himself to Marshall Cutter, who was fiddling with a large gold wristwatch that Charlie could see had a rather complicated dial.

'It seems you're in danger again, Mr Cutter,' Charlie said in a mild voice. 'Have you any idea who pursues you with such relentless passion?'

'None at all,' Cutter said. 'My people have been on the job for some time.' He cradled the glass in both his hands and looked to Pearce. 'Hell, we play rough in the States, but I don't know that I've damaged someone enough for them to go this far.'

211

'How much do you have to do with the Jericho Institute these days?' Charlie said in the same easy tone.

Cutter looked surprised at the question.

'Nothing,' he said. 'Lawrence Brady took control a couple of years ago. He's doing a damn fine job as well. The profits have been good since he started.'

Charlie placed his empty glass on the mantelpiece and his chin came down as he thought.

'How long are you staying in the country, Mr Cutter?' he asked eventually.

'Just till tomorrow,' Cutter replied. 'This evening was a farewell dinner.'

'I think I ought to warn you that we believe the Jericho Institute could be connected in some way with these threats to your life.'

'That's crazy,' Cutter said in a forceful tone. 'There's no advantage to them in having me out of the way. Hell, Brady has complete control.'

'Nonetheless,' Charlie said, 'we feel there is a definite link. Tell me about Lawrence Brady,' he went on. 'Do you know him, Mr Pearce?'

Pearce shook his head. 'No, I've not had the pleasure.'

Charlie turned to Cutter, who sat back in the deep leather armchair before he answered.

'There's not much to know. Brady is a man in his late fifties, a widower, no children. He made a considerable amount of money mining in South America and Australia. You may or may not know that I had difficulties a few years ago.'

Cutter hesitated and Charlie Mars didn't speak, so he continued.

'Marshall Electronics suffered a catastrophe. Our Californian factory was destroyed – a fire.'

'Weren't you insured?' Charlie said sympathetically.

'Sure, for the buildings and equipment, but we lost four of our best people and the work they had been engaged on for three years. It was all there in the laboratories and on the computers. The work of a generation gone. It was touch and go for a while until Brady came up with the cash for the Jericho Institute.'

Cutter turned at this point and held out a hand towards Pearce.

'And an old friend let me join him in a very successful venture.'

Charlie looked towards Pearce who seemed embarrassed by the gesture.

'Hell, Marshall has been as much responsible for the success of the Rainbow Division as anyone. Perhaps more than anyone, I'd say.'

Charlie suddenly straightened up from where he lounged against the mantelpiece and created the impression that he was about to go on to other things.

'The duty officer will tell you where we have made arrangements for you to stay,' he explained to Cutter. 'We will make sure of your safety.'

Then he turned to Hanna.

'I've got to go to a party, and Sybil is away at the moment. I don't suppose you would care to come?' he said with a certain persuasion.

'Why, I'd be delighted, Charlie,' Hanna replied. 'Where is it?'

'Chiswick,' Charlie said, 'but you'll know some of the other guests.'

Chapter Nine

Pamela Hurst closed the door of 27 Lynton Road behind her and trod the snow-packed path with care. She carried an umbrella to protect her newly-set hair from the swirls of snow, and had tied a chiffon scarf over the carefully arranged ringlets as an extra precaution. Her strapless silver dress was low at both front and back so she had thrown her husband's raincoat over her shoulders, and she wore a pair of wellington boots rather than the silver-lamé shoes she had left by the radiator in the entrance hall of her house.

Only the darkness and the shortness of her journey permitted her to venture outside in such unflattering costume – and the knowledge that she was only going to visit another woman. She unlatched the gate to Number 25, stood in the scant protection of the tiny porch and pressed the bell twice. Wind was gushing about the roadway and, despite the umbrella and the scarf, she was sure her hair would be in ruins.

She began to shiver as she pressed the bell once again. The door opened enough for Pamela to see Mrs Maynard standing in the dim hallway.

At first, Pamela thought she must be ill; her hair was unkempt and she looked drawn and tired.

'It's me, Mrs Maynard – Pamela Hurst from next door,' she said brightly.

'Yes,' the woman said and her hand clutched the housecoat close to her throat as if to protect herself.

'I just wanted to tell you that we're having a little party tonight, and there may be some noise. I do hope you won't mind.'

214

Mrs Maynard shook her head and Pamela looked at her with concern.

'Would you like to pop in later? It's just some of Anthony's friends from the cricket club. We've had a bit of luck with the business and we thought we'd celebrate. After all, it is New Year's Eve.'

Mrs Maynard shook her head again.

'No thank you, Pamela. I'm afraid I'm not feeling too well, but it was kind of you to ask,' she said with a thin smile.

'Well, if you change your mind, just pop in,' Pamela said cheerfully. 'Happy New Year.'

'Happy New Year,' Mrs Maynard replied, and she had closed the door before her neighbour reached the gate. Moments later Pamela let herself into Number 27, quickly slipped on her silver shoes and thrust the umbrella, raincoat and wellington boots into the cupboard under the stairs.

In the living-room her husband Anthony was blowing up a balloon. He tied a knot in the neck with a deft movement and placed it on the sofa where a collection of others gently bounced together. He studied her while he began to blow up another balloon and realised how excited she was. The extraordinary events of the day had clearly stimulated her so that her eyes looked wider, and the new dress emphasised her excellent figure. She took off the chiffon scarf and shook her head before the mirror where she had written HAPPY NEW YEAR in large letters with an old lipstick.

'Do you like my hair like this?' she asked as she patted the ringlets.

He put down the balloon and stood behind her to encircle her waist with his arms. She looked at his face reflected in the mirror and recognised his expression.

'Not now, darling, there isn't time,' she said quickly.

He caught her bare arms and pulled her back towards him just as the bell chimed. She disengaged herself and made for the door. As she did so, the sound of squeakers and toy trumpets came to her. Two men stood on the doorstep in party hats. They both held cardboard boxes of drink in their arms.

'Come on, Jacko, Barbara,' the heavier man called back to

a couple at the gate who also carried boxes and were wearing similar hats. They came laughing up the path with their loads.

Pamela Hurst held the door open as they passed her and proceeded down the passageway to the kitchen, where they placed the boxes on the table. Charlie Mars adjusted the joker's hat that he wore and removed his overcoat.

'Mrs Hurst,' he said as she joined them in the kitchen, 'how charming you look. May I introduce Dr Hanna Pearce, Chief Inspector Lear and Mr Reginald Tyson.'

Pamela shook hands and noticed that Mr Tyson looked flushed and a little bewildered.

'There will be lots more coming, Mrs Hurst,' Charlie explained. 'Inspector Lear will check everyone at the door in case outsiders are carried away by the festive spirit and attempt to gatecrash the party.'

Anthony Hurst joined them, and Pamela noticed the glance he shot towards the dark-haired woman, who had now removed her coat and didn't look at all like a doctor to her.

'What exactly do you want us to do?' Hurst said.

There was a crackling sound from one of the cardboard boxes and Charlie Mars reached in and took out a walkie-talkie.

'Excuse me,' he said and muttered a series of brief instructions into the piece of equipment. When he was finished he turned to them again. 'If you could have a party on the ground floor, Mr and Mrs Hurst, we will get on with our task. A lot of people will be arriving soon. Some of them will remain downstairs with you and some will be busy in the attic.'

He watched as Anthony Hurst reached over and put his arm protectively around his wife's bare shoulders.

'And please don't worry. I can assure you that you will be perfectly safe.'

Anthony Hurst shrugged, then took his arm from around his wife and reached into one of the cardboard boxes and drew out a bottle of gin.

'In that case, would anyone care for a drink?'

'That's the spirit,' Charlie Mars said, and he turned to Inspector Lear. 'How about the photographs?'

A brown manilla envelope was produced by Mr Tyson, and Charlie took out half a dozen enlargements which he examined under one of the spotlights that illuminated the kitchen.

'Yes,' he said softly, 'I see.' He laid the pictures on a butcher's block that stood next to the door and continued to study them until the doorbell chimed again.

'Let me get it,' Inspector Lear said, moving with surprising swiftness for a man of his bulk.

Four noisy youths in casual clothes and carrying guitar cases passed him at the door, followed by six others manhandling black-painted amplifiers and pieces of electronic equipment. Most of them continued up the stairs, but two men remained to unpack a tape-deck and speakers which they placed against the wall that divided the two houses. They located the power points and, at a nod from Charlie Mars, they switched on the sounds of a pop group warming up their instruments.

More people began to arrive. Some behaved as partygoers, accepted drinks and mingled in the living-room, making small-talk and devouring the bowls of nuts and crisps. Others climbed the stairs. Two groups had arrived with carry-cots. Pamela Hurst followed one pair up the stairs on her way to use the bathroom, and through an open bedroom door she watched as a young man with short fair hair and a blond moustache took a gun from the carry-cot and snapped a magazine into the heel of the handle. It was a familiar action to her; she had seen it done many times on television. So it was a moment before she appreciated, with a slight shock, that this was actually happening in her own house.

Below, the sounds of the group tuning their instruments gave way to music so loud it seemed to cause the entire building to vibrate. As Pamela Hurst rejoined her guests in the living-room, she noticed that her husband was paying particular attention to the dark-haired doctor. She had to admit the woman was beautiful. Even though she wore a plain dark skirt and a blue silk blouse, Pamela could tell the clothes were expensive and worn with the same unconscious style that professional models learned from observing the rich.

She looked around the room to make sure that everyone was attended to, and then realised with a feeling of slight foolishness that this was not a normal party at all. The guests were there to work; they had to seem to enjoy themselves. As she had no duties as a hostess she suddenly felt liberated.

To hell with it, she thought, I'm going to have a good time.

The only person who did not seem to be shouting conversation above the noise of the tape was Mr Tyson. He stood in the corner next to a table loaded with food, morosely eating segments of pork pie. Pamela walked up to him.

'Would you like to dance?' she called out above the thundering music.

'Sorry?' he mouthed back and cocked his head towards her. She pointed to the centre of the room.

'Dance?' she mimed.

A look of astonishment passed across his face, followed by a grin of pleasure, and he put down his glass of red wine and took her in his arms. Above them, Charlie Mars stood on the narrow landing. He was drinking a cup of black coffee and yearning for a cigarette. Cables snaked around his feet and rose like vines into the open attic above him. An extension speaker from the party below was blasting sound into the roof while two technicians attached sensors to the dividing wall between the two houses.

Outside, in the swirling snow, black-clad figures swarmed on the outside of Number 25. Charlie walked into the larger bedroom, which overlooked Lynton Road. It was a strange sight. The double bed had been dismantled and was propped against the wall. In the cleared space a mass of electronic equipment was being fussed over by a patient young man who occasionally beat time to the rock music as he adjusted various tuning devices on the TV display screens he had set up on Pamela Hurst's large Victorian dressing-table.

Charlie leaned against a stripped-pine wardrobe and waited.

'How is it going?' he asked.

'Nearly there, sir,' the young man said without looking up from his work. Finally he leaned back and reached into his pocket for a packet of cigarettes. He lit one and inhaled with evident satisfaction. Charlie could have struck him out of envy.

'Ok,' the technician said to himself and reached down to a switch. The screens came alive and produced a series of glowing images. Charlie glanced up and saw that Hanna Pearce had joined them.

'I hope you don't mind,' she said. 'I thought I ought to get away from Mr Hurst for a while.'

Charlie smiled and beckoned her over. She stood next to him and looked down at the glowing screens.

'Do you understand this stuff?' Charlie asked and Hanna nodded.

'I think so. It's a thermal picture of the house next door. You can read the temperature of various parts of the rooms from those screens.'

'Clever, isn't it?' Charlie said.

'We use it for locating diseases.'

'That's what we're using it for,' the young man said, still without taking his eyes from the screens. Hanna was reminded of Lewis by this quiet remark.

Gordon Meredith entered the room. He was wearing a black cotton combat suit. Around his waist was a holster and ammunition webbing.

'We should have sound in a few minutes,' he said to the technician.

Sandy Patch followed him. They both studied the photographs Tyson had provided. These had been Sellotaped to the mattress propped against the wall.

'What do you think?' Charlie said. There was a pause.

'Not great,' Gordon said.

'Why?' Charlie asked with an edge of concern in his voice.

'They're all packed together in there,' Sandy Patch said.

'Too close for comfort,' Gordon added.

'Will it be dangerous?' Hanna asked.

'Not to us,' Gordon replied. 'The trick is keeping three of them alive.'

Charlie reached out and took a cigarette from the packet on the dressing-table. He lit it and drew a long pull of smoke into his lungs. Then he glanced at his watch.

'Let's leave it until midnight,' he said. 'We might be able to work something out.'

The chimes of Big Ben began to toll the New Year, and at the final stroke 'Auld Lang Syne' hammered out. The party guests sang lustily, and at a signal from Charlie Mars the sound system was switched off.

The front door of Number 27 opened and a conga line of cheering people came out into the snow of Lynton Road. The line passed up the pathway of Number 25, and the man in the lead began to ring the bell as the crowd chanted and swayed.

Wearing a pair of headphones, Charlie Mars crouched forward over the monitor screen, in the bedroom. He could hear a conversation in German. Then two women, whom he could identify as Joyce Maynard and her mother, explained in strained voices that it was a British ritual to knock up neighbours for the New Year.

'It's working,' the technician said, as they traced two shimmering images of light which left the attic and began to descend the staircase inside Number 25.

Sandy Patch and Gordon Meredith watched the screens across Charlie's shoulder. The technician swung away from the screen and tapped the photographs.

'Those are ours – here and here.'

Sandy and Gordon swarmed back into the attic and waited by the dividing wall. Below them Mrs Maynard opened the door of Number 25, and the conga line pushed past her and avalanched into the hallway. Mrs Maynard was snatched out of the doorway and bundled back into the crowd and the startled man in shirtsleeves, who was standing behind her, holding a shiny revolver, crashed back into the hallway as he was struck in the throat by the elbow of the man who led the conga.

Reaching across his body, Tim Lloyd wrenched open the cupboard beneath the stairs, located the mains switch and threw the lever.

'Lights out,' the technician shouted as he monitored the

220

screen which now showed a slight fade as the electricity supply in Number 25 died away.

'Go,' Charlie Mars shouted up into the attic.

In the total blackness of the attic at Number 25, Joyce Maynard crouched on the sofa that lay under the angle of the roof and clutched for her companion. Instinctively she pulled Dr Lionel Reece down, so they both sprawled on the floor. Suddenly there was a shattering crash and Joyce felt a series of numbing blows as bricks from the dividing wall between the houses thudded down upon her braced back. The explosion was followed by a light of searing intensity, so bright she could see the weave of the dust-covered carpet her face was pressed against. She shut her eyes tightly.

The flare that Sandy Patch had fired burned with a fierce white light, blinding the three men who stood frozen in the glare. With their own eyes protected from the light by dark goggles, Sandy and Gordon leapt into the rubble-strewn attic. One of the men swung a stubby sub-machine gun towards the sound, and Gordon's shots hit him in the left shoulder, broke his collar-bone and grazed his throat. Sandy held his sub-machine gun in both hands and stepped one pace forward. The two remaining men held handguns, but they were so dazzled by the burning flare that they could do nothing to stop Sandy clubbing them to the floor.

The flare fizzled out and, in the dimness that followed, Dr Reece and Joyce Maynard felt themselves being gently guided by careful hands.

When gradually sight returned, Joyce found herself in the bedroom of her childhood with her mother's arms around her.

'Happy New Year, Joyce,' Charlie Mars said in a relieved voice.

She reached out and took the mug of tea that was offered to her. It was very sweet.

'I'm afraid I don't take sugar,' she said and tried to hand the mug back to the policewoman.

'Doctor's orders,' Charlie said. 'It's supposed to be good for shock.'

'Here, you have it, Mum,' Joyce said, handing her the mug, and Mrs Maynard took it without argument.

Joyce looked around the small room and Charlie followed her gaze. There was only the single bed she sat on, a white-wood dressing table and a matching wardrobe. The wallpaper was pale blue with small pink intertwined flowers.

'My dad decorated my room like this for me when I was fourteen,' she said gently. She reached up and touched a spot on the wallpaper where there was a discoloration. 'I stuck a picture of David Bowie up here. Dad went mad.'

She looked round at Mrs Maynard, who had not drunk any of the tea.

'Do you remember, Mum?'

Slowly, as they watched, tears filled the older woman's eyes and she nodded her reply. Joyce clasped her in her arms.

From the next room Charlie Mars could hear the high-pitched, frightened voice of Dr Reece.

'Who is in authority here? Please let me speak to him.'

Charlie smiled reassuringly at Joyce and went into the next room. There Reece stood with Hanna Pearce, who was attempting to light the quivering cigarette in his mouth.

'I'm in charge, Dr Reece,' Charlie said in what he hoped was a soothing voice. 'What can I do for you?'

Charlie could see Reece was close to hysteria. He kept running a nervous hand through the long, straight hair that flopped over his eyes. After each attempt to thrust back his hair he would scratch with the same hand beneath the left side of his neck, just under the jawbone. The other hand seemed to flutter about his face as he smoked the cigarette Hanna had managed to light for him.

'It's my wife. She's in danger,' Reece said.

Charlie exchanged glances with Hanna.

'Your wife is quite safe, Dr Reece,' Charlie said.

'Where is she?' Reece said, and they could see he was close to nervous collapse.

'She's in our protection with George Selby. They're both out of danger.'

'Who are you?' Reece demanded. He dropped the cigarette and Hanna bent down to retrieve it from the carpet.

'We're civil servants,' Charlie said in the same soothing voice. 'As soon as you've answered some questions you will be with your wife.'

Hanna stood just beyond Reece's line of vision and slowly shook her head at Charlie.

'All right, Dr Reece,' Charlie said. 'We'll arrange for you to join your wife immediately.'

The policewoman who had been distributing tea now joined them in the room. She took Reece firmly by the shoulders and guided him to a chair.

'Just sit down here for a minute, love,' she said and Reece meekly did as he was told. Charlie and Hanna went out and stood on the landing.

'Shock,' Hanna said. 'You won't get any sense from him for a while.'

'Damn,' Charlie said and he slapped the banister to emphasise his frustraton.

'I'll go and see how Joyce and her mother are,' Hanna said.

Charlie nodded and looked down at the cigarette that burned in her hand, but he resisted the impulse to inhale a lungful of smoke.

Sandy Patch came up the stairs carrying a large, squarish black briefcase. He held it out to Charlie.

'The bomb boys just opened this outside,' he said. 'We found it in the attic. It's full of papers.'

Charlie took the briefcase from Sandy and made his way back to the bedroom at next-door, where the scanners had been only a few minutes before. They had already gone. The bed was back in place and Tim Lloyd was placing the ornaments back on the dressing-table.

Charlie sat on the bed and took a wad of papers from the case. They were telex printouts, but on a brief examination he could make no sense of the random language. They seemed to be holiday instructions and time schedules. There was also a sheaf of drawings. Charlie put them to one side and continued to study the random words. Meredith put his head around the door.

'Inspector Lear is just leaving, sir. Do you want to say thank-you?'

Charlie stood up.

'Yes, I'll be right there. Keep your eye on this stuff,' he said to Gordon.

Inspector Lear was putting on his overcoat in the hallway.

'I'm going now, Charlie,' he said above the din that still came from the living-room. 'I'll drop Mr Tyson off. The rest of my team are still enjoying the party,' he said, indicating the noise that showed no signs of abating.

'They deserve it,' Charlie said. 'They did a fine job.'

Inspector Lear grinned. 'Remember that next time we have a cock-up,' he said as he opened the front door.

Charlie grinned back.

'The snow's stopped. Come on, Mr Tyson,' the Inspector said to the swaying figure who had been leaning against the wall.

Charlie realised that the other man was very drunk.

'Happy New Year,' Lear called as he helped Tyson through the open door.

'Happy New Year,' Charlie said and he closed the door behind them.

He looked into the living-room, where the music had suddenly become quieter. Couples swayed close together. In the darkness he could see Pamela Hurst with her husband's arms around her. Charlie stood alone in the hallway for a moment and thought of Sybil. Then he climbed the stairs, back to the bedroom.

Joyce and Hanna were there with Gordon. Joyce was sitting on the bed scanning the wad of telexes and making notes on sheets of paper that had been torn from an old exercise book. She was passing these to Hanna, who sat at the dressing table. Beside her were the diagrams Charlie had glanced at briefly.

'What have you got?' Charlie asked, but Joyce held up a silencing hand without looking up from the work she was doing.

'Give us a few minutes,' she said in a preoccupied voice.

Charlie motioned for Gordon to join him on the landing. He could still taste the cigarette he had started earlier.

He patted his clothing in the vain hope that he might have

224

something he could smoke, and then he remembered that a new year had begun and he silently renewed his resolution about tobacco.

'Where's Sandy?' Charlie asked.

'He had a party to go to. I told him to push off,' Gordon replied.

'What about you?' Charlie said.

Gordon smiled. 'Janet's already downstairs. I'll join her in a minute.'

'You chaps did well,' Charlie said.

'No we didn't,' Gordon said flatly. 'We fumbled the flare after the explosion. It cost us a few seconds – we could have killed everybody.'

'Don't be too hard on yourself. It worked.'

Gordon shrugged. 'We have to be hard. It's the way we stay alive.'

'Go on,' Charlie said with a certain gruff warmth. 'Join the party.'

He watched Gordon walk down the stairs, and a soft voice behind him called his name. It was Hanna. He rejoined them in the bedroom and the two women looked up from the papers they had before them. He could tell from their expressions that it was serious.

'Bad news?' he said and Hanna nodded.

'This isn't my field but it's simple enough for anyone with a rudimentary knowledge of chemistry to follow. It really terrifies me that anyone could be so irresponsible.'

'Explain,' Charlie said curtly.

'Did you know that all kitchens contain bacteria, no matter how houseproud the housewife is?'

'No,' Charlie said. 'I thought only dirty kitchens had germs.'

'You can't kill them all. No one can. Luckily the average human being is pretty tough and can cope with the kind of bacteria we all have to face in our daily lives.'

She paused and looked down at the notes she had been working on.

'Dr Lionel Reece has discovered a way to mutate the bacteria you find in an ordinary kitchen stove. What's more,

225

you complete the process by cooking them in the very stove you find them in.'

'So how dangerous does this make the bacteria?' Charlie said. Hanna paused again.

'I would need my notes checked by someone who was a specialist in this field.'

'Give me your opinion, Hanna – in layman's terms,' he said, and she looked up in surprise at the firmness in his voice.

'It would be like turning the germ of the common cold into something roughly equivalent to the Black Death,' she said quietly.

There was a silence in the room and from below they could hear the partygoers singing 'Auld Lang Syne' once again.

Lewis and the girl Annie followed David Neil's footsteps in single file along the dry river bed. They stayed close together as they moved through a landscape that had begun to pulse with colour. It was as if a magician had passed a wand across the terrain where the water from the storm had unlocked the desert flowers that now studded every plant they could see. But the lushness of their surroundings was an illusion. Despite this rainbow of colours, the land was already dry again.

Neil stopped and they looked down from the embankment to the bed of the wash. They had been following the dry river all day as it cut its way through the landscape towards the east. Now it turned sharply and headed north. Instinctively, Lewis and Neil looked at the white plastic container which was about one-third full of cloudy water. The sun was getting low but it still burned wherever it touched their skin.

'Shall I make a fire?' Annie said.

'I'll do it,' Neil said easily. 'We only want a small one, made with very dry wood.'

'I can do that,' she said.

'OK,' Neil replied. 'Make it there.' He indicated a hollow place tucked beneath the east side of a rock formation. The

226

girl studied the spot for a moment, then she began to search for tinder.

Neil sank to his haunches and looked east. Lewis squatted down beside him.

'This is it, then?'

Neil nodded. 'Last water stop we can rely on.'

They left Annie on the higher ground, searching for wood, and they slipped down the side of the wash. Slowly they walked to the point where the river bed turned. They crouched down close to the outer bank and, using the knife and a couple of beer cans, they began to dig in the soft earth. At first it was bone dry but gradually they began to scoop out oozing mud. Eventually they had made a wide hole that slowly filled with scummy dark brown water. Neil scooped up a palmful and tasted it cautiously.

'Not bad,' he said with a grimace. Lewis stood up and looked towards the setting sun. The skyline had turned to crimson, and cast a glow like a great fire across the desert.

'We'll drink as much as we can tonight and in the morning,' Neil said. 'After that it's luck and the power of prayer.'

Lewis drank some more of the water before he spoke.

'I calculate they'll be with us by about mid-morning tomorrow.'

Neil had begun to strain the muddy water through a piece of material into the plastic drum. 'I think you're right. They'll be travelling lighter than us, with a chopper in support.'

Lewis gazed across the desert, where the light was turning from coral to Prussian blue.

'We'll wait for them around here, near the water.'

'Let's go and take a look,' Neil said.

Annie sat crosslegged on a flat rock and watched them as they returned to her. Lewis passed her the water.

'Drink as much as you can,' he said.

'I thought you drank as little as possible in the desert,' she said.

'The more you've got inside you, the slower you'll dehydrate,' Neil told her.

227

She took the container and began to drink steadily. They watched her with concern until she looked up at them with a certain exasperation.

'I'm not a horse, you know,' she said.

They turned away and began to busy themselves with the equipment. Lewis checked the contents of the canvas roll-up he had carried throughout the day. The rifle which he had propped against a rock slid over and fell into dusty dried earth around the base. Annie noticed that Lewis was unconcerned.

'You don't take much care of that rifle, mister,' she said.

Lewis glanced up. She pointed down to where the weapon lay in the dust. Lewis grinned.

'What do you know about guns?' he asked, but there was no challenge in his voice. She picked up the rifle and cradled it in her arms.

'My daddy had a hunting rifle he cared about more than anything in the world,' she said, and he could hear the bitterness as she spoke. 'I saw him kiss it more times than he did my mother.'

Lewis took the rifle from her and carelessly laid it aside.

'That's a modern assault rifle with a built-in sniper-scope,' Lewis explained. 'It was designed so you could run over it with a tank or bury it in sand or snow. All you have to do is give it a shake to clear out the barrel and it will still fire. Guns have changed a lot since your daddy's day.'

Neil came and sat next to them, and unwrapped the dried meat. They each took a piece and began to chew on the fibrous strips.

'What are you going to do about those guys coming after us?' Annie said.

'What guys?' Neil said.

'Come on,' she said flatly. 'You're treating me like a horse again. I saw that helicopter to the south.'

'Maybe it wasn't looking for us,' Neil said.

The girl took a drink of the cloudy water before she answered.

'Then why didn't you signal to it with the mirror you keep in your pocket?'

Lewis and Neil remained silent, so she continued.

'It was bigger than the last one they sent. That means more people on board. They'll be tracking us – at least, that's my guess.'

Lewis took the container from her and drank before he passed it to Neil. He swilled some of the water around his mouth and spat it out.

'That's my guess, too,' he said to her. 'Have they got trackers who can do that?' he asked Neil.

'If they use Indians. There are still some who know how.'

He stood up and climbed to the top of the rock that rose above their campfire.

'Can you see anything?' Lewis said.

'Come and take a look,' Neil said, and Lewis climbed up and joined him.

Neil pointed to the west and Lewis saw the pinpoint of light that marked the campfire of their pursuers.

'They must be pretty confident to light up like that,' Neil said softly.

'I'm never that confident,' Lewis said.

'Nor me,' Neil replied.

They stayed watching the distant fire for a while.

'We'll have to hit them hard,' Lewis said. 'Otherwise they've got all the cards.'

Neil nodded.

'Are you staying here?' Lewis asked.

'Yeah, for a while,' Neil said in the same soft voice.

'I'll be with Annie,' Lewis said.

He scrambled down to where she sat by the fire with her legs drawn up to her chin, massaging her feet.

'How are you?' he asked.

She looked up at him. 'I've been in better shape.'

'Are your feet troubling you?'

She grinned. 'You sure speak nice.' Then she shook her head. 'They're OK.' She straightened out her legs. 'Talk to me some more.'

'What about?'

'Anything. Tell me about your home town. Where you lived when you were a boy.'

Lewis looked away from the fire and up at the sky. He could feel the desert losing the heat of the day.

'My father was in the army. I didn't have a home town. My sister and I travelled with them. Then we went to school in Britain.'

She waited and then questioned him again.

'Did you go to a fancy private school?'

Lewis smiled. 'No, my mother was a school teacher when she met my father. Some friends of hers were teachers. I lived with them for a time and went to the local school.'

'Didn't your daddy want you to go to a fancy school?'

'No,' Lewis said, 'he went to a fancy school and he hated it.'

'Did you say you had a sister?'

'Yes, a younger sister.'

'I've got a sister, too. Do you want to see a picture of her?' She held out the locket that hung around her neck and Lewis opened it. In the light from the fire he looked at the two faces. 'That's my mother and that's my sister, Carrie.'

Lewis looked at the pictures for a moment, and then stirred the fire till it glowed brighter.

'Where are they now?' he asked.

She took back the locket and looked down at the photographs. 'My mother is dead. I don't know where Carrie is.' She snapped the locket shut and put it carefully inside her shirt. 'Carrie used to work at Kate's. She was a cocktail waitress as well. I was working in San Diego when I got a call from her. She said she'd been invited to this big party and she'd met the boss, a guy called Brady, and he'd asked her to go to Los Angeles with him for the weekend. I got a call from her, and then nothing. I haven't spoken to her since.'

'What happened?' Lewis said.

She shrugged. 'I don't know. I got a couple of postcards but they didn't say where she was.'

'What about the postmarks?'

She rubbed her brow slowly. 'They were both from Los Angeles.' She paused for a while and then she said: 'I think something has happened to her. I had a feeling . . . '

'So that's why you got a job at Kate's?'

She nodded, then raised her head, and he could see that her eyes were full of tears.

'Do you think something bad has happened to her?'

Before Lewis could answer, Neil sat down beside them.

'We'll have to be ready by first light,' he said, and he curled up and seemed to be asleep immediately.

The girl waited for Lewis to answer but he did not say anything. Eventually she also lay down to sleep. Lewis stayed awake for a time thinking about the face of the girl in the locket.

David Neil could see the two figures while they were still a good way off. One wore a pale-blue shirt and a wide-brimmed hat. The other was thin and sticklike. They both moved with a shuffling gait, more than a fast walk, not quite a run.

'They must be crazy jogging in this heat,' Annie said.

'They're Indians,' Neil replied. 'Yaquis, they know the desert.'

'Can they really track people?' she asked.

'My wife had a silk dress once,' Neil said. 'It was pink. Right down to the floor. We were going to a dance. She looked great to me, but she said she couldn't go because there was a grease spot on the hem the size of a pinhead.'

He nodded towards the figures in the distance.

'The desert is like that dress to the Indians. They know every part of it. When someone like us has walked across it, they can spot it like she could the grease.'

'I've never heard of Yaquis,' Annie said. 'Are they like Papagos?'

Neil continued to look towards the Indians. 'No, the Papagos are farmers. The Yaquis came up from Mexico, and taught the Apaches how to fight when they reached here from Canada.'

'Canada?' Lewis repeated.

Neil turned to him. 'Sure. Indians moved about a lot. The plains Indians came from the east.'

They turned back and watched. The figures came on and then suddenly stopped.

'They've seen us,' Neil said. 'Stand up.'

They emerged from the shade of the canvas awning they had draped over some scrub and stood on the rock. The Indians waited for a few minutes and then came on at the same pace. Neil and Annie stood quite still and the Indians stopped about twelve feet from them.

The one in the shirt was quite young. His face was smooth under a wide-brimmed black hat with a rounded crown. He wore jeans and moccasins with leggings up to the knee. Around his waist was a Magnum revolver in a heavy leather holster, with a walkie-talkie slung to it. His companion was old and nearly naked. He wore a breech-clout and long moccasins. There seemed to be no flesh on his body – just muscle covered with dark leatherlike skin. They both stood quite still, their faces expressionless, waiting.

'My friend is pointing a rifle at you. He never misses,' Neil said in a quiet, unemotional voice. The young Indian's hand moved a fraction towards the butt of the Magnum. Without taking his eyes from Neil, the old man raised his hand in restraint.

'This business is not your concern,' Neil said. 'Leave the radio and go.'

Annie could now see the helicopter low on the horizon.

'They called them,' she said. Neil nodded.

The old Indian took the walkie-talkie from the boy's belt and laid it on the ground. The girl looked at the old man's face and thought she could detect an expression of approval as he studied Neil. He spoke rapidly in a guttural dialect and the young boy said in faultless English, 'My grandfather says their helicopter is armed with heavy-calibre machine guns. He also said we wish you no harm.'

Neil studied them for a moment then he waved towards the east. 'Why don't you two just keep going,' he said. 'There's going to be trouble here soon.'

The old Indian seemed to understand Neil's words. He gestured to his companion and they slipped down on to the bed of the wash. Neil watched them until they were out of sight, but Annie was only aware of the helicopter which ceased hovering and started to head towards them. Neil walked over and picked up the walkie-talkie.

'Let's see if they're poker players,' he said. Then he switched on the set. 'Hello, gunship. Hello, gunship. Remember the money?'

There was a pause and a voice replied, 'What money?'

Neil grinned. 'I won fifty thousand dollars from Reicher. I've still got it. Kill us and the money goes with me.'

The helicopter was nearly upon them. It stopped in flight and began to hover.

'Where's the other guy?' the voice asked.

'He's dead,' Neil replied. 'I buried him after the flood. So what do you say about the fifty thousand bucks?'

The voice spoke. 'What's the deal?'

'I hid the money back in the Grand Hotel in Jericho. You drop us at the highway near traffic, and I tell you where the hiding place is.'

There was no reply for a while.

'We'll work something out,' the voice said. 'Stay where you are. We're coming down.'

As the helicopter began its descent Annie could see the machine guns poking from both sides. The wind from the blades ripped the sparse foliage around them and blew dust and gravel across the rock they stood upon. A loudspeaker from the helicopter began to blare.

'Stand apart and stay where you are. Make a wrong move and this is what will happen.'

One of the side guns opened up, and the landscape to the left of them began to disintegrate into a dust storm under the massed firepower of the rotating Gatling guns.

Neil switched on the handset again. 'OK, we're impressed.'

A single figure, dressed as a Jericho guard and carrying a handgun which he had not drawn, climbed out of the chopper and walked towards them, making sure to leave the ship's guns a clear line of fire. He approached them carefully, and when he was close enough he reached forward and snatched the fighting knife from Neil's waistband and took the girl by her wrist to spin her around.

Then he held the point of the knife against her solar plexus. Neil could see the look of triumph on the man's face. He was young but had run to fat, and the hair had receded from a forehead that was red from the sun. He smiled and Neil could see a row of jagged teeth.

'Now you tell me where the money is or I'm gonna spill her in front of you.'

Neil looked at him with contempt.

'We've got a sniper concealed,' he said in a conversational tone. 'He can take you and the chopper crew before you can locate him.'

'Prove it,' the man said with disbelief.

Neil tossed the walkie-talkie into the air and two shots slammed into the spinning object, which shattered like a clay pigeon.

'Drop the knife or you're dead,' Neil said.

The guard did as he was told and Neil picked it up.

'Now go and tell your friends to come over here.'

As the man started to walk towards the ship, Neil said to the girl, 'It looks as if we're getting a ride out of here.'

But as he spoke the Gatling guns facing the river-bank opened up, blasting the side of the wash like a giant shotgun. It began to scythe towards Lewis's concealed position. In the roar from the engines and the thunderous chatter of the machine gun, they did not hear Lewis's shot.

The gunner pitched forward and dangled from a safety harness, and the pilot reared the helicopter up to swing around and bring the gun on the other side of the ship to bear. He made the mistake of presenting the cockpit to the river-bank. Lewis's shot hit him below the Adam's apple. The bullet punched through the sternum and severed his spinal column.

Out of control, the helicopter spilled to the side, the rotor blades tearing chunks of rock and gravel from the ground until the blades broke free. Like a giant thrashing insect the body seemed to writhe to the edge of the wash, until it tumbled onto its back in the riverbed and the engine died. In the sudden silence, Lewis rose from his position and crossed the wash to where Neil and Annie stood.

The guard standing with them looked down at the wreck in stunned disbelief. Neil had taken his revolver, and he held it loosely by his side.

Lewis joined them. 'That's a pity,' he said.

'It would have been kind of nice to ride,' Neil replied.

'OK,' Lewis said. 'Let's see what we can use.'

They scrambled over the carcase of the helicopter and found the second gunner was still alive, but unconscious, with a deep gash in his forehead. They took the water and emergency packs of food from the wreck, and Neil looked down at their fresh supplies.

'I think we're going to make it now,' he said. 'But we've still got some walking to do.'

'Let's eat before we start,' Annie said and she began to break the sealed cellophane wrapping from a beef sandwich.

Lewis took one of the bottles of fresh water from the helicopter and drank. After the muddy concoction from the riverbed it tasted sweet. He raised the bottle again and noticed that grey clouds had started to fill the sky from the south. By the time they had finished eating, the rain had started to cloud the desert with mist.

Charlie Mars stood and drank coffee at the window of his flat in Clifford's Inn as he watched the birds eating the bread he had thrown into the snow below. It was almost light, and the pathways that led between the ancient buildings already showed footprints left by those few people who had early business about the chambers on New Year's Day.

He glanced down at a silver-framed photograh that stood on the table by the window. It showed Sybil and the girls dressed for a wedding. The girls were very young, and he couldn't remember who the celebration was for.

He ran his finger along the smooth top of the frame, then picked up the telephone next to it. He took a slip of paper from his waistcoat pocket and dialled the number Lewis had given him. After a while a man's voice said 'Hello.'

'May I speak to Lewis Horne,' Charlie said very clearly.

There was a long pause, then a woman with a deep voice spoke. 'Who do you want?' she said.

'Lewis Horne,' he repeated. 'I'm his Uncle Charlie.'

There was a longer pause, and the woman said: 'He ain't here.' But she didn't hang up.'

'It's most urgent that I speak to him. Have you any idea how long he is going to be?'

Charlie could feel her reluctance to speak, but he sensed she cared about Lewis.

'Are you really his uncle?' the voice said.

'Yes, I am.'

'Can you prove it?'

Charlie thought before he spoke.

'Let me see . . . he has good manners but he can do surprising things occasionally. He plays the piano very well. He has a friend called David Neil.'

'They took both of them away a couple of days ago.'

'Who did?'

Charlie had to wait a long time for the reply.

'Some guys.'

'What happened next?'

There was another pause.

'I think they're in bad trouble.'

The line went dead.

Charlie replaced the receiver and thought for a time. When he finally moved from the window it was getting on for ten o'clock. He was surprised that the pathways below had not already been trodden flat by a first rush of clerks and secretaries coming to prepare the offices for the barristers who kept more gentlemanly hours. Then he remembered it was New Year's Day and there would only be the porters, slowly scraping the snow to the verges.

He was about to leave the flat when the telephone rang. He closed the front door again and picked up the receiver.

'Mars,' he said in a preoccupied voice.

'Charlie? It's me, Sybil. I'm coming home. All's well here. It wasn't heart trouble at all, just Christmas indigestion. God, old people can be as bad as children at times.'

'When will you be home?' he said.

'Tomorrow, I hope. If I can get a flight.'

'Do your best,' Charlie said almost gruffly. 'It's boring here without you.'

'Is everything all right, Charlie?' she said.

He knew it would be pointless to lie to her.

'Lewis is missing,' he said. 'But I expect he'll turn up.'

'I'm sure he will,' Sybil said with conviction. 'I think we would feel something otherwise.'

Charlie smiled. 'Happy New Year. I'd almost forgotten.'

'I'll see you tomorrow, I promise,' she said.

Charlie found a certain pleasure in the deserted streets. London was as silent as his village in Oxfordshire. Occasionally a lonely car would glide slowly past but there were no pedestrians in Bloomsbury.

When he got to Gower Street he found Hanna Pearce waiting in the hallway with Sergeant Major Watts and Roger Kent.

'I want to talk to you, Charlie,' she said and he could hear the determination in her voice.

'Ah, there you are,' Claude Henderson boomed across the hallway and they watched him ushering a small man with a fringe of scruffy grey hair from the direction of the Duty Room. The man wore a very old dark-grey overcoat over a tweed suit. Despite his lack of weight, he carried himself with a certain authority.

'May I introduce Professor Alex Williams from the Ministry of Defence.'

'Professor,' Charlie said and they shook hands.

'I have the stuff here,' Claude said to Charlie and Roger Kent. 'It's taken me most of the night to make a clear translation. Of course, we wouldn't have done it without Skylark. She was superb.'

Charlie could see that Claude was pasty with fatigue and he needed a shave.

'Let's go to my room and have some coffee.' He ushered the party up the stairs.

Penny Rose had lit the fire, and a glass container of coffee was bubbling on the heating machine when they entered the office.

Charlie turned to the man from the Ministry. 'Have you come to any conclusions?'

The professor lit a cigarette.

'I haven't had a chance to look at anything yet,' he said. 'I arrived only moments before you did. Perhaps if I could be allowed to study the documents for a time I can give my opinion.'

'Certainly,' Charlie said. 'Would you like to be alone?'

'That will not be necessary,' Williams said, and threw the half-consumed cigarette into the fire.

'Why don't you make the professor comfortable at the end table, Claude?' Charlie suggested. 'Then I should pop along home. You look as if you could do with a rest.'

'As soon as I've heard the professor's conclusions,' Claude said.

'It won't take too long, I can assure you,' the little man said.

Charlie could see that Hanna was still anxious to speak to him.

'Shall we go next door?' he said in a soft voice.

She followed him into Penny Rose's office.

'Pop down to the Duty Room for ten minutes will you please, Penny, and take any of my incoming calls from there.'

Penny left the room with only a tiny glance of interest at Hanna, who leaned against a desk with her hands against her sides and studied the tips of her soft leather boots. When Penny had closed the door, she looked up at him and he could see the assertive thrust in her jaw.

'Where is he, Charlie?' she said in a determined voice.

'I've told you, Hanna. He's in Arizona,' Charlie said.

'Where in Arizona? It's a big state,' she persisted.

He drummed his fingers for a moment and then made up his mind.

'He went to a small town in southern Arizona called Jericho.'

'Why?'

Charlie rubbed the back of his head. 'Because there seem

238

to be a lot of nasty people there and we wanted to know what they're up to.'

'Where's he staying in this town?'

Charlie coughed and looked with interest at a potted plant on top of the filing cabinets where he leaned.

'Well actually, it's a sort of hotel called the Grand.'

'You're not telling me everything,' she said relentlessly.

Charlie thrust his hands deep into his jacket pockets and rocked on his heels.

'It's a house of pleasure as well,' he said finally.

'A house of pleasure?' Hanna repeated in a baffled voice and then slowly her expression changed. 'A bordello?'

'Er, yes,' Charlie said.

Hanna's chin seemed to become even firmer.

'All this time I've been out of my mind with worry and he's been in a sporting house in Arizona,' she said in a voice that was close to an explosion. Then she saw the expression on Charlie's face. 'There's more,' she said with an edge of concern.

He nodded. 'He's been missing for a couple of days.'

'Where?'

'We don't know, Hanna.'

She stood up very straight. 'I'm going to find him.'

Before he could answer, Claude knocked and entered.

'He's ready,' Claude said and they could hear the exhaustion in his voice.

They followed him back into Charlie's room, where the professor sat at the desk chewing the earpiece of a pair of wire-framed spectacles. Roger Kent stood at the fireplace reading from a leather-bound book.

When the professor was sure he had the room's full attention, he carefully put his spectacles on and glanced down at the papers before him.

'As you correctly surmised, Dr Pearce, these are the instructions for the manufacture of a quite deadly virus. Dr Reece has produced an elegantly simple solution to the problem and I cannot fault his design.'

The professor removed his spectacles again with a rather theatrical gesture.

'Does this mean *anyone* can make the virus from those instructions?' Roger Kent inquired.

'Oh, yes,' the professor replied in an almost light-hearted tone. 'What they don't say, of course, is how to distribute it to the population. It will only communicate in food or the water supply, so to all intents and purposes it is an exercise in futility.'

'I don't follow,' Charlie said.

'It's quite simple,' the professor replied. 'Dr Reece has quite cleverly tricked his captors.' He put down the glasses on the desk in front of him and began to enjoy the lecture. His long, dry, sticklike fingers waved in front of his face to emphasise his words.

'He has produced for them a very nasty little creation indeed but human beings can't spread it amongst themselves, so it cannot reach epidemic proportions.'

'Could he have done so had he wished?' Kent asked.

'Oh, yes, quite easily, but as it stands I cannot see how anyone could put this formula to practical use.'

'Thank you, Professor, you've been most kind to render this help at such short notice,' Roger Kent said, and he rose to his feet and shook hands warmly.

'I'll see the professor to the car and then pop off,' Claude said.

'OK, Claude,' Charlie said. 'Ring me when you're rested.'

'You seem worried,' Roger Kent said when they had departed. Charlie looked up from the tattered rug before the fireplace.

'Yes, I am a bit.' He turned to Hanna. 'A little while ago you said you wanted to go and find Lewis in Arizona. Do you mean that?'

'Every word,' she said with utter conviction.

Charlie didn't speak for a minute. He stood by the fireplace deep in thought. Finally it was clear he had made up his mind about something. He turned to Hanna.

'I want you to give him a message.'

'Is it important?' Roger Kent asked. 'In view of what Professor Williams just said?'

'I think so,' Charlie said very softly.

240

Kent looked at each of them in turn.

'How can you be sure that you will be able to get into this place?' he said.

Charlie looked from Roger Kent to Hanna.

'There are two types of people who can always get into a brothel, Roger . . . '

They waited for him to continue.

'Gentlemen with money and good-looking women.'

Chapter Ten

Salvatore Angelini switched off the windscreen wipers and watched the heat of the sun turn the rain-blackened road ahead to a pale grey. On each side of the highway where the run-off from the surface brought extra moisture to the edge of the desert, spring flowers grew in colourful profusion. He loved Arizona. Although the temperature was climbing into the nineties outside, the air-conditioned cabin of his truck stayed cool enough for him to wear a thick wool plaid shirt and a sixty-dollar straw cowboy hat with a swooping brim and a bunch of feathers in the band.

The tape in the deck played a selection of Dean Martin songs about the glories of Italy, while he thought about the steak his wife would have ready for him to lay on the barbecue when he made it home in Tucson. Steak, Chianti and Barbara – the six-foot blonde from Minnesota whom he had married two years before. A girl who was as Italian as Nancy Reagan. No wonder he always smiled when people asked him if he missed New Jersey.

The uneven reddish-brown desert stretched out each side of the highway, relieved only by the primitive shapes of the tall saguaros cacti.

About half a mile ahead three figures stood waving by the roadside. Salvatore could see no vehicle. Desert hikers, he thought as he slowed down to stop. Then he realised it was an act he would never have committed on a New York State turnpike. Stop a truck on the east coast for a hitchhiker and you'd end up with a gun up your ass and your load on its way to Canada.

They looked harmless enough, and as he drew closer he could see one of them was a woman. Reaching forward he touched the butt of a snub-nosed .38 which Barbara had bought him as an anniversary present. The feel of the varnished grip reassured him and he put on the brakes. The massive articulated vehicle came to a hissing stop and the three hitchhikers climbed into the cab.

'Hi,' Salvatore said as he examined the trio. They looked tired. The men had grown a few days' beard and they'd taken a lot of sun. The girl was beat, so tired she looked drugged. 'There's some Tab in the icebox,' he said gesturing towards a large container at their feet.

The shorter of the two men reached down and took three frosty cans from the container. He pulled the ring on the first and handed it to the girl. She drank greedily and then held the still-cold empty can against her sunburned cheek.

The dark man took a long pull, then turned to the driver and said, 'Thank you for stopping. It was kind of you.'

'Hey, are you British?' Salvatore said in an interested voice.

'I am,' Lewis said. 'My friends are American.'

Salvatore looked at them with renewed interest.

'My old man was in England for the invasion. You know, World War II?'

They nodded. 'He said it rained all the time and everything is green. The whole goddamn country's covered in grass. Is that a fact?'

Lewis smiled. 'It's pretty green.'

The driver switched off the tape. 'What the hell are you doing walking in the desert?'

'We're looking for film locations,' Lewis said. 'Our pick-up broke down. We had to leave it.'

'You were lucky,' Salvatore said. 'This is rough country. So you're in the movie business?'

'TV,' Neil said. 'We're doing a programme for public service on the Sonora Desert.'

'Yeah?' Salvatore said. 'I'll watch out for it. Great country, Southern Arizona, don't you think?'

'We like it,' Lewis said.

'Sure,' Salvatore said. 'I tried California but it's full of crazies. I came here six years ago and met my wife. We wouldn't live anywhere else. She's a Baptist.'

The driver talked on, and after a few minutes Annie dropped off to sleep leaning against Neil's shoulder. Finally they approached the outskirts of Tucson and Annie woke up again. The short sleep seemed to have refreshed her. She stretched her arms sideways and Salvatore watched with pleasure.

She was a good-looking woman, he thought, although she did look a bit chewed over after her walk in the desert.

'Where can I drop you?' he asked.

'The first Holiday Inn next to a shopping mall,' Neil said and they searched the low, pastel-shaded buildings until they saw what they wanted. They climbed out of the cab and Salvatore waved goodbye.

'Say,' he shouted as they crossed the sidewalk to the mall.

They stopped and looked back.

'What's the name of your movie?'

'*The Desert Song*,' Lewis called back.

'Great, I'll watch out for it,' he said and he engaged the gears and rumbled away.

They stood in the sliproad next to the highway and Lewis put his hands in his pockets.

'I hate to tell you this but I'm broke,' he said.

Neil unbuckled the wide leather belt he wore, unclipped a couple of studs near the buckle and carefully extracted nine one-thousand-dollar notes.

'Some of my winnings,' he said with a smile. 'I hid the rest in the Grand Hotel.'

They shopped for nearly an hour and then, with their arms full of packages, stood at the reception desk of the Holiday Inn.

'Gentlemen, ma'am?' the clerk said with studied politeness.

Neil cleared his throat and Annie elbowed him out of the way and leaned on the counter.

'A double room for Mr and Mrs David Neil and a single for our nephew, Mr Horne.'

Lewis looked back as the bellboy led him along the corridor and Neil gave a resigned shrug.

Lewis made a bundle of the clothes he had worn in the desert and crammed them into a plastic carrier bag. Then he soaked in the bath for a long time. When the hot water had softened his skin, he set about removing whatever cactus spikes he could reach among the countless embedded in various parts of his body. When he had plucked as many as he could, he lathered his face with shaving foam and raised the razor for the first stroke. But suddenly he decided he would keep the half beard he had grown. Wrapped in a towel he reached for the telephone.

Charlie Mars woke up and picked up the receiver on the third ring. He switched on the bedside lamp and saw that Sybil had also woken, but was still half drugged with sleep. He reached out and touched her fair hair before he answered.

'It's me – Lewis. Sorry to ring so early,' came a distant voice.

Charlie sat up further and ran a hand through his tousled hair. Sybil could sense the importance of the call. She turned and looked up at her husband.

'How are you?' Charlie asked as casually as he could.

'Fine,' Lewis replied. 'A bit footsore, but otherwise the same as usual.'

'Have you made contact with Hanna?' Charlie asked.

'Hanna?' Lewis said. 'Is she here in America?'

Charlie took a deep breath.

'She left for Jericho two days ago. I know she's there. Signals got a message from her.'

'What the hell is she doing here?' Lewis said, his voice showing his concern.

'She has a letter for you, from me,' Charlie explained. 'She insisted on taking it.'

'Yes,' Lewis said, 'she can be insistent.' He paused to think. 'I'd better get back to Jericho, Charlie. I'll make contact as soon as possible.'

'Incidentally, Hanna's father is over in Tucson,' Charlie said. 'He's staying at the Arizona Inn.'

'Why is he here?' Lewis asked.

'He took her out there very fast in his own jet, and he wanted to stay near her,' Charlie explained.

'What name is she using?'

'Her own.'

'Goodbye, Charlie,' said Lewis.

He dressed quickly in the new clothes they had bought in the shopping mall and checked his appearance in the wardrobe mirror. The heavy cotton Western-style shirt and grey slacks looked respectable enough, despite the half-grown beard. The soft brown leather jacket was expensive enough to cancel out the raggedness of the beard.

Satisfied, he left his room and walked down the corridor. Neil and Annie were both wearing bathrobes when he entered their room.

'I've got to get back to Jericho,' Lewis said. 'I've called London. There are problems.' He glanced around the room, which was now littered with empty boxes and discarded wrapping paper. Neil swept himself a clear space on the bed and sat down.

'Yeah, I've got problems, too. The Marine is in town.'

'Harry Selig, here in Tucson?'

Neil nodded. 'He's staying at the Arizona Inn with Forrest Pearce. I didn't know they knew each other.'

'They all know each other, the rich and the mighty.'

'Anyway, I've got to go and see him.'

'Give me some money,' Lewis said.

Neil took two thousand-dollar bills from the dressing-table and passed them to Kate.

'I'll meet you in Kate's saloon tonight,' Lewis said.

'They won't let you guys back in town,' Annie said.

Neil smiled. 'We won't be asking permission.'

Lewis stood in the car park of the Holiday Inn and watched the young man park the red Toyota. Although the bodywork was shabby, the tyres were good and he could tell from the engine tone that the car was in good shape mechanically. The youth was aware of Lewis's interest. He slammed the door shut, and Lewis nodded.

'Hi.'

'Hello,' the youth said.

246

'Is this your car?' Lewis asked.

A wary look came to the youth's face. A cop, he thought. Why do they look like rock stars these days?

'Sure, it's my car,' the youth said, and he reached into the open window and took a set of documents from the glove compartment.

Lewis waved them away. 'Sorry, I didn't mean to be rude. It's just that I had one of these when I was at college.'

'A new model?' the youth said in a more relaxed voice. 'You must have been loaded.'

'No,' Lewis said proudly. 'I won it on a quiz show. I answered ninety-seven questions about the Beatles. Got one hundred per cent correct.'

'That's great,' the youth said dismissively and made to pass Lewis. Lewis moved slightly to block his passage between the cars, and slapped the hot bonnet.

'Yes, sir. I had that car for five years. My wife took it with her to San Francisco when she divorced me.'

The youth smiled noncommittally and made another attempt to edge past. Lewis slapped the bonnet again.

'How much is this car worth?'

The youth paused for a moment.

'Five hundred bucks?' he said tentatively.

Silently Lewis held out a thousand-dollar bill.

Twenty-five minutes later he was clear of Tucson and heading south for Jericho.

The trailer site sprawled on each side of the road that led out from the Jericho mine to the smelting plant. No-one had ever planned the area. It had grown haphazardly, in the manner of a shanty town, but like all communities it had found its own levels of respectability. The road out of Jericho passed through its guarded entrance, between a sheer, rocky gorge, then headed west before it curved to the south.

To the north of the road the trailers were lined in an orderly fashion, and some even had trellis-work and tiny tended gardens. Children's bikes rested against the stoops, and washing was hung in greater profusion. This was where the married men lived and, for the most part, their wives added a certain order and civilisation.

South of the road was squalor – and the sour-sweet smell of failure. Lewis had seen the bottom of the heap in a lot of countries. It was the same everywhere: half the people struggling for a respectable life, the other half snarling in the mire.

Lewis pulled the Toyota off the road on the southern side, next to a trailer where a youngish woman with pale skin and lifeless hair stood patiently filling a paddling pool with a plastic hose.

'Excuse me, ma'am,' Lewis said.

The woman turned and shaded her eyes from the sun.

'Yeah,' she replied in a listless voice.

'Can you tell me where Jim Davies lives?'

She pointed along the road.

'You can't see it from here. It's behind that big red camper with the tall TV aerial. It's the one with the dog outside.'

Lewis followed her directions and stopped next to a ramshackle, rusting caravan that had once been silver. It sagged to one side, and lying next to the wooden steps was a brindled dog thag eyed him malevolently when he got out of the car. He banged on the door and eventually there was the noise of someone moving about inside.

Finally the door swung open and Jim Davies stood blinking in the sunlight. He wore an ancient pair of boxer shorts and a singlet that was grey with age. The fetid air from within made Lewis step back.

Davies peered at him for a moment, then a flicker of recognition and fear crossed his face.

'What do you want, mister?' he said and glanced around to see if they were being observed.

'I've brought you a present, Jim,' Lewis said, and he held the brown bag so that the old man could see half of the Jack Daniel's bottle.

'Come in,' Davies said with another nervous glance around.

'You come out,' Lewis said.

Davies gestured for him to get back into the car, while he

248

withdrew into the trailer. A few minutes later he re-emerged wearing his blue overalls.

He slid into the passenger seat and Lewis passed him the bottle. He took it and drank four good swallows before he offered the bottle back. Lewis shook his head.

Davies took two more pulls, looked ahead through the windscreen, and spoke. 'You're a wanted man, mister. What do you want with me?'

Lewis took a thousand-dollar bill and laid it on the ledge before the windscreen.

'I want to make you happy, Jim,' Lewis said gently.

The old man looked at the money hungrily.

'What do you want me to do?' he said. 'I ain't got the stomach for anything dangerous.'

'Tell me exactly what you do at the Institute, and at what time.'

'Is that all?'

Lewis took the thousand-dollar bill and put it back in his pocket.

'And get me into Jericho tonight.'

The old man thought for a while and then looked at the bottle in his hand before he spoke.

'You've got a deal,' he said.

The red Toyota stopped at the checkpoint in the tunnel that led into Jericho from the trailer park end of the town. The guard leaned into the car.

'You're getting pretty fancy, Jim,' he said as he glanced around the interior.

'Son, this is just a Jap rollerskate,' Davies said. 'When I was your age I had a Buick convertible women used to throw themselves into when I drove down Sunset Boulevard.'

He gunned the engine as the guard waved him on. Davies drove past the mine and up into the main street of town where he turned the car into the car lot opposite the Grand Hotel. He waited until two figures passed up the alley to the saloon entrance before he opened the boot of the car. Lewis eased himself out of the cramped space and took a deep breath of cool night air before he reached back into the boot and took out a battered straw cowboy hat from the dark recess.

'It's gonna rain again,' the old man said just as a series of lightning flashes jabbed down, lighting Jericho for a moment in a silver light. The thunder that followed seemed to make the ground beneath them shake as if an earthquake was about to split the mountainsides. Rainspots the size of plums began to patter down on the dry earth.

'Meet me at eleven o'clock in Kate's,' Lewis said as he ran for the entrance of the saloon.

He paused in the doorway, pulled the stetson low over his brow, threw his shoulders back, stuck his right thumb in his belt, and walked into the saloon with a slow, swaggering gait. Few people looked up as he hunched over the bar and asked one of the girls for a beer. He took the glass and ambled slowly to the back of the saloon, where he sat in semi-darkness and watched the thin crowd that had assembled in the early evening.

The jukebox played the same Dolly Parton record that Lewis had heard on his first day in Jericho. Kate sat at her table with a cup of coffee in front of her. The barman was making an elaborate cocktail with the concentration of a scientist mixing dangerous chemicals. Three of the girls were dancing, and two cocktail waitresses stood waiting for their orders to be filled.

Jenny, a short blonde, took her consignment away and Lewis watched Hanna Pearce start to load drinks onto her tray. He moved his chair slightly so that he could see the full length of her figure. Her hair was piled up on her head and the long dress she wore was low and made of some silky, grey-blue material that was cut to reveal most of her back. Like the other waitresses she wore long white gloves.

Even across the room he could see the heavy make-up that emphasised the shape of her eyes and cheekbones. When she picked up the full tray she paused for a moment and glanced in his direction, and then passed on to the table where a noisy crowd of engineers from the mine took the drinks and bantered with her.

Gradually she worked her way around the room until she got close to him. The saloon was only half full, and the tables around Lewis were still empty. Hanna put down her tray on the table before him and placed a fresh beer mat near his hand. He looked up into her eyes.

'Of all the gin joints in the world, why did you have to come into mine?' she said softly.

He leaned back and pushed the chair opposite away from the table with his foot. She sat down and leaned towards him.

'Where the hell have you been?' she said.

He waved towards the west. 'In the desert, taking the waters.' He studied the low-cut dress. 'You should wear that kind of thing more often,' he said with admiration.

Hanna smiled sardonically. 'I do wear this kind of thing more often. It's by Yves St Laurent. I bought it when we were in Paris.' Before he could answer she said, 'I know, we'll always have Paris,' then she leaned down, slipped off a shoe and massaged her foot.

He wanted to reach out and touch her but he sipped his beer instead.

'This job is a killer on the feet. I'll never be curt with a cocktail waitress again.'

'I thought you spent your time walking around hospitals,' Lewis said.

Hanna slipped the shoe on again.

'Not in four-inch stiletto heels with the patients grabbing at my ass.'

Lewis shook his head sadly. 'This kind of work has coarsened you, Hanna.'

Looking past her, he could see Kate watching them. He lowered his head so the brim of the hat covered his face again.

'Charlie says you've got a letter for me.'

'Yes, but I can't get away for a while. There's some kind of party going on here tonight. The guys at the Institute graduate tomorrow.'

'What time will you be free?'

'Not until after eleven.'

He looked towards Kate who was still watching them.

'Do you know if my old room is empty?'

She nodded.

'I'll meet you there.'

She swept up the tray and walked away. He watched her appreciatively and thought that it was a strong man who didn't make a grab for her.

David Neil parked the hired car and entered the discreet elegance of the Arizona Inn. General Harry Selig was alone in the library. He sat on a long, comfortable sofa reading a book, and looked up to study Neil through half-moon glasses. The Marine nodded for Neil to sit down in a nearby chair.

'Coffee?' he said. 'It's still hot.'

Neil poured himself a cup and waited for Harry Selig to speak. The Marine laid his book down on the table, next to the coffee-pot, and slipped the glasses into the waistcoat pocket of his dark grey suit. Neil glanced at the Marine's clothes. White shirt, black knitted tie. He was dressed so plainly that the West Point class ring he wore seemed opulent – like the jewellery of a Levantine prince.

'How are you, Major Neil?' he said in a light, cheerful voice.

'Fine, sir,' Neil said warily.

'Good,' the Marine replied, then he sat back on the sofa and folded his arms across his chest.

'Now, would you mind telling me what you and your British buddy have been up to on your vacation? I take it that's what you've been doing in the desert for the last four days?'

David Neil took a sip from his coffee.

'Let me tell you about our vacation,' he said.

The Marine sat and listened attentively while Neil related the events that had taken place since Lewis Horne had arrived in Arizona.

When Neil had finished, the Marine nodded his head three times.

'I see,' he said. 'And what do you plan to do next?'

'Captain Horne has gone back to Jericho. I've arranged to meet him there tonight.'

'Well, here's someone who will be glad to hear that you have returned.'

Neil followed his gaze and saw Forrest Pearce enter the library.

'Hello, Major,' Pearce said when he joined them. 'Is Lewis Horne with you?'

'He's gone to Jericho, sir,' Neil said.

Pearce stood for a moment, his hands thrust into his jacket pockets, and exchanged glances with General Selig.

'My daughter Hanna is there, Major. Do you think she's in any danger?' Pearce said quietly.

Neil thought about saying something reassuring, but he realised that Hanna's father was too shrewd to be satisfied with platitudes.

'I don't know,' he answered. 'It's a pretty dangerous place at the moment.'

'Thank you for being frank,' Pearce said, then he turned to General Selig.

'My emotions tell me to go there myself, but I suppose you would advise against that?'

'I would,' Selig said.

'Lewis Horne is there, sir,' Neil said. 'He's a good man.'

Pearce smiled at him, but there was a sadness in his face.

'I know he's a good man, son,' he said. 'I just hope he's lucky.'

Neil stood up. 'It's time I moved,' he said.

'Good luck, Major,' Selig said. 'If I haven't heard from you in the next twenty-four hours, I shall be coming myself.'

'And he'll have company,' Forrest Pearce said.

They watched David Neil walk away from them in silence, both thinking of their vigorous days.

'Drink?' General Selig said, and Forrest Pearce raised his eyebrows in agreement.

As they walked to the bar, Selig placed a hand on Pearce's shoulder.

'They're both good men – Neil and Horne. They'll take care of her.'

They walked on for a few paces before Pearce replied.

'Jesus, I hate getting old.'

'It has its compensations, Forrest,' Selig said.

Pearce looked at him sideways. 'Just name one.'

'You've got to be over sixty to appreciate a really great dry Martini.'

'I must admit,' Pearce replied, as they entered the bar, 'they need a mature palate.'

The only other person in the bar turned and smiled when they got close to him.

'Marshall,' Pearce said. 'I didn't know you were in Tucson. You know General Selig?' The men shook hands.

'Of course I know Harry Selig,' Cutter said and he took a handful of the little fish-shaped biscuits from a bowl on the counter and began to throw them one by one into his mouth.

'So what brings you here?' Pearce asked.

Cutter finished off the biscuits and dusted his hands together before he raised a glass of whisky that clinked with ice.

'I came down to do some final work on *The Silver Spoon*. They say she's just about airworthy.'

General Selig raised his eyebrows questioningly.

'Marshall has rebuilt a B17 we once flew in the war,' Pearce explained.

'I've also been doing some private checking on Brady,' Marshall said.

'Did you learn anything?' Selig said and he nodded approvingly to the barman, who was waiting for a verdict on the Martini. Cutter shook his head.

'I got a couple of private investigators, professionals, to take a look at Jericho. They gave me one report – Brady has sealed up the place like a prison. They were going back, they said, but since they last called me I've heard nothing.'

Cutter looked over his shoulder towards the sound of the piano. In the centre of the room a man in a dinner jacket was playing a selection of Gershwin. He turned back to Pearce and Selig.

'I've asked around town. I've still got some friends here. Brady has recruited a private police force.'

'Has anyone got any idea what he's doing?' Pearce said.

Cutter put down his drink and laid both hands on the bar.

'I believe they've hit another rich vein. When I sold him the place I had a clause in the contract that if the income from the mine rose above a certain amount, I retained a percentage of the profits. It's my guess he wants it all. People get very sentimental about money.'

'And about daughters,' Forrest Pearce said.

Cutter looked towards General Selig.

'What's the matter with you guys?' he said with concern.

'Hanna may be in trouble,' Pearce said. 'I'll just have to wait and see.'

'Tell me about it over dinner,' Cutter said and he beckoned to the barman for the bill.

David Neil waited until he was clear of the city limits, and then he began to push the Mercedes he had hired. The empty landscape flickered past as he hammered towards the mountains to the south.

By moonrise he was in the foothills. When he judged that he was close enough to the tunnel into town, Neil found a place to conceal the Mercedes near to the road, behind a low screen of trees. He stood for a time, growing used to the environment, then he opened the boot and took out a light-weight seersucker jacket. Not ideal climbing clothes – but useful for concealing the shoulder holster and Colt .45 army model he rigged under his left armpit. God Bless America, he thought. Where else in the Western world could you buy a gun in a shopping mall?

He buttoned the jacket and took out a backpack, slung it onto his shoulders and started to walk at a steady pace towards the mountains that rose above him. Progress was easy until the last hundred feet. After a wide belt of shale he began a final ascent of almost sheer rock.

Patiently he picked his way to the summit, feeling for every hold with his fingertips until at last he lay on a narrow ridge looking down on the rooftops of Jericho. He was close to the tunnel exit. Too close, he thought. With great care he edged along the ridge until he felt he was at a safe distance, then he located a crevice in the rock that suited his purpose.

Taking a small steel grappling hook from the rucksack, he wedged it securely into the fissure before he checked the nylon rope, attached it to the grappling hook, and threw two lengths into the void. When he had adjusted a harness to his satisfaction, he clipped onto the rope and abseiled down the rockface to the edge of the road that led down to Jericho. When his feet touched the ground, he looked towards the mouth of the tunnel that glared with light, but all was quiet.

He hauled on the other length to release the rope, and gathered it together. Within a few minutes he had concealed the equipment and was moving towards the Grand Hotel.

Kate was sitting in her office reading *Vanity Fair* and dreaming of Manhattan, when David Neil's shadow fell on the page. She glanced up and a slow smile came to her face.

'I can always tell a bad penny,' she said in her gravelly voice.

'Nice to be back again, Kate,' he said softly. 'Have you seen anything of Lewis Horne?'

Kate closed her magazine and sat back in the swivel chair.

'He's downstairs in the saloon with the phoney dame who turned up a couple of days ago looking for you,' she said. Neil leaned against the desk and put his hands in his pockets.

'How do you know she's phoney?' he asked.

Kate leaned back in her chair and laid the magazine on the desk, then she folded her arms.

'Honey, cocktail waitresses don't buy their clothes from Paris and Fifth Avenue. Wearing a lot of make-up and chewing gum will fool a man, but not another woman.'

'Are they safe in the bar?' Neil asked.

'Sure, Reicher has got men watching for you both, but that beard Horne's wearing is enough to fool them. Reicher doesn't hire his help for their brains.' She looked at Neil. 'Of course, they'd recognise you; no-one's that dumb.'

She stood up. 'Wait a minute.'

She returned a moment later with a key which she handed to Neil. 'It's Horne's room. Go and let yourself in. I'll go downstairs and announce your arrival.'

He did as he was told, and after a few minutes Lewis let himself into the room.

'Where's Hanna?' Neil asked.

'She stopped off at her own room,' Lewis replied. 'She's collecting a few things for me.'

There was a muffled knock on the door and Lewis opened it. Hanna entered holding a make-up case and a bottle of vodka. She took an envelope from the case and handed it to Lewis. He opened it and discarded the sheets of handwritten paper inside, then took the bottle of vodka and opened it.

'Do you have a handkerchief or some cotton wool?' he said to Hanna.

'Cotton wool – in the make-up case,' she said. He took a ball and soaked it in vodka and swabbed the envelope. The gummed seams came apart and he continued to liberally soak the envelope in alcohol. Words started to appear, dimly at first and then in greater strength, like a photograph developing in a dish of chemicals.

Lewis spread the soaked sheet of paper on the mirror of the dressing-table and read the message from Charlie Mars.

'What does it say?' Neil asked.

Lewis looked up. 'Skylark broke their computer code. I can get into their system.'

'First, you've got to get into the Institute,' Hanna reminded him. He turned to her.

'Go down to the bar. At the end where the Mexican girl serves you'll find an old man in a blue work shirt with about two days of grey stubble on his face. Tell him Lewis has got the rest of the dough, and he'll come back here with you.'

When she had gone, Lewis opened Hanna's make-up case and searched until he found a small pair of scissors. Then he began to crop his beard closer to his face.

'Pretty good,' Neil said in admiration of his work. 'You're starting to look like a bum again.'

He had reduced the whiskers to a stubble by the time Hanna returned with Jim Davies.

Lewis observed him in the reflection in the mirror. It was

clear that Davies was very drunk, his head nodded erratically and he blinked constantly in an effort to keep his red-rimmed eyes in focus. He stood swaying in the centre of the room, but was saved by some remote inner balance that kept him from falling to the ground. Lewis stood before him and studied his face carefully for a few minutes.

'OK,' he said to Neil. 'Get his shirt and pants and put him on the bed.'

The old man let them lay him down, and as soon as he was on his back he passed into sleep. While Hanna and Neil undressed him, Lewis opened Hanna's make-up case and set to work. Twenty minutes later he was finished. He stripped himself, and put on Davies's shirt and pants, letting the shirt bag out and the trousers hang low on his hips. He tried a shuffling walk across the room.

'How does it look?' he said.

'Not bad,' Neil said, 'but you're exaggerating the walk too much. Try it again.'

Lewis repeated it.

'Yeah, that's it,' Neil said, and Lewis grinned.

Hanna shook her head.

'That won't do.'

'What?' Lewis said.

'Your teeth. They're forty-five years too young,' Hanna said, and she scrabbled into the make-up case and found an eyeliner pencil.

'Suck your teeth and then bare them,' she ordered.

Lewis obeyed and she applied the brown grease pencil.

'Right,' she said finally. 'Go to the other end of the room.'

They looked at him with critical eyes.

'It'll work,' Neil said at last.

'Only if you're this far away,' Hanna said. 'Any nearer and it's easy to see the make-up. You'll never get past the guard on the door if he looks close.'

'People don't look too closely at old drunks,' Lewis said. 'Besides he sits inside at the desk and operates the glass door from a distance. I'll make it.'

'What's Davies's procedure?' Neil asked.

Lewis sat down and made sure his whitenened hair did not

come in contact with the antimacassar protecting the velvet chair. Then he began to recite the old man's work schedule.

'Davies cleans the corridors, the toilets, the lecture theatre, the refectory, three classrooms and the entrance hall. All the offices are done at seven-thirty by a Mexican woman who does the work under the supervision of the secretarial staff.

'They arrive one hour before the bosses. Davies is a slow worker; he usually takes six hours to do his job, although he can finish in half the time if he wants to. He stores his equipment on a trolley which is kept in a small closet next to the men's room on the top floor. Each floor has a water point where he can fill his bucket.

'He steals a certain amount of food from the refectory every night. The supervisor knows this. He pays off the guard with a bribe and takes care of the supervisor once a week. The payoff depends on the value of what he has stolen. Sometimes, when it's something larger than usual, he uses the trolley to take the stuff from the Institute to his car. The guard is used to this. He never checks on him because Davies doesn't enter any of the high-security parts of the building.'

Neil and Hanna exchanged glances.

'Where's the computer room?' Neil asked.

'Second floor, next to the lecture theatre.' Lewis looked at his watch. 'Time to go,' he said.

Hanna stood before him and he grinned.

'Better not kiss me goodbye. You'll spoil my teeth,' he said. She reached out and held his arms for a moment.

'Now I know how you'll look when you're old,' she said. 'That's if you get to be old.'

'I'll do my best,' he said. He looked at his watch again. 'I'll be back. Keep a light burning for me.'

'Do you want to take a gun?' Neil asked.

Lewis shook his head.

At that moment Davies moved in his sleep and made a snorting noise as he turned on his side. He began to snore loudly. The sound broke the tension.

'On the whole,' Lewis said, 'I think I'd rather be doing what I'm up to than have to stay here and listen to that.'

259

Neil took a pack of cards from the sideboard.

'Go on, beat it,' he said. 'I'm going to take this dame for every cent she's got at gin rummy.'

Lewis half-raised a hand in a farewell salute and slipped out of the room. Neil and Hanna stood by the open window and watched him as he entered the street and shuffled towards the Institute.

Lewis took the plastic identity card from the pocket of Davies's work shirt and clipped it to his chest. Just inside the mahogany doors of the Institute was a glass screen. Lewis rapped and the guard inside looked up from his desk and pressed the control button. The lock buzzed until Lewis pushed the door open. The guard continued to read his copy of the *Enquirer*.

'I sure would like some chocolate,' he called out without looking up from the paper.

'I'll see what I can do,' Lewis replied and he jabbed the button to call the caged lift. When he reached the top floor only the tiny emergency lights were on, casting shadows across the marbled and stone corridors. He found the control box and switched on the mains. The clip of his footsteps echoed as he made for the room where Davies's trolley was stored.

Working swiftly, Lewis set to and cleaned the toilets, replacing soap, towels and paper from a store he had found. He polished the brass fittings and swabbed the floor of the corridor.

When the work was done he switched off the main lights in the corridor once again and stood by the door to the secretary's office where he and David Neil had first been held captive. The panel set next to the door glowed, and Lewis remembered the key: it was the first five bars of 'There's a Small Hotel'. The door clicked open and he slipped into the darkness. He stood still and lit a bookmatch which he shaded with his hands.

There were two sets of blinds at the window: Venetian and plain roller. When he had pulled down both he switched on the lamp on the secretary's table. He sat in the chair and looked down at the desk before him. To his right, an angle extension to the desk held a computer terminal. Lewis sat and studied the desk top and his surroundings.

It was neat and Spartan: just a blotter, a flip-top calendar and an appointments diary. There was also a small enamelled elephant. Behind the desk was a pin board with photographs, postcards and illustrations cut from magazines. Lewis noticed that several of the postcards showed elephants. He thought for a moment, and then started to flip over the calendar. There were notes on nearly every page.

He opened the desk diary and turned the pages. The secretary had made masses of trivial notes in the same small neat handwriting. He sat back in the chair, folded his arms, and began to think about the person who normally sat at this desk. It was clear that the woman acting as Reicher's secretary was efficient, painstaking and extremely forgetful. He switched on the screen and thought for a moment as it glowed into life. Any such girl, he reasoned, would be nervous about not remembering a vital piece of information. Where would she keep it? Somewhere close. He spun the chair and reached out, circling with his hand. When it contacted the notice board it touched between two postcards. He unpinned them both and turned them over. He studied them for a few moments, then found a series of numbers and letters faintly pencilled in the corner of one.

Lewis tapped out the letters written on the postcard and a list appeared on the screen. He worked for ten minutes until he had what he wanted. He punched the necessary code and Reicher's diary appeared. There were only two entries for the following day: Professor Jochin Hyach was due to deliver the Gospel lecture; then came the graduation ceremony.

He was about to shut down the system when he remembered the word 'students'. He called up the list and fifty names appeared on the screen. At first glance he recognised six of them. Taking one that he didn't know, he hit the code next to the name and studied the information on the screen. It read like a horror story.

At the age of twenty-four years, Eduardo Santanos had murdered fourteen people including a father, mother and three children. He had killed the mother to make the father talk. When he had extracted the information he attempted to eliminate the children because they were witnesses. But one of them had lived.

Lewis called up three other names at random. Each told a terrible story. He wondered what Gospel they would receive the following day, these Children of the Devil.

Taking the codes, he let himself out of the office and took Davies's trolley down to the next floor. The three classrooms were located there. He checked them all and found a door with a security lock off the third room. Behind this door, in the centre of the small room, were three large black boxes a foot deep and the size of a small coffee table. He tried the weight of one, it was easy enough for him to lift. He sprang the two catches that held the lid down and looked inside. Lettered in gold Gothic type on the inside was the single word 'Gospel'. There were three rows of orange plastic lids set into circular slots. Lewis unscrewed one and found that it secured a plain aluminium container. He replaced the plastic lid and traced the work Gospel with his fingertips before he shut the box once again.

Leaving the trolley behind, Lewis made for the floor below. To one side of the corridor were offices, the other side of the building was divided between the refectory, the computer room and the lecture theatre.

He checked the refectory first. It consisted of a large store-room that contained freezers full of individually prepared meals and cupboards packed with canned food and boxes of confectionery. The only cooking equipment was a row of microwave ovens.

There were half a dozen tables in the larger room, with moulded plastic chairs set around them. He passed the computer room and entered the lecture theatre. Clearly it was still kept as it always had been since the Institute was built. Dark wood-panelled walls, a raised dais flanked by doors which led to the computer room, banks of pew-like seats with desk tops. The only modern touches were small display terminals at every seat, set at an angle so that the students could have a clear view of the lecturer.

Lewis used the code to get into the final room. It was in

total contrast to the lecture theatre. Neon-strip lights cast a harsh bright light on the rows of plain cabinets. There was no colour in the windowless room, just muted tones of grey. He sat down at one of the desks and checked his watch. He had more than an hour before Hanna and Neil would be expecting him.

After a few minutes of study, he tapped in the code which Skylark had provided, and began to explore the material stored in the electronic cabinets. Nearly two hours had passed when he stopped to massage his eyes with the heels of his hands. Finally he leaned back and switched off the terminal.

The guard had left his desk and was standing by the glass doors when Lewis brought the lift down to the entrance hall. He had opened the outer doors so that the lights shone out onto the narrow street and he could watch the rain lashing down. Lewis wheeled Jim Davies's trolley towards him. The guard turned as he shuffled the last few yards and automatically stood aside.

Lewis passed a box of candy into the man's hands.

'Give me a hand with the trolley, buddy,' he said in a fairly good imitation of Davies's whining voice. 'My Toyota's just around the corner.'

The guard looked down at the box of Hershey bars.

'I'll just get my rubbers,' he said and he walked over to the desk and took a long oil slicker from a peg on the wall. 'What the hell have you got on here?' the guard asked as they manhandled the trolley down the steps.

'Soup,' Lewis replied.

'How many cans?' the guard said as they negotiated the final step.

'What do they care?' Lewis said. 'A few lousy cans of soup ain't gonna break 'em.'

The guard wiped the rain from his face as Lewis pushed the trolley away into the darkness. He blinked for a moment but the figure he watched had already gone.

'Jesus, we almost gave you up,' Neil said when Lewis entered the room once more. Lewis placed the box on the table and glanced around. Davies still lay asleep on the bed. The room was heavy with smoke and Lewis could see the ashtray was filled with the stubs of Neil's cheroots.

He stripped off Davies's clothes and put on his own once again.

'What the hell is this?' Neil said, gesturing towards the cardboard box.

'I don't know,' Lewis said, 'but it's worth fifteen million dollars to the people who are due to receive a can each at ten o'clock this morning.'

Lewis sat down and took one of the aluminium containers from the box.

'This is Gospel,' he said, then he turned to Hanna. 'I want you to listen very carefully to what I am going to tell you, and commit the relevant points to memory.'

He stopped and took her hand.

'It's important, Hanna.'

She nodded and he continued.

'With the code supplied to me I entered their computer. Their whole programme of intent is stored there. I now know exactly what the Jericho Institute is used for. It is a staff college for terrorists. Two years ago Brady's organisation began to bribe their way into all the international information exchanges about terrorist groups. Everything they obtained they stored in the computer at the Institute. The programming is brilliant. They now have a data base on terrorists that is as advanced as anywhere in the world. Even information from the Eastern-bloc countries is in there.

'Early last year they contacted every terrorist group in the world and offered them the same deal; strictly business, unencumbered by idealism, they offered refuge for those members who were wanted and an opportunity to study, under the best of tutelage, the most advanced methods of waging urban guerrilla warfare. Bombing, kidnap, extortion, psychological warfare are all on the curriculum. Students are given hypothetical situations and then test their game-plan on the computer.

'The cost of this exercise is astronomical, and so are the fees. The organisations that send their star pupils here raise the tuition costs by robbery and blackmail in their own countries. The final lecture, which takes place in a few hours' time, guarantees a new method of bringing terror to the particular government they wish to overthrow.'

Lewis paused from his monologue and Neil lit another cheroot. The storm had finished and the sound of running water came from the street.

'Dr Lionel Reece's formula,' Hanna said.

'Exactly,' Lewis said. 'How to brew a piece of chemical warfare in your own kitchen.'

'So what has this stuff got to do with it?' Neil said as he tapped the box.

'I'm not certain,' Lewis replied. 'But maybe the army will know. There are references in the computer but no actual description of what Gospel does. Dr Jochin Hyach is going to deliver that information at a lecture to the student body at the graduation ceremony this morning.' He turned to Neil. 'Your remark about practising medicine in Belsen was right on the button. We think he's a man called Hyach who was a boy genius in the Third Reich's chemical warfare programme. He's still wanted for experimenting on human beings.'

Lewis noticed Hanna's reaction to his words.

'Will you be able to remember what I've told you?' Lewis said to her.

'Sure,' Hanna said. 'It's a simple enough tale even if it is a trifle gruesome.' She paused. 'How am I going to get out, and if I do, where do I go?'

Lewis pointed to the figure asleep on the bed.

'He's going to drive you out in the boot of his car. Then you've got to get to the Arizona Inn in Tucson. This is the most important part, Hanna.'

A wary look came to her eyes and she searched his face.

'Go on,' she said.

'Tell Harry Selig he's got to make sure that the Air Force destroys the Institute at twelve o'clock tomorrow.'

He stopped and he could see the fear in her eyes.

'It must be a total job, Hanna, even if it means hitting other buildings. They've got to kill everyone inside.'

She tried to draw away but he held her hand.

'Listen, the saloon downstairs is as safe as a nuclear shelter.'

'That's if you're there. I know you, Lewis Horne, you like to roam around a lot.'

He held her hand even tighter.

'You've got to do this, Hanna. You must give me your word.'

She studied him for a moment.

'If you promise me you'll be here in the cellar.'

'We'll be there, Hanna,' Neil said. 'I promise.'

'OK,' Lewis said. 'Now let's get this tired old man into his wet clothes.'

Chapter Eleven

Hanna stopped the Toyota a few hundred yards from the Arizona Inn and adjusted the rear-view mirror so she could check her appearance. It had been a long night and it showed. The heavy make-up she had applied in the Grand Hotel looked cheap and vulgar in the early morning daylight. Tendrils of hair had escaped from the carefully arranged pile on top of her head and now hung in wisps around her neck and face.

She thought about making repairs, and then shrugged when she looked down at the state of her evening dress. Even three thousand dollars of haute-couture silk could not withstand the battering she had subjected it to. The real damage had been done when Davies had smuggled her out of Jericho sharing a cramped space in the back of the Toyota with a spare tyre and some old tools encrusted with oil and grime. Only her silver shoes seemed to have escaped unscathed.

She sighed, got out of the car and slammed the door. Immediately a young man in black trousers and a white shirt, who had been standing in attendance before the discreet foliage-clad entrance of the hotel, switched his attention to her as she crossed the road and approached him.

When it was clear that she was heading for the Inn, he set out to meet her. He was still ten paces away when he began to speak.

'Lady, you can't leave that . . . ' he managed to say before Hanna halted and froze him with an imperious stare.

She was not by her nature or upbringing a bully but, when necessary, she knew how to exercise the power that lifelong wealth and privilege endows. The youth stopped and eyed her warily. He was sensitive enough to realise that his first impressions had been wrong. His assessment of Hanna's standing in the social scale had risen by several points. Now she knew that she wouldn't have to use the big freeze. She smiled and walked on.

'Be a dear and park that for me, will you?' she said, and the last word was delivered over her shoulder.

'Certainly, ma'am,' she heard him say in a firm, respectful voice.

Forrest Peace had a cup of coffee halfway to his mouth, but lowered it to the saucer again as he watched with astonishment his daughter cross the restaurant floor towards the table he shared with General Selig and Marshall Cutter. The general followed his stare, and all three men looked up at Hanna as she paused for a moment, then she sat down in an empty chair at their table and reached across to take her father's untouched coffee.

'Jesus, Hanna,' Forrest Pearce said. 'You look like . . . '

'A hooker?' Hanna said sweetly. 'Is that why none of you stood up – or have manners changed so much while I've been in Jericho?'

The three men began to mutter their apologies but Hanna waved a hand to dismiss their mumble of words as she gulped down some coffee. Forrest Pearce was aware that a group of people had appeared in the doorway of the restaurant and were watching their table with interest.

'I think we'd better retire to my room,' he said firmly, and he led the other men across the floor.

Hanna stood up and drained the coffee cup before she followed them. A couple of elderly ladies breakfasting at a nearby table watched the procession with obvious interest and disapproval. They studied Hanna's tousled hair, heavy make-up and revealing evening dress with censorious eyes. She winked as she passed them, and pointed after the retreating gentlemen.

'You'd think the old goats would have had enough after last night,' she murmured conspiratorially. 'Still, business is business' – and she hurried after the three men into the gardens of the hotel.

268

They crossed the geometric garden by a brick pathway that was wet from the sprinklers that played over the dark-green leaves. The dusty pink of the low hotel buildings contrasted with the carefully tended flowerbeds and high box hedges that divided the grounds into secluded segments. The pathway led to a bungalow suite that overlooked the garden.

Once inside the sitting-room the air-conditioning made Hanna shiver as the cold air brought a chill to her bare shoulders. The three men sat themselves in easy chairs around the room and then looked expectantly towards Hanna, who chose to lean against a chest of drawers. There was a vase of flowers beside her; the scent of them was heavy despite the sterile freshness of the processed air.

She glanced at the clock on the mantelpiece: 6.55.

'General Selig,' she said quietly. 'In about five hours time, Major Neil and Captain Horne want you to make an air strike on the mining Institute in Jericho.'

Selig exchanged glances with her father and Marshall Cutter, then he turned back to her.

'Did they say that specifically?' he asked in the kind of voice adults use to coach children in a difficult task. The tone irritated Hanna.

'Just as specific as I'm being, General. Captain Horne's words were quite clear. He expects you to instruct the Air Force to bomb the Institute with the intention of killing all the occupants.'

'There are American civilians in Jericho, Hanna,' General Selig said.

'There also happens to be an Englishman there that I care for.'

'You'd better give us the full story,' Forrest Pearce said.

So Hanna began.

After thirty-three minutes Hanna stopped talking. She rubbed her arms and looked around the room.

'Does anyone have a cigarette?' she asked.

Marshall Cutter produced a pack and she inhaled gratefully. For ten minutes more she continued.

'So there you have it. Fifty of the world's most dangerous terrorists have been instructed in how to manufacture a virus of devastating power that destroys the central nervous system in human beings.' She paused to add emphasis to her final sentence. 'And with their diploma, each will be presented with something extra special: a container of Gospel.'

She could feel the effect that this final word had on the three men. There was a tension in the room and each of them carefully avoided her stare as she looked in turn at their faces. Finally General Selig shifted in the armchair and straightened his shoulders with a slight shaking motion.

'Gospel?' he repeated noncommittally.

Hanna nodded. The silence that followed was so profound she could hear a distant hedge-trimmer. She turned her head and watched a Mexican gardener come into view. Slowly he moved across her line of vision as he carefully shaved a tall box hedge into a sharp rectangle. When he had gone from sight she turned back to the three men. She had given them enough time.

'Yes, General. Gospel. I imagine, from its name, that it's another type of chemical monstrosity that spreads efficiently.'

She shook her head as she gazed at them.

'Where in God's name do you find the people to make these terrible things?'

'I made it, Hanna,' Forrest Pearce said quietly.

'You, Dad?' Hanna said.

Pearce held up a hand with the palm open.

'One of our companies. It amounts to the same thing. And I think you're guilty of pre-judgement.'

Hanna held out her own hands.

'If Gospel isn't dangerous, why are you frightened that terrorists will get hold of it?' She looked at them in turn again. 'You are frightened, aren't you?'

Pearce got up and stood by the fireplace, as if to warm himself against non-existent flames.

'First, I must tell you I am in no way ashamed of Gospel. In fact, to the contrary, I am rather proud of the achievement.'

Hanna watched her father's face. She could tell that her words had hurt him.

'I'm sorry, Dad, but . . . just what is it?'

Pearce looked up at the ceiling.

'It was developed by the Rainbow Group down at San Diego. They were looking for an agent to make fertilisers more efficient. They certainly found it.'

'Explain the principle,' Hanna said.

Pearce looked to General Selig, who nodded.

'Of itself,' he continued, 'Gospel is quite harmless. Put it in water and it imitates the molecular structure at an incredible rate.'

He paused briefly.

'Mix it with anything else and it does the same. As it imitates the structure of the water, it carries whatever additive you have chosen and combines the process. There you have it.'

Hanna thought for a moment.

'So you could put a tiny amount of vaccine in the water supply and Gospel will imitate it until all the water carries the vaccine?'

Pearce nodded.

'Oh my God,' Hanna said. 'Or some disease?'

'Right,' General Selig said. 'So you see, you're asking us to bomb Jericho which has a nasty set of home-made plagues bottled up, and a large supply of Agent Gospel. It's the rainy season in Arizona. We just don't know what the repercussions could be.'

'And if you let these guys go, the same problem could crop up anywhere in the world,' Marshall Cutter said. 'There are only two roads: in and out. Can't the army seal up the place?'

General Selig stood and joined Pearce at the fireplace.

'It would take more than the army to contain those mountains. Of course, we could try an airborne drop.'

'Lewis told me to say you can forget using troops,' Hanna said. 'The mountains are riddled with mine shafts. Brady has more than a hundred exits planned from Jericho.'

She pushed herself away from the chest of drawers and stood before her father and General Selig.

'By now they would have hidden the Gospel in the basement of the Grand Hotel. It's like a nuclear shelter down

271

there. Lewis says that as long as it doesn't take a direct hit, the Gospel will be safe.'

Selig folded his arms and lowered his head so that his chin rested on the black knitted silk tie at his throat. He stayed in that position for at least a minute, then he walked to the telephone, punched the buttons, and waited for a brief moment.

'Harry Selig,' he said. 'I wish to speak to the President.' He turned and winked at Hanna. 'Hello, Jack. Harry Selig. Can I speak to him . . . yes, Jack, very important . . . '

There was a pause and once again the only sound in the room came from the hedge-cutter in the garden. Then the General's head snapped up again.

'Hello, Mr President. I need your help, sir. No, it's the Jericho business. I haven't given in a report yet, sir. Briefly, I'm in Tucson. I need to bomb somewhere. No, sir, it's in America. Yes, sir, imperative . . . If you contact the commanding officer of the Monthar Davis base here and authorise the venture, I can take it from there. Yes, sir, I'll remember. Thank you . . . ' There was another pause and his tone of voice altered. 'Jack, hello. OK, the details are as follows . . . '

Selig talked rapidly for some time and then hung up. He turned to the room.

'What did the President say?' Hanna asked.

Selig grinned.

'He said for Christ's sake make sure we don't hit Mexico.'

Lewis dreamed he was with the New Model Army once again. It was night in winter and the troops were bivouacked in open country. The ground was hardened by frost, and a biting wind made the camp fires gutter. This time the men did not watch him like a stranger. Now he walked through unnoticed. There was to be a battle, he could feel it. All around him soldiers saw to their weapons, while officers and NCOs moved through the lines with grim purpose. He stopped by a company of musketeers grouped about a powder keg by the light of a lantern held clear of the barrel. They filled their charges and cursed the gusting wind. There was a drumming of hoofbeats and a rider entered the lines.

The horse had been pushed hard; its flanks were foaming with lather. The rider reined back and the great charger came to a snorting halt. When he had dismounted, Lewis could see the face of the horseman was lined with fatigue. The man swayed slightly and he looked around, then he saw Lewis and started to walk towards him.

As he did so he reached inside his leather jerkin and produced a sealed letter which he held out before him. Then Lewis became aware of another noise and he woke slowly to the sound of girls laughing. He lay, with his eyes still closed, and felt the touch of cool air on his face. For a moment he thought he was waking in Charlie's Mars's house in Oxfordshire to the sounds of the girls playing on the lawn beneath his room. But he suddenly caught the acrid scent of a cheroot.

He opened his eyes to see David Neil standing by an open window looking down into the street. Lewis got up from the bed and joined him.

'The ladies are going out for the day,' he said.

Lewis scratched his itching beard and looked down on the group below. Just across from them a small bus was standing in the parking lot, with its sliding doors open. Kate's girls stood around it in excited groups. Some carried baskets and wore light summer dresses – while others were more casual in shorts or jeans. The loud chatter of voices was occasionally punctuated by shrieks of laughter.

'Do you know what they remind me of?' Neil said.

'A team leaving for an away match,' Lewis answered.

Neil swung his head in surprise.

'You're damned right. I know it's crazy but I keep thinking of my high school.'

'I was thinking of a cricket team. I suppose some things are the same everywhere.'

As they watched, the barman crossed the road from the hotel and they saw that he was wearing a baseball cap and white slacks with a shortsleeved sports shirt. He shouted for them to get into the bus, but they seemed to want to delay the moment of departure and prolong the pleasure of anticipation. Eventually they were coaxed aboard and the bus pulled away.

273

'What are they celebrating?' Lewis said.

'It's Sunday,' Neil replied. 'They're going to the Mission at San Xavier.'

'We should have asked them to light a candle for us,' Lewis said.

As he finished speaking there was a thunderous roar as a jet fighter flashed low over the town heading west.

They moved away from the window and sat down in the overstuffed chairs.

'Damned fast, that plane,' Neil said. Lewis nodded in agreement.

Neil looked at his watch and then drew the army Colt from his shoulder holster, unclipped the magazine and tried the pull on the trigger. Reminded by his actions, Lewis raised himself to stand on the edge of the bed and he retrieved the leather bag he had concealed above the canopy. When he produced the revolvers, Neil whistled with admiration.

'Pretty fancy, eh?' Lewis said with a grin as he buckled the belt around his waist.

But then it was Neil's turn to smile. The gunbelt had been made for a man with a far larger girth than Lewis's. He let go of the rig and the holsters slipped to the floor. Lewis stepped out of the gunbelt and slung it over his shoulder.

'It suits you better like that,' Neil said and held out a hand. Lewis handed him one of the Colts. Neil took the gun and spun the chamber. When it clicked to a rest he cocked the hammer and then eased it back into place. Neil studied the decorations on the pistol for some time and let out a low whistle.

'These are just beautiful. They're worth a fortune.'

'How do you know?' Lewis asked.

Neil held up the gun and traced the mane of a horse's head engraved above the mother-of-pearl plate on the butt. Lewis took the gun and looked carefully. At first he could see nothing, and then he realised that the curling mane of the horse spelt something. He turned to hold the gun in the bright sunlight and gradually deciphered the inscription. It read: *To General Nelson A. Miles from the grateful citizens of Tucson.* Lewis looked up at Neil with a questioning expression.

'General Nelson A. Miles was in command of the troops who finally subdued Geronimo. There were big celebrations for him in 1886, and the people of Tucson presented him with these guns. They were stolen the next day.'

Neil reached out and tapped the gun in Lewis's hand. 'It looks like they've turned up again.'

Suddenly there was the noise of raised voices from below. The confusion continued for a few minutes, then there was an urgent knock on their door and Kate slipped into the room. They could see from the way she moved that there was trouble.

'Reicher's men,' she said softly, 'looking for you.' She glanced around the room and noticed the ashtray full of cheroot stubs. She tipped them into her hand and threw them out of the open window. Her actions made Lewis and Neil suddenly aware of how much the room smelt of tobacco. Kate looked around and took one of the scent containers from the dressing-table. She began to spray the air. Lewis and Neil picked up glass bottles and did the same.

'That'll have to do,' she said. 'Come with me.' She opened the door a fraction and glanced along the corridor, then she turned and gestured for them to join her. They followed her out of the room and along the passage. At the end there was a short flight of steps leading to a door.

'These are my rooms,' she said as she opened it with the key. They entered a room which, in contrast to the others, was decorated as a modern apartment. Instead of windows there was a large photographic mural of the Manhattan skyline at night. The windows of the buildings in the photographs glowed with opalescent light, so that the low lamps in the apartment were unnecessary. Everything in the room was in tones of white and grey. Kate gestured for them to stay with her as she moved into a bedroom. There she opened the doors to a closet and felt behind the dresses hanging there. They heard a click and Kate gestured for them to follow her into the darkness.

Forrest Pearce looked back from where he sat in the front of the automobile beside General Selig, and he smiled with approval at the clothes his daughter now wore. The housekeeper at the Arizona Inn had found her a pair of jeans, some training shoes and a red sweater. Her hair was loose and she wore no make-up. Pearce thought that she looked much as she had when she was a little girl. Hell, why not, he remembered. After all, it wasn't that long ago. They had waited a long time for her. She'd just been eight or nine when her brother was killed in Vietnam. Then it was as if he'd turned around and she'd grown up. Sometimes he felt cheated out of her childhood.

Hanna looked through the blue tinted glass of the limousine at the endless vista of aircraft that stretched to the horizon. They were laid out in blocks, like the geometric streets of an American city. Bombers, transports, fighters, helicopters stood in the blazing sun. Billions of dollars worth of hardware. The abundance of a superpower cocooned and stored in the dry desert air.

Hanna drummed on the seat next to her and she felt a dry, hard hand cover hers. Marshall Cutter squeezed gently and smiled at her.

'It's OK, honey, he'll be fine.'

She leaned against him and rested her head on his shoulder.

'Can you guarantee that, Uncle Marsh?'

'I've known a lot of guys like Lewis Horne,' Cutter said. 'Take my word for it, survivors survive. It's the poor dumb sons-of-bitches who get knocked down by automobiles you've got to worry about.'

Forrest Pearce turned again and pointed out of the window.

'Just look at that stuff.'

'Makes you glad to be a taxpayer, doesn't it,' Marshall Cutter said.

Forrest Pearce smiled. 'Feel proud, Marsh. Remember we bought most of that stuff.'

'This place makes a profit,' General Selig said. 'The only United States base in the world that gives money back to the Government.'

The car stopped before an administration building, and a

276

lieutenant escorted them to the commanding officer's quarters.

'Paul,' Selig said as he shook hands with the stocky figure who stood up when they entered the plain room decorated only with two flags and framed photographs of groups in flying kit.

'Sorry to be a nuisance on a Sunday.'

'Don't be,' General Elmstead said with a lopsided gr⸱ 'My grandchildren were as impressed as hell. They were over for breakfast when the President telephoned.'

'You know why we're here, Paul,' Selig said. 'What's your opinion?'

The stocky figure took some time before he answered.

'I won't try and snow you. I'm not sure we can do it.'

'Why?' Hanna said forcefully.

The general turned to her. 'From the look of the place on the map, it's a problem.'

'What kind of problem?' Selig asked.

Before he could answer, one of the telephones on his massive desk rang.

'Send him in,' he said. The door opened and a figure in flying overalls entered. 'This is Colonel Taylor,' the general said.

The pilot removed a pair of dark glasses that had given him a rather sinister appearance. Immediately his face took on an almost boyish look.

'Well, Jack?' the general said.

The pilot shook his head.

'The whole town's the size of a pool table, sir. If I'd have blinked I would have missed it.'

The general exchanged glances with Selig before he turned back to the pilot.

'Can you hit a single building?'

Taylor shook his head again.

'We could take out the whole town but not one building.'

'What about choppers?' Selig said.

'No,' the pilot said. 'Those buildings are too tough. Rockets couldn't do the job. It needs something slow and heavy. It sounds crazy but our technology is too advanced.'

There was silence in the office.

'How about a B17?' Marshall Cutter said.

The colonel nodded. 'Great, but it's been some years since we had any.'

'What's a B17?' Hanna asked.

'A Flying Fortress,' Forrest Pearce said. 'The kind of aeroplane I flew during the war.'

Hanna turned to Cutter. 'Didn't you say . . . ?'

'That's right, Hanna. I've got one.'

'Where?' the general asked in an incredulous voice.

'About three miles from here, over at the Puma Air Museum,' Cutter said.

'And it still flies?' the general asked excitedly.

'Sure,' Cutter replied.

'We won't have time to fit laser bomb-sights, sir,' Taylor said.

'Son,' Cutter said, 'they trained us to drop our load into pickle barrels during World War II. I can still remember how to do it.' He turned to Forrest Pearce. 'How about you, you old bastard? Do you think you can still drive a Fort?'

Hanna looked at her father with sudden concern.

'You're not thinking of flying it, are you, Dad?' she said with dismay in her voice.

Pearce took her hands with a smile.

'Honey, we're only going to be up a couple of hundred feet. We used to fly so high you could ice-skate on the wings, and there's no Luftwaffe waiting for us. A job like this is a milk run.'

The air force general looked to Colonel Taylor.

'The film will be ready now, sir. We can take a look at the problem.'

'What do you think of the idea?' the general said.

Taylor shrugged. 'If Mr Pearce lined up with the mountains exactly, and flew steady as a rock at the right altitude and at the correct airspeed, we could calculate the moment for Mr Cutter to release his load.'

'You do that, son,' Cutter said, then he addressed the general. 'Paul, will you be kind enough to show us where we should park *The Silver Spoon*?'

*   *   *

278

'Stay where you are for a minute,' Kate said to Lewis and Neil.

They did as they were told until a match flared in the velvet darkness. Kate found a switch and a string of naked light bulbs lit their surroundings. They were in a windowless corridor that stretched before them like a long tunnel.

'Watch your step,' Kate said. 'Some of these boards are rotten.'

They followed her for some time, the ancient boards creaking beneath their feet, until they were confronted by a blank end to the corridor. Kate pushed against one corner and the wall groaned as it pivoted open. They entered darkness. Gradually they saw that everything was coated with a thick, whitish dust. The room seemed to be carved out of stone.

They had emerged through a section of the panelled wall. There were deep buttoned sofas and low armchairs and tables. Around the walls were paintings in heavy frames, but no colours, just the same dust. Kate lit another match and put it to a gas-mantle.

'What was this?' Neil said in a hushed voice.

'Jericho Gentlemen's Club,' Kate replied. 'The wives watched them going in the front door, and the ladies at the Grand Hotel saw them coming out back there. It's been closed for a spell. There ain't many gentlemen in Jericho any more.'

'Who knows about the tunnel?' Neil asked.

'Just me, I guess. I don't think anyone else remembers. Look at the place,' she said and she gestured around the room. Then she reached over to a dust-encrusted table and shook free an ancient newspaper which she handed to Neil.

He took the brittle pages, and parts of the paper flaked away, but they could still read the text. A story at the bottom of the page caught Lewis's attention. The headline read 'GUERNICA DESTROYED BY BOMBS'. A thought suddenly occurred to him.

'How close are we to the Institute?' he asked.

'Next-door,' Kate replied.

Lewis and Neil looked at their watches. It was close to noon.

279

'Go back to the hotel,' Lewis said to her. 'Make sure every-one who works in the Grand goes down to the saloon. Tell them that if they don't do as I say, they could die.'

Kate could tell he did not exaggerate. She nodded.

'When Reicher's men have gone, flash the lights in the corridor and we'll come back.'

'I understand,' Kate said.

Lewis moved towards the far end of the room, where a fine crack of light showed. It came from a tiny gap between two shutters. Lewis eased the crack wider with his fingertips. The windows were grimy but the recent rain had washed the glass enough for him to see down onto the street. He had a partial view of the entrance to the Jericho Institute, where groups of men and women stood talking before the steps in the morning sunshine.

They wore sober clothes, the men in suits and ties and the few women among them neat in formal dresses so that Lewis was reminded of churchgoers lingering after a service.

A thin white-haired figure stood ram-rod straight by the doorway. When he turned to look up to the sky for a moment, Lewis recognised Hyach, the doctor who had been in Reicher's office the night they had tortured Annie. As he watched, four more of the group came over from the direction of The Silver Queen. The men on the steps greeted them and they entered the Institute with the students following them.

Neil gave a short whistle and Lewis saw him beckoning from the far end of the room.

'The lights just flashed,' he said. 'Come on.'

Brushing the white dust from his shirt, Lewis followed Neil along the creaking tunnel.

Hanna settled back into the cool, padded vinyl of the seat and felt a moment of relief as the lights dimmed and the glare from the harsh neon gave way to the soft glow from the illu-minated lectern where the intelligence officer stood to the side of the screen.

'Are you ready, sir?' he asked, and General Elmstead nodded. He pointed to the back of the room.

'Let her go.'

White-on-black numbers flickered onto the screen for a moment, and then a blur of grassland which flashed into scrub, rocks, mountain rim, a jumble of rooftops, and then the mountains again. The lower part of the film had shown a strip of instruments.

'Ladies and gentlemen,' the intelligence officer said as the few seconds of film came to an end. 'That was Jericho filmed from the nose of a jet fighter.' He pointed to the back of the room again. 'OK, give it to us frame by frame.'

The same images came back to the screen in a slow, jerky motion.

'The instruments you see at the bottom of the picture tell you the altitude, airspeed and compass direction the aircraft was flying at,' the intelligence officer said. 'Dr Pearce, will you be kind enough to identify the buildings during the flyover?'

Hanna stood up and took the pointer from him, and as the frames ticked up on the screen, Hanna read them off.

'Thank you, ma'am,' he said when Hanna had finished and returned to her seat. 'So there you have it' – and he made a final sweep of the last frame that was still projected onto the screen. 'Dr Pearce has identified the building in question and you can all see the extraordinary problems one would have in guaranteeing destruction of the Institute without taking out the entire town. I'll hand you over to Colonel Parker now, who is in charge of arming *The Silver Spoon*.'

Hanna sat in the comforting darkness and thought how laconic these people taking part in the venture appeared to be. Everything seemed to be approached without emotion, as if they were planning a rather dull shopping trip. And it's the British who are supposed to be unemotional, Hanna thought, as a stocky figure took his place at the lectern and murmured thanks to the previous speaker.

'Can you put up my graphic, please,' he said quietly.

The aerial photograph vanished and a crude sketch of a bomb appeared on the screen.

'Mr Cutter, I understand you're bombardier on this mission?'

'That's correct,' Cutter replied.

'Well, we only had time to produce one of these babies. It's armed to explode ten seconds after release from the aircraft, which should be enough time considering the low level of the drop and the amount of building it has to penetrate. My boys have rigged a press-button operation for you, rather than the switch you used in World War II. The bomb itself is in a tough jacket – but it's got to be. Those buildings are pretty rugged. Despite the casing, the shrapnel effect will he minimal. We're relying on the high explosive content, and the compression the walls of the Institute will give, to do the job. Any questions?'

The colonel paused for a moment to look around the audience, then he stepped down and took his seat once again.

General Elmstead took his place.

'Sergeant,' he called out and the room flooded with light once more. 'I think that's pretty clear,' he said. 'Colonel Taylor will be flying with you as co-pilot. He will watch the altitude on your approach. If you line up correctly when you come over the mountain, the two crosses marked on the bombardier's bubble will cover the two peaks at the head of the valley. So if Mr Cutter released his load at exactly that moment, he should hit the Jericho Institute.'

He leaned forward and pointed to emphasise his point.

'Remember, the crucial part is altitude and line of approach. If you're a few yards on either side, it's been a waste of time. Captain Kenton is your navigator. His intention is to take you on a wide half-circle by flying in an easterly direction at first, so that you're over the target at precisely 12.15.'

The general looked around the room once more.

'Well, that just about wraps it up. There's time for some coffee before take-off. I don't know about you but I'm ready for a cup.'

Outside the briefing room, two long tables bore coffee pots. A young officer helped Hanna. She stood alone drinking slowly and watching her father who stood with Cutter in another corner of the room. They wore light flying overalls and it seemed strange to see him in uniform.

'Time to go,' General Elmstead called out eventually.

They moved out of the building and into the cars outside. Hanna rode with her father and Marshall Cutter. When they were clear of the administration buildings they began to cross the great expanse of shimmering concrete to where *The Silver Spoon* stood alone, its polished steel gleaming in the hard sunlight. When they got out of the car, the heat radiated from the runway with a relentless ferocity.

Forrest Pearce kissed Hanna lightly and moved towards the aircraft. Marshall Cutter could see the anxiety on her face. He took her hand briefly and smiled.

'It's OK, honey. Remember no-one is shooting at us.'

'I know,' Hanna said.

He winked and rejoined her father. With a certain amount of effort they pulled themselves through the hatch in the belly of *The Silver Spoon*. The rest of the crew climbed aboard. After a few minutes there was a series of whining coughs, the propellers turned, reluctantly at first, and then the four great Pratt and Whitney engines smashed into life.

Despite the security of the mission, the word had spread around the base, so that the path of *The Silver Spoon* was lined with spectators. Compared with the sleek jets that scattered the airfield, the B17 seemed like some medieval armoured monster but she still possessed a certain grandeur.

Hanna felt her throat constrict as the great silver machine's engines roared into full throttle.

Forrest Pearce sat in the pilot's seat and for a brief moment felt a wave of stomach-churning panic. The controls and instruments before him seemed strange and baffling. It's small, he thought, so damned small.

As if reading his mind, Colonel Taylor spoke: 'Doesn't seem much of a size these days.'

The words shook Pearce from his panic and automatically he began the system of checks that had once been second nature to him. When the engines reached the correct pitch, Pearce spoke the one word, 'Navigator?'

'Cleared for take-off, sir,' the voice replied.

He released the brakes and the aircraft began to move forward. As they gathered speed Pearce could feel the response from *The Silver Spoon*. He watched the speed increase until he began to ease back on the joystick. For a moment she seemed reluctant, but the four great engines hauled the aircraft on and finally she soared from the runway.

Kate was waiting at the end of the tunnel. The apartment was a wreck. The contents of the closets lay strewn on the floor; the bedding and the upholstery of the furniture was slashed open. As they walked through the wreckage, goosedown and powder rose in clouds around their feet.

'The whole place is like this,' she said as they left the apartment. 'They were looking for you guys.'

Lewis could see into the rooms as they moved along the corridor. Each one had received the same treatment. The air was sickeningly sweet from spilt make-up and smashed scent bottles. Kate stopped in the entrance hall and lit a cigarette. She looked disdainful amid the wreckage.

'Looks like a Halloween that got out of hand,' she said philosophically.

'Trick or treat, Reicher style,' Lewis said, and looked up at the brass and wood clock that hung over the reception desk.

With an audible click the hand moved to one minute before twelve.

'Who's still here?' Lewis said.

'In the hotel?' Kate asked. 'Just me and the Mexican girls. The others were going to Tucson after church.'

'Anyone else in town you want to be safe?' Neil said. 'Think now, there's not much time.'

'It's Sunday,' Kate said. 'Everyone decent's away.'

Lewis nodded and the big clock clicked again and began to chime twelve.

There was a crash of applause in the lecture theatre of the Jericho Institute. Professor Jochin Hyach stood on the small stage and looked up at the faces in the tiers rising above him. The rest of the faculty sat in a semicircle behind him. Next to the professor, on a low table, were the three black boxes. Hyach bowed slightly to acknowledge the success of his lecture on the application of Reece's formula. He waited until he judged the clapping had gone on long enough, then he raised his hand and there was silence. He paused for a moment, and then began to speak once again.

'Graduates of the Jericho Institute,' he began in a dry, precise voice. 'It gives me great pleasure in presenting you today with the final gift that this establishment can bestow upon you. As you know, this ceremony was to be performed by our founder, Matthew Brady, but he has been prevented from being here today. However, he sends his heartfelt good wishes and has asked me to congratulate you on the exceptional dedication you have brought to your time here.

'When Matthew Brady first brought forth his dream for the Institute, he was greeted with scepticism in many quarters. The cynical mocked his singular vision, and the timid expressed doubt that so revolutionary an idea would flourish in an age of mediocrity. Well, you are the proof that his dream was not in vain. You are the fruit of his genius. Until Matthew Brady founded this Institute each revolution had to relearn the process of urban warfare.

'To be sure, fragments of knowledge were shared, like a suppressed religion. Lessons were passed on by word of mouth, and experience was bought by the deaths of martyrs. Like candles in the storm, you fought the mighty winds of governments who sought to snuff you out. But now you can shine brightly with the strength of a new sun, and Matthew Brady has brought this great work to fruition. Here at the Jericho Institute is a fountain of knowledge which will change the world. Each of your movements will, henceforth, be able to gain instant access to the most precise knowledge on the state of readiness which any of the world's security forces may bring to bear on you.

'As a final act of good faith, you have all been instructed in Dr Lionel Reece's brilliant work. Until now, of course, this has been of no practical use because no method of distribution has been available. Today I bring you a further miracle.'

Professor Hyach gestured towards the shining black box beside him, and paused once again before he spoke the single word: 'Gospel.'

Lewis was the last person left in the entrance hall of the Grand Hotel, and he was about to make for the saloon when the door crashed open and two of the girls entered shouting abuse at each other. They stopped when they saw Lewis looking at them with an expression of shock on his face.

'What's the matter, honey?' the taller girl said. 'Ain't you ever heard a lady swear before?'

'I thought you'd all gone to Tucson,' Lewis said and he looked up at the clock once again. It was eleven minutes past the hour.

'Annie got sick,' the tall girl explained, 'then they started having an argument about religion. The snake said she didn't want no Roman Catholic propaganda and Juanita said she felt real bad so we decided to come back.'

'Where are the rest?' Lewis said in an urgent voice.

'Outside, still arguing, I guess.'

Lewis ran into the street where the girls were grouped around the van, shouting at each other in the bright sunshine. The barman was trying to placate them but they all ignored him.

Lewis attempted to seize one of them by the arm. She shook him away and continued to scream in the face of her opponent. Lewis drew one of the silver pistols from his waistband and fired it into the air. They all stopped shouting and looked at him in surprise.

'Get into the saloon,' he ordered.

Subdued, they shuffled ahead of him.

'Faster,' he shouted and they began to scramble through the doorway.

Just as he was about to follow them, three shots echoed along the narrow street. One shattered the rear windows of the bus at the kerbside and one clipped the doorway of the hotel. Lewis turned and saw Ram Reicher raising a pistol to fire again. The bullet struck the pavement at Lewis's feet and ricocheted along the street. Reicher aimed again and Lewis could see blue-clad figures coming from the police building. He threw himself into the doorway.

'They're in the hotel now,' Ram Reicher called to his brother. Supporting his plastered leg on a single crutch, Bull hobbled out of the police barracks to join them.

'Give me that,' he said, and he took an Uzi sub-machine gun from one of the guards and held it with his free hand.

'Let's go,' Ram Reicher said and the group made their way towards the Grand Hotel. 'Half of you go through the saloon,' Ram ordered when they reached the doorway. 'The rest of us go through the front door.'

Ram took cover behind the van as two guards fired long bursts into the entrance hall.

'Now,' Ram shouted and they rushed the doorway. As they ran forward a thunderous roar filled the street, and Ram looked up from behind the bus to see the dark underbelly of *The Silver Spoon*, with an open bomb-bay, appear over the rim of the mountains. As he watched, a fat black bomb spilled slowly from the aircraft. Instinctively, Ram threw himself into the entrance of the Grand Hotel.

'Going up,' Forrest Pearce shouted on the intercom of *The Silver Spoon* as the load fell from the aircraft and he banked the B17 in a tight, climbing turn. From the bombardier's bubble in the nose of the aircraft, Marshall Cutter watched in alarm as the detail of the approaching mountainside came into pin-sharp clarity. Then there was clear blue sky.

Professor Jochin Hyach gestured for assistance and two of the faculty stepped forward and opened the box beside him.

'As I call your name, please step forward and receive your graduation prize,' he said, and he consulted the list on the lectern. 'Jean-Pierre Armand,' he intoned and the young man rose from his seat and approached the professor, who unscrewed one of the orange plastic caps inside the box and drew out the can of Campbell's tomato soup that Lewis had substituted.

Hyach was still staring at the can with astonishment when the massive bomb smashed through the bank of windows on the top floor of the Jericho Institute at an angle of forty-five degrees. The hardened steel nose passed through the concrete floor like a knitting needle thrusting through cheese, and the tail fins sheered off as it cut through two more floors.

Professor Hyach just had time to see the faces of the students react in amazement, before the bomb that had sliced through the ceiling came to rest before him and vaporised the room.

Ram Reicher lay on the marble floor of the Grand Hotel and felt the shock waves of concussion pass through the rock that Jericho was built upon. It was like a great hammer striking, and the valley held the noise long after the explosion. Then there was a silence, except for the sound of glass shaken from windows falling in tinkling fragments onto the street outside. The two men who had entered the front door before Bull Reicher now crouched blinking in the aftermath of the bomb. The one kneeling by the staircase carried a short, stubby machine-pistol.

Ram Reicher got to his feet and edged over to him.

'How much ammunition have you got?' he said.

The guard turned to him, his face blank with shock. Ram kicked him in the ribs. It seemed to work. He shut his half-open mouth and checked his webbing belt.

'Three magazines,' he said.

Ram turned to the other guard, who sat propped with his back against the reception counter, his right hand holding a Magnum loose in his lap as he clutched his solar plexus with the other.

Ram stood over him and the man looked up. Ram could see the dark pool of blood forming between his legs.

'I got shot?' he said in a surprised voice.

The effort of lifting his head to speak altered his weight

and he slid sideways into an awkward heap, and with a last low sigh he drew his legs up to his bloody chest.

'Stay here,' Ram said to the other guard. 'I'm going to check downstairs.'

He moved across the hallway and opened the door leading to the saloon. From the top of the stairs he looked down and saw that his brother Bull had herded Kate, the barman, the Mexican servants and the girls into the far corner opposite the bar. Three guards covered them. He joined his brother at the bar, where he snapped open the chamber of his Magnum and banged the butt on the counter so that the empty shells clinked onto the surface.

'What are we going to do?' Bull asked.

Ram reloaded the Magnum before he replied.

'You and me are going to stay down here,' he said softly. Then he walked over to the corner.

The guards looked at him expectantly.

'OK, boys, you've done a good job.'

He reached forward and took two of the girls by their arms and dragged them from the huddled group.

'Now I'll tell you what I want you to do,' he said in a rasping voice.

'You two take these ladies with you and clean out those dudes. There's only two floors and the corridors are real narrow, so get these girls to walk in front of you, and when you come to a room, have them go in first. Those guys are gentlemen, so they ain't gonna kill hookers.'

The guards pushed the girls before them towards the staircase. When they came into the hallway they saw Willard covering the top of the staircase. They were next to him before they realised there was no magazine in his machine-pistol.

'We're here, boys,' a voice said softly and they turned to see Lewis Horne and David Neil standing in the doorway of Kate's office. One of the guards made a fractional movement and Neil shook his head.

'Do you really want to die for the Reicher brothers?'

Carefully they both laid down their guns. Lewis gestured to the door and the two men hesitated. He waved with the pistol and they walked swiftly into the street.

'Now I want you two girls to do exactly what we say,' he said.

A few minutes later Neil fired three short bursts from a machine-pistol and he and Lewis moved out of the doorway of the hotel. One of the girls stood in Kate's office and counted to sixty, then she threw the main switch to the hotel's electricity supply. In the basement there was sudden, inky darkness.

The other girl, holding the sub-machine gun Neil had given her, opened the door to the staircase and threw it into the saloon. As it hit the third step the hairpin Neil had lodged in the firing mechanism jogged free and the weapon began to Catherine-wheel down the stairs, firing the magazine.

Instinctively the Reicher brothers aimed towards the sound. Suddenly the lights snapped on again. Crouching near the bar with guns level were Lewis and Neil, who had entered the blacked-out saloon from the alleyway. Both Reichers turned to them and began shooting. The shelves behind Lewis and Neil shattered as the glass and bottles exploded.

Kate was standing close to Bull Reicher and he pulled her in front of him. It was a mistake. As Kate struggled, his next shot went wide and ploughed into the woodwork at the far end of the bar.

Lewis took a moment to aim with the silver engraved Colt .45. The first shot hit Reicher in the shoulder, so that he released Kate and spun to the right. The second entered his ribcage under the outflung arm and ploughed around the chest cavity.

Ram levelled the machine-pistol, but Neil's shot hit the magazine and twisted it out of his hand. Ram snatched the Magnum from his waistband. As his gun hand came up, Neil's second shot hit him in the wrist and passed through the hand into his heart. He was thrown back by the impact and lay still for a moment before he gave a final twitch and clicked to stillness.

Kate looked down at the two bodies and then slowly up at Lewis.

'Was that just a lucky shot, when he was holding me?' she said.

'He knew what he was doing, Kate,' Neil said.

She looked back at Lewis.

'Prove it,' she said and she took a short glass on the bar and slid it along the long counter. Lewis raised the Colt .45 and hit the glass just before it fell from the end of the bar.

Hanna stood next to General Selig in the control tower of the Monthar Davis Airbase. She looked out over the great expanse of runways towards the mountains, as if she was willing some message to appear in the clear sky. Then an easy voice came to them from the loudspeaker close by, and cut through the murmur of voices.

'Goose One to Condor, Goose One to Condor.'

General Elmstead picked up the hand microphone.

'Condor to Goose Flight. Come in.'

'*The Silver Spoon* dropped its load right in the pickle barrel. Primary target totally destroyed. You won't be needing us.'

'How's she looking?' Elmstead asked.

'She's rolling home like a high-school hayride.'

The two generals exchanged satisfied glances, before they noticed Hanna's expression.

'He said "You won't be needing us",' she said coldly.

General Selig nodded.

'If *The Silver Spoon* had missed, you would have bombed the whole town, wouldn't you?'

Selig nodded again.

'They knew that, Hanna.'

She was about to protest when she realised that he spoke the truth. Instead she gripped the back of a chair and looked again towards the distant mountains.

'Thank God for Dad and Uncle Marsh,' she said softly.

Chapter Twelve

Lewis and Neil climbed aboard the last helicopter and looked down on Jericho as the pilot hovered for a moment before turning north over the mountains. Neil nudged Lewis and pointed to where he had concealed his car the previous night. He had to raise his voice above the clatter of the engine.

'Avis are going to have to hire Pinkerton's to find that,' he said with a certain amount of satisfaction.

Lewis leaned towards him so that he could catch the words.

'What happened to the knife?' he asked as his mind began to go back over the last few days.

'Annie's got it,' Neil said.

'I thought you were going to give it to your father,' Lewis shouted. 'It's not a very romantic present for a woman.'

'She's taking it to my old man. I've sent her to my folks' house.'

Lewis knew there was more. He looked at Neil and waited. Neil looked back with a serious expression.

'She's asked me to marry her.'

'What did you say?' Lewis said.

'I told her she'd have to ask my father's permission.'

'Do you think she'll get it?'

'It's a cert. The old man'll be crazy about her. So am I, Lew.'

'I wish you good fortune,' Lewis said.

Neil smiled. They looked down at the landscape for a while until the pilot turned to them.

'I've just got a radio message for you guys from General Selig. He says to conceal any weapons when we get to the base. There are a lot of media people around.'

Lewis held the twin Colts for a moment before he slid them into his belt and covered the handles with his jacket.

'They sure are pretty guns,' Neil said.

'They kick like a mule. Hitting that glass was the luckiest shot of my life,' Lewis admitted.

'If Kate had known that she wouldn't have given them to you.'

Lewis looked back towards Jericho but all he could see was the distant range of mountains and he had no way of telling which concealed the little town.

When they landed at the airbase they were driven to the administration building and escorted to the briefing room where Kate and the staff of the Grand Hotel were waiting. The girls chattered with excitement, and the Mexican staff sat huddled and anxious.

'I guess they stuck everyone else from the town in the stockade,' Neil muttered to Lewis.

They all looked up expectantly when the door opened and General Selig came into the room. He was wearing uniform and was accompanied by a young Air Force officer with a dark complexion.

'Ladies and gentlemen, my name is General Selig, and this is Captain Montez who will translate for our Spanish-speaking friends.'

He looked around the room before he continued.

'What happened in Jericho is a matter of National security and therefore highly secret. We have issued a statement to the media that there was an explosion due to a build-up of gas in the mine and that we have evacuated the town because of the possibility of further danger. Luckily, it being Sunday, there was no shift on duty. Because it's a slow news day there are a couple of people from the wire services plus the local press and a TV crew. I must emphasise that if you deviate from this story you could be in serious trouble.'

Selig smiled as he spoke but there was an edge to the warning. The girls began to mutter to each other as Captain Montez translated. Kate raised a languid hand and the general looked in her direction.

'Yes, ma'am,' he said.

Kate lit a cigarette before she spoke. 'General, what you just said is bullshit. We can say what we damn well like. But we're loyal Americans.' She waved towards the girls. 'Hell, we're in the business of keeping secrets. I know things that would tarnish the buttons on your soldier suit, but I won't, so just ask us nicely.'

The general knew when to retreat. He bowed slightly.

'I apologise, ma'am. On behalf of the President of the United States I ask you to keep this secret.'

'One more thing,' Kate said.

'You have my attention.'

Kate gestured to the Mexicans. 'Citizenship for these folks.'

'You have it,' the general said crisply.

When Captain Montez translated, there was a happy exchange of glances from the Mexican girls. General Selig looked at Kate once again.

'May I bring the ladies and gentlemen of the Press in, now?'

'Let 'em roll,' Kate said and she sat back in her chair.

A few minutes later four reporters filed into the room, two young and two old, but all with the bored expressions of men covering a dull story on a slow day. They were followed by a thin woman with a mane of hair and an irritable expression. She was accompanied by a bearded young man carrying a mobile camera.

The thin woman elbowed her way to the front and nodded to the cameraman. She thrust the microphone she carried towards Kate and said: 'Tell me, what was your job at the mine?'

Kate studied her for a moment and blew a thin blue stream of tobacco smoke in her direction. Then she uttered the words that were to make her famous across the nation.

'Honey, I'm the Harlot of Jericho,' she said.

The reporters were galvanised. They began shouting questions. Lewis and Neil took the opportunity to slip away.

Some time later General Selig found them drinking coffee next to a dispenser in a recreation room.

'Jesus, what a woman,' he said. 'We could have taken Iwo Jima with her. We wouldn't have needed the Corps.'

'Any word on Brady, sir?' Neil asked.

The general shook his head. 'We may have something in a couple of hours. Why don't you two take off and meet me back here at six o'clock?'

'Where are the others, sir?' Lewis said.

'Forrest Pearce and Hanna have gone to the Arizona Inn. Cutter's got *The Silver Spoon* in a hangar to strip one of the engines down. He said it sounded a little rough on the return trip.'

'I'd like to get off the base, sir, but we don't have any ID,' Lewis said.

'Here's the man who can fix that,' the general said, and waved towards Captain Montez who had entered the room. 'Take care of these guys, will you, Captain?'

Half an hour later Lewis and Neil walked to the car pool, escorted by a sergeant. Neil handed Lewis a key before he got into his car.

'I'm staying with my folks tonight,' he said. 'You can use Paul and Florence's place if you care to. Don't worry if you bump into an old Mexican lady. She goes out there a couple of times a day to look after the dog.'

'Thanks,' Lewis said. 'I'll see you at six o'clock.'

When he got to the Arizona Inn, Lewis found Hanna in the lobby.

'I've got to buy some clothes,' she said. 'My father is packing but he said he'd like to see you before he leaves for New York.'

'I've got to do a bit more work later,' Lewis said. 'But I should be through by dinner time. I'll meet you here at eight. When we've eaten we can drive out and spend the night at a house I've borrowed near the Ricon Mountains.'

She leaned forward and kissed him.

'In that case, I won't bother to buy a nightdress,' she said, and the girl at the reception desk lifted her head to glance in their direction.

Hanna smiled. 'Sorry, Captain. I only do it to make you bashful.'

Lewis received directions from the girl on the desk, who eyed him with a certain interest, and then he strolled through the peaceful gardens to Pearce's suite. When Hanna had said he was packing, Lewis imagined her father slowly pottering around the room and occasionally stuffing clothes into an old suitcase. What he actually found was enough activity to turn the suite into a scene resembling a branch office of the Pearce Corporation.

Two secretaries were clearing a desk and packing files and papers, a valet was instructing one of the bellboys on the order he wanted the cases loaded into the cars, and an assistant was hovering over Forrest Pearce with a handful of papers while he stood at a desk shouting into a telephone.

In the corner of the room a television set was on, with the sound muted. Pearce waved for Lewis to sit down while he continued with the call.

'OK, Henry, I've got to go now, and the line is terrible. Call me in New York after nine o'clock our time if you've seen the Minister of Trade by then. Otherwise tomorrow.'

He put down the telephone and the assistant held out the papers for him to take.

'I'll deal with those on the plane, Mark,' he said, and instantly the young man drew back.

'Let's take a walk in the garden,' Pearce said to Lewis. 'Wrap it up here,' he said to the assistant, then something caught his eye on the television screen. 'Lord, here she comes again.' He jabbed the remote control and the sound came onto the television set just in time to hear Kate say, 'Honey, I'm the Harlot of Jericho.'

Pearce watched a few moments more of the interview, then ushered Lewis into the garden.

'She's been on every news broadcast for the last hour,' Pearce said with a shake of his head. 'What an extraordinary country we've become. One sentence and she's as famous as George Washington.'

They walked at an easy pace along the red-brick pathway without speaking, then Pearce turned to Lewis. 'Things

296

seem to be getting pretty serious between you and Hanna. You know she's going to be very rich one day?' he said.

'Yes,' Lewis replied after a pause.

'So what's the problem?'

They walked on before Lewis answered.

'Hanna isn't too keen on my line of work.'

'How do you feel about her?' Pearce asked.

'I've never cared for anyone the way I do about Hanna,' Lewis said carefully. 'But the job isn't nine to five. I don't know if it's fair to give a woman that much worry.'

Pearce's voice became fatherly.

'You can't live your life like that, son. When I married Hanna's mother, the life expectancy of an Eighth Air Force pilot was three months.'

He looked sideways at Lewis again.

'Of course, that was about two thousand years ago, when marriage was still in fashion.'

You foxy old bastard, Lewis thought. Now, if I say I want to marry her, I'll look like a fortune hunter. If I don't, I'm compromising her virtue.

'Your war was over in 1945, Mr Pearce,' Lewis said flatly. 'There's no sign of mine coming to an end.'

Pearce stopped and turned to face Lewis.

'How about walking away? By all accounts you've done your share.'

Lewis smiled and shook his head.

'Yes,' Pearce said. 'Hanna told me that would be your reaction.'

He looked around the garden for a moment.

'Nice spot, this. I had some good times here,' he said almost wistfully. Then he held out his hand. 'I imagine that I'll be seeing you again.'

They shook hands and Lewis watched him as he turned away and walked back towards his rooms.

Lewis held out his identity card to the guard on the airbase gate.

'I have a message for you, Captain, from General Selig,'

the man said as he handed back the card. 'He says for you to meet him in General Elmstead's office.'

Lewis found a parking space and handed the car keys back to the sergeant on duty. He was about to enter the building when he heard a whistle and turned to see Neil striding to catch him up.

'What did your father say?' Lewis said as they made for General Elmstead's office.

'He kept the knife. He wanted to keep Annie as well but my mother made him give her back.'

When they were shown into Elmstead's office, the two generals were standing before the desk studying papers. Selig looked up and held out a telex message to Lewis.

'Brady?' he said. The general nodded.

'We found him in Miami.'

'How?' Lewis asked.

'Good staff work,' the general said. 'After he left South America there was no trace of him through the usual channels. He had no family or close friends, but the barman in the local cantina he used down there remembered that he always read the same paper every evening. It was the *New York Times*. We found his new address on the subscription list. He just couldn't break the habit.'

Lewis studied the telex for a time.

'You found the girl as well?'

'Yes,' Selig said.

'Let's go and get him,' Lewis said to Neil.

They stopped the car outside the hangar and walked from the harsh, bleaching sunlight into the cool interior, and paused for a moment so that their eyes could become accustomed to the shadowy light. Across the vast floor they saw three men working on one of the engines of *The Silver Spoon*. The sound of tools clinking on the machinery seemed to be amplified by the walls of the hangar. Marshall Cutter stood beneath the wing, looking up as one of the mechanics made an adjustment. He glanced over to where they stood and then turned back to the other men. He muttered to them for a moment, and they replaced the engine cowling and pulled themselves into the cockpit entrance.

'We'll try her in a minute,' he shouted. 'I've just got to see these guys.'

Cutter walked towards them, wiping his hands on a piece of cloth.

'We found Brady,' Neil said. 'The real one.'

'Good.' Cutter then studied their faces. 'So?'

Lewis thrust his hands deep in his pockets.

'It's over, Cutter. We've worked it all out,' he said in a matter-of-fact voice.

'Go on,' Cutter said.

'Do you want it from the beginning?'

'Sure,' Cutter said confidently.

'We know it was you who organised the Jericho Institute. The real Brady lived in South America. He used to do consultancy work for one of your subsidiary companies. No-one knew him, he hadn't been in the States for thirty years, and he had no family. So you pensioned him off in Miami and took his identity so you could buy the Jericho Institute from yourself in his name.'

'Why would I want to do that?' Cutter said, and he continued to work carefully on his hands with the cloth.

'Marshall Industries was going down the tubes. The Electronics Division had turned into a money pit – that's why you sabotaged the works for the insurance. Forrest Pearce knew you were having difficulties, and because of your friendship he offered you half of the Rainbow Division, but you didn't have all the capital you needed.

'So you hit on the idea of the Jericho set-up. The profits made up the money you needed for your share of the Rainbow Division.

'Pearce and you were equal partners. If anything happened to either of you, the other got the whole company. That's why you sent hitmen to the south of France, and you tried again in London. They weren't after you; they were going to kill Forrest Pearce.'

Cutter laughed. 'Sheer fantasy. You can't prove any of this.'

'Yes, we can – even how you stole the supplies of Gospel.

299

You put the whole plan on the computer at Jericho,' Lewis said.

'What computer, Captain Horne? All I saw at Jericho was a heap of rubble.'

'You're right,' Lewis said. 'But I was in there last night. I hooked up the program to the telephone and dumped the entire contents on the main frame at Langley. The CIA has got everything.'

'Where are your witnesses?' Cutter said in a voice that was still full of confidence. 'This is no evidence. Anyone could have written that stuff into the computer.'

'Anyone could have, but you had your entire life recorded. Every transaction you made in your own, or Brady's name, every nickel and dime you possessed. You couldn't tell your secrets to a human being, Cutter, so you ended up confessing everything to a computer.'

Cutter looked at them without speaking. He stood in the hard shaft of sunlight that entered the hangar doors while Lewis and Neil were back in deep shadow. Lewis could see a trickle of sweat run from his hairline to his jaw.

'Carrie Thompson was traced this morning,' Neil said, 'through the monthly payments you made on the apartment in Los Angeles.'

Cutter put the rag he carried into his pocket of his stained overalls and let his hands hang at his sides.

'She knows nothing of this,' he said.

'We know,' Neil said. 'Our people talked to her. She even thinks you're a hero doing some kind of secret work for the Government. That's why she hasn't contacted her family for so long.'

Cutter reached up and brushed the trickle of sweat from his chin.

'We know you met Carrie in Jericho,' Lewis said. 'She first knew you as Brady, then when you took her away you had to tell her you were really Marshall Cutter.'

'I never did her any harm,' Cutter said quietly.

'Yeah,' Neil said, 'but you nearly killed her sister. She was the red-headed girl, Annie, whom your hoods tried to murder in the desert.'

'I didn't know that,' Cutter replied. 'Are you sure?'

'Annie showed me a locket in the desert,' Lewis said. 'It had both their photographs in it.'

Slowly, Cutter put his hands into his pockets. He looked down and traced the tip of his shoe along the edge of the shadow that divided him from them.

'So this game is over,' he said when he looked up again.

There was a rising note of anger in David Neil's voice when he replied, 'This wasn't a game, Cutter.'

'Yes, it was,' he answered sharply and he took his hands from the overalls once again. 'It's all a game. Some people get to play if they've got the guts and the ambition.'

'What about the rest of the people in the world?' Lewis asked. 'Don't they count?'

Cutter shrugged. 'Somebody has got to buy the tickets.'

Neil shook his head in disbelief.

'Well, it's over for you, mister. You just struck out.'

Cutter gestured towards *The Silver Spoon*.

'Don't be too sure. You see, there's one of my boys in the mid-upper turret with twin Browning machine-guns pointed at you. When I give him the signal he's going to turn you into hamburger.'

Cutter began to back away from them but his boast had saved their lives. Lewis and Neil had begun to move as he spoke. Ten feet from where they had stood was a row of heavy-duty oil drums.

They reached them just as the Brownings from *The Silver Spoon* began to punch holes through the walls of the hangar.

'Aim for the co-pilot,' Lewis shouted, and he thrust one of the Colts into Neil's hand. Before they could return the fire, the four massive engines of *The Silver Spoon* coughed into life and the backwash from the propellors threw a whirling mist of dust and debris into the air inside the hangar.

In the sudden fog Lewis and Neil moved swiftly away from their cover and further into the shadows as the concentrated fire from the Brownings punched great holes into the oil drums and sent them rolling crazily across the concrete floor.

Lewis and Neil crouched down and took deliberate aim as *The Silver Spoon* trundled from the hangar and out onto the runway. By the time she had cleared the hangar doors they had emptied the Colts.

'How did you do?' Lewis asked after a few moments.

'I could have sworn I clipped the pilot,' Neil said. They continued to watch *The Silver Spoon* begin to rise from the runway. When she was about twenty feet from the ground, she started to slip from horizontal. Slowly the starboard wing lowered towards the ground. It seemed for a moment the aeroplane would clear, but with sickening deliberation the tip made contact and the great silver bird started to cartwheel until she exploded in a massive ball of flame and black greasy smoke.

Neil handed the Colt back to Lewis, who glanced at it for a moment before slipping it into his waistband. Then he looked back again at the burning plane.

'Game, set and match,' he heard Neil say to himself.

The dream came to Lewis again. There had been a battle, and the moor, dusted white by frost, was dark with bodies. A sickly pale sun, low on the horizon, showed through the overcast sky and gave enough reluctant light for him to search for the messenger. Across the field the dead of both armies lay scattered in disorder, their original neat symmetry broken by the fighting which had taken place. In death they now mingled with the enemy.

Why? Lewis thought. What passions had caused this terrible sacrifice? Then he saw the messenger waiting for him, holding his charger by the bridle. He stood in the manner of soldiers after battle, stooped with weariness, body and mind drained to exhaustion. When Lewis drew close, the man raised his head and held out the letter again. This time he took it and broke the heavy wax seal to unfold the square of paper.

Despite the fading sun, the letters stood black and bold on the parchment. Then he felt a crushing weight upon his chest. The battlefield faded and he looked up into the face of a great black beast. It was Duchess the Great Dane who crouched over him, her paws on his chest.

302

'Lewis,' Hanna called again, and he saw that her head was nestled in the crook of his arm. 'Are you all right?' she asked. 'You called out in your sleep.'

'*Deuteronomy*,' he said. 'Chapter II, verses 22 to 28.'

He looked into her puzzled face.

'Remember that.'

She repeated the words. He pushed the dog aside and reached for a pair of jeans on the chair next to the bed.

'Wait here,' he said and he padded barefoot from the bedroom and into the corridor. Duchess followed him, her claws making the tapping sound on the bare, polished boards. He found the bookcase and scanned the shelves until he located a heavy Bible with a battered leather binding. He opened the pages and confirmed it was the King James version before he returned to the bedroom.

Hanna sat up when he entered, drew in her legs and rested her arms on her knees. For a moment he was distracted by her nakedness, but he sat down next to her and opened the book.

'What was it again?' he said.

'*Deuteronomy*, chapter II, verses 22 to 28.'

He found the place and began to read aloud.

' "For if ye shall diligently keep all these commandments which I command you, to do them, to love the Lord your God, to walk in all his ways, and to cleave unto him: Then will the Lord drive out all these nations from before you, and ye shall possess greater nations and mightier than yourselves. Every place whereon the soles of your feet shall tread shall be yours: from the wilderness and Lebanon, from the river, the river Euphrates, even unto the uttermost sea shall your coast be. There shall no man be able to stand before you: for the Lord your God shall lay the fear of you and the dread of you upon all the land that ye shall tread upon, as he hath said unto. Behold, I set before you this day a blessing and a curse: A blessing, if ye obey the commandments of the Lord your God, which I command you this day: And a curse, if ye will not obey the commandments of the Lord your God, but turn aside out of the way which I command you this day, to go after other gods, which ye have not known." ' '

Then he closed the book and looked at her.

'That's it,' he said. 'It's really very simple.'

'What is?' Hanna said.

Lewis placed the Bible on the bed between them.

'Why the New Model Army fought again the King. To them it wasn't political; it was a commandment from God. I've been looking at the motives of the politicians and the ruling classes. To the soldiers it was obeying their religion. They believed in what they did; it was that simple.'

Hanna put an arm around his waist and rested her head upon his shoulder before she began to speak.

' "Such men as had the fear of God before them and as made some conscience of what they did, the plain russet-coated captain that knows what he fights for and loves what he knows." '

He looked down at her.

'That's Cromwell. How do you know that?'

She smiled. 'Charlie Mars told me. I asked him what makes you go on doing what you do and he read me that.'

Lewis sat in silence for a moment and there was an expectancy in the tiny room. The dog could feel it. She leaned forward, still, but full of anticipation.

'Will you marry me?' Lewis said finally.

Hanna reached down and picked up the Bible between them. Then she answered.

'Hold this and say it again.'